The Tale of Hansuli Turn

The Tale of Hansuli Turn

TARASHANKAR BANDYOPADHYAY

Translated by Ben Conisbee Baer

COLUMBIA UNIVERSITY PRESS

NEW YORK

COLUMBIA UNIVERSITY PRESS

Publishers Since 1893

New York   Chichester, West Sussex

Copyright © 2011 Columbia University Press

LIBRARY OF CONGRESS CATALOGING-IN-PUBLICATION DATA

Bandyopadhyaya, Tarasankara, 1898–1971.
[Hansuli Bankera upakatha. English]
The tale of Hansuli Turn / Tarashankar Bandyopadhyay ; translated by Ben Conisbee Baer.
p.   cm.
ISBN 978-0-231-14904-4 (acid-free paper) — ISBN 978-0-231-52022-5 (e-book)
I. Conisbee Baer, Ben. II. Title.

PK1718.B2985H3613   2011
891.4'4371—dc22   2009035408

Columbia University Press books are printed on permanent and durable acid-free paper.
This book was printed on paper with recycled content.
Printed in the United States of America

C   10 9 8 7 6 5 4 3 2 1

To Philip Conisbee

(3 JANUARY 1946–16 JANUARY 2008)

Introduction

Tarashankar Bandyopadhyay's *Hansuli Banker Upakatha*, or *The Tale of Hansuli Turn*, as I have translated it, tells the story of an India modernized by the forces of war in the mid-twentieth century. The novel was written across the cusp of India's formal accession to independent nation-statehood and was published in various versions between 1946 and 1951. It first appeared in a much shorter version in a special annual Durga festival issue of *Ananda Bazar Patrika* in 1946. (During the celebration of Durga Puja in late October in Bengal, many periodicals bring out a special issue publishing new writing, often by younger up-and-coming authors.) *Hansuli Turn* was greatly expanded and revised over the following five years, appearing in several editions during that time.

Hansuli Turn is unusual in at least two respects. First, it tries to represent sympathetically the frightening (and seductive) shapes of the new from within the imaginative universe and philosophy of the old. Second, it takes as central a set of subaltern protagonists, drawn from the very lowest and most marginalized strata of rural society. In our context, the term "subaltern" began to come into general use in the mid-1980s, following the work of the Subaltern Studies group of historians of South Asia. It names the shifting and heterogeneous positions that are cut off from the lines of intellectual and social mobility, and institutionalized agency, in colonial and postcolonial society.[1] In *Hansuli Turn*, as in other places, the representation of subalternity turns on the philosophical paradox of its coming to a crisis and exceeding the codes by which it remains subaltern.

Those who have read some mid-century Anglophone Indian fiction, and perhaps some works in translation, will probably notice something of a shift in milieu with *Hansuli Turn*. Rural society in India is extremely differentiated and diverse, and it would be a mistake to assume that all novels about rustic protagonists, peasants and others, are dealing with common types of figures or even with subalterns at all. A very well-known Anglophone novel such as Raja Rao's *Kanthapura* (1937), for example, takes as central a group of male and female Brahmin village activists who are connected with metropolitan movements. It is only in the novel's extraordinary climactic moments that the village's subaltern ("Pariah") women steal the initiative from the upper class/castes and burn the settlement in protest.[2] Moreover, the central peasant characters of Premchand's *Godaan* (1936), perhaps the most famous Hindi novel of the early twentieth century, are a cut above the Kahars. (There is no qualitative ranking implied in my comparisons with these other works, simply an effort to indicate to readers who are perhaps not familiar with this literary territory that *Hansuli Turn* is carving a particular place for itself.) Thus, although subalternity cannot ultimately be located in any specific sociological or empirical group, *Hansuli Turn* contrasts with other mid-century literary landmarks by explicitly embracing the task of making a new kind of literary representation of the subaltern.[3]

It would, however, be misleading to give the impression that the primary way to come to terms with Tarashankar's writing is through Anglophone writing of South Asia in the 1920s, '30s, and '40s. I mention Rao and Anand here for heuristic reasons, assuming the greater likelihood of U.S. readers' familiarity with their works rather than with the milieu of non-Anglophone modernist writers in India in general and in Bengal in particular. Although Anglophone works of this period presuppose a class-fixed national and international readership, a writer such as Tarashankar does not presuppose exactly the same public, though he does assume a largely metropolitan one. This is the Calcutta or "educated society" named in the dedication to *Hansuli Turn*, but also the "educated society" of the *mufassil* or country town. His literary milieu is no more "local" or parochial than others (Bloomsbury, for example, or Greenwich Village), but contains its own dynamics and tendencies that are too complex to summarize here.

Suffice it to say by way of introduction that the reader, feeling her way toward what Gayatri Spivak has called "transnational literacy," must come to sense this novel's insertion into a Bengali literary milieu.[4] She must also—and the novel itself begins to teach us about this—come to sense its own regionalism within that virtual space of a "literary milieu." On the one hand, the spectacular and lengthy comparison between Eastern and Western regions of Bengal at the very opening of the novel appears to be redundant to the plot and constitutes a parenthesis that diverges conspicuously from the momentum of the opening's urgent mystery (4–6). But it places the reader in relation to a sedimented coding of "Bengal" that is not just social, political, and historical but also cultural and literary. On the other hand, the novel is an account of a much more general problem of literary representation: it is an experiment in how to "do" novels in

India, of how to make "tale" (*upakathā*) into "novel" (*upanyās*) across divisions not specifically defined by region.

***

The novel's main protagonist and focalizer, meaning the character whose "vision" is given words by the narrator, is Bonwari Kahar. Much of the novel is vectored through his thought world, his imaginative universe and philosophy, which, along with the other village elders such as Suchand Kahar, exemplifies the values of the "old" world for the novel. Bonwari is a subaltern figure, though drawn from the upper spaces of subalternity. He is the village headman and protector of its dharma (broadly speaking, ethical and religious principles), to whom responsibility means a complex relationship of loyalty and subordination to the quasi-feudal masters of village and town, and adherence to the prescriptions of gods and forefathers that comprehends any threat to these as a threat to the moral and existential order itself.[5] *Hansuli Turn* represents a space in which precolonial temporalities, structures of myth, memory, and ritual, practical arrangements of everyday life, and imaginative patterns are powerfully residual.

However, I must immediately qualify the statement that emphasizes the contrast between new and old in *Hansuli Turn*. The old is not to be taken as referring to some kind of pristine, archaic tradition brought into contact with the novel's key indices of modernity (the forces of war and capital as the machines of development in the twentieth century). The Kahars, the untouchable collective protagonist of the novel, are not traditional in any uncomplicated way. As they are depicted in *Hansuli Turn*, they too are the product of an earlier wave of transformation, the British colonization of India, displaced from an unknown elsewhere and brought to their present location and function by the vicissitudes of colonial capital and indigenous class/caste hierarchy. As the novel's narrator tells us:

> The real meaning can be found in the old papers of the Chaud-hury house. All those papers have now almost disappeared, de-voured by termites. There are still a few whole bits and pieces in piles of termite-eaten paper. Among them the total statement of revenue accounts for the year 1818–19 can be found—the whole Bansbadi ward was wasteland—there was neither pond nor settle-

ment there. There is mention of about ten huts situated in Jangol village, all were Sadgop farmers. In the papers of 1842–43 you see—a new land settlement, in the name of the illustrious Mister Jenkins saheb, indigo planter. Whatever wasteland there was at Jangol had almost all been incorporated into this new landholding, along with the entire Bansbadi ward. On the upland west of Jangol, the ruins of the indigo offices and a pond called Lake's Pond can still be seen. Water from Lake's Pond used to flow down through brick channels and fill brick-built indigo fermentation tanks. The place is overrun by brush now, and wild pigs have set up an outpost right there. Once they've taken a land settlement at Bansbadi ward, the sahebs dig a pond there and turn all Bansbadi's wasteland to indigo cultivation. It's in order to do just this that these folk of Kaharpara come to Bansbadi. Many people had come. Among them, a few of these Kahars put cottages here. Some had found jobs at the indigo office, patrolling with fightsticks and keeping watch at the sahebs' gates when needed; for this they'd been given some land in lieu of salary and, in keeping with local custom, had received a title befitting their function as tenants of rent-free land on call twenty-four hours a day—Ostoprohori, or Atpoure. Twenty-four-hour guards. The Behara Kahars would till the indigo fields and carry the palanquins of the sahebs and their ladies when required. (19–20)

This story is told and retold by the narrator and within the narratives of the Kahars themselves, and the permutations of these retellings are material for the novel's elaboration of the relation between "tale" (*upakathā*) and "history" (*itihās*).

The Kahars are thus the collective product of prior waves of internal migration and diaspora—a class of armed guards and palanquin carriers created by the colonial planters that is then transformed into a class of landless sharecroppers for the needs of the indigenous landowners, and finally wage laborers in the small-town wartime industries. On the way, the Kahars also become a "criminal tribe," a colonial-era category for a large number of rustic groups outlawed by the British, an appellation they are portrayed as struggling to avoid in the novel. The Kahars are therefore thoroughly modern hybrids occupying the broad and shifting territory of untouchability between the autochthonous or aboriginal "tribal" groups of this western region of Bengal, and the caste Hindus and their erstwhile colonial rulers. *Hansuli Turn* vividly dramatizes this hybridity through the huge and general trope of reproductive heteronormativity, as the skin tone of the Kahars lightens while they work for the whites and some of their features come to resemble those of the Bengali landlords once the planters have departed. In spite of all the surrounding codes stipulating caste purity and avoidance of pollution, the Kahars appear as the exception that makes the rule of caste segregation possible. In many other ways, *Hansuli Turn* gives the lie to notions of the intact practices, values, and mind-sets of a fantasmatic "village India." In spite of the novel's conclusion, we must bear in mind that the Kahars never "belonged" to the land in the first place. The novel tells us that their particular marginality and rusticity was itself always a result of a chain of social transformations that led to their temporary stasis and isolation, to their stagnation, perhaps, in the place depicted. *Hansuli Turn* dramatizes this stasis and isolation in its opening pages with the motif (to which it often returns) of the circular or oxbow river bend within which the Kahar hamlet sits, as if cut off from the wider world by a physical boundary. As the novel's development makes clear, while the Kahars *are* both cut off and exploited in various ways, the isolation is a matter of social spaces and boundaries rather than of the figurative geographical circumscription that expresses it. There is much traffic in and out of the enclosing river bend, but this traffic actively denies the Kahars social or intellectual mobility. The drama and tragedy of *Hansuli Turn* comes from one of the main protagonists, Karali, a youth whose crisis precisely involves a movement toward a social and intellectual mobility that clashes with the values of the village's elders and the indigenous landlords.

Yet as often as making such obviously historical statements, the novel's narrator refers to the "ancient" or "primordial" (*ādim*) character of the Kahars, as if they represent some kind of anthropologically interesting survival of the primitive within the modern world: "In their eyes that primeval epoch's stare lights up; that's to say the darkness-piercing forest-animal stare of humans from the age before the discovery of fire!" (87). This conflict of different modes of imagining and representing India's rural oppressed is one of the most powerful sites of aesthetic and rhetorical tension in *Hansuli Turn*, something that contains and determines the novel rather than being contained and resolved by it. Readers will recognize that it is a tension shared by many other so-called "primitivist" modernisms, not just those of Bengal or India.[6] Perhaps more so than in any other region of India, literary artists of Bengal have been fascinated by the residual aboriginal elements in their social and cultural landscape. That story is too big to tell here, but a thread of this nature could certainly be traced, linking nineteenth-century writers such as Sanjib Chandra Chattopadhyay through Rabindranath Tagore to Bibhutibhushan Bandyopadhyay, Tarashankar, and today's Mahasweta Devi.

Thus, if the novel exemplifies an attempt by an upper-middle class Brahmin author to represent social and epistemic change in a class and caste emphatically not his own, then it does so in ways that pose provocative questions and render the work difficult for recuperation within postcolonial studies as a novel of "resistance" by the colonized. Beside its modernist primitivism, there is no simple colonizer/colonized, East/West contrast in this story. *Hansuli Turn* explores the fault lines within the colonized, and thus complicates the postcolonial paradigm. The novel offers multiple taxonomies of difference within the untouchable world and within the ranks of an indigenous rural society being transformed by colonialism. It asks us to imagine a world of peasant farmers (Sadgops and Mondols), landlords, landowners, and rural gentry (Ghoshes, Chaudhurys, and unnamed Brahmin gentry) from the vantage point of the landless sharecropper eking out a living in village or country town. The ebbs and flows of collective and individual fortunes are not static in this world.

Whites, Englishmen or "sahebs," are a sinister offstage presence for most of *Hansuli Turn*. The Kahars live in the ruins of a former indigo plantation. A railway line (metonymic signifier *par excellence* of the imperial network) runs past the village, and the rhythmic to-and-fro of the train is used as a timepiece by the Kahars to measure out the workday. The reader who has seen Satyajit Ray's first and best-known movie *Pather Panchali* (1955), based on the 1929 novel of the same name by Bibhutibhushan Bandyopadhyay, will recall that its most famous scene involves the children Apu and Durga running though a field of kash reeds to watch a steam train pass by. This scene of confrontation between impoverished middle-class rustic Brahmin children and the ambiguous forces of imperial "modernity" is displaced in *Hansuli Turn*. Our protagonists are far lower on the social scale than Apu and Durga. Yet the train has been assimilated and in a sense normalized as timekeeper, and the rail line is now a different kind of narrative pointer to an "outside" (of the Kahars' immediate world and of the text itself). Karali shuttles between village and town, and constantly tries to recruit the young men of his group to take up work in the factories. Yet Karali's *temporary* and cyclic migration out of the village and back is set against the backdrop of the prior *permanent* migration women are obliged to enter if they take up the same kind of workshop or rail-line employment. These women, named only once in the novel, fleetingly appear and disappear from the narrative along this line: "So many women left home to work construction on this line—Panchi, Khuki, Bele, Chitto, Nimmla. Khuki and Bele left the locality—with two Muslim stonecutters. Chitto and Panchi went off with a Hindusthani line mechanic. And Nimmla took off with another mechanic. Karali was that Nimmla's son. The bitch even went off leaving little five-year-old Karali" (89-90). The novel points to a story of a women's diaspora that it leaves untold as it focuses on change coded by male intergenerational struggle. (The predicaments of gendered subalternity are—more or less—occluded in *Hansuli Turn*; I would ask those interested in this question to read carefully the figures of Suchand, Noyan's Ma, Pakhi, and the male-to-female transvestite Nasubala). The real equivalent of *Pather Panchali*'s fascinating, monstrous, and mysterious train, sign of some vast and as yet unknown alien structure, is *Hansuli Turn*'s squadrons of military aircraft that fly low over the Kahar hamlet as World War II unfolds. Indices of crisis in several ways, the aircraft subvert and overwrite the now normalized (clichéd) motif of the steam train of empire. The airbase and airplanes become the sign of some offstage imperial and existential catastrophe, rather than of a systematic occupation of new territory; or, as they come insatiably to eat up irreplaceable resources and space toward the novel's end, they become the signs of a late imperialism driven headlong by crisis.

Hansuli Turn stages the agonizingly difficult way the forces of colonial modernity can in some sense be understood as emancipatory for India's most marginal people. It is complicity with the very structural violations of war and "modernization" that paradoxically enables Karali to break with the feudal violence that prevails over the Kahars. The novel presents this dilemma as a double bind, particularly as its focalization is so powerfully vectored through the figure of Bonwari, unable to imagine an outside to feudal strictures except in terms of cosmic and moral-existential catastrophe. Karali takes a job in the wartime rail workshops, actively recruits the villagers to do likewise, and comes to an emergent understanding of the injustice of caste segregation. *Hansuli Turn* represents this process of change through Karali's work and speeches, and also through the outward signs of the body as he undergoes a transvestite makeover from loincloth-clad village boy to uncanny uniform-clad proletarian.[7]

The novel depicts the horizons of rustic feudal hierarchy being ruptured by the world of wage labor and British military structure. As the war machine touches the subalternity of Karali, it causes that subalternity to exceed its own bounds, and this overflow can be given the name of "crisis" inasmuch as it enables the signs of a different order to begin to challenge and displace the signs of the prevailing one. Thus, for example, Karali openly questions the casual abuse and insults by which the rural landlords address the Kahars, and the proverbial wisdom through which the Kahars accept these appellations ("the foot is not equal with the head"): "Karali said—All that don't seem wrong ta chief, though; they've got used t'all a that. I'm sayin'—scum, what's that for, Mister; scum? So saying, he walked off quickly. Talking as he went—Scum jerk bastard shit-eating louse, right on the tip—right on tippa gentymens' tongues. Gentymen! Under their thumb! Ah—" (124).

The change is drawn beginning with Karali's mode of investigation into the source of the terrifying forest whistling announced in the novel's first lines. He uses a flashlight to search in the surrounding bamboo groves. The word "torch" (here meaning flashlight), lexicalized into Bengali from (British) English and metonymically associated with Karali, already announces a difference from the rest of the Kahars, as the use of electric light is associated with whites and with the police. At this inaugural point, Karali's flashlight is "extremely weak" (16); the transformation is at an early stage. Karali is, in a metaphorical sense, reaching for a certain "enlightenment," linked by the rhetoric of the novel to the rational capabilities of the colonial apparatus, just as his rationalizing explanation of the mysterious forest whistle is at odds with the village elders' metaphysical one. From the beginning of part four the visible signs of a change accelerate, and a series of references to clothing suggests the becoming-other of the young man:

> [Bonwari] glanced toward Karali and was utterly undone with astonishment. Karali was wearing long pants and a jacket. (224)

> Suddenly one day he turned up wearing those clothes and said—I've taken war work. . . . Shoes on feet. Blisters sprouting, corns rubbing, but he'll not give up the shoes. (228)

> Karali has become a coolie leader inside these very workshops. Wearing a coat, wearing long pants, shoes on feet, cap on head, he gives orders. (277)

Nowadays dresses like the soldiers an' says,—*Military*! Wears
shoes an' puts a cap on 'is 'ead. (364)

As the novel ends and the forest is cut down by wartime timber contractors, the intensity of the light penetrating the village's former gloom com-
pletes the illumination brought from the beginning by Karali's "extremely
weak" flashlight. A brilliantly ironic phrase rewrites the destruction of
the bamboo's irreplaceable ecology, life space, locus of differentiated
memories and particularities, as its substitution by the *image* of equality.
"Pagol said—They leveled out [*samān kare*] Father's shrine makin' it a
motorcar lot, Bonwari-bro" (360). *Samān* means equal as well as level, so
that in the symbolic site of the old divine hierarchy is installed no more
than an image of equalization, light, and rectitude: now the road runs
"straight" to the town (360). The promise of enlightenment contained
at some level in the colonial project becomes an emblem of betrayal of
the enlightenment ideal. None of the foregoing argument is to claim that
Hansuli Turn endorses the mission of colonialism as enlightenment (nor
do I endorse the notion that colonialism and enlightenment are simply
one and the same). The novel confronts us with a literary staging of the
problem in the form of an unresolved double bind: being touched by the
colonial apparatus as both a good and a bad thing for the subaltern. In
doing so, it refuses the reader the false comforts of an easy indigenism or
nativism, a sense that the old, quasi-feudal values were better, just as it
confronts us with a representation of colonization as the false herald of
enlightenment and equality.

***

I suggested above that *Hansuli Turn* offered in its time the most significant
effort by a literary author from the upper classes and castes to imagine
and portray epistemic and social change in a space drastically different
from his own. I added that the novel renders visible the fault lines within
the colonized rather than homogenizing them for the aesthetico-political
effect of a too-neat contrast between colonizer and colonized. Perhaps
the most interesting and provocative place these methods converge is in
the staging of the language of the novel. This dramatizes a problem of
literary representation, of how to tell the "tale" of a subaltern group; but
it approaches the challenge rhetorically, or structurally, as a reflection on
the transformation of a "tale" in one kind of language into a written novel
in another kind of language, across an abyssal social divide. The mecha-
nisms of this dramatization involve interesting and experimental muta-

tions of syntax, semantics, and rhetoric that make *Hansuli Turn* stand out not only in Tarashankar's own oeuvre but also within Bengali and other South Asian literature of the period.

The "*upakathā*" or "tale" of the novel's title is referred to again and again in the novel itself. The word *upakathā* conveys the somewhat folksy sense of "tale," but can also literally mean a subnarrative, a smaller, tangential thread woven into the dense texture of an epic, for example. Suchand Kahar, the oldest woman resident of the Kahar community and the main custodian of its narrative, hands the tale to the novel's narrator in its closing pages: "This tale's gonna end wi' me, yeh. But if ya can, keep it in writin'" (372). The final part of the novel contains several images of writing associated with death, then ends with two scenes of a possible new writing: this one (where the narrator is asked by Suchand to preserve in writing the very tale that gives the novel its name), and the closing image of Karali, who "cuts into the sand, cuts into the sand," to make "the tale's Kopai merge with history's Ganges" (373). Thus Suchand's request of the reader/narrator is to re-elaborate her tale, her *upakathā*, in writing, a moment wherein the novel dramatizes its own origins in a subaltern space of story not its own. In other words, I prefer to read this novel as a strange sort of chase or hunt, figuring out the trail of its own originating impulse in the subaltern imperative to preserve a tale. I prefer this reading to one that would simply point an accusatory finger at the upper-class/upper-caste novelist appropriating subalternity in his representations so as to incorporate it into a monocultural, monotemporal novelistic universe, neatly slotted into the space/time matrix of the modern nation-state. I have shown in depth elsewhere that through Suchand's fictive call for the "tale" to be preserved in writing, the novel poses the problem of bridging divides of class and caste as a formal, literary problem.[8] This extends to the way *Hansuli Turn* handles the creole Bengali of its Kahar protagonists.

While many translations and also Anglophone South Asian novels contain glossaries at the end, or explanatory footnotes, *Hansuli Turn* contains a strange "glossary" of sorts within the main text itself. The narrator frequently steps in to gloss creole words or phrases, always using the same word to announce this move, *arthāt*. This is a very colloquial and everyday word and expression of explanation, best translated as "that's to say," or "which is to say." I have used both these phrases to translate it, as well, sometimes, as simply, "or." For example, "His bodily frame—they call it 'spindlish,' that's to say sliverlike; but what a head he has" (54). Using this device, almost inconspicuous in his Bengali though often somewhat awkward in translation, Tarashankar manages to activate the relation between the field of "standard" Bengali and its creole. In my other writing on *Hansuli Turn* I have elaborated how this literary gesture does not simply represent a moment of clarification for a metropolitan readership, but is the sign of another scene of meaning that cannot yet register within the public sphere.[9] Ultimately, this novel leaves the drama open-ended and seeks to suggest that the uncanny words, rhythms, and subnarratives of the rustic tale could be written into the future in a different way. This new story would, for better or worse, break with the dominant representation of the "we" of the public sphere and the "they" of the creolized subaltern. Hence, its closing moments stage the upwardly mobile militant Karali scratching or inscribing a link to "history," but also include the transvestite dancer, Nasubala Kahar, and the crazy balladeer, Pagol Kahar, continuing the story in other forms.

THE AUTHOR

Tarashankar Bandyopadhyay (1898–1971) is one of the main figures in twentieth-century Bengali literature, the author of more than fifty novels and hundreds of short stories.[10] Tarashankar was born into a prosperous Bengali Brahmin landowning family in the rural town of Labhpur, Birbhum, Bengal. Being of the highest caste, and also a landowner, he cannot be said to be a "subaltern" writer, even though a large number of his novels attempt to represent subaltern spaces and protagonists. Like many young men of his generation, Tarashankar was radicalized during the 1920s in the period of the Gandhian Non-Cooperation Movement and was imprisoned briefly in 1930. During these years he built up a rich stock of experiences as a village activist in Birbhum, his native district on the western border of Bengal. While the relationship between an author's "life" and their "work" is not always direct, Tarashankar's intimate involvement with the textures of rural life at many levels undoubtedly enabled his writing. Tarashankar reports in his literary biography that Rabindranath Tagore said to him, "I've never read anyone who writes about rural people like you do. . . . Not standing at a distance. You'll go and sit with them and become one of them."[11] Because of this period of activist experience, Tarashankar at his best stands a little to the side of the prevailing "Santiniketan" aesthetic that often sentimentalizes and fetishizes the folksy and picturesque aspects of rural (and especially aboriginal, or "tribal") life.[12]

Tarashankar's first publishing break came with a short story in the avant-garde Kolkata-based literary journal *Kallol* (Clamor) in 1929, and he remained associated with the metropolitan avant-gardes through the 1940s. He was associated with the All-India Progressive Writers' Association (PWA), an organization that emerged as part of the Comintern's Left Front international mobilization against fascism, during the late 1930s and '40s. Tarashankar was also a leader (he became president in 1942) of the Anti-Fascist Writers' and Artists' Association (AFWAA), a branch of the PWA. He remained aligned with these literary-political movements into the 1950s, though he broke with the communists in important respects around the end of the '40s.

In India Tarashankar is best known for a series of novels and short stories from the 1930s and 1940s that deal in with the patterns and textures of rural society. Part of an existing strand of Bengali fiction writing, these novels displace the expressionistic urban-centered grittiness of the teens and '20s into a new framework. The rural scene is depicted as the cutting edge of social transformation, while the (imagined) past of rustic Bengal lives on as hallucinatory afterimage in grotesque or macabre gothic modes within a rapidly changing milieu (the 1938 short story "Jalsaghar," made into a movie of the same name by Satyajit Ray in 1958, is a good example of this). In the great rural novels of this period, Tarashankar charts the breakdown of older quasi-feudal structures that both persisted in and were renewed by colonial rule. Several novels of this period have been translated into English: *Kalindi* (1940), *Ganadevata* (1943), *Panchagram* (1944), and *Aragyaniketan* (1953).[13]

Finally, Tarashankar is currently best known in the West for the famous film adaptations of his work by director Satyajit Ray. Ray's movies *Jalsaghar* (The Music Room) (1958) and *Abhijan* (Expedition) (1962) are both based on short stories by Tarashankar. Additionally, there are more than twenty other film adaptations of his short stories and novels in Bengali cinema. This includes an adaptation of *Hansuli Banker Upakatha* by director Tapan Sinha (1962).

ABOUT THE TRANSLATION

The work of translation is the work of solving problems for a reader of a language other than that of the original. A translation is, in both senses of the word, a "solution" of the puzzle of a text. It dissolves that text in another linguistic medium (here the metaphor is chemical solution); and it also "solves" the text as mathlike problem by making it legible to someone who does not share the original's language. In this latter sense, each translation represents a very close "reading" of the original and the production of a tangible or legible monument out of that reading. Such an act of reading unavoidably erases the original, making it illegible in the very movement it makes it legible by repeating it in another tongue. Such are the paradoxes of the translator's work.[14] Translation makes indeterminate the relation between ruin and monument. And as in many arithmetical or algebraic solutions, there is of course a remainder. A question is in what mode the remainder will appear, if it can appear at all? What to do with all the rhetoricity and texture of the original that *did not* carry over? The puzzle of the text to be translated does not have one correct solution like a crossword, but seems to have an infinitude of possible solutions. Each one, at the level of word, space, sentence, paragraph, or chapter, appears to the translator as a temporary fix, an improvised dance over the structuring guidelines of the original that could and would be performed differently another time. This is true no matter how satisfying a particular solution may be when it is arrived at. In other words, translation, no matter how gracefully executed, is as much of a (new) problem as it is a necessity and a solution. Indeed, it is often the case that the more graceful the execution, the more problems and remainders are covered over by the surface beauty of the translation. I have "solved" the problem of *Hansuli Turn* according to the grace and clumsiness of my own ability to dance across the abyss between two languages, so here I wish to make some of those moves visible.

The structure of any text is articulated by rhetorical patterns, silences, spaces, signs, and marks that are not words. These are sometimes the hardest aspects of a text to "translate," if they are even translatable at all. A simple example is the representation of direct speech in *Hansuli Turn*. In keeping with prevailing Bengali conventions for representing direct speech in modern prose publishing, Tarashankar introduces direct speech using a long dash (—) and does not demarcate it from the rest of the text with inverted commas. (This has also historically been a convention for representing direct speech in European languages, including in English.) I have carried over this aspect of the orthographic idiom of the original into the translation rather than add speech marks and phrases such as "she said" and "he replied" to the novel. To carry over, and thus in some sense to "translate" the often playlike layout or appearance of the page is an important concern because this dramatic style of presentation of direct speech has been a significant feature of the novel in Bengal. As

Partha Chatterjee has observed, "it was remarkable how frequently in the course of their narrative Bengali novelists shifted from the disciplined forms of authorial prose to the direct recording of living speech . . . it is often difficult to tell whether one is reading a novel or a play." Chatterjee goes on to argue that this playlike representation of direct speech is an attempt to develop a prose style "modern and national, and yet recognizably different from the Western."[15] Although this is the stuff of a larger debate, I have found it important to preserve the visibility of this aspect of the novel so that the reader can judge its effect for him- or herself.

This translation is based upon the version printed in volume 7 of the *Tarashankar Racanabali* (Collected Works of Tarashankar) published by Mitra and Ghosh of Kolkata (1999). It is the representative standard version of the novel in its final form, though the other widely available edition from Bengal Publishers (2002) is perhaps in more general use. Although I have endeavored to render a translation that is both accurate and readable, I have not attempted here to produce a critical edition that would tabulate the important editorial changes between the various editions of the novel. I hope that in future someone will do so.

A few words are necessary to outline some of the other main protocols of my translation. I have not given "correct" (often Sanskritized) transliterations for proper names, but have rather rendered them in the regular alphabetic system to approximate the way they would sound when spoken. Thus "Bonwari" rather than "Banwāri," "Kaloshoshi" rather than "Kālosasi" and so on. In the present context, to render Bengali in Sanskritic diacritics would clutter the printed page unnecessarily, betray the Bengali word as *parole* (as spoken), and give a misleading impression of the phonic fit between the two languages.

Moreover, while the narrator "speaks" mainly in the "standard colloquial" version of Bengali, the distinction between creole and "standard" is not always maintained. Sometimes creole words bleed into the narrator's discourse, especially when it is a matter of proper names. This may be initially confusing, though like everything in the novel, it establishes patterns that the reader becomes accustomed to very quickly. I have kept strictly to the novel's own deployment of these words between the "standard" and creole variants. Some key examples of this are:

a) Chandanpur is the name of the local country town. The creole version is "Channanpur," and the narrator varies somewhat unpredictably between the two.

b) Neem-oil Prankrishna is one of the Kahar protagonists. He is mostly referred to by the interchangeable abbreviations "Pana" or "Panu" by narrator and characters alike. The same goes for Prohlad Kahar ("Pellad"), Notbor Kahar ("Lotbor"), Noyan Kahar ("Loyan"), and Roton Atpoure ("Oton"). The key protagonist, Bonwari Kahar, often has his name shortened to "Beano" by his friends.

c) Two of the central female figures are Gopalibala Kahar and Kaloshoshi Atpoure. Their names are often shortened to Gopalibou and Kalobou, the "-bou" suffix being an untranslatable appellation for a married woman (Mrs. So-and-so would be slightly too formal).

d) The local landlord family is called Ghosh, and consists of several brothers and their wives. Sometimes the middle brother is called "Mejo Ghosh" (which I have translated literally as "Middle Ghosh," as we say "Big John" or "Freddie Junior"); sometimes he is called "Maito Ghosh," which means the same thing but which I have retained in this form to mark the difference. Another group of rural overseers and bosses is called Mondol, which is often rendered in creole as "Morol" for characters and narrator alike.

The hardest decision to make while translating *Hansuli Turn* was to recast the colloquial term that the novel's protagonists use for the play of erotic desire. The word used in Bengali is *ranga*, meaning "color." There is no near equivalent in the English language that connotes the often subtle, sometimes bantering, and electric sense of erotic tension designated by *ranga* while retaining the reference to hue, staining, or coloration. I have translated *ranga* as "heat," having in mind the way that erotic affects are colloquially designated in this way in the English language (the object of desire being "hot," "having the hots" or "being hot" for someone, being in heat, being warmed or inflamed by desire, burning, ardent, fervent, and so on). I have translated the word *ranga* consistently as "heat" in this way so that the reader can see where each change has been made. Or rather, for the most part, I have represented creole *anga*, with the *r* dropped, as "'eat" without an *h*. The poetry of hue, stain, or color as a way of naming the affective movement between two people is of course irremediably altered by translation into a thermodynamic principle, though the sense of mutual contamination remains in the new medium. Moreover, some other connotations of "heat" (*tāp*) in South Asia are laden with a philosophical and religious significance that, while it can include erotic affect, is certainly not restricted to that. I can here only mark and account for what has been lost in translation and offer the reader these guidelines for calculating and making up the difference him- or herself.

And then, finally, there is the problem of how to translate the actual simulations of more extended creole speech in *Hansuli Turn*. I have developed a pattern of translating the creole that does not sacrifice the novel's dramatic and frequent shifts of register to the flattening effect of rendering everything in a standard English prose of translatorese. This is an adventurous work of fiction, and therefore the translation has been obliged to take a few risks. I have amalgamated aspects of several different English-language dialects and regional accents in order to mime the alien and strange effect of Kahar creole in Bengali. The literary criticism on this work tells us that the language of the novel struck its original readership as odd, jarring, and sometimes comical in its original context. It is a modernist novel, and correspondingly creates certain effects of "distanciation" in its language even as it also aims at a more vivid "realism." A comparison might be the contemporary or near-contemporary modernist experiments of William Faulkner, Zora Neale Hurston, Claude McKay, or James Joyce. While pertinent comparisons may also be made with the representations of rustic speech to be found in Thomas Hardy or D. H. Lawrence, the mechanism by which, in *Hansuli Turn*, Tarashankar frames the creole Bengali (the *arthāt* device explained above) puts this particular novel in the company of the more obviously "experimental" works.

The main point here is that this is a translation: there is no *one* idiom that can be used to make an equivalent to the language of the Kahars. In my view, it would not be correct to pick out a single creole or dialect of the English language and stay with it consistently, as that would risk falsely fixing in the reader's mind a specific social group in Europe or America as an adequate equivalent. The Kahars are *a bit* like plantation slaves, as they are *a bit* like Italian rural bandits, *a bit* like Welsh provincial farmers, and even—the young men and women at least—*a bit* like urban Cockney wide boys and Chicana cholas. But South Asian social groups are not exactly the same as the ones we in the United States are familiar with, and so I have wished to maintain a sense of the strangeness of a complex and different group whose dialect cannot quite be pinned down to a familiar place. In my translation, the Kahars do not speak an English that is spoken by any empirical group. I have tried to maintain a sense of equivalence without identity, and have therefore tried to map the confusion of the novel's language with another kind of confusion.[16] Method to the madness, of course; initial and final consonants are often dropped, idiomatic insults are rendered more or less idiomatically in

English, and so on. Yet every reader will both "read in" the dialects they know already and hear in their head when they read the words on the page, and have those modes of speech defamiliarized by the one I elaborated as I followed Tarashankar's lead. I hope that the translation lends its words to the sounds of many dialects, in bits. This may reflect one of the novel's unspoken presuppositions: that the plurality of creoles precedes the purity of a single tongue. Every translation closes many doors on the plurality of the original, but it can perhaps also mime that plurality in its own way, giving the reader a sense that the original *has* a plurality or infinity, even if it cannot communicate the original's specific performance of infinitude.

Ben Conisbee Baer
Birbhum and New York

NOTES

1. The subaltern historians adapted the term from the writings of Italian Marxist philosopher Antonio Gramsci. One of the most useful early statements of the Subalternist position may be found in Ranajit Guha, "On Some Aspects of the Historiography of Colonial India," in *Subaltern Studies Vol. I*, ed. Ranajit Guha (Delhi: Oxford University Press, 1982), 1–8. For broader elaborations of the question see also Gayatri Chakravorty Spivak, "Subaltern Studies: Deconstructing Historiography," in Spivak, *In Other Worlds: Essays in Cultural Politics* (New York: Routledge, 1988), and the well-known essay "Can the Subaltern Speak?" now updated in her *A Critique of Postcolonial Reason: Towards a History of the Vanishing Present* (Cambridge: Harvard University Press, 1999), 244–311. There is by now a very extensive debate on subalternity beyond the limits of South Asian history.

2. Raja Rao, *Kanthapura* (New York: New Directions, 1963). See Senath W. Perera, "Towards a Limited Emancipation: Women in Raja Rao's 'Kanthapura,'" *Ariel: A Review of International English Literature* 23, no. 2 (October 1992): 101–110, for an analysis of the role of women in *Kanthapura*. The novel also contains a powerful scene of class/caste difference when the Brahmin Gandhian activist Moorthy enters a "Pariah" (untouchable) household for the first time in his life and in spite of himself is seized with visceral horror at this transgression: "he thinks surely there is a carcass in the back yard, and it's surely being skinned, and he smells the stench of hide and the stench of pickled pigs, and the room seems to shake, and all the gods and all the manes of heaven seem to cry out against him" (72). *Hansuli Turn* gestures toward the focalization of such a scene from the side of the Pariahs, so to speak, as well as from that of

their superiors. I use the word "untouchable" rather than the now more acceptable term *dalit* in this introduction. *Dalit* came into widespread currency as a militant appellation in the 1970s, but *Hansuli Turn* deals with a group largely, but not entirely, cut off from the currents of *dalit* militancy that were emerging even in the novel's own times.

3. Mulk Raj Anand's pathbreaking English-language novel *Untouchable* (London: Wishart, 1935) was one of the first works of Indian fiction largely to stage its narrative through the focalization of a subaltern untouchable figure, here a member of the urban underclass. For an extended discussion of *Untouchable* in these terms see Ben Conisbee Baer, "Shit Writing: Mulk Raj Anand's *Untouchable*, the Image of Gandhi, and the Progressive Writers' Association," *Modernism/Modernity* 16, no. 3 (September 2009).

4. A starting point for thinking about the practice of "transnational literacy" is Spivak's "How to Read a 'Culturally Different' Book" in Francis Barker et al., *Colonial Discourse/Postcolonial Theory* (Manchester: Manchester University Press, 1994), 126–150. Spivak's first extended discussion and naming of this practice is in "Teaching for the Times," *The Journal of the Midwest Modern Language Association* 25, no. 1 (1992).

5. "Feudal" is strictly speaking a misnomer when used to describe the social structures of rural India in the colonial period (and before). However, for the nonspecialist in Indian history, the term "feudal" or "quasi-feudal" as I use it here is intended to give a loosely analogical sense of a social order based upon hierarchical rankings of mutual obligation, service upon the land, and extra-economic coercion. For discussions see R. S. Sharma, *Indian Feudalism* (Calcutta: University of Calcutta, 1965) and Irfan Habib, *Essays in Indian History: Towards a Marxist Perception* (New Delhi: Tulika, 1995).

6. The most significant body of research on the critical possibilities of primitivism in South Asia has come from art history. See Partha Mitter, *The Triumph of Modernism: India's Artists and the Avant-Garde, 1922–1947* (London: Reaktion Books, 2007).

7. Compare with the subaltern protagonist Bakha transformed by British military uniform in Anand, *Untouchable* as well as with the masquerading British/Indian counterespionage agent Kim in Rudyard Kipling's *Kim* (1901) and the rewriting of Kim as unknowing orthodox Hindu masquerader in Tagore's *Gora* (1910).

8. Ben Conisbee Baer, "Creole Glossary: Tarashankar Bandopadhyay's *Hansuli Banker Upakatha*," *PMLA* 124, no. 3 (May 2010).

9. Conisbee Baer, "Creole Glossary." See also Conisbee Baer, "Arthāt Tārāshankar," *Gangeo Patra* 20 (April 2008).

10. As is conventional in South Asia, where respected figures are generally referred to by their first names, I call him Tarashankar. The best general introduction to the work of Tarashankar in English remains Mahasweta Devi, *Tarasankar Bandyopadhyay* (New Delhi: Sahitya Akademi, 1975).

11. Tarashankar Bandopadhyay, *Amar Sahitye Jiban* (Kolkata: Paschimbanga Sahitya Akademi, 1997), 93. My translation.

12. Mahasweta Devi writes that "Tagore had said [to Tarashankar] that Santiniketan remained an alien place to the residents of the district," Devi, *Tarasankar Bandyopadhyay*, 16. To explore these issues fully would take far more space than available here. Santiniketan is the name often given to the university founded by Rabindranath Tagore in 1921. It is actually the name of the place the university is located, in the same district in which Tarashankar was born and grew up. As a name for a cultural tendency, "Santiniketani" refers especially to the visual arts and literature produced by students or faculty of the university, or those in its broader cultural orbit. My point is not that all works produced within the orbit of Santiniketan romanticize tribal/rural culture, but rather that Tarashankar's best writing manages to establish alternative topoi for these themes.

13. *Kalindi: The Caprice of the River and the Greed of Men*, trans. Leila L. Javitch (New Delhi: Munshiram Manoharlal, 1978); *Ganadevata: The Temple Pavilion*, trans. Lila Ray (Bombay: Kutub-Popular, 1969); *Panchagram (Five Villages)*, trans. Marcus F. Franda and Suhrid K. Chatterjee (Delhi: Manohar Book Service, 1973); *Arogyaniketan*, trans. Enakshi Chatterjee (New Delhi: Arnold-Heinemann Publishers, 1977).

14. I have developed this understanding of translation from Paul de Man's account of reading in his essay "Shelley Disfigured," in de Man, *The Rhetoric of Romanticism* (New York: Columbia University Press, 1984), 92–123.

15. Partha Chatterjee, *The Nation and Its Fragments: Colonial and Postcolonial Histories* (Princeton: Princeton University Press, 1993), 8.

16. I have learned from and been inspired by Gayatri Spivak's example in her translation of Mahasweta Devi's 1980 novel *Chotti Munda and His Arrow* (Calcutta: Seagull, 2003). There for the first time she took on the task of rendering in dialectal idiom the creole Bengali of the Munda (and other) protagonists, remarking in her introduction that "the sustained aura of subaltern speech" makes it seem "as if normativity has been withdrawn from the speech of the rural gentry" (vii). I am not aware of any other translations from Bengali that have tried this, and I have of course made other kinds of choices in rendering the different creole of Birbhum. Tarashankar is an important precursor for Mahasweta Devi's work, and although his representation of subaltern creole does not usually give the impression that "normativity has been withdrawn from the speech of the rural gentry," it does put the two modes of Bengali into play with each other in ways that authorized Mahasweta's own representations. I borrow the word "confusion" at this point in the main text from Jacques Derrida, "Des tours de Babel," tr. Joseph F. Graham, in Gil Anidjar, ed., *Acts of Religion* (New York: Routledge, 2002).

With greatest respect
Kalidas Ray, Poet
Most esteemed

Dada,

The Rarh's "Tale of Hansuli Turn" is not unknown to you. The earth of that place, its people and their aberrant language—all these things are very familiar to you. Their lifespirit's black hue and sensuous bumblebee hum are woven together with your images and songs of rural life. I don't know how the subject of these people will go down in educated society. I have put it into your hands. Yours—
Labhpur, Birbhum

TARASHANKAR
ASHARH, 1355

Part

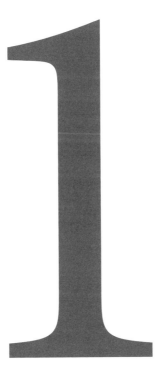

One

At night in the thick jungle of Hansuli Turn someone's whistling. No one knows if the spirit's a god or a demon. Everyone's terrified. Especially the Kahars.

* * *

Almost at the midpoint of the Kopai river there's a famous river bend called Hansuli Turn—meaning that where the river doubles back on itself in a very tight curve, its figure is just like a crescent-shaped hansuli necklace. In the rains, as it encircles the green fields, the hilly Kopai's red-earth-filled, water-brimming bend looks like a golden hansuli on a dark girl's neck. In the spring months, when the water flows clean and clear, then it's like a silver hansuli. That's why the bend is called Hansuli Turn. Within the river girdle, surrounded by the thick bamboo groves of Hansuli Turn, the settlement of Bansbadi occupies about one hundred acres inside the ward of Jangol. North of Bansbadi, on the other side of a few small paddy fields, lies Jangol village. Bansbadi's a small village. Around the four sides of two ponds are thirty or so Kahar huts. Genteel society in Jangol village—potter Sadgops, farmer Sadgops, spice-merchant-caste homes, as well as one barber-caste and two weaver-caste houses. Jangol's boundaries are broad; maybe one and a half thousand acres of good cropland, and lots of fallow too—about a hundred and fifty acres of it abandoned on the Saheb Tracts that used to belong to the English indigo planters.

Recently the respectable caste-Hindu masters, the gentlefolk of Jangol village, have had quite a fright. The Kahars of the little hundred-acre-bounded Bansbadi village, which is to say Hansuli Turn's Kahars, said— The good sirs are "scairt." Meaning scared. They would be. It seems someone's whistling at night. For a few days the whistle came from exactly midway between Jangol and Bansbadi, from the first westward curve of that Hansuli Turn—thick with wood-apple and saora trees, a terrifying place for ordinary mortals, the Brahmin ogre's den. Then for a few days it rose from the thorn-infested jungle on the Kopai riverbank on Jangol's eastern side. Then for a few days the whistle rose from a little farther off—

moved toward Hansuli Turn. Now the whistle rises from somewhere in the middle of Bansbadi's bamboo groves.

The gents have done a lot of investigating. They blasted gunshots into the night, went yelling out of the village a couple of nights with guns, sticks, clubs; came, went, and looked all around in the light of powerful, footlong flashlights. Yet not a clue did they find. But the whistle still rang out nonstop. The police station is twenty or thirty miles away. It was reported there too. Sub-Inspector came for a few nights, but he couldn't get a single lead either. Yet it's true that the sound keeps circling around the riverbank. Hearing all this, he made a conjecture.

Sub-Inspector is from East Bengal—he said, something's happening in the river. "Life by a river, year-long worry-giver." Think, ruminate a while. If you mull it over then you'll get it.

"Life by a river, year-long worry-giver"—the phrase is obviously a saying from oral tradition, coming down through the generations in the land. It's never a false statement, but just as the land splits the sayings split too, and thus, in Jangol village of Hansuli Turn's Bansbadi, this saying doesn't fit right. It doesn't fit this western region of Bengal. It was meant for that other region of Bengal. A member of the Ghosh family of Jangol village does business in Calcutta. He buys and sells coal, and also trades in jute. Sire Ghosh has been all around that other part of Bengal. He says—Now over that side's a river country. Water and land all mixed up. Rivers running full a twelvemonth; tide comes in, water pours over riverbanks, brimming in green fields; flow tide then ebb tide, and the field water just going back down into the river; when the river course empties, banks surface. But it's still a couple feet below the banks at most, no farther down. So what's the river then, this or that, one or two? Like the flow of Ganges-Jamuna, dark and eerie; their folks get the shakes setting off to cross from one side to the other. And just one stream? Where one stream comes and joins from, where the flows split and go—can't tell. It's like a seven-stranded water necklace—not a hansuli! River bends ever end over there? "Eighteen Bender," "Thirty Bender," river looks different every turn. Betel and coconut trees both sides—not in rows—not orchards—like a forest. And so many other trees, so many creepers, so many flowers, if you haven't seen you couldn't imagine. You want to see more than you ever can. Narrow little creeks going from the big river into the thick coconut and betel forests, creek on creek. Tiny boats plying those creeks. Little villages of tin-roof bamboo-wattle huts hidden under coconut and betel shade. These narrow creeks go by one village and right through the middle of another—from one village right into the next. The little boats of that land are like our oxcarts. Harvest going up from field to yard by boat, going from yard to market, to trade post and harbor; this village's folks going around in those same boats to their marriage kin in that village, newlywed girls going to their in-laws' places, girls coming home to their parents' places; groups of pals going to fairs and games. Farmers going to fields—going by boat too, sailing off alone with their sickles and plows in a boat. River with no end, no beginning, like the Milky Way in an autumn sky—sitting at the head of the tiny boats, like banana-stick rafts on that river, rudder gripped in left hand and armpit, scull in right hand and foot, moving along. Ghosh son bursting with talk about that land can't say it all. Sitting on those riverbanks—'course it's a worry.

As he speaks of worry, fear spreads in Ghosh son's eyes—sometimes he gets goosebumps. If you go farther down, that seven-stranded necklace of a river merges into one again. Then the river is shoreless. As if the seven-stranded gold necklace around the neck of Lakshmi of Wealth has turned to the python's grip on the neck of Monosha of the Snakes; river's even hissing like a python. Rising, swelling, wave on wave, like the swaying of a thousand cobra hoods. With all this, sometimes a few bits of black cloud appear in the sky—flashes of lightning play right upon them, as if someone's firebuilt fingers beat out the music of the "Terror Drummer" of those Black Clouds. Heaven and hell shake with the beat of his dreadlocks. Then the python flings and flings its huge shape and dances, striking with its thousand hoods—crazed in an orgy. Storm beats the river water. That storm washes everything away—homes and villages, trade posts and harbors—humans, cows, the insect world. Suddenly no tempest, no storm, everything seems to be peace and quiet, nothing anywhere—suddenly on the riverbank half a village stars to shudder and shake, turns and rolls straight over into the fathomless womb of the pythonlike river. Folk there have to keep one eye on the lap of the sky all year round—looking out for bits of black cloud; and the other eye to the earth's breast, like sandalwood covered in green grass and crops—looking for signs of cracking. Yep, yearlong worries there, all right.

Sub-Inspector's from that place, that's why he said what he said. But Hansuli Turn's an altogether different kind of place. Hansuli Turn's a place of iron-willed earth. People battle with the earth here far more than with the river. If it's "parchtime," the height of cruel summer, that is, the river dries and turns to desert, sand as far as the eye can see—on one side water no more than knee-deep somehow trickles along, like a motherless little girl with feeble body and miserable face, somehow inching forward. Then earth becomes stone. Grass shrivels away, earth heats up like forged iron; hoes and shovels won't cut, strike with a hoe or shovel and the blade bends; hit with a pickaxlike thing and it'll cut a bit, but with each blow sparks fly. Waterways and lakes, ponds and tarns fill with cracks. Then it's only the river that keeps folks going; it's the river that gives water. Here, worry about the river isn't yearlong.

Here, four months' river worry. From Asharh to Ashwin, the rainy months. After Asharh, the motherless little girl grows up. Youth fills her body. Then suddenly one day she becomes a witch. Just as a Kahar girl suddenly fights with mother-father-brother-sister-in-law, curses the neighbors, leaves home for the village, hair flies loose, cloth drops from the shoulder, eyes spit fire, she pelts rocks at anyone who comes for her; runs off directionless, completely out of her mind, tarnishing family honor; so does that full river one day suddenly rise in flood. A witch incarnate! No mercy—no mercy, gone completely out of her mind, she takes off screaming and calling like naked Kali, raising a rumbling roar as if with a hundred mouths, directionless. Village, settlement, field, corpse-burning ground, carrion pit, from home's Lakshmi shrine to garbage dump—she tramples and scatters whatever's in her way as she goes. And for a day or two, even. Occasionally it's massive; it's four or five days later that good sense returns. When her rage passes, the Kahar girl sits quietly at the edge of the village, comes step by step into her backyard, lies down and weeps or sings softly, you can't quite tell which—and just like this the Kopai comes down to her banks; having sprung her banks, she sinks a little below them and flows on with a gentle sound. She'll do this six or seven times, no more, in the space of four months. Maybe once during that time, or perhaps once every two or three years, she's yet crazier. The Kopai's just like a Kahar lass.

But the girl's done wrong, ruined honor. Even if Kopai floods don't smash your home you do still suffer, indeed. When the water goes down, steam rises from the sodden fields; countryside fills with flies and mosquitoes. Humans move; above moving human heads, swarms of droning mosquitoes also move; human bodies shiver; bites bring up swollen welts on limbs. Flies sit in layers upon cows' bodies; unable to dislodge them by tail swipes, cattle shake their horns nonstop, sometimes jump with all four legs in the air. Farmers help out; bind spliced palm leaves together like a broom, and with this swat flies and drive them off. Just a few days after, "maloyria" fever starts.

There's more—misery of the Kopai's flood. Every two or three years the Kopai hill river of the Santal Parganas suddenly floods. It's called "Flash Flood," and now and again a "gubagha," a leopard, or two gets caught in that flood current, is washed down to these unlikely bends of Hansuli Turn, gets caught in the bamboo-grove edges of Bansbadi village's riverbank. Sometimes dead, sometimes alive. If alive, the leopard makes a home in these bamboo groves. Then come bears; one or two a year of those bastards. Strange, those fellows, when dead, never remain trapped in the bamboo groves when they die. Live tigers hardly ever turn up; same with dead. In a whole generation there were two—one dead and one alive. The Ghoshes of Jangol pulled the dead one out and showed its skin to the district Saheb, thus gaining a gun. It was the Kahars who killed the live one; the spice merchants got a gun by showing its skin. If a bear comes it's still the Kahars that kill; every flood time, if they see one on their searches of the bamboo groves after every flood, they give chase and kill with club, cudgel, spear, pike, bow and arrow, and celebrate, dancing wildly; transfixed by their own bravado, they down huge quantities of liquor. And it is here there are wild pigs that, in spite of the Kahars' clubs, cudgels, spears, pikes, have set up a regular outpost. Not, of course, in Bansbadi's bamboo thickets, but a bit farther away in the Saheb Tracts. With the ravages of the Kahars, they don't get away with settling in the Bansbadi area. Their great gathering place is in the brushland, in the ruined offices of the indigo works. At night a horde of swine runs grunting along the river's edge, digs up earth with tusks, eats roots. Now and then one or two are thrown off the horde and enter the village. Someone stumbling across them gets hurt. Then the Kahars take up arms against them. Not arms, traps. They have an amazing ruse for killing wild pigs. In the middle of two-foot strips of bamboo is tied a foot-long, strong, wiry cord with a sharpened hook at the end. As bait on the hook, banana and fermented liquor dregs. Ten or so of these things are scattered on path and field. Drawn by the sweet smell of liquor dregs, the damn pigs come snuffling along the ground and gobble them up with delight; hooks stick straight through their tongues or jaws. They then try to release the hooks by pulling with their hoofs—which has the opposite effect, as the hook's wire enters the hoof cleft and the hoof cleft gets stuck on the bamboo strip at the end. At one end the hook catches in the tongue, at the other end a cord-yoked hoof catches on the bamboo strip; the poor piggy bastard has one leg up and stands there like that on three legs. In the morning, the Kahars all come with clubs in hand, beat the pig to death, and drag it off for a sacrificial feast.

Sometimes crocodiles appear too. Nearly all are fish-eating. When they come the crocodiles get down into the Jangol gentry's fish-filled ponds. They don't want to come up. *Boom-bam*, the gents bring rifles and fire bullets; the crocodile surfaces, dives, and sticks up its snout in a different corner. Sitting up on the banks, puffing their pipes, the Kahars watch with amusement; yet by the riverside of Hansuli Turn's Bansbadi there are deeps where a huge, voracious man-and-cow-eating crocodile comes—folks here call it "ghariyaal." Then the Kahars don't sit quiet. They come out in a posse; yellow turmeric smeared all over, they carry spades, axes, staves, spears, and a very long bamboo pole with a rope noose tied on one end. All along the riverbanks they hunt for the crocodile's den. If they find sign of the devil's lair in a hole at the edge of the bank they excitedly block up the mouth of the hole while digging into it from above. Then they slaughter the devil trapped in the crevice. Sometimes they'll cleverly pull it up in the noose and brutally beat it to death over a few days. If the crocodile isn't found in the hole then the cowherders bring a herd of buffalo from their neighborhood down to the deeps. The buffalo disturb the water and bring the ghariyaal crocodile out. Then it's time for crocodile slaying. It's a virtual demon slaughter. And while you could never really compare the bastard crocodile with a demon, the Kahars' frenzy—well, the only thing to describe that is the annihilating dance of Shiva's entourage.

In short, in this place—there's not much worry about the river in Hansuli Turn; apart from the little spells of "maloyria," the weight of what little worry there is falls solely on the Kahars of Bansbadi. But now this whistling business has also totally thrown them. In the first place they didn't think it was thieves or bandits; the thing was some romance. They'd gotten annoyed. Because around here, ninety-nine out of a hundred romantic heroines are girls from their homes. But within a few days this notion had already passed. Now the idea is that Lord of the Brahmin demon's shrine has gotten furious for some reason. Maybe, having departed this wood-apple forest and saora woodland, it's he roaming along the riverbanks, letting the denizens of Hansuli Turn know about it by whistling. They'd been imagining all sorts about this. In house after house they're smearing the gods' niches with rouge and offering pennies, and, seeing the indifference of Jangol's gentry masters to the matter, they're falling into despair. What more can the poor Kahars do? With such little understanding? Yet one evening they sat down to meet. But the Kahars have two hamlets now, "Behara" hamlet and "Atpoure" hamlet. Bonwari, headman of Behara Para, shook his head in despair about the Atpoures and said—An offerin' once a year, so they don't do it well. There'll be a "noo" offerin'!

Neem-oil Panu's proper name is Prankrishna. As there are two Prankrishnas in the hamlet, the neem tree in the yard of this Prankrishna's house is prefixed to his name and he's called Neem-oil Panu. He said—Y'know what chief, there's summat I was too scared to say for ages, man. When it came up, like, know what I mean, an' all was said—when the thing's been goin' bad, then it's not right to keep quiet 'bout it no more. Whatcha say?

The eyes of everyone at the meeting fell on him. Very slowly Bonwari pulled himself closer and asked—Ya gonna tell whaddappened, then?

Panu had opened his mouth, but before he did a piercing pipe sound rang out. That whistle sound! The sound's coming—from the bamboo groves south of Bansbadi village. Startled, everyone pricked up their ears and stayed quiet. Bonwari sat facing northward, his tobacco pipe in his left hand; he lifted his right arm over his shoulder and tipped his forefinger backward, indicating a southerly direction to everyone. Behind, southward in the bamboo border, the whistle is sounding.

Again the whistle rang out! Oi!

***

Abandoning their work, with anxious faces, all the Kahar women came down into their yards and stood afraid. Some had cooking spoons in their hands; others were putting children to sleep, children still in their laps; some were combing their hair, handfuls of hair in their left hands, combs in their right; some had gone to take dung cakes off the back wall of the house by kerosene lamplight, and in that kerosene light they came running, still carrying a handful of dungcakes, and stood among the crowd. Only Suchand Kahar, stone-deaf old woman, remained gaping into the others' faces; with the hem of her upper body's clothing shamelessly open, she was fixing a long tear in the worn-out, sewn-up patchwork of her wrapper's scarlet border; she just remained sitting, questioning all around her with a silent scowl. Unable to understand a thing, she finally screeched a question in her usual harsh voice—What?

Embarrassed by her mother's deafness, Suchand's daughter, Bashan, that's to say Bashanta, turned and said—Damn you.

Suchand asked again, yelling even louder this time—Ey, whaddappened? What y'all standin' up for?

This time granddaughter Pakhi, that's to say Bashanta's daughter, Pakhi, shouted close to her face—Wh-i-i-i-stle!

—Whistle? That's one o' them lads from Jangol doin' it.

—Nah—nah. Gesturing with her hands, she explained—*That* wh-i-i-i-stle!

At that very moment, the whistle rang out again.

Pakhi shoved her grandmother and said—Listen ta that. But fearful Suchand clamped a hand over Pakhi's mouth and sat straight up. She could hear. And she stood up. Since entering middle age she's worn the merest cloth over her breasts at home and outdoors, and this only at her daughter's request. And to that very purpose she'd been sewing up the ripped hem at this moment—but she forgot to pull the tattered hem over herself as she stood. Trailing the torn hem, she put her face right up to Bonwari's and yelled loudly—Are ye gonna gi' God's sacred offerin' or ya gonna mess around?

Bonwari yelled loudly too, gestured vigorously, arms and legs moving—Does God's offerin' just come from you an' me, auntie? What can we do if gentry do nothin'?

—So we're gonna die? Ooever gets deaded, you lot'll be the first to go!

—Say what I'm s'posed ta do? What God pesscribes, that'll be. If we're standin' guard on village southside, an' we're, y'know—the garbage o' creation, then yeh, 'course we'll be first ta die.

Neem-oil Panu spoke up—No, chief. If anyone comes to 'arm, it'll first be that Chaudhury 'ousehold o' yours. That I know.

A deep surprise and questioning appeared on Bonwari's brow and in his gaze, and he asked—What's all this about then?

Suchand said—What? What ya said?

—Nothin', dearie. Not speakin' ta you. Siddown, won'tcha.

Pakhi came and took Suchand's hand, led her aside, and said—Sit 'ere.

Panu said—That offerin' that just went, chief—there was a mark on the goat.

Everyone spoke up in amazement—There was a mark? The women shivered—Ooh no!

Panu revealed the details. A dog had left a tiny bite mark on one of Panu's baby goats.

—Was such a little 'un then, next some bastard's dog comes along an' just grabs 'im on 'is back leg. Right then Lotbor's Ma seen it, 'ad a broom in 'er 'and; chased the dog off wi' a whack of the broom, but two teeth'd gone in. Wi' turmeric an' stuff on, it 'ealed up. Was thinkin'—I'll castrate it for fattenin'. Wi' this an' that I didn't, the goat got big. Then I was thinkin', one of these days I'll gi' the chop an' share 'im out to the neighbors to eat. This year, know what I mean, what did the bastard goat go and do—went into the Chaudhury 'ouse; an' it'll eat—planted by the gentry for fun—what's it called dad, that flowerin' bush. Now 'e's grabbed an' tied up. Searchin' an' searchin' I went there. I went an' the Chaudhurys' agent slapped me about. Then 'e shows me the bush and says—"I paid five rupees for this shoot and brought it from Calcutta. Now you need to pay the price for it." What'm I s'posed ta say? I saw—tree leaves an' roots weren't damaged by the damn goat's eatin'—shrub 'ad totally shriveled an' died on the train. I begged at 'is feet. Finally got out of it by givin' the goat. I said—"But listen sire, goat's marked, chop 'im up it'll be tasty, but you better not give 'im as no offerin' in no God's shrine, sire." I swear to ya by my son, wi' a hand on that Lotbor's 'ead, chief, I told 'im twice—"Marked goat, a marked goat, sire, better not offer it at no shrine." Now what do I see at the seat of the Bahmin demond, in 'is shrine at Lord's offerin'—that goat first ta get the chop from the Chaudhury gents. "Awmighty" knows—t'ain't my fault.

Suchand hadn't moved far. Sat just nearby, she'd fixed Panu's face with a stare and was listening to his story; light from the oil lamp in her hand was falling entirely on Panu's face. Now she's able to understand almost everything. She heaved a deep sigh and spoke, shaking her head—Not good, not good, this is never good.

The whole meeting was plunged in dreadful silence. It seemed that God had spoken those words through Suchand's mouth—Not good, not good, this is never good.

Everyone sat stunned.

In that terrible silence of the assembly Suchand began again—Whatever's at Hansuli Turn's there by grace o' this Father. Three generations ago those Chaudhurys were regular 'ouseholders, agents in the sahebs' indigo office. Office was in a broke-down state even back then. That time came Kopai's "'nihillation" flood. That was long back, 'fore our time; 'eard it from me pa. Kopai started flooding at midday. In the first watch o' night, h-u-r-r-i-c-a-n-e! Everything went under, right up to the big edge of "lakey" pond. Indigo Saheb an' Missus climbed a tree. Then all night, whooshin' roarin' floods moved—floods moved. Pitch dark all over. An' poundin' rain. Like there'd be no tomorrer after that night. So then it's third watch o' the night—an' it's like there's light an' music comin' from middle o' the river, far from Hansuli Turn. Straightaway outta the glowin' 'eart o' the river a "lumernated" wedding-barge-lookin' boat started comin' over the deeps at Hansuli Turn, playin' all kinds o' music. Saheb 'ad seen it—'e dived in the water. Missus told 'im no. Saheb didn't listen. Then what's Missus do? Missus came down too. Up to 'is waist in water, Saheb went ta grab the boat. Lord suddenly came out from that Father's shrine. Givin' me goose bumps ta say it—Suchand was really shivering— that shaven 'ead, shinin' white skin, 'oly beads 'round 'is neck, that sacred thread, 'e wore red robes, clogs on 'is feet—Lord walked across water in 'is clogs and said—"Where you going, Saheb? To grab the boat? Don't do it, it's not your boat." Saheb paid no mind to that. Said—"Scram or I'll put a bullet in you." Lord laughed—"All right, take the boat then." Well, no sooner'd 'e said that than the bottom drops out of Saheb and Missus's waist-deep water, and straight off a whirlpool sucks 'em down, spinning oo knows where—whooshin' away. Chaudhury was right near Saheb, sat on another tree branch. Lord came and called to 'im—"Come down." Now Chaudhury's shaking wi' fright. Lord laughed and said—"Eh sonny, no fear, get down. You won't go under." Ye wouldn't believe it, kid— Chaudhury got down, water's no more than knee-deep. Lord laughed, then pointed an' said—"Did you see you needed a boat? That's your boat. Worship me, bow your head to God, feed guests, give alms to beggars, pity the poor, speak kindly to the unhappy. The wealth of he who had it I've given to you. It'll continue as long as my word is followed—He'll remain steadfast. If you don't follow, He'll leave; ye can suffer the consequences." For him—that very Lord—such contempt! Lakshmi of Wealth up and gone. Nothin' we ain't done against dharma. Finally a tainted, dog-bitten, secondhand goat offerin' at that Lord's shrine! Does God stick around for this! Aye, it be God—it's surely God whistlin'. Gonna leave, so 'e's lettin' us know.

Dusk darkness was gradually thickening. On Hansuli Turn's sandbank, just touching the village flank, curving parallel with the river, ran the village's bamboo border. The river bend is round like a hansuli necklace loop, and so its parallel bamboo curve or bamboo levee is circular too. They've surrounded Bansbadi like garland threads of green and scarlet. A ring of darkness advanced from those very bamboo groves, centering on Kaharpara's surrounded huts. Eerily, overhead light to illuminate the assembly in the yard was blocked. Owls with cracked voices screeching and flying. Bats fluttering—startling overhead breeze with skittering wings. Now and again a couple of them scrap, clash wings, squeaking like kites. Meanwhile, having heard in Suchand's story a description of the Lord of the wood-apple and saora forest's great spirit, those ochre robes of his, this shaven-headed, bead necklace and glowing sacred thread-wearing figure; and then having heard about the crime of the dogbitten goat offered to that very Lord—well, everyone was frozen absolutely stiff with terror. A child in someone's lap began to wail. The agitated assembly cried—Aaaah!

His mother put a breast in the boy's mouth and tried to rush him out of there, but she didn't dare enter her home alone.

Suddenly Suchand spoke again—Pana, but it's definitely your fault too, at Lord's shrine.

Panu was unprepared for such an accusation. Besides, his throat had gone dry from fear; who knows why his fear was greater than anyone's. He heard Suchand's words and tried to reply, but couldn't.

Then, agreeing with Suchand, Bonwari said—Ye said right, auntie. Was Panu's goat.

Suchand had herself been talking alone for some time—no matter that she couldn't hear. As soon as Bonwari spoke it mattered anew. Suchand considers herself one of those Kahar elders who have the right to pronounce judgment in such weighty problems. Suchand wouldn't stand for such "disspect" if anyone disputed this. She keeps a sharp eye out for it. Not hearing Bonwari's words, she got the idea—he's contradicting her, slighting her words by whispering. She fixed a steady gaze on Bonwari, leaned slightly toward him waving her hand, and said—I've seen plenty like you, Bonwari—goddit! Little boy o' back in them days. Yer ma dead, "muvverless" boy—that skinny tum. Drank me milk and put flesh on yer ribs. Me bod was like a Bhagalpur cow's, milk in me tits like a she-buffalo. Now 'ere youcome talkin' over me? You mark my words, you'll see—all the village folk'll see too—won't make year's end, Panu'll come to 'arm.

Panu shuddered. Panu's wife was standing a little way off among the women; she began a soft, sad weeping.

Now Bonwari shouted—That's exactly wha' I'm sayin' though, dearie! I'm sayin' what you're sayin'.

—Sayin' that?

—Yeh. I'm sayin', 'ow can Panu's fault be undone when it's 'is goat?

Suchand's dull eyes began to gleam—a smile of satisfaction at her own sagacity also blossomed on her mouth—Aye-aye! Ow undone?

An upset Panu asked—Yeh, I mean, like, say 'ow to undo it? Listenin'? I'm sayin'—tell me what's the "counterpesscription"? As he finished his question, his voice rose to a scream.

—Counterpesscription?

—Yeh.

Suchand thought a bit. Led by Bonwari, the others began to discuss this.—Right, tomorrow we're all going to the Chaudhury 'ouse together. Let the 'ole thing be said openly.

Suchand said—You gi' another goat, Panu. An' we raise the dough from the 'amlet for an offerin' at Lord's shrine one day. If Jangol folks are "neggetful"—we do their duty. What you say, Bonbihari? Anythin' else in the counterpesscription? Lord's a god, right—'e'll figure out our meanin'.

Bonwari nodded again and again—Yeh, sure, that's right. What's everyone think then?

Everyone nodded. Prohlad, Gopichand, Pagol, Panu the Second, Omon, they all agreed—So be it, an offerin' it is.

At this very moment a hideous shriek suddenly split the night darkness as if ripping it to shreds. Some animal scream. The shriek's intensity as agonizing as its edge was unbearable. Scream of a young wild pig. Probably dropped away from the herd somehow, jackal saw a chance, grabbed it. Nothing but a baby pig can scream that razorlike scream. Except a hare—a wild, earthcolored hare. Could also be a hare's scream.

At this very next moment a dog came running, barking loudly. A huge, black, swaggering dog, baying vigorously, startled the village meeting and, taking no notice of anyone, leaped through the middle of the meeting onto the trail of that scream. The dog's body collided with Suchand's. Suchand panicked at the dog's blow and the sound of its barking in her ears. The next moment she screamed out—Ai Bonwari look, another evil! That dirty bastard—ye'll all 'ave to do antoniement fer 'is evils, fine that bastard for it. Punish. Punish. Punish.

Before Bonwari could even reply, a hiss came from Suchand's granddaughter among the women—Bashanta's daughter, Pakhi. She spoke up—Why, whassat bastard done ta ya now? Usin' a broke broom ta sweep out yer own ashes! So much anger on *that* bastard.

Now the women started to smirk. Isn't the contagious play of heat an amazing thing in human life? Folk around here, Hansuli Turn people, they call man-woman love "heat." Not "heat"—they say "'eat." They call Hari "Ari," Hanuman "Anuman," Hrishikesh "Ishikesh," Heramba "Eramba." Meaning that where there's an initial *h* in a word, they make it a vowel. Otherwise it won't come off the tongue. An *h* in the middle of a word comes out beautifully. If a man and woman are in love, they say— Them two's 'eatstruck. Yep, heat. Deep red heat. A droplet's touch of that red heat changes the hue of a mind filled with another. The women had been standing in terror, work abandoned, speechless, still as clay manikins, listening to Suchand's horror stories, convinced of that ghastly future, unable to see a way out; now, touched by that heat during Pakhi's outburst, they became instantly mobile, allowed faces to smile. Heat was at work.

The name of that bastard of Suchand's is Karali. Karali's a boy from this hamlet. Karali works in the rail workshops at Chandanpur town. He remains independent from all Kaharpara in talk and outlook. He wants to follow no one, accepts nothing. What he earns he spends. Leaves for Chandanpur in the morning, comes home in the evening. He got back home today, heard the whistle, set out with dog and flashlight. Pakhi's secretly been filled with heat for this Karali. That's why she spoke out against her grandmother. They're shameless when it comes to this. Kahars don't know how to keep anything covered up if they're in love; for shame, for fear, for resentment of the neighbors. It's not one of their habits, they just can't do it. That's why now and then an adolescent Kahar girl rages up like the flooding Kopai and storms out of the house into the street. What's more, Pakhi is daughter of Bashanta, the history of whose lovelife is notorious in these parts. There was once even a ditty all about it. Folk would sing—"O—Come, hear of Bashanta's 'eat."

That's a huge story. Yet Bashanta's daughter Pakhi's story goes this way somewhat independently. She was married in this very village. To the son of the former Kahar headman's house. But bad luck—he's sickly, asthmatic at this age. Meanwhile, Pakhi's fallen in love with Karali. When Karali got accused like this before the assembled village community, Pakhi spoke against her grandmother right there in the meeting.

Grandmother isn't exactly one to roll over for Pakhi; she's Suchand, after all. Suchand too stared Pakhi right in the face a while and suddenly said—Hah, can see yer smeared in 'eat. Look 'ere, that bitch! Seen the lad wimme own eyes, down at that shrine o' Lord's wi' that black mutt, gone ta kill pigeons with 'is sling.

Just then someone, that's to say Karali himself, spoke up from the back of the meeting—Lord told me, when ye're firin' yer slingshot 'ere, one day I'm gonna come down on that Suchand's back wi' a bang. Watch out crone, it's you's in danger. He laughed aloud. The young women's smirks rippled more powerfully at his burst of laughter.

Bonwari gave a sudden, harsh warning—Oi, Karali!

Smiling, Karali said—Oho, what "clamity"! That a warnin' then?

—Siddown, siddown. Bastard, you siddown.

—Old it, I'm off.

—Where you goin'?

—I'm goin'—he smilingly spoke—off ta see, what's all this fuss? That's why I let the dog go.

—No. It's not up ta you ta see what it's all about. That we do know. S'all happenin' cos o' your lot's evils.

Karali burst out laughing and said—What? That Bahmin demond Lord? Pah.

—Watch it, Karali. Yer face'll rot off!

—Look a' this! Me face'll rot off, so why y'all warnin' me?

Meanwhile, somewhere in the bamboo groves, the dog's yelping suddenly took on an angry, warning growl, as if he was about to attack. He must be seeing something right now, rushing off to snap it up. Switching on an extremely weak-beamed flashlight, Karali dashed along the pondside and disappeared into the deep darkness of Bansbadi's bamboo border. The whole meeting was stunned. What boundless guts Karali has, what willful recklessness! Only Pakhi edged forward a little into the darkness and called—Don't go. Eh, don't go I tell ya. Oi there, maniac! Look 'ere. Eh, stubborn idiot! Don't go! Don't go!

Her words were drowned by the dog's heartrending scream of pain.

Bonwari said—Bastard's gonna die, I told ya so Auntie Suchand.

***

The dog came running back, howling in pain. Such an agonizing howl.

Right behind him Karali came back. —Kalua, Kalua!

Kalua looked at his master's face and tried to keep still, but he couldn't stay still. As if the most terrible agony was chasing him. Kalua started turning round and round. Within a few hours he collapsed on the ground, started scratching his face, immediately began whining.

Karali sat by his side and started stroking his body, but the dog was getting like a mad thing; he even jumped to bite master Karali. He began to thrash, started chewing at the earth, sometimes raised his head to whine—made an expression of unbearable torment and again began scraping his face in the dirt.

Sitting motionless, Karali was watching. His flashlight beam going from weak to weaker. Surprised, terrified, he suddenly said softly—Blood!

—Blood!

—Yep.

He pointed—at Kalua's nostrils. Streams of blood rolling from nose and mouth. Finally a horrible thing happened. Two eyes suddenly ballooned up and burst. Streams of blood spurted straight onto black fur. All Kaharpara saw the sight and quaked.

In a voice of fearful assurance Bonwari said—Lord!

Maybe, with his clog-clad left foot, Lord had stomped on the dog's neck.

Two

That very day, night's end, then dawn.

In depths of sleep Bonwari screamed aloud. His wife, Gopalibala, woke with a shock, shoved him, and shouted—Oh dear—say—oh dear! Oh dear!

End of Phalgun month, twentieth already past. Land of hard soil. It's been very hot here lately, mornings get really hot; but at night's end it is chilly-cold. Bonwari said—Body's tinglin'. He had not slept well all night. Hugging the bedsheet to his body, he'd found a bit of restful sleep in the early dawn. All of a sudden he woke up screaming and gibbering. Gopalibala shoved and pulled him—Oh dear! Oh dear!

Torn from sleep, Bonwari looked around groggily for a moment. Then sat up.

Gopalibala asked—Whaddappened? Havin' a bad dream, dear? Why'd ya scream so!

She was trembling with fright too.

—Yeh. Get me 'baccy ready, will ya?

—What dream was it, eh? Why'dya start babblin' in fear like that, dearest?

—Lord was comin'. Bonwari clasped his hands and touched them to his forehead.

—Lord! Gopali began to shake.

—Yeh, Lord. What auntie said's right, Gopali. He was quiet for a moment, then said—Oi, quick wi' the 'baccy! I'm goin' down river's edge via Atpoure Para when I've smoked. Else probly won't see none of 'em. Gotta give an offerin' fer the Lord. Need a donation from Atpoure Para.

Porom Kahar is headman of Atpoure Kaharpara. Bonwari will go to him.

Bansbadi is an entirely Kahar village—well, not a village exactly, it's a hamlet of that there Jangol village. Yet in the landlord's record office it's counted as separate from the ward—taken as a separate village. Beside two ponds are two Kahar hamlets. Behara Kahar and Atpoure Kahar. There've always been more folks in Behara Kaharpara, a settlement of nearly twenty-five little cottages; to the east, the indigo fields' great irrigation pond and the indigo levee's four sides enclose the Beharas' settlement. Bonwari of Kosh-Shoulder house is headman of Behara Para. The Behara Kahars carry palanquins. Bonwari's forefathers used to carry a palanquin for one krosh, a two-mile road, on one shoulder without changing shoulders—so that's why their home is called "Kosh-Shoulder" house. Their clan is some tough clan. Tall and broad, big and hefty figures, but seeming somehow rough-cast, or as if they were constantly fumbled in the making; not a bit of polish.

A few furlongs west of Behara hamlet is the Atpoure Kahars' settlement. The Atpoure Kahars live in a few cottages around a middle-sized pond called Stubborn Dike. Atpoures don't carry palanquins on their shoulders; they put themselves above those Beharas. Using extremely fine phrases, they try to demonstrate their superiority. They say—Atpoure is Ottopohori.

Which is to say "Ostoprohori," twenty-four-hour guard.

The real meaning can be found in the old papers of the Chaudhury house. All those papers have now almost disappeared, devoured by termites. There are still a few whole bits and pieces in piles of termite-eaten paper. Among them the total statement of revenue accounts for the year 1818–19 can be found. The whole Bansbadi ward was wasteland—there was neither pond nor settlement there. There is mention of about ten huts situated in Jangol village, all Sadgop farmers. In the papers of 1842–43 you see a new land settlement, in the name of the illustrious Mister Jenkins saheb, indigo planter. Whatever wasteland there was at Jangol had almost all been incorporated into this new landholding, along with the entire Bansbadi ward. On the upland west of Jangol, the ruins of the indigo offices and a pond called Lake's Pond can still be seen. Water from that Lake's Pond used to flow down through brick channels and fill brickbuilt indigo fermentation tanks. The place is overrun by brush now, and wild pigs have set up an outpost right there. Once they've taken a land settlement at Bansbadi ward, the sahebs dig a pond there and turn all Bansbadi's wasteland to indigo cultivation. It's in order to do just this that these folk of Kaharpara came to Bansbadi. Many people had come. Among them, a few of these Kahars put cottages here. Some had found jobs at the indigo office, patrolling with fightsticks and keeping watch at the saheb masters' gates when needed; for this they'd been given some land and, in keeping with local custom, had received a title befitting their function as tenants of rent-free land on call twenty-four hours a day—Ostoprohori, or Atpoure. Twenty-four-hour guard. The Behara Kahars would till the indigo fields and carry the palanquins of the sahebs and their ladies when required. The pond had been dug to irrigate the indigo fields, so it was called Indigo Levee, and another name was Whitey's Levee—"whitey's," that's to say sahebs', levee. The pond's water is good. In those days no one was allowed to go into this pond, as water for the sahebs' use was taken from there; now and then some of the head saheb's friends came visiting and white folk would go bathing in the tank. Even went in naked to bathe. From that time forth, beauty came to live in several Kahar homes. From that time on, the color of Porom Kahar's clan was luminously fair. Auntie Suchand's grandaddy's, that's her father's father's, color was exactly like a saheb's. Auntie Suchand's color is fair too. Daughter Bashanta isn't very fair. But her daughter, Pakhi, is quite the amber-jewel bird; the head of the Chaudhury household's son died an untimely death of drink, but if he hadn't the young Pakhi's face would now have shown an amazing resemblance to his. The same large eyes, the same well-formed nose, even her hair has the same kind of wave. Of course Master Chaudhury is now penniless, and stingy to boot, yet he is fondly affectionate toward Bashanta's daughter Pakhi. Bashanta's connection to that household isn't broken even now; she still goes to that house, trades gossip, brings daily milk, but doesn't ask for money.

The grandfather of this Master Chaudhury was rent collector for the sahebs. He's supposed to have been a wealthy man, supposed to have been a young buck as tyrannical and arbitrary as he was wealthy; so arrogant he'd take his steer to water where the tiger drinks. If it isn't *he* who was delivered by the Great King of the wood-apple forest—the one they call Lord around here—in ochre robes, clogs on his feet, club in his hand, holy beads on his neck; the one who wanders all around at night with his shaven head and his gleaming chest all decked out with a pristine holy thread. Gentlemen of Chandanpur say—The Kahars necessarily made those things into a tale. What really happened is that the indigo business folded here too, just as it did everywhere else. But the Kopai flood and the folding of the business coincided. In the days things were going badly for the saheb businessmen, already talking about giving up the trade, right then one night the Kopai suddenly flooded. Guess the Kopai never flooded like that time.

That flood even sunk the factory buildings. Folk say Saheb and his Missus were washed away in that same flood. But what Auntie Suchand said, *that* was the real story. *That's* the story Bonwari believes. Mister Saheb and his Missus were sucked down by a whirlpool for ignoring Lord's word. Otherwise, Saheb, Missus—how could such folks who'd come sailing across the Seven Seas get drowned in a Kopai flood? Lord's game,

Lord's ruse, all of it. Master Chaudhury didn't just get the bounty of God's grace, he got the saheb Company's entire property for a song. Karma of Lord's will.

The Kahars worked as bearers in the days of the Chaudhury Lords, too. The Chaudhurys had two palanquins. There were several litters. And the Atpoures worked as twenty-four-hour guards at their mansion.

***

Let that old story rest; I tell today's story. Arriving at Porom's home, Bonwari saw that even this early Porom had already gone out. Porom's wife, Kaloshoshi, is a granddaughter of this very village. Daughter of Gorachand Atpoure's daughter. Kaloshoshi grew up right here in this village. Gorachand never had any sons—she'd raised the daughter of her eldest girl. There wasn't the usual awkwardness of talking to a wife-type when speaking with Kaloshoshi, as, unlike the others, she wasn't an outsider who'd married into the village. Besides, isn't it true that once there'd been a secret bit of heat sparking between her and Bonwari? That's a long story. In those days even a god might have gone crazy for a Kahar maid like Kaloshoshi. But nobody won her heart. Bonwari did. But alas, "fate's writ"! How's an Atpoure Kahar maid going to marry a Behara Kahar? Alas, "fate's writ"!

The thought of those days makes Bonwari's chest heave if it comes to mind, even at his age. They'd rise in the night and couple by the Kopai. Kaloshoshi would sing. In the sky a "moony moon" would rise.

The lads of Atpoure Para would go after him; how hard they tried to catch Bonwari! But zilcho! Yet another day they failed to get him. Bonwari would laugh and sing—"Quick as a lizard boys, so long; see me once and then I'm gone!" They'd burn with fury. Their leader, Porom, would get into fights all over the place on the feeblest pretexts. There's no counting how many times Porom traded smacks and punches with others. Finally, Kaloshoshi fell into Porom's grasp. Kaloshoshi's destiny. No end to her misery once she's in Porom's hands. After he'd married Kalobou, Porom fell for another girl from a different caste; what's more, he got into bad company and into banditry. In her rage Kalobou went off to Chandanpur to earn some small change, and there she started fooling around herself. While Porom was locked up she got work as a drudge in Chandanpur gentry houses and became a favorite of Singhji, one of their footmen.

After Porom returned from his incarceration, Kaloshoshi came back to the village. She'd gotten a really bad name, was terribly disgraced—however great a person may be, their disgrace is always greater.

Today, smiling from ear to ear, Kalobou gave a warm welcome—What a treat, seein' your face a' mornin'! Sit.

—Porom-bro's took off, say where?

—So ya came fer bro then? Kaloshoshi laughed.—E left a bit 'fore ye came. Still a bit left ta burn in this pipe. Smoke some 'baccy.

—See what danger, eh!

—Why? Wha' was danger? Siddown, don' worry 'bout gossipin' wi' me for a bit. Kalobou drew her cloth wrap over her face and smiled.

—Eh, ye're gettin' a grin now?

—Ya what? I'm not gonna grin, seein' you?

—Look, didn' you 'ear a whistle las' night evenin' time?

Now Kalobou is afraid.—Yeh, 'eard it bro.

—So?

The "so" was like this—the moment night's darkness lifted, Kalobou forgot the worry.

Now Bonwari sat down. Picking up the pipe and puffing away, he told Kaloshoshi the whole story of the hideous and terrifying death of Karali's dog. He said—I'm tellin' ya sis, 'e copped it blood comin' out 'is mouth, an' 'im clawin' at 'is own 'ead. At the end, what a—

Bonwari took the pipe from his mouth—boundless terror bloomed in his mouth and eyes; the hairs on his body stood out like thorns.

Kaloshoshi was listening open-mouthed. She stood there loglike, broom in hand. Bonwari told her about the dog's eyes bursting. Said—Blew up like blisters, then *spla-a-a-t* they popped. An' blood gushin'.

Kaloshoshi shuddered—Oh my God!

Bonwari said—That's why I came ta Porom-bro; gotta do the counterpesscription.

—Course ya do! When ya live in Lord's "puttekshun," 'ow else ya gonna survive 'is wrath?

—That's it. So what you all doin'?

—Us? Kaloshoshi suddenly flared in sharp resentment against her husband.—My destiny's the broom, an' 'is destiny's ash—geddit brother, 'is destiny is ash. This place is done for. Don'tcha geddit? If 'eadman's a real 'eadman, 'e thinks 'bout others. Ain't that you, bro! But that—"Phorom" Atpoure. Night an' day thinkin' 'bout 'isself, land 'n' dough, then dough 'n' land. Last night we all 'eard the whistle. All gettin' scared. But what'll 'appen? Eadman went ta Channanpur, ta big gentry's landlord office. Gentry's buyin' up all the Saheb Heights, ain'tcha 'eard?

Bonwari was taken aback. This was valuable information to him. He asked—S'mornin' got up an' went straight there then?

—Where else? I'm tellin' ya brother, 'e 'ad a dream at night an' speaks out—mumblin' that stuff. "Ditch," "squeezewater," "cut it, cut it," "I'll chop 'ead off with a shovel"—this stuff.

Bonwari had become completely distracted. The big gentry at Channanpur are kinglike beings, huge coal business. Now suddenly they've an eye to land. Buying up wasteland wherever it is. They'll have the land dug. Have some dug for themselves and farm; get tenants on the rest. Porombro's a very sharp man. Keeps his ear to the ground. He's certainly gone to show his face where the gentry hold court. And what's *he* doing? No, dammit, dammit, dammit!

The thought of all his business affairs flooded Bonwari's mind. He must get to the landlord agent's office in Jangol. Rice threshing is finished; annual debit-credit accounts still haven't been reckoned. He needs to go there right away. Then he really must get to Channanpur. Bonwari's barely listening to Kalobou's talk now.

Kaloshoshi had been saying—So I'm lyin' next ta this one, an' even if I fell sick or me body went bad an' I die moanin', well, they wouldn't even wake up. Y'know why? Cos—snorin' so much ya couldn't 'ear! If you could 'ear that snore.

Kaloshoshi brought the cloth wrap to her mouth and began to laugh.

Bonwari abruptly got up. Propping the tobacco pipe, he said—Well sis, I'm off then.

—Siddown, siddown. Why don't I put more 'baccy in for ya.

—But I got work to do too, sis. Gotta go ta landlord agent's office. Then—. Bonwari trailed off. He didn't say what the purpose of his going to Channanpur was. After all, Kaloshoshi isn't one of his own.

Kaloshoshi looked him in the face with a close-lipped smile and spoke with a note of regret—Oh well, suppose so! Men are all the same! That there work, work, an' more work! A strange expression spread across her face.

Bonwari was caught a little off guard. Trying to smile, he said—Hey sis, we may work, but it's all for you. What "earns" we make, right inta yer 'ands they "gies."

Saying this, he left Porom's house. If he hadn't, even this statement wouldn't have interrupted Kaloshoshi's flow.

Lots of work. Will it do for Bonwari to sit a few minutes? I do love you, Kaloshoshi-sis, but what to do? Once heat's force has stricken the mind, does it ever leave off? No matter their meeting an eon later, still if they meet, smiles break out on two pairs of lips. This surely was a lasting kind of heat. Once touched, no amount of scrubbing'll wear it out of the "'eart." But what's the use of weeping and misery for those who have no options? Your ma's dad wouldn't put you in Bonwari's hands on account of that there "Behara Kahar" stuff! And once you'd been married to Porom, could Bonwari still smile and exchange a few words? And Bonwari's no longer that kind of person. There's something called the dharma of duty. He's headman of a hamlet. Oh my! Oh my! "Lawd," you must save Bonwari. Tiger, boar, snake, storm, flood—Bonwari doesn't say save me from them; you must save Bonwari from all these reasons to be bad.

Lots of work. Back at the hamlet, must talk to Auntie Suchand—make sure she goes 'round every house and collects a donation and some rice for the offering rites. The girls who'll go to Channanpur carrying dungcakes on their heads and taking milk, who sell the milk and dungcakes and will then get to work in gentry houses there, they've got to be told—if anyone gets the chance to see Porom at landlord's office, they should straightaway tell him he must come home. He's made this arrangement in case he doesn't get to Channanpur today, in case he somehow gets stuck at the boss's office. No shortage of ways to get stuck at the boss's office. Clean out the threshing yard; if not, cut some bits of wood off that tree trunk; if not, add a new coat of clay to the cow fodder trough; in the midst of the dying clump of banana trees that old trunk's rotted, dig it out and chuck it. And accounts? Sitting to do accounts will take ages.

***

As he returned from Atpoure Para to his own hamlet, he first had to stop by the yard of Karali's house. Karali's digging a hole in this yard, and Pakhi is telling him off.

—Gonna be such a stink when it rots!

Karali keeps digging earth. Lad's frame sure is tough. He's turning out really strong! Beside this, the body—developed muscles, especially on chest, back, arms, legs; and sweating too—every limb gleaming. Today's Sunday, the lad's holiday, so he's not gone to Channanpur and has started digging Kalua the dog's grave.

Pakhi is yelling—You 'eard wha' I'm sayin'? Or not listenin'?

—Stop that yellin' an' naggin'. Karali gave a curt reply as he cut away at the soil. He's going to make a grave for Kalua the dog right here. Karali couldn't bear it if kites, vultures, jackals picked Kalua's bones clean.

—S'gonna put the house in a fix. Foul stink's gonna make ya puke when ye eat.

—Whassat ta you? Don't come ta my 'ouse then!

—Ooh monster, ooh louse! S'there a bigger two-faced bastard than you? Don't they say—"Can't stand a beatin' from the 'and that'll kill me"; that's your story. Don't get that stink on me, ain't gonna come ta yer 'ouse. Nasu-sis is 'uman too. Ow's 'e gonna be able ta stay?

Bonwari couldn't not go into Karali's house. Seeing Bonwari, Pakhi spoke up—Hey uncle, look, looka what 'e's doin'! Gonna bury the dog at 'ome—gonna make a "fooneral grave." You stop 'im. Nasu-sis ain't 'ere, so 'e's just doin' whatever 'e wants.

Bonwari said—Hey there, whass goin' on? Oo's makin' a shit'eap in yard of their 'ome? Ya mad or crazy?

A visible crack had opened in the ground beneath the blows of Karali's spade—wedging it open with the shovel, teeth gritted, his life's strength applied, Karali was trying to lever up a lump of earth. He didn't offer any response. Pakhi said—Now 'e's sayin' once 'e's buried the dog 'e's gonna go to the bamboo edge ta search.

—Ta search the bamboo edge! There was no limit to Bonwari's shock.

—Yeh. What's makin' the whistle, 'ow'd it kill 'is Kalua, 'e'll seek it out.

Clamity! O God! O Father Kottathakur—the boy wants to drive out your playful game! One evil will bring tenfold ruin! Immediately he became furious.

—*Karali*!

Karali was startled to hear this tone, threw down the shovel with a jump and stood aside. He turned to look Bonwari's way.

No one can expect this tone of voice from Bonwari. Bonwari's usually an exceedingly nice and pleasant man; in spite of being hamlet headman, there's no headman's harshness, no headman's arrogance. He is all happy-smiling, singing-dancing, sweetly spoken; if someone's having a falling-out with someone else he'll get the two of them back together, get it all patched up with slaps on the back; to see, you'd think it was Bonwari's own business. But there is another Bonwari who hardly ever shows himself. Before appearing, he first gives notice by taking this tone; *that* Bonwari was awakening.

If that Bonwari awakes he'll attack the rebel in a flash; knock him to the ground with demonic strength, come down on his chest, crush his throat with his left hand, try to grab the tongue with his right; then you can't drag that Bonwari off without six or seven big strong men.

Bonwari's eyes were turning red. He started to advance toward Karali. Coming up to him, Pakhi now said in a frightened voice—No, uncle, no. E's not really gonna do all that.

But Karali was standing motionless, looking at Bonwari with a steady gaze. One moment his eyes widening in dread, the next moment rebellion flaring up.

Bonwari shoved Pakhi aside. Pakhi tried to grab his arm from behind—Uncle! Uncle! But Bonwari was silently advancing.

Helpless, Pakhi finally fled out—Oi sister, sister, help! Oi sister! Sister, that's to say Suchand. At this time only a Suchand can stand in Bonwari's way.

Bonwari was becoming more and more enraged; no one had ever shown such disrespect. He kept coming forward. Yet Karali held still.

Finally, though, Karali could hold on no longer, it was as if his courage suddenly gave out; in a second he leaped onto the yard wall, over and down the other side, and fled into the fields. Bonwari ran for a bit, but he's getting old. If he runs, he gets out of breath. With a palanquin on his shoulder, doing "beharin," carrying in the usual way, changing shoulders and sometimes resting, he can easily do twenty-five miles on foot; but he can't run like this anymore. Bonwari had to stop. Down there at the edge of the village stood Auntie Suchand, calling. Lads and lasses all gathering. Prohlad, Roton coming forward. Bonwari had to turn back. Let the son of a bitch go—let him go for now; but where'll he go? Does he have to come back or not? Whose place will he return to?

***

Morning in the month of Phalgun, so the Kahars were at home. Pressure of work and chores was light just now in Kaharpara; agricultural work in fields and meadows had finished, rice threshing on the threshing floor had also come to an end; and spring harvest nearly over; nobody's wheat ripening nor even beginning to ripen; everyone's chickpeas, lentils, mustard in that same state. No more work left to do in potato fields. Just needed digging up. From the beginning of Chaitra month they'd need a bunch more people again. Some folks had sugarcane—late-growing cane that would be crushed in Chaitra month too. Now the only job was at boss's house, figure out the debit and credit accounts—that account's in the hands of the bosses. Thus all the men were also home. So Karali escaped.

Prohlad and Roton are the same age as Bonwari. They came up, took his arms, and led him back. Prohlad said—If Karali ain't brought in line, Oton, it'll be a bad scene. No one'll obey anyone no more.

Roton said—If that 'appens, won't be no more "susternants" in t'village—s'a totally "shoor" thing.

Bonwari did not say a word.

The route they took to enter the hamlet brought them right past Neem-oil Panu's house. West of the neem tree, just where shadow falls in the morning, Panu lay on a palm-leaf mat, prepared tobacco, and welcomed the headmen.—Siddown, Bonwari-bro, Oton-bro, uncle Pellad—sit, smoke 'baccy.

Little by little, everyone gathered. Even Suchand came and stood. She said—Don' get too mad, Bonwari me son, I'm gettin' the lad brung back ta beg at yer feet.

Bonwari didn't say anything to this either.

Suchand said—I've a'ready been mortified, geddit son—in a mess at my old age 'cos o' that little slut born o' me bitch daughter. Gotta fish-bone stuck in 'er throat that won't come up, won't go down neither, yeh. Without that wreck Karali the 'ole "ooniverse" gettin' lonesome an' empty. Now everyone laughed at the old woman's gestures. Not just gestures, the old woman also cut a little dance. Bonwari saw this and a faint smile appeared on his face too. Panu led a goat out out of his cottage by the ear and said—Looka this, Bonwari-bro, this one. Got back las' night, me an' the wife, an' decided we'll make 'im the Lord's offerin'. E's my biggest one, an' 'is body's all right. A right strong goat.

Bonwari stroked the goat's body with his hand, felt its spine, and said—Look after 'im real careful fer a couple days, son. We'll gi' the offerin' day after tomorra. There's Sat'day; an' another day.

Roton said—Won't ya tell Atpoure Para?

Shaking his head to show his disappointment, Bonwari said—Well, an' why get me "tempey" bad! In the mornin'—get this first—crows, cuckoos callin' wakes me up. All night worryin', got no sleep. In the wee hours me eyes close fer a bit—y'know, right then I 'ad a dream. Like I saw the Lord 'isself come an' stood afore me, right above me 'ead. Woke up babblin'. Goddup. Goddup an' went to Porom's place. Porom 'ad gone out that sunup. So I'd said to Kalobou—Tell ya, tell Porom if 'e comes.

Looking at Bonwari's face, both Roton and Prohlad smiled faintly. The whole meeting—men and women, they all smiled. Of course they all hid their smiles.

Bonwari was able to feel the slight, luscious touch of the hidden laughter's current. To change the subject, he said—E went to yer gents' house at Channanpur. Ain't the gents buyin' up all the Saheb Tracts. They'll break up the uplands and make farm plots. I 'eard they're gonna distribute "lickle-bits" of it.

Straightaway everyone's mind turned around; greed for Bonwari-and-Kalobou stories became greed for tales of land. Now this is some news, for sure. That bit of upland belonging to the indigo-plantation sahebs, that bit where they'd put their buildings to be safe from floods, where the plantation was, *that* same upland's going to be broken into plots? They'll distribute some plots? And at dawn one of the other group's gone and is already begging to be assigned some of those plots of land? In a flash everyone was excited. Land! Land!

Bonwari said—Been thinkin' 'bout sommat. Ye listenin', Oton-bro, Pellad-cuz?

Roton and Prohlad looked at Bonwari excitedly and slowly came closer.—Whassat ya say? But everyone's getting the point. When a bunch of chickpeas is moistened they'll sprout, and then just as all the shoots come out of the chickpeas together, emerge and rise, breaking through soil, so is this news the nectar of dormant hopes; and the shoots of the Kahars' inner desires wish to emerge as one. Sitting tight together, looking into each other's faces, in contact with each other, they're understanding quite clearly what's on each other's minds. And yet it's good that this has come from Bonwari. It is good that Bonwari speaks up. One day it will all come out, and if he takes land and keeps it secret from the other Kahars it's an undharmic thing, unfitting for a headman. He said—We all go ta Channanpur too. Them plots at Jangol's Saheb Heights ain't outta yer reach; sett'ment'll be bid at hunnerd-fifty acres. All together, we do 'alf, one acre—. Bonwari looked at everyone.

They were all on tenterhooks, eyes burning—like sparks of fire in coal.

—Whassat ye say?

Suchand can't quite understand the situation. Standing a little way off, she was surprised to notice that the annoyance and anger at Karali's behavior suddenly dissipated and seemed to turn into an outbreak of delighted glows on everyone's faces. What's this surprising news harboring the reason for the delight of all and sundry? Besides, she had noticed that the way Bonwari was talking had a certain air of counsel and advice about it.

Coming forward, she spoke—What? Whassup Bonwari? What y'all sayin'?

Laughingly, Prohlad said—Shove it! Now sound the summons drum an' call the 'amlet together.

Looking him in the face, Suchand said—Ya makin' fun o' me Pellad, ya little freak?

Even though she cannot hear, Suchand can tell unmistakably from the speakers' movements and expressions that it's her they're mocking. Now the old woman is most certainly going to scream and make a scene. The only way out is to tell her. If he tells her, the old woman will forget the sting of the mockery. Therefore Bonwari has to tell her, and he does. Sitting next to her, shouting and gesticulating, he told her everything. Suchand said—Yeh, tha' makes sense, fer sure. That side o' the river, d'ya geddit—

Bonwari got up. The day will end by the time Auntie Suchand's "d'ya geddit" is got. It's already gotten late under the influence of that devil Karali. Worried, he abruptly got up. Then, yelling, he spoke to Suchand— So yer gonna collect cash an' rice fer the offerin', right auntie?

—Fer offerin'? Lord's offerin'?

—Yes dear. If not, no benefit.

—Ah—aaah! If not, no benefit! Oo's gonna unnerstan' that? Listen up, gonna say sommat else.

—What?

—If ye tek land, then saccifice 'nother goat at the offerin'. Do it by Lord's leave; sprinkle on the uncut earth—'ow many unknowed, un-thought, un'eard troubles there are—y'unnerstan'—or whatcha say?

Everyone considered what she was saying. Everyone looked at Bon-wari. Even Suchand's gaze remained on his face. Inclining his head, Bon-wari said—Yes, yes, that's a thing worth sayin'. Yep. Well said, auntie.

—What ya sayin'?

Bonwari yelled—*That's gonna be, dearie.*

Suchand said happily—Aaaall-right. Now look, it were back in me dad's day—

Bonwari stopped this with a shout—Seven o'clock terain's crossed t' bridge. We'll 'ear ya later.

The rail line runs past the eastern side of the village. The line leaves Channanpur station, crosses the Kopai river by bridge, and goes on its way. At Hansuli Turn, you can see the bridge very well from the edge of Bansbadi's indigo-levee pond. The trains crossing that bridge have been adopted as the timekeepers of Kaharpara's life. There is a train at six in the morning. Then when the seven o' clock train's signal comes, the men go out to work. Today they're getting a bit late. Then, when that train signaled at seven comes, the women who go out do so, to work, to sell dung cakes, to sell milk.

Suchand remained staring toward the train. If a train goes onto the bridge she must listen to its sound attentively. Faint sounds of a deep clanking echo in her ears, and Suchand holds these profoundly dear. Suchand says—When train goes over the bridge a'night and I'm lyin' in me room wimme eyes closed, it sounds like a buncha 'oly singers playin' drums.

The men quickly headed out.

Bonwari addressed everyone—We can't go the day after tomorrer, s'gotta be tomorrer, so ye better remember, yeh! If not, bosses'll say— Why didn't you tell me before, how's my work going to get done now?

***

Bonwari is a sharecropper tenant for the Ghoshes of Jangol. The relationship has lasted two generations, from Bonwari's father's time. The Ghoshes of Jangol have had this relationship with the Bonwaris since the time they were utterly ordinary householders. When he was a young man, a whelp of a boy, old Sire Ghosh—who up and died one day—found himself suddenly fatherless; he'd go around like a vagrant and play female roles in that latest fad of the Channanpur gentry, the theater. His widowed mother, young wife, and widowed sister were at home. But there was no way of getting by. No land, no rented plots, not a bit of work. The boy doesn't think, no time to think; so, thinking hard to pass the time, the widowed mother gets from Bonwari's father enough wood to make a rice husker. The thread of the relationship began here. The time Bonwari's father had pulled out a large tree trunk from the recent Kopai flood, she'd taken a section of that. Ghosh Missus sold the wife's earrings to get a carpenter, had a rice husker made out of the wood, and began taking in rice-husking work. Bonwari's ma would occasionally help with this work too. In this situation Ghosh Missus constantly begged her son to turn his mind to earning a living, was constantly disappointed, and finally, like a madwoman, caused a scene. One day, late at night, when the boy came back singing from a theater party and demanded his dinner, his mother brought a shard of smashed plate and, truth to tell, a handful of ashes, set them before him, and said—Eat! The boy stared into his mother's face in shock for a while, then got up and left the house.

And he was really gone, for about five years. In this situation, Bonwari's parents got even more entangled in the miseries of the Ghosh family. First it was Bonwari's mother; then, sucked in by her, his father. Bonwari's father used to take raw paddy from Channanpur gentlemen's houses for turning into husked rice, and if the Ghoshes had prepared the rice he would deliver that to Channanpur. A completely one-sided arrangement. Because the Ghoshes would get the rice earned in exchange for converting it from paddy. What's more, if Ma Ghosh or Sister Ghosh needed anything at all, they would go themselves to Bonwari's father. Wood, palm leaves, field fish, baskets full of cow dung fuel, he would bring it all to the Ghosh house—what else could people like Bonwari give? So they gave, and this was of great help to the Ghosh people. Ma Ghosh gave fried snacks. Her cooking was "ambrojia." Then one day Ghosh returned, having made a fortune. Lakshmi of Wealth arrived at that Ghosh house. Ghosh bought an estate—from those Chaudhurys of Jangol. Land by the river, by the cowpath; if flood comes it goes right under water, and what's more, herds of cows on the cowpath daily stick their mouths into the harvest. Five acres of land, and paddy on two acres of that would always get gobbled up. But the saving grace is low rent—the yearly rent of five acres of land is twelve and a half rupees at the rate of two and a half rupees an acre. Ghosh's Ma said—Tarini's my elder son. He'll work the land. Give him a share of land.

Bonwari's father was called Tarini.

If Lakshmi's wealth comes to your world, doesn't it all happen, the ruined and abject become resplendent—a beauty appears on their faces; malice fades and becomes benevolence, a poison tongue's venom is washed clean by gushes of honeylike ambrosia. At his mother's words, Ghosh paid obeisance with hands on her feet and said—Can there be a "no" to your word? Tarini is my elder brother. Brother Tarini himself will work my land, you understand, Tarini?

Smiling, Tarini had said—Now look 'ere Missus, look whatta "fixt" ye've gotten me into! Where's me steer an' plow, then? Best you get the steer an' a plow, I'll stay a tiller.

—Get a steer and plow. I'm giving you the money. What's to fear, you can pay it back slowly. So Ghosh had said.

Tarini had been dumbstruck; he had served the pure castes, received such a reward and been blessed; he'd gone home and wept that day. Since then there have been steers and plows at the Bonwari place. Since then the Bonwaris have been farming the Ghoshes' land. Father Tarini died,

Sire Ghosh is also no more, the sons of Sire Ghosh are now a wildly successful lot. Middle son does business, rushes around here and abroad, rakes in the cash he makes and stores it up in the *bank*. Now what fear fills this very Bonwari at the Ghoshes' house. Now he cannot just go straight into the house as before, now he cannot give the same kind of advice to Big Ghosh. He cannot demand money for manure in the same way anymore. How indeed can he effect a hurry for accounts? Bonwari got there and saw that Big and Middle were both drinking tea and were engaged in some intense counsel. He paid obeisance and squatted down on the terrace. Soon after, he found a more comfortable position leaning on a post. Then began to nod off. He had not slept well all night; sleep was coming in the cool breeze of a fresh morning. A very gentle breeze blowing from the south. Chilly cold of dawn breaking with the rising of morning sun. He's having various jumbled dreams in his light sleep. Kaloshoshi, Karali, Porom—and a whole bunch of other people gathering on the Saheb Tracts. A grunting, ox-calf-sized, black, tusked wild boar coming out from the overgrown factory buildings on the Saheb Tracts, coming swift as an arrow. It's gored Karali. Porom is fleeing. Kaloshoshi is clinging to Bonwari. But Bonwari is able to flee by giving Kaloshoshi a quick shove. Who's behind him making that clomping sound? Bonwari could understand who. Lord's coming. No more fear. Feeling assurance in his fright, reviling the wild boar, he raised a powerful cry—*A-a-a-a-a-p!*

Sleep's touch instantly vanished. First he looked around in confusion, then got his bearings back and sat. The Ghosh brothers are laughing.

—What's up Bonwari, why did you yell?

Smiling sheepishly, Bonwari said—By yer leave sir, summat 'appened, like!

—Summat 'appened, like! What happened?

Bonwari remained silent. He was embarrassed of course—to admit, I was dreaming and I screamed out like this.

—You what? You were dreaming you say?

—Aye, by yer leave.

The middle one bursts out laughing. Asks a question—And what dream, pray?

—By yer leave, was dreamin' I was bein' chased by a tusky wild boar.

Now both of them exploded in laughter. Bonwari began smiling too, and straightaway began scratching his head. He said—Them tusky beggars are real mean, man! You've no idea. Then, taking the opportunity given by their subsiding laughter, said—By yer leave, me account, if ye could lookit an' settle up. Some noo farmin's just come up.

—Account! Can do. Come tomorrow. Or the day after.

—By yer leave, can't come tomorrer or next day.

—Why? What you doing tomorrow and the next day?

—By yer leave, village 'as raised contributions fer an offerin' to the Lord.

—Offering to the Lord! So untimely? What's up?

Bonwari tries to tell them the whole story in detail. His wish—to collect a contribution from Middle Ghosh too. But after listening for a short while Middle Ghosh said—This is you lot—"Get out of bed, blind man! Can't tell if it's day or night!" It's all the same to you lot. Pah, Lord Father's whistling! Such a load of—ugh!

Bonwari was disheartened. But, pulling himself together, he was now starting to say something. But the words were not said; he jumped up anxiously, cupping his two hands to his ears. Because it seemed a sudden uproar was breaking out in the distance.—Fire! Fire!

Fire! Bonwari dashed outside. Fire where? Moving toward the hollering, he ran out of the village. Yes, yes, huge amounts of smoke rising into the sky from that southern end of Bansbadi. Twisting coils of smoke, pile on pile, hiding the tops of the bamboo edge; thick clouds of smoke like monsoon clouds.

Bonwari's chest pounded—"Lord's fiury"!

***

No—the Kahars' luck is good. Even in his fury the Lord's showing a little mercy.

No fire in the village. Fire's caught beneath the bamboo edge groves. Bamboo leaves falling in the month of Magh. Numberless leaves from dense bamboo groves gather in piles upon the forest floor. Fire's caught in those dry fallen leaves. Who knows how it caught? The day's getting scorching; nighttime dew on drying leaves; fire's finding good fuel. The bamboo groves, like a green wall, are almost completely covered by smoke.

People are standing in shocked amazement on the edge of Bansbadi. No one dares venture inside. Neem-oil Panu, Prohlad came back from Jangol before Bonwari. They had gone in, but had run out in fear and agony. Fear—that whistle is sounding. Agony—from smoke.

Lord's wrath, finally become fire, burning up at the edge of the village; sending a warning. Bonwari came to a sudden stop and pantingly said— Lord's wrath! Lord's fiury!

Prohlad says—No, Karali's set the fire, 'e poured "keracheen" oil on the leaves an' 'e's set the fire. E's still inside that smoke.

In an instant Bonwari became wild with rage; he descended into the smoke-filled bamboo groves.

Yep, whistle rising too. Lord's raging as well. Bonwari moved forward, trailing the sound.

Karali is standing right before the spot where the sound is rising. He's standing staring fixedly upward, chest fearlessly puffed out. Tears streaming from his eyes. He's wiping and looking up again. Below, fire's dancing on a stack of dry leaves. In the heat the bamboo edge is starting to resemble a fire fortress, heat pummeling the body; Karali doesn't heed that either.

Bonwari approached, an image of menace.—O Lord, forgive us. I'm throwing the loser into that fire. Use your holy powers to put the flames out. Save Bansbadi, save Hansuli Turn—save. In that terrifying tone of his he shouted—Karali!

Karali looked at him as if startled, then turning his gaze back, beckoned Bonwari and called—Come, come.

He didn't budge an inch. Bonwari's fury grew greater. He approached, saying to himself—I'm coming I'm coming, just wait.

From far behind another sound comes floating—Uncle! Uncle! Uncle! Pakhi's voice. In tones seeming to crack with distress and anxiety. But Bonwari's heartless today. He's Kaharpara's Lord of Justice. Like Daksha son of Brahma, he is sovereign Lord—the Punisher.

Bonwari pounced on Karali in terrible rage. Bonwari, son of the Kosh-Shoulder house, a stone-built man carved by God's massive hand.

But Karali didn't budge, and, most amazing, even wrenched one of his arms free of Bonwari's grasp. He attacked Bonwari with the terrible power of that arm. Incredible, Bonwari's feeling—Karali's strength seems greater than his. No, bamboo leaves are slipping back from under Bonwari's feet. It's because of this handicap that Karali's getting the better of him. Suddenly Karali screamed—Quit—quit—s'fallin'. Quit.

It was as if his strength had grown a hundredfold with the intensity of his excitement. He threw Bonwari down effortlessly, let go, and stood up. He began to dance. That—that—that bastard's fallin'. Bonwari leaped up.

Karali immediately came and pulled and shook his arm and said—That—looka that, yer Lord's fallin' from toppa the bamboo. Yee—haa!

Agonized and weakened from heat and smoke, a gigantic snake is falling from the top of the bamboo clump. Fat as a hill chiti snake and similarly mottled in color, but not so long. There's the difference from a hill chiti.

Bonwari looked at it wide-eyed and said—You-u-u-ge chain viper! Yeh, they can really roar some.

—See 'ow big 'e is, eh? That's the whistle sound. Bastard!

The snake has fallen into the fire and is writhing in pain. Dying. Karali's bombarding it with stones. His aim is infallible.

—Uncle! Uncle! Pakhi calling from thataway. In the middle of the smoke she doesn't know which direction they're in. She's calling with anxious apprehension. The call circling around. Pakhi has searched and is going back.

Karali yelled a response—This way—this way. Come on. Come on. Call all the 'amlet lot! Lookit yer Lord burnin'! Lookit. Call 'em all. Call—call.

Meanwhile a swollen part of the snake's stomach has burst in the fire's heat. A thing has fallen out. Karali went forward, Bonwari too. Bent down to look, what *is* that? Yuck, a baby wild pig. The one screaming so piercingly last night.

Pakhi came running and grasped Karali's hand. She's panting.

Karali said—Looka that. Pakhi was dumbstruck to see the snake. Before long all Kaharpara's folk came rushing. They stayed a while amazed, curious, speechless, then Bansbadi was abuzz with talk.

Karali spoke up with a grin—Eadman, ya gotta gi' the Lord's offerin' all fer me, pal. He burst out laughing.

Pakhi told him off—Shut it.

But Karali broke into laughter. It's like a huge joke.

Pakhi punched Karali in the back and said—Ya suicidal maniac, ain'tcha got no sense o' proportion?

Three

Every single person in Kaharpara was stunned and stupefied hearing Karali's statement and seeing his burst of laughter. Karali says what? "Ya gotta gi' the Lord's offerin' fer me, pal!" He's got some balls! O God, O Father Kalarudra, O Babathakur!

Bonwari was staring fixedly at Karali. Only today he seemed to see Karali anew. Bonwari looked at him just how a person looks when he sees that a stone he's gathered to make a pestle sparkles and glows in the light; how he turns it to and fro with surprise, fascination, reverence. The lad looks so much sweeter than when he was a child. And seeing him today, Bonwari's mind awakens to the sweet taste of that look; today Bonwari's getting a fresh taste. It seems all Kaharpara's getting it too.

A lean, rangy figure, by standard measure no doubt six feet tall; slender waist, broad chest; rounded, muscular arms; two straight legs; long, mango-shaped face; large eyes; snub nose; but of all this, making that figure sweetest of all, the very sweetest parts are his lips and teeth. If he smiles they make Karali look really beautiful.

The group of youths has surely been eyestruck by this face. Most of the hamlet's young men are secretly followers of Karali. But the one looking most on this face is Pakhi. She's learning by heart the form and spirit of Karali's body. For her, in life, everything and Karali lead in the same direction.

Bonwari too was seeing the beauty in the power of Karali's body. Yep, lad's sure getting strong. It was as if he'd noticed this figure in an instant while Karali was digging the dog's grave at his cottage. But that time Bonwari both saw and didn't see. Today, at this moment, there's no way Bonwari cannot see him. It's coming back to Bonwari—he'd leaped on Karali in the bamboo groves, leaped on him with merciless rage, wishing—I'll slam down hard on his chest and strangle him, throw him in that blazing firepit if he dies. But—. How it happened isn't coming back clearly to Bonwari! His feet had slipped on bamboo leaves?

Did his head spin in the smoke? Something happened. Karali got on top of him? He was thinking, maybe Karali'll laugh out loud and say to these assembled Kahars, Babathakur's disciple Bonwari, chief too, I saw 'im an' took—

Pakhi approached Bonwari. She called—Uncle!

Bonwari stared into her face. Then, suddenly smiling, said—Karali's a smart 'un. E's understood right.

Karali spoke up enthusiastically—Exactly same thing 'appened twenny-eight miles down the rail line too. Unnerstan'—twenny-eight miles—real jungly, las' time exactly same whistle used ta come up. Got there in the evenin' pushin' a cart, saheb's in the cart. Rifle in 'is 'and. Unnerstan', 'e 'eard the whistle an' says—Stop cart! Then starts shinin' a flashlight, shinin' shinin', one place flashlight hits 'e caught sight o' the snake. That's it, lifts the gun, *ba-boom*!

Prohlad said—Now then, this time burn the snake good an' proper. It's not a kharish or a cobra, it's a chiti fer sure—an' a big un. If t'ain't a Berahmin it's upper-crust Kayastha-thingy, not a doubt. Really gotta do the proper cremation rites!

Although Neem-oil Panu is the same age as Karali's group, he goes around with the wise elders like Prohlad. He is first to nod his head in agreement, and says—Absolutely. An' is it only a pure-caste, Pehlad-bro? Vennerble, wise old snake. Gonna be a real old 'un, pal.

Karali said—Nope. I'm takin' it. Let 'em see, let 'em all see. Ow you lot used ta bolt yer doors in fear soon as dusk fell. Let 'em see. Saying this, he began to laugh again.

Neem-oil Panu looked Bonwari's way and said—Chief!

Bonwari said—That—. He didn't know what the right thing to say was.

—What? Speak? Ye've stopped on "That"! said an annoyed Panu. —What "scipture" says gotta be done, ain't it? Or—what?

—T'will be done. When body dies ya don't burn straightaway. Folks come, look. Better not leave a dead body overnight 'afore burnin'. Let it be kept fer now—after that we'll burn a'night on river's edge.

Karali was really pleased. He said—Why'd ya say that better not, chief?

Bonwari said—Cos ya don't obey the chief, like.

Now Karali was embarrassed. Smiling a lovely smile, he said—I obey, like, I really obey, obey in me mind. Unnerstood?

Neem-oil Panu said—Butcha don't obey now. Ya walk all over th' ancesteral teaches o' Kaharpara, gi' the finger right in chief's face, goin' takin' work in them filthy infidel Chandanpur workshops. Makin' a tonna money—

Karali became frightful in a flash. He screamed out—Bastard!

Opening his arms in restraint, Bonwari said—No.

Karali paused in surprise. Held Bonwari's face with an angry look. Bonwari said—There'll be no scrappin'. Peno's wrong, no doubt. I'll bring 'im in line.

Karali said to his followers—Bring a pole. We'll load up an' go.

Prohlad said—Best leave a broad spot. Loadsa folks gonna come look. They've experience of this. The killing of a tusked wild boar is a regular thing around here; they've inherited teachings on this subject too. From time to time one or two people are also injured by boar tusks. Two or three stabbed by tuskers each year, and the nature of this place's people is—come rushing to look as soon as they hear. Having seen the tusker itself, now they go take a look at the injured person too. And if it's a tiger or crocodile, well, it goes without saying. About twenty-five, twenty-six years ago a cheetah washed up; floating in that Kopai flood, it gets stuck in the bamboo border. That one was alive. It has to be said that was in Bonwari's dad's day. Those others were lords. Bonwari, Prohlad—back then these two were Karali's age, both laborers. On the instructions of the lords it was they who'd built a bamboo cage and caught the cheetah. They'd split strong mature shoots of bamboo in half and stuck them into the ground like bars; stronger than an iron cage. In that cage was tied a goat kid, and the cage was set up in the Bansbadi woods. One, two, three whole days the cheetah was prisoner. Then, set up for stabbing to death. After the killing the district folk came rushing. First of all, Sire Ghosh came and shot a bullet into the dead cheetah. Bullet in its temple. Then the crowd watched as he had a raised bier brought from Jangol and put the creature up there. What a crowd! Some of them threw rocks at the cheetah, some jabbed it with their staves, some pulled its tail, three or four young lads even had the guts to jump up and beat it with their fists. Yet others embraced it and lay down for joy. Thinking of all this, Prohlad and Roton's group spoke in accordance with ongoing immemorial custom. Nor was there any need to worry about space. Unloading has happened in the same place forever; it's been in that yard of Bonwari's—a huge empty space.

But Karali's intentions were different. He began to move right on past Bonwari's yard toward his own house, carrying the snake dangling from an eight-foot bamboo pole on his shoulders with another's help. Prohlad, Roton, Panu said—Put it down just 'ere.

Karali said—Uh-uh. Gonna take it ta my place, me.

Prohlad, Roton, Panu were astonished at Karali's nerve. They stared at Bonwari.

Bonwari laughed long. He spoke dismissively—Let 'im go, let 'im go, little man. Besides, it's 'is own drama, that's fer sure, boys. Then, giving Karali a couple of fond slaps on the back, he said—Yep. Ye're a right heroic laddie, ain'tcha.

Karali smiled. Smiled a smile of pleasure. And immediately seemed to get a little embarrassed. Remembered that he must show a little respect to Uncle Bonwari. He said—But you come too.

—All right. I'll go, come on.

***

Karali threw defiant glances at everyone as he set in down in the house's yard. None of the headmen and elders came along. Although there was no sense of insult, they were still getting upset. Karali took this chance to make a joke, pretended to be suddenly surprised, and cried out—Ah man, it's twitchin'!

Immediately the group of women screamed in terror, backed off pushing and jostling. The men began shoving each other out of the way. Karali let out a loud guffaw. Said—Whatta buncha scaredy-cats—ye'll die o' fear, die o' fear.

Then he said—Run off, the lotta ya, flee, I'm tellin' ya. Worse fer you if ya don't. Get lost. Pakhi, bring it out.

The liquor bottle, that is. The victorious hero will drink with his girlfriend and his pals. He's got a group among the youth of the Kaharpara; and although on the outside that group follows headman Bonwari, in their inner hearts Karali is their real gang leader. Among them Roton's son Notbor is foremost.

Notbor circled defiantly once around the snake and said—Hey, if ye tell 'em ta bring pennies then ya won't see none. Oh yeah, won't see zilch this time.

A young woman said—Damn! Kills a snake an' now comin' over so brashwise! That's to say, cockily.

Karali said—Grab 'er, Notbor, we'll sing, she'll 'ave ta dance. Grab.

Now the group of young women fled. They don't trust this group of young bucks one bit, and what's more the bottle of booze is appearing. A few swigs in the gut are enough for mischief!

Notbor said—Ah, shame Nasu-sis ain't 'ere today!

Meanwhile, Karali was drinking a bit. He said—Hah, if he'd been 'ere woulda been crazy. Bitch's always wanted at a weddin'.

Nasubala is Karali's cousin on his father's side. Real name's Nasuram. Nasuram's strange character. Just like the young women in thought, attitude, speech, conversation. Hair on his head like the young women; he ties it in a bun, wears a ring in his nose, wears earrings in his ears; glass bracelets and red bangles on his arms, he wears a sari like the girls. He gathers cow dung with the young women, breaks kindling, mops rooms, goes to Channanpur to deliver milk, goes to do odd jobs. A lovely sweet voice—he sings and dances. Song and dance—these are his biggest obsessions. He dances in the Ghentu spring festival group; in the women's ritual dancing of Bhanjo it's he among the women who leads the finest dance. He even takes part in ritual fasting with the young women. It's he who's mistress in Karali's house. Karali was married and he kicked his wife out; he didn't like the wife, he'll marry again. Nasu too had been married, Nasu too kicked his wife out; he won't marry again. To stay in Karali's home, to become Karali's younger sister and a sister-in-law to his wife—this is his desire. It's Nasubala who dances and sings songs in the bridal chambers at marriages in the hamlet. And not only in the hamlet, in the village and beyond, wherever a grand wedding takes place, it's almost always Nasu who is asked. Tying up his bun, painting red dye on his feet, putting on a colorful sari, putting a red mark on his forehead, that's to say applying a dot, Nasu sets off; then after the celebration he returns. Brings back something or other for Karali.

Today it was the lack of this very Nasubala that Karali felt most of all.

—Nasu-sis ain't 'ere, why not let Pakhi dance then? This was spoken by Karali's devoted follower Mathla. Mathla's real name is Rakhal or Akhal, but because of his disproportionately large head the Kahars, likely putting their trust first in their own grammar, made it Mathla, Big 'ead.

Mathla's suggestion wasn't dirty. But Karali frowned nevertheless. Pakhi loves him, one day maybe she'll tie the knot with him. Will she dance in front of this lot?

There's a heat in Pakhi's eyes, she's drunk a bit of prime liquor, her mind too is turning toward a dance in Karali's honor; but she looked at Karali's face. She saw, could understand Karali's thoughts, spoke abruptly—No. Whyn'tcha call yer wife?

At this very moment the grating sound of Suchand's voice rose somewhere nearby; in an instant the whole hamlet was alarmed.

—O Father, no! O Ma, no! Where'm I gonna go, then?

Laughing aloud, Karali said—Looka the crone's "abdabs"! Which is to say, look at the old woman's screams of fear. Then, jokingly, he said—

Bring 'er 'ere, bring 'er 'ere, bring the crone 'ere—*she*'ll dance. I'll make the crone dance like a Turkish dervish. Sees a frog an' dances, why not if she sees a snake?

She didn't need to be summoned. Smeared head to toe in mud, wearing a short cloth wrap, Suchand came and stood in Karali's yard. Behind her, a few other aged women. She fixed the dead snake with a steady gaze for a while, then suddenly began to beat her chest and weep. Her voice rang out with a sound announcing dreadful misfortune.

—O me dearest Babathakur! O no, me Father's familiar, no! Oh no, what'll be! Alas alack, Ma! As she spoke she sat down hard on the ground, shaking violently.

The heavens of all Kaharpara were filled with the sound of terrified, anguished wailing. Karali, Pakhi, Notbor, Mathla, everyone came out— Whassup?

Small village enclosed in Hansuli Turn's bamboo-ringed light and shade. In that village's tale, contained in the words of women's rituals of this place from so long ago, there's this: "In the village was an old childless woman; she did the women's rituals, kept up dharma and karma, it was her joy to sorrow with the village's sorrows. If she couldn't find anyone weeping in sorrow, she'd set off in search of a sorrowing bird or beast. On such mornings she'd sit and think and say to herself—'I'll weep, I'll weep, decides my mind, but weeping will not respite find. There's an elephant dying in the great forest, I'll go; I'll embrace it and weep.'"

In Hansuli Turn, old Suchand is perhaps that same old woman of their time. When the snake died, the old woman wasn't home. If she had been, there's no telling what she'd have done. She'd gone to cut grass. Old Kahar women and men of Bansbadi who can no longer do manual work can't live by doing nothing. The ancestral rule is this: do whatever work your body can do. They go out at noon and cut grass for cows-calves-goats. Baskets on hips, carrying sickles, they cross to the other side of Hansuli Turn—to the cattlemen's hamlet on the other bank of the Kopai, to cut grasses in Buffalo Pit marsh. All over the vast marsh grows a great abundance of grasses. They also pick water chestnuts, gather bindweed, cress, greens, and a few eels—they catch these too. And so the old woman had gone to that Buffalo Pit marsh. On her return she heard the whole story and came dashing to see the snake. Saw it, screamed, and wrought terror on the hamlet.

The old woman widened her eyes in awe before the snake. After a few moments she wiped her eyes with the corner of her wrap, clasped her hands, touched them to her forehead, and reached toward Babathakur's shrine, saying—O Father, O Father, O Father!

—Oi, crone! Karali yelled an objection.

Pakhi said—Dammit! See this act! See 'ow she's set to cryin' in middle o' the day! Now snake's become Father!

—Tis so, 'tis. The old woman wept. Weeping, the old woman said in a singsong way—O, that's me Babathakur's familiar! Babathakur goes out a-journeyin' mounted 'pon its top. O, seen it wimme own eyes, me! T'was goin' 'appily off ta sleep in a nook in Babathakur's silk-cotton tree above the deeps, I seen the beast meself.

After this, absolutely no doubt remains. The most ancient arbor above the rapids is Babathakur's silk-cotton tree; when this astounding, whistling, mottled, venomous snake lived there in that very nook it was protected by Babathakur; his familiar—where's the doubt in that! Men and women of Kaharpara gave a collective shudder; in one voice the young women cried—Oh my God!

Karali became terrified, and then enraged too. He's able to guess what will happen next. The entire hamlet will break out lamenting. All his heroism will be ground to dust. But he couldn't think what to do! His friends looked aghast. As if they were getting scared too. He wished he could flee to Channanpur. Bring back Junior Saheb from there, the one who killed just this kind of snake that day beside the rail line; the saheb who with his own hands chopped down the ancient saora tree beside the river, the tree that was the banshee's refuge. Let him come and jab the dead snake with a stick, let all Kaharpara be punished.

Suddenly Pakhi screamed. She went right up to her grandmother and said in a sharp voice—Now look oldie, this dawn at third watch I told ya don' start cryin'.

Deaf Suchand couldn't hear the words. She was moving sorrowfully inside her own mind—It'll be ruin, o, it'll be ruin. This village got no plenty. Ah—ah—O woe, woe!

Pakhi didn't try any more useless yelling. She came, took the old woman's arm, and led her out from their cottage threshold, shouting— Siddown 'ere an' cry.

Despite being led by the hand, Suchand at first couldn't understand what Pakhi was thinking. But now there was nothing left to understand. At that moment she became frightful, and in that same moment descended from the unworldly realm to Bansbadi's worldly history. If not, then Pakhi can't be held back, Pakhi and Karali can't be frightened into obedience by fear of God. So she began to tell the story of Pakhi's disgraceful birth; how else could her character get that way?

In epic proportions, Suchand screamed to the heavens the story of Pakhi's life and its many appalling acts, from her disgraceful birth until now. As a final reproach she said—Casteless bitch—scumcaste—bastard child, think ye're so great? Gonna kick me outa me own 'ome?

Then she said—An' 'ow come? Oo else'd 'ave the sauce but this Pakhi? Oo else could it be but this girl o' Bashanta's? So what if it's Suchand's own daughter? Suchand won't tell lies devoid of truth. She doesn't hold back just because it's her own daughter. Those filthy schemes of Bashanta's; when Bashanta gets on heat for that drunkard son of Sire Chaudhury in Jangol, Suchand knows then that she'll have to suffer the consequences. To this very day Bashanta takes milk to the Chaudhury house for free, year round, under the spell of that heat. She doesn't even speak of this. When this bitch Pakhi was in Bashanta's belly, Suchand went hunting and found a feeble, lame son of a Kahar; she got him with huge bribes, forced the fatherhood responsibility of Pakhi upon him, saved Bashanta and Pakhi. There was wrong done—she'd done wrong. Bashanta should have been thrown on the street. Or else it was her duty to make Bashanta destroy this evil-gotten fetus. Everyone knows the evil that was to come. The blood of those Chaudhurys, of Bashanta in her veins, oh, she'll get their fix of heat! Evil Pakhi's gone mad under the spell of Karali. Hooked on that fix, perverted casteless bitch seeing wrong as right, right as wrong.

Suddenly Pakhi hissed—Bitch, t'ain't 'cos Chaudhury blood's in me veins that me fix is stronger. But why ain't the fix o' the daughter o' yer own belly left off till this day, eh? I say, oose blood's in yer Bashanta's veins? Eh?

Pakhi's scream startled the buzzard circling right in the overhead skies; or at least it seemed that way. The buzzard that had been gliding right overhead with unmoving, outstretched wings appeared, just at this moment, to powerfully flap its wings and speed away from the place. Nor had a single word remained unclear to Suchand. Suchand gazed fixedly after it. Then she looked here and there, as if she'd begun searching for something.

Pakhi said—So I don't know what ye're like? Ya won't tell me about yer own 'eat yerself?

Suchand dashed off and came running back from under Neem-oil Panu's neem tree with a broom in her hand—I'll clean out yer poison today, I will.

Pakhi ran away and came back with an enormously long bamboo baton—Come on then, you come on. I see ya.

Just then Bonwari suddenly appeared. Suchand's screaming grew louder. Pakhi stopped screaming and went indoors, taking the baton. This is an absolutely normal event in Bansbadi's Kaharpara of Hansuli Turn. Such is the flow of this place—thus quarrels break out and thus they are settled. Just as it had suddenly blazed up, firelike, so it was quickly extinguished. This is just how fights stop if Bonwari appears.

Bonwari's face was grave. His thought, his bearing, were full of modest dignity. He said—Hush, everyone quiet.

Again Suchand began to yell—Oh no, O my—

Stooping to her ear, Bonwari shouted—I'll listen after this.

—After this?

—Yeh. Maito Ghosh is comin' ta see snake.

—Oo's comin'?

—Maito Ghosh of Jangol. My boss.

The old woman was terrified too. Everyone stared anxiously toward the Jangol track. From the rear Panu called—Move, move aside. Make way.

The crowd split in two. Ghosh of Jangol was standing there.

Four

Karali's eyes flamed.

If he sees Maito Ghosh of Jangol, Karali is fearstruck to the same extent an inner hurt awakens. However much pride he takes in working in Channanpur's workshops, in some unknown, secret part of his mind a greater pain is accumulated. It's this Maito Ghosh who drove him off to those Channanpur workshops. That's tied up with the history of Karali's mother. There's little shame here in the light and shade of Hansuli Turn. But nonetheless, a mother's shame is the greatest of all shames. What's more, there's the pain of a mother's loss. And there's the painful memory of the first day she quit this Bansbadi.

All that's an old story. A story fragment in the tale of Hansuli Turn, a few stanzas out of a whole ballad. It embarrasses headmen like Bonwari to recite those stanzas. Youths tell them in nooks and corners. Young women whisperingly speak them among themselves if the subject of love's heat arises. Only Suchand yells them out. She says—Hah! What's 'e gotta be ashamed of? "If the eggplant's shape's a joke, didn't it get it from its folk?" is the thing she says. This is passing from generation to generation of Kahars. This story they'll tell openly. Karali was a child then, his father died when he was three. When he's five years old his mother abandons him and runs off with some man from that Channanpur station. That rail line's being built then, people coming from all over the country and laying the line, putting a bridge over the Kopai, the whole thing causing a huge fuss. The young women of Hansuli Turn used to go to Channanpur to work on building construction. They were banned from have anything to do with that huge deal of a rail line. Bonwari himself was headman then, and the prohibition was his. If you go there you lose caste—no dharma there. If the winds of those workshops blow on the bodies of them who live by farming, it's not well for them. Those winds, that "sattink." Or stink. The farmers' patron goddess, Lakshmi, can't bear it. But enough of that. Left a widow, Karali's Ma goes off to Channanpur to work in the gentry's houses and in her greed for money sets up "'idden" relations with the folks in the station workshops. Then one day she took off somewhere, giving up all attachment to the child. Who'd even bother searching? And what would happen if you did look?

Karali began to weep. But at Hansuli Turn that's nothing new. So many such incidents, so many weeping boys; the relatives take them in. If they don't have any relations then the headman takes them. Even surrounded by neglect, they somehow grow up. If they make it to ten or twelve years old, no more worry. Then they can stand on their own feet, feed and clothe themselves from their very own earnings. Retained at Jangol's Sad-gop houses in exchange for rice, clothing, and a monthly income of four annas. They graduate to being cowherds.

In all three branches of Karali's family there was one aunt—that Nasu's Ma; it was she who took Karali in. People used to call Karali ghost boy. Karali would go out looking for his ma. He'd go looking in the Buffalo Pit marsh, he'd search in woods alongside the Kopai river, beside ponds, under the silk-cotton tree, there where Babathakur's shrine is; some days he'd get halfway along the field path to Channanpur. He'd weep, saying, "Ma, ma." Then, inventing some game, he'd become absorbed in that, or, tired, would fall asleep. At Babathakur's shrine he'd observe lines of ants for hours, watch the building of a termite hill. He'd gather flowers from the tendrils of a flowering-creeper-covered wood-apple tree. On days when the Kahars made offerings at Babathakur's shrine, he'd go along there after the offering—he'd collect oblations of candy, molasses, and eat them. He'd have to go to war with the ants. The Kahars left small cups of milk there, and he'd drink what little there was. Sitting beneath the silk-cotton tree by those river deeps, he'd see flocks of parakeets—they'd fly, tails dancing, bring rice stalks in their scarlet beaks; how often they'd battle with the snakes that came to steal their young. Karali would help the parakeets, he'd hurl rocks, harry the snakes. He knocked one or two snakes down from the tree with his rocks. At some point, the passion of play would suddenly vanish, then he'd go searching for his ma again. Slowly he got older; he was touched with shame at the history of his mother's disappearance, then he gave up looking for her. Then one day— just when he'd reached the age of twelve—Bonwari put him to work as a cowherd in the household of the Mister Ghoshes. He'd graze cows, gather cow dung, do odd jobs. He occasionally helped Middle Ghosh onto the train at the station, and Middle Ghosh would give him a quarter-bit every single time.

Karali had really liked Maito, that's to say Middle, Ghosh, and feared him to the same extent he liked him. One such as this, with a box bed, with such fancy clothes, who can so carelessly throw away a quarter-bit; a man who gets up into a rail carriage and takes off to travel in distant lands; the Kahars fear such a man as much as they like him. One day this liking suddenly became poison.

Ghosh beat on him with a shoe. Bonwari grabbed his shoulders and forced his head down, and Middle Ghosh thrashed his back with one of his open-heeled shoes. Here's how it happened. One of Middle Ghosh's clients had sent him a basket of extra-special mangoes. Karali had gone to Channanpur station to fetch this basket of mangoes. You don't get men as good as Station Master anymore. The goods that come to the station, a king's trappings; every single Station Master always pinches a few bits of this and that from them. But that Master never dipped his hand into anything of anybody's. Only what was owing to him per receipt—that he would indeed take. Ghosh's mango basket was well wrapped, stitched and glued. But the sweet smell of those very best quality mangoes was lusciously filling the goods room. If you so much as entered the room that scent would go in your nose and fill your chest, dragging saliva from the back of your tongue until your mouth was wet and drooling. Master had a little daughter who was tempted by that smell, clamored for mango to eat, and finally began weeping. Yet Master didn't take out a single mango. But Karali couldn't hold back. He took out two mangoes himself and gave them to the little girl. He said—Me boss ain't like that, good Master. Then just as Karali was leaving the station the guard grabbed him. Wouldn't let him go without getting two mangoes. Not simply wouldn't let him go; he got a knife out of his pocket, cut off a bit of mango, ate, sang its unending glory, made Karali taste a slice of mango, and only then released him. There's his crime. Ghosh couldn't have caught Karali for four mangoes too few; he caught him because of the smell of mango on his hands and mouth. Middle Ghosh grabbed the mango basket and took it down from Karali's head. When it was set down, he grabbed Karali's right hand, put it to his nose, and sniffed it. Next he called Bonwari and said—Smell his breath, Bonwari. Bastard's taking mangoes out on the way and eating. Bonwari at first stood there hanging his head in shame. Where will he put this shame? Karali's a boy of his own caste group, it's he who got him a job in this household. Above all, he's hamlet headman and Karali's a boy of that same hamlet. Subjects' evils pollute landlords and kings; therefore it's the right of landlords and kings to punish subjects. Society's evil pollutes the chief, the headman; therefore the task of chief and headman is—to close the no-good, undharmic road to man and woman. Shame shame shame. There's God, there are Brahmins, there are respectable householders—they're your bosses; they may eat, but don't they give you the favor of their leftovers? Bonwari wanted to take a red-hot iron rod and burn Karali's tongue off. But Middle Ghosh carried out the punishment himself. He said to Bonwari—Grab, grab the bastard's neck and shove his face in the dirt. So Bonwari grabbed. Middle Ghosh himself took off his shoe and gave a "youge" thrashing. And Middle Sire drove Karali away too. Some wages were owed; he didn't pay them either. Station Master heard the story. He was crushed to dirt with shame and it was he who summoned Karali and gave him work as a coolie in the station warehouse. But there's nothing to be made by this work at a little station. It's tough going to fill your belly. So after a word with Line Inspector he's finally allowed to join the coolie gang. And that's why Karali is today's Karali; and it's because of all this that he wants neither to honor Bonwari nor to tread in the shadow of the Ghosh house. No matter that this all happened an age ago, and no matter that opinion judges him to be in the wrong, Karali still can't forget what happened or admit that the wrong was his.

When he saw Middle Ghosh, Karali's eyes at first began to burn. But the next moment his mind did a dance. Bonwari had grabbed his neck, Middle Ghosh had beaten him. Today Bonwari is praising him, Middle Sire has come to see the snake he's killed. Today for once he'll see what Middle Ghosh has to say, with what praise-filled gaze he will look Karali's way.

He came down from the yard and waited with outpuffed chest, really. Ghosh was standing right near the snake. Moving the pressing crowd aside, Bonwari advanced and paid obeisance. But Karali neither came forward nor paid obeisance. He had some kind of word with Lotbor and started to smile. Bonwari signaled with his eyes a few times, summoning him to go and lie at Sire Ghosh's feet. Karali saw and, seeing, made as if he had not seen; he just stood there like this. His ears were pricked, though; who's saying what, he was listening to every single word. Restlessly awaiting the words to come out of Middle Ghosh's mouth—that's what he was listening for. Every single person showed amazement, applauded Karali's heroism. But after watching and listening for a bit, smiling faintly, Middle Ghosh said—Nah, not so big. Even in the zoo there's hill chitis a lot bigger than that. Not to speak of the jungles of Assam. Snakes so big there that they'll kill a tiger if they get in a fight with it. If one of them falls on the rail line when a train's coming, well, the train gets stuck.

Bonwari agreed with this statement. He said—Yes, by yer leave. Middlin' snake.

At this point Karali came forward haughtily. He's going to carry the snake out of here right now. Take it to Channanpur station and show it to the gentry there, show it to Saheb. Beside them Ghosh is a worthless nullity. The son of one of the Jangol gents said—But this isn't a hill chiti—it's a chain viper. No one's seen a chain viper this size before. And this is a hell of a snake.

Smiling faintly, Ghosh said—That's just the same species, see, chiti species. Then, staring at Karali, he said—Well, aren't you just becoming the hero. Expect your mind's a bit sharper too, eh. What you doing these days?

Holding his head high, Karali tried to answer solemnly, I works the coolie gang on the 'ail line. But what an incredible thing, a solemn tone didn't come from his throat at all. He began to reply, swallowed twice, and shut up. His chest began to pound. In reply Bonwari said—E does coolie work on the 'ail line these days.

—Oh, right! Well, haven't you come up in the world then! And what else are you doing? Thieving at night? With that body you're building up and your mind sharp and bent as a fishhook, you'll be able to master the tricks of that trade.

Karali's body began to feel wobbly. He stood with bowed head. The way Middle Ghosh spoke had everyone smirking. Grinning, Bonwari said—By yer leave, no. E don't do none o' that thievin'. No chance 'o that sorta thing in my day at Kaharpara. Ooever'd do that'd 'ave ta get outta the village. But Karali's a total lowborn. Lowborn an' tricky in equal measure.

Laughingly, Middle Ghosh said—In that case, he's bound to end up a thief. And if not a crook, then he'll turn out a perverted freak—I've told you so, Bonwari. Then he took the leather-trimmed money bag out of his pocket and, tossing a one-bit coin, said—Take.

Middle Ghosh was instantly transformed into the most astounding kind of nobility before all the people. Next he said—Haul that thing off. Stink's rising already. Once they heard this everyone began to breathe in deeply. Isn't a stink rising? Stink? Even Bonwari started to breathe heavily. Although he heaved a strangled or tormented sigh, Karali did not disregard the one-bit coin; picking up the coin, he tucked it into the waist of his loincloth and said to his companions—Tek. Hup. We'll tek it ta Channanpur stishan. Hup.

Today, right this minute, Karali regretted again that Nasu-sis wasn't there. If he'd been there he would've been able to make a comeback to Ghosh. If Nasu-sis had been there he'd not have been able to resist tightening the wrap around his waist, pulling up his veil a bit, looking at Ghosh, and answering him back.

Ghosh said—Nah, not so big.

Quick as a flash Nasu would've put his hand to his cheek and come back—Oooooh my! Well, what *would* ye call big, sir?

Ghosh would've mentioned the chitis in the jungles and hills of Assam or someplace.

Wagging his finger, Nasu would've said—Where'll I find a cobra, dad? Our little grass snakes is cobras. Assam or Blighty or whatever place ye're on about, they can keep their boa corn-stricters. This 'ere corn-stricter of ours, to us that's real big; they say gold's cheap down in Lanka, folk down there's got gold on every limb; in our land glass bangles, tin bangles, they's our golden bangles.

How many more ditties he'd have come up with. Karali kept thinking and thinking about Nasubala. And it would have been so great if Nasu-sis had been here today! Middle Ghosh had managed to dull the shining glory of such a huge feat. Yet with Ghosh now out of sight, a little of his courage returned. He rebuked Mathla, saying—Whass this? Din'tcha 'ear what I said, or what? Tek, hup! Mathla had put his shoulder at one end of the bamboo pole for carrying the snake; at the other end was "Lota," or Nota, which means Notbor.

When Ghosh had left the compound, Karali took the one-bit coin from his waistband and said—Looka this thing—this bit any good? Fakey, ain't it? He addressed Mathla and Notbor, who'd carry off the snake hanging from its bamboo pole. Before either of them could even answer, Neem-oil Panu came up. Said—Where, give, let's see!

He looked and said—Nah, it'll work. Good 'un fer sure. Besides, that's a bit from master Maito Ghosh's bag. E don't keep no money but the noo shiny kind.

Karali said—Huh.

Panu said—That time I was given cash 'e poured a pile of it onna couch from the bag. Money was just like gold, shiny-red money—so much.

Panu also joined them as a bearer; he'd go to Channanpur with them too. A lot of money to be made at Channanpur, no doubt about that. Karali didn't mind this. Let the little jerk come along. Panu himself lent a shoulder. The python left for Channanpur.

After a few moments Karali suddenly stood back and slapped Panu's face with a resounding smack—Bastard, why're ya movin' like the blind? Movin' like a blind man? Whatcha keep bumpin' me feet for? Can'tcha even see us no more? Bastard! Money just like gold, "shiny-red"! Bastard, wherever ya go to, get off there. Think ye're wi' me?

Mathla said—Karali's sayin' right. Think ye're wi' us today, then? Go an' toady wi' the 'eadman. Are ya wi' us today?

Notbor cautioned him—Oi, shuddup. Jus' look an' see if chief's co-min' or not now.

Because of the narrow, raised fieldpath on the one hand, and the snake dangling from the bamboo pole on their shoulders on the other, there was no way the two of them could turn to look.

But Mathla turned his neck, looked, and said—Nah. Where? E ain't comin'.

Karali spoke in the Hindi he could muster—Whoever comes'll come. Nuffink to do with me. Nope. Then suddenly said—Why aren't Kahar lads callin' out the palky-bearer's call, the jerks? Call it out. This really got to Mathla and company. With the dead snake mounted on its palanquin, they swung their arms and began the call—Ploh heen—ploh heen—ploh heen. Suddenly from behind they heard Bonwari's throaty yell—Wait, wait. Heeey! Wait. They all stopped. Had to stop. Legs did not lift again. It was only Karali who got agitated—Whass all this! Whass this tyranny!

Bonwari's face appeared blankly stern. He came and stood. Said—Come back.

—Come back? Why?

—Gotta be burned.

—But we'd said it'd be at night.

—Nope. Burnin'll be right now. All Kaharpara's gotta take the ritu-al bath. And then in a voice full of resentment and anger he suddenly added—It's you's gonna ruin the village, ya know—ye're the root of all trouble.

Karali was stunned.

Bonwari heaved a deep sigh. Said—Come on back. Gotta foller the counterpesscription on whatcha done.

Karali said—No. Up with it you lot, up.

But none dared to lift. They stood there like clay figurines.

Karali spoke again—Ye listenin'? Up!

It's as if no one can hear him. Bonwari said—Go back, unless ya wan-na die spewin' blood from yer mouths.

Now the snake went up. With the snake on their shoulders, everyone began moving back toward Bansbadi. Only Karali didn't start back. He set off very quickly in the direction of Channanpur.

Bonwari stared after him for a while, then turned away.

Suchand is keeper of whatever archaic ordinances belong to Kaharpara. Those ordinances have been forever intact, as they were this day.

Bonwari took his leave of Middle Ghosh and arrived home to see Suchand sitting there. Suchand arrived after fighting with Pakhi. She'd come after telling Pakhi—If I ever come back in this 'ouse, if I ever 'ave cookin' earned by the sweat o' yer ma's brow, well then I ain't got no caste, I'll be outcaste. I'm gonna stay at Bonwari's.

Bonwari knows how to show respect. He says—Sure thing, auntie. Ya gave me lotsa milk when I was a little boy. Ye'll stay, that'll be my good luck, sweetie. What, whaddappened then?

Suchand went into a detailed description and said—Bonwari, if it ain't Lord's familiar, or if it ain't no daughter o' Monosha o' Snakes, then what am I talkin' about!

It was as if Bonwari's—headman of Kaharpara's—vision had been slumbering all this time; now it awoke. And he was happy. Incredibly happy. The painful memory of snake killing was lifting like a cloud in his mind. He touched auntie's feet.

Auntie blessed him—May ye live long, son. May yer lifespan be as long as the hair on my head. Then, wiping her eyes with the hem of her wrap, she said—Ah, me ma's been burned up in the fire, but what lovely looks, what beauty! Oh it's ruin, son!

Bonwari immediately started racking his mind for the counterprescription. Counterprescription—ritual offering to Babathakur. Offerings with booze and meat, drum and gong, dried rice and sugar, cloth and rouge. His headman's responsibility comes above all other deeds of karma; he must first look to the good of the village. O Father, Lord! See to the village's well-being. You must give punishment, so give it to the evil-doer. But Karali has to be brought in line. He's really getting outsized. Hot blood of a young buck. Bonwari was suddenly bursting with rage. And today, inside those smoke-shrouded bamboo groves—. With frustration Bonwari tried to recollect how it was his feet had been carelessly slipping back on the bamboo leaves. And yet it's his disgrace. It's a really shameful thing to him.

Bonwari headman joined his hands at his forehead and paid obeisance to Babathakur. He took a glance upward and then made a silent vow to the Lord—O Lord, I've made arrangements for the offering. I'm vowing once more—I'll give a new goat for it. You keep the Kahars safe.

Suchand asked—Tell what ye're doin'.

Bonwari said—I'm gonna make an offerin' fer this, auntie, vowin' another goat.

—Whatcha doin'? Nother goat?—Looking steadily into Bonwari's face, Suchand repeated her questions.

Bonwari explained again—Yeah, yeah, I'm makin' a vow—a vow.

—Vow?

—Yeh. Gonna do Lord's offerin' wi' two goats.

Holding up two fingers, Suchand said—Gonna gi' two goats?

—Yeh.

—Fine, fine. But that one used ta do a lotta good, sonny—that one. Ah, what a whistle!

Bonwari said—Gonna burn Father's familiar. Everyone in Kaharpara must bathe. Tell everyone. I'm off ta call 'em. He hurried off.

On Kopai's banks a pyre was built and Father's familiar was cremated. All Kaharpara bathed and went home. Bonwari went and paid obeisance at Father's shrine—O Father! Save us Father. Burn up the infidel, Father. Master of the Kahars, keep the Kahars safe and sound.

Five

Dang-dang-dang—dadang-dadang—br-ur-ur-ur-ur-ur-ur—dang-dang—
dadang-dang—

At Babathakur's shrine at dawn while it was "murksome," which is to say still dark, the drummer started drumming the dawn in. Sunday new moon—time turning out well, Babathakur's offering would take place. With flowers and leaves, oil and rouge, incense and lanterns, dried rice and sugar, milk and bananas, liquor and meat, cloth and gratuities—beautifully done offering.

Kaharpara rises before drumming even starts—women and men. Only children stay asleep. Today they got up too. They clamor to visit Babathakur's shrine. Suchand widens her eyes and says—Watch it, t'ain't no yearly offerin'—no makin' merry 'ere. Offerin' fer a wrongdoin' that's made Father scowl, then boys'll go make a ruckus, mess about, splash dirt 'round, weaklings—they'll make filthy dirty—it'll be wrong on wrong. Watch out! First let them two goats get the chop wi'out any messin', Babathakur'll take the offerin' happy; after, skip an' dance, music an' song, booze an' drunk craziness—it'll be everythin'.

Bonwari went all around the hamlet and said—Take care, everyone take care! Lord's makin' everyone in the 'ole 'amlet take the rap fer Karali's wrong-doin'; don't be makin' the wrong worse. Exacted a high price. No more.

Prohlad said—Sheer expense!

Bonwari's doing the spending, Panu's keeping account in his mind. The Neem-oil lad's very good at this sort of thing. His bodily frame—they call it "spindlish," that's to say sliverlike, but what a head he has. He can keep so much in his mind. Panu kept count orally—Yer expenses are a lot. Two paisa over three rupees twenty annas cash.

On top of this there's yet more expense, all sorts of things being given from home; they're really pricey. Two goats, one sheep, twelve ducks, twenty to twenty-five pounds of rice must be given—food offerings for the musicians, for the ritual-performing priests. All this costs a lot. To those who toil from morn till night for five annas a day, meaning they're getting a mere nine rupees six annas a month, it's really a lot! In the Ka-hars' life, therefore, this really is awesome and spine-tingling.

The jitters became yet more intense when it was time to clean up Babathakur's shrine. As jujube shrubs were being cut away, three or four stinging kraits sprang out of the termite hills beneath them. Kahars aren't all that scared of kraits. Stinging kraits have forever made their homes on Kopai banks, in Jangol meadows. The Kahars live alongside them somehow. From time to time the kraits chase them; they too chase the kraits and beat them to death with pestles. Yet this snake caste is Brahmin, so once killed they're all reverentially "kemmated," that's to say cremated, by fire. But at Babathakur's shrine, the krait had a different meaning. Especially after it became known that this pythonlike chain viper was Father's mottled familiar, Bonwari couldn't help but see the kraits as its entourage. He said—Watch out! Don't lay hands on 'em. So saying, he himself clasped his hands and paid obeisance. Snakes then rearing their heads, hissing. Striking earth here and there. But they don't have the courage to venture forward either. Snakes can recognize members of the snake-charming Bede gypsy caste by their body odor, and they flee in fear because they're Bedes. Perhaps they feel just that fear at a Kahar's body odor; they generally don't want to approach.

Bonwari said to the snakes—Get, get; get fathers, get outa here. Give a bitta room. Snek an' 'ooman, that's to say snake and human, mustn't set up 'ome together; now you gi' some room. Let's finish offerin' to yer Sovereign, our Babathakur; afterward ye can reign over yer own place again!

The snakes indeed made way. The Kahars remained cautious, though. You never know; although they're the entourage of Babathakur's familiar, there's still no trusting that kind.

But that beating, ringing drum sound, they'll get well out of the way for that. Incense smoke besides; lots of people coming and going.

The goodly priest took eight annas from cash expenses; a seven-yard piece of cloth—price five bits a pair—comes to ten annas; a measure of wine, five and a quarter annas; molasses drops, candies, sweets, and other things—Bonwari and company call these items "stuff"—their price is five and a quarter annas; the man who makes the sacrificial cut, six annas; one and a half jars of booze, eighteen annas; and the drummer's taking four annas; the last four annas go on oil, rouge, incense, incense burners, lamps, and so on. Priest's taking one of the chopped heads of the goats, sacrificer's taking the other, drummer's taking the sheep's head. Priest's taking the piece of cloth. They were all pleased, saying—Faultless offering, chief. Just a day late's all! Ye missed the Saturday. Never mind. The priest said—New moon Sunday—very good. On new moon Sunday ye'll eat fish thrice. Lord'll be happy and eat meat and drink liquor.

So Babathakur, pleased, accepted the meat and liquor offering full-handed and content. The sacrifice went off without the slightest slip. At the third watch the sacrificial drum sounded—*dang-dang-dang—denak-dadang—lag-dang-dang-denna—*

The Kahar headmen then drank some of Father's ritually leftover wine offerings—a little wine filling fasting bellies; heads reeling. They all stood with hands pressed together. Suchand stared with bulging, reddened mango-stone eyes and began calling—O Ma—O Ma—O Ma!

With their mouths, the boys began to speak the sounds of the instruments—*Kha-jing-jing jinak jingjing lag jing jing jina—*

The offering finishes just at the sacrifice. The sacrifice is done in an instant—flawless sacrifice. Ducks chopped and then let fly. Ducks chopped and the headless bodies tossed. They flew a bit, then fell.

Sure, there was Panu's goat, and Bonwari himself has given a goat too. Roton's given the sheep. Bonwari paid the fine for the crime of killing this snake. Karali did evil, Bonwari did penance. If he doesn't, who will? Come what may to Karali, it's Bonwari who must look out for the hamlet's welfare, the village's welfare. Everyone in the hamlet's given their heartfelt thanks to Bonwari for this. Roton's given a sheep on behalf of his own disobedient son—Lota, Karali's pal, that very same loser who carried off the supernatural snake swinging from a bamboo pole. Suchand gave a duck. Gave it under the force of sheer devotion. Bashanta also gave two ducks; there was not a pair of chopping blocks, left and right, for such a sacrifice—yet she gave two ducks wishing there were. Pakhi partners Karali. Bashanta's secret dedication was one duck for Pakhi, the other for Karali. Kaloshoshi sent a duck too—sent it in secret. Though everyone from Atpoure Para joined in this offering, Porom wasn't excited about it. There's no friendship between him and Bonwari. Porom won't let the Atpoures join in anything Bonwari does as headman. Here the Atpoures disobey Porom's word. But Porom doesn't join in. Yet if the folks of his own neighborhood didn't listen to what he said and went and took part, then the least he had to do was show up as headman. The remaining eight ducks came from eight other homes. Whoever had a duck couldn't not give. No duck, what to do? Who doesn't long to offer to Lord, who doesn't want the chance to receive his leftovers? Every house gave candies, sweets, five pennies. Beside that, booze. Master Ghosh had donated the price of three jars, but Bonwari didn't buy more than one and a half. They bought one and a half jars, and with that as their cover they fooled the vendor and made another three jars of liquor in the village themselves.

The offering's done. Carefree now. Let's go, everyone, let's go. Take Babathakur's leftover candies, drink up, cook food. Victory Babathakur! O God, may you do us good.

Suddenly Karali elbowed through the crowd and stood there. Three ducks in his hand. Nasubala and Pakhi behind him.

—Eadman, I'm gonna sacrifice three ducks.

Bonwari stared at him with a look of unbearable rage. What's this mess-up—what's this hitch! Fury stopped the words in his mouth; all Kaharpara was frozen still. Panu came forward. Extending his long, skinny arm he pointed to the road and said—Scram.

—Scram?—Karali asked.

—Yep. Tek yer ducks. Ain't gonna tek yer sacrifice.

—Ain't gonna tek?

—Nope.

Karali yelled—Eadman!

Now Bonwari approached. Said—Why the yellin'? Why the yellin'?

—I'll smash Pana's face in. Earin' what 'e's sayin'?

—Whass 'e sayin'?

—Can't gi' me ducks. Won't tek me sacrifice.

—Yeh, won't be took—my orders.

—Why? Why not tek?

—No, no. Won't be took. Yer nose should be ground in dirt—

Karali interrupted—Me nose should be ground in dirt?

—Yeah. Ya gotta pay a fine. Fronta everyone—

—Wait, wait. If I do this, ye'll tek the ducks?

—Yep.

—And if I don't ya won't?

—Nope.

Without another word, quick as a flash Karali tore the three ducks' heads off with his bare hands and said—Lord, eat if ya will; don't eat if ya won't. Do whatever ya feel. Our talk o' duck eatin', our sacrifice, it's all over. He said this and left, his mouth reciting the sounds of the sacrifice's instruments—*Kha—jing jing—jenak—pujo—*

He tore the heads off and hurled them, then left, taking the duck bodies. The whole hamlet stood motionless.

Only Bonwari yelled out—Leave it, leddim go. C'mon everyone, get 'ome, 'ave a drink. Call to Father right now. He spoke and called out—Say, "Shi-va—dharma ronjo."

All cried out in one voice.

The drum began to sound the end of the offering—*Dang-dang-dang-dang-dang-dang-dang—dang dang—*. A lengthy playing. It was done. Offering done.

Karali in an ill-fated moment, his ill-starred birth; the unease he caused at an offering like this. Let him. Bonwari doesn't have the leisure to worry about it. The offering may have been finished, but the work was not. Lots of work. Not easy doing headman stuff. Got to weigh up a lot. Got to think of a lot. Ritual leftovers'll have to be distributed. Leftover candies, leftover sacrifices, leftover wine. In order to give to all the homes from which a duck or other sacrifice doesn't come, a couple of legs from each sacrifice are taken and chopped up all together and that's divided up between each home. Two more legs cut from his own sacrifice must be sent to the Ghosh house. He went with those two himself. Before this, he took a good look at his own outfit. Oh yes, very nice. Fine. Today he's wearing his fresh, one-piece knee-length loincloth, its pleated end passed down between his legs and tucked into the waistband; on his shoulder is hanging a clean, folded cotton scarf; on his forehead there's a circle of rouge. Ghosh was delighted to get the meat; he gave Bonwari a cigarette. He said—Yes, today we can really call you a top-notch headman. How could you possibly be that without a cigarette?

Bonwari tucked the cigarette behind his ear, performed a devoted obeisance, and turned homeward. He'd already drunk two cups of liquor before this. He was feeling quite fearless before the world; he said—S'a blessin', s'all youses' blessin'. The "livins" of Bonwari's forefathers was in the bounty o' Ghoshes' leftover wastes. Bonwari began to weep with emotion.

Consolation would only make things worse—Middle Ghosh knows this from experience; he is also not unaware that rebukes cut very deep too. So he spoke brusquely—It'll be fine, Bonwari, we'll discuss it all tomorrow. You've lots of work over in your hamlet today. Better make sure nothing goes wrong.

Now Ghosh really wants Bonwari out of there. For one thing he's a Kahar; and he's drunk too, a stink coming off his body. But a drunken Bonwari doesn't shut up so easily; he said—Yes, by yer leave. Undred times yes. Words o' wisdom. But if there's life in Bonwari's body, that won't 'appen. There'll be bloody murder. That Karali—that bastard crook—'e killed the godly snake in 'is 'ot blood; you see what I do to 'im. Drive 'im off—I'll drive 'im off from 'ere.

Big Ghosh's wife spoke—Yes, very good, now go home. It's already evening, you're giving an offering today, you'd better go light a lamp over at Lord's place and tell the drummer to get drumming. Go. Get it set up now.

Now Bonwari quickly stood. He's forgotten to set something up. Just right; such smart people they are, all that learning inside their "innards," such needful stuff'll just come right to their minds! He folded his hands and said—By yer leave, I'm goin' now.

—Yes, come again—Middle Ghosh can keep a straight face better than anyone at these moments. Everyone else was faintly smirking, but Ghosh was absolutely serious, as if holding an anxious conversation with his agent about a property auction.

Bonwari left; rushed with hurried strides. Lamp must be set, drummer must be told to beat the tattoo at Father's shrine. He's messing up. There's no work today more prone to slip-ups than this headman business. A king's faults ruin a kingdom, a chief's faults ruin a village; subjects' evils destroy a king, a village's evils bring a thunderbolt onto a chief's head. O God!

As soon as he got back to the hamlet he started hollering—Lamp— need a lamp. Gi' a fresh wick. Get some oil from the pot, ya better not give cookin' oil.

He sent Panu to Bayenpara, the musicians' quarter. The drumroll must be sounded.

He walked two steps with the lamp and came to a sudden stop. Breeze blowing. His wife, Gopalibala, came forward and put a "creel," that's to say a basket, in his hand.

Bonwari said—Great! Yes, women really are smartest when it comes to all these jobs. Well done. He screened the lamp with the creel and left. To get to Lord's shrine he must pass by the banyan tree's clumped foot at the northern edge of Atpoure Para. A really dark spot. Lamplight hidden by screening basket. The foot of the tree is eerie. Bonwari suddenly paused, hearing a sound. Who's making that sound like sniffly weeping?—Who?—Who's there?

A pale figure sitting at the foot of the tree. Bonwari approached.

—Who? Lifting the basket from the lamp, Bonwari was surprised. Kalobou? Kaloshoshi? What's this? What's this? Yes, that's Kaloshoshi for sure! There seemed to be a drum beating in his chest. In darkness, under this tree, alone, Kaloshoshi!

Kaloshoshi was crying; she'd come from home in distress. Porom had given her a thorough beating. She'd sent the duck sacrifice to Bonwari in secret, but it doesn't remain secret from Porom. Nobody let on, but Porom figured it out for himself. Porom had paid a visit to that place of the Lord's; although he wasn't taking part in the offering, he'd gone to pay obeisance. Right then, when the priest was smearing rouge on the duck's head for the sacrifice, he began to get suspicious because the duck was one of his. But he didn't kick up a fuss there. Back home he made a count of the ducks and found one too few. He dragged Kaloshoshi into the house without saying a single word, and beat her mercilessly; there were many signs that this secret offering was not out of devotion to Kaloshoshi's Lord at all, but rather out of affection for Bonwari, the offering's organizer; Porom's said this again and again to Kaloshoshi in the most repulsive way—Dunno when I'm gonna die, but I know everythin' else, unnerstan' everythin', geddit? Finally, he'd called Kaloshoshi some disgustingly obscene names. Beating's pain made her livid, and her resentment against God and fate took this chance to awaken. So she left the house and came to sit and weep under the banyan tree outside the village.

But with Bonwari she dissimulated. She kept the real story secret and said—I'd come to pay 'beisance ta Lord. Made a vow.

Bonwari said—Why were ya cryin' then, sis?

—Was cryin' 'cos o' pain in me mind.

—Pain in yer mind?—Bonwari began to weep. Pain in Kaloshoshi's mind! That pain immediately troubled Bonwari's soft, alcohol-sodden mind.—What's yer mind's pain, sis?

—Me pain's me own, bro; the one ta talk to'll unnderstan' what's ta be unnerstood. I said—If I could only die.

—Why, sis? Whatcha make such a vow for, sis? What's yer pain, what ye missin'—won'tcha tell me?

—Ow ta go on? No son, no kids! Usband; no, butcher—

Putting his hand on her head, Bonwari said—It'll 'appen—it'll 'appen. I'm tellin' ya, you'll get a child. You see.

The lamp's light suddenly went out. It wasn't a breeze blowing from outside into where the lamp was sheltered in the basket. No breeze, the light was put out by a puff from Kaloshoshi. She clasped Bonwari's empty hand eagerly. The tang of liquor is coming from Kaloshoshi's mouth too.

In Hansuli Turn, beneath the bamboo groves, darkness of earth's ancient times still lives on. As soon as it gets the chance it rushes in thickly, from dark bamboo groves into settlements. Just as the lamp went out, that darkness rushed in like a flash flood from the heart of the Kopai. Bonwari and Kaloshoshi, drunkenly aroused, were obliterated in that pitch blackness. Kaloshoshi told Bonwari everything at length. Bonwari wept profusely. He spoke of his pain too. He's childless too. He knows the misery of childlessness. Such a big headman, a few acres of land, a bit of pasture, so many cows, a plow, a steer, what will become of all this? What's it all worth? But today he's got no recourse. And besides, he's not going to keep the truth hidden from Kaloshoshi now, at such a moment; he never loves his wife as he does Kaloshoshi. But what's he going to do? They do have a custom of making companion marriages, but for him— Bonwari shook his head. Such a thing would be possible if it were someone else. He's Bonwari—hamlet headman.

Kaloshoshi said—Is that even me place, bro! I ain't sayin' that. Suddenly Kaloshoshi jumped. Said—Someone's there! I'm off 'ome. Go, put the lamp in Lord's shrine an' go back ta the 'amlet.

—Wait, I've lit the lamp again.

Now Kaloshoshi said—Ye're bringin' a lamp, where's incense? Is it just done wi' a lamp or what?

Right. Kaloshoshi's saying right. Kaloshoshi, the woman who came back from Channanpur; who else beside Kaloshoshi could've said it?

Kaloshoshi had worked a long time as a "lowclass" drudge in gentry houses of Channanpur. The gentry say—Lowclass drudge. Their girls clear the garbage heap of leftovers and fishbones, scrub utensils, wash children's dirty clothes, get to eat twice a day, receive new cloth twice a year, earn between four annas and one rupee—depending on whose house it is and what the work is. The Kaharpara girls go to the Sadgop farmers' houses in Jangol at dawn, do their work, and return home. Channanpur's a long way from here, you can't go there, and anyway there are a lot of low-caste people there; it's them does that place's work. It's only Kaloshoshi who's spent a couple of years working at the great gentry houses of Channanpur. That's the time Porom was in jail for two and a half years on a charge of banditry. It was then that one of the big gentry's armed guards, a Hindusthani, Mister Bhup Singh, had fixed Kaloshoshi up with some work in a big gentry house in Channanpur. That's where Kaloshoshi lived then. Mister Bhup Singh then became Kaloshoshi's master. There's certainly scandal in the affair; there was nasty gossip; but merely blameworthy conduct isn't an unforgivable wrong in society. In their society, this isn't such an awful act that it can't be wiped away. Because Mister Bhup Singh's from an upper caste, a Chotri, with a holy thread around his neck; and besides, he's the gentry's armed footman. Let that rest. When Porom came back, he brought Kaloshoshi home. That's the place Kaloshoshi came back from knowing all these manners and customs.

Bonwari now went back to the hamlet and fetched incense and a lamp.

***

The lamp flamed for a few moments and blew out in the breeze.

The incense began to burn, began to coil with the breeze blowing around the reptile-infested wasteland of Lord's shrine. Back in the village the carousal's starting, drums beating, singing songs in chorus. Ah, but no Pagol Kahar today! Pagol Kahar is Bansbadi's balladeer, he composes songs, sings songs; if he'd been here, more folk would've come. Quite a few have gathered anyway. The thick voices of the old with the clear, strong, sweet voices of the boys; thick voices and clear voices, being artfully woven together like horn and oboelike shanai. The women are also drinking liquor. They've formed their own party. The main singer at their party is Suchand; today she's delighted. Lord's offering's been made, an offering worthy of the name, sacrifice, drums, liquor—no mistakes. She's drunk three half-quart milk jugs' worth of liquor. Now Suchand's dancing, now she's singing, now she's telling horror stories from the olden days. Stories of who got secretly hot for whom back in their day, who was in love with whom—smiling faintly, she's recounting all those tales. Now she's telling stories of the sahebs in the indigo-plantation days, of the Kahars' miseries when the plantation shut down.

—That's one o' Kaharpara's "fammins." Me ma used ta say, me dad's ma used ta say, 'twere a "terr'ble" thing. Fate o' the Haris—misfortune o' the Doms. Came the flood. Off floated factory in that flood—that's Kaharpara! Kaharpara an ocean o' water. What a torrent! Buildins fell down. Dead cows, calfs, goats swole up, some got stuck in bamboo groves, some floated off. Folks took son, grandson, ma, sis, an' sat up in the trees. Young boy in ma's lap so deep in sleep 'e slipped out of 'er arms an' fell wi' a splash in the floodwaters. There was an uncle of our Bonwari's—dad's big bro, then 'e was two year old—'e fell down. Ow many more people's boys fell. On a tree branch, *ker-chunk*, Pehlad's granddad died, 'ung by 'is neck! The granddad o' that bastard Karali was in 'is ma's belly then. Filled it up fer ten months. The boy was born on a tree branch. That's 'ow 'e got the name—Shosthidash. The tree was a shosthi tree. People called 'im "Tree-boy Shoshti." Why's that bastard Karali such a maniac? Cos 'e's a shoot off Tree-boy Shoshthi.

Then she started to laugh aloud.

Bashan said—Damn, now what's she laughin' at?

Pakhi is staring unblinkingly with bulging alcohol-reddened eyes; she's looking out at that other get-together, weaving daydreams in her mind. Listening to sounds coming from the party at Karali's house. Karali's holding a separate party at his house. Karali fears none, admits defeat at no one's hands; today he didn't even bow down to Ghosh, Bonwari! Those three headless ducks being cooked up. Bottles of prime liquor coming from Channanpur. Nasubala's dancing. Their party's gotten crowded. Pakhi's mind is dancing. She's wanting to fly off, fly just like the thickening clouds that billow up and dance their flying way in Asharh. Love's heat coupling with an arousing drunkenness in her mind. She *will* go to Karali's place. If only this party would break up, or if they'd all get a bit more drunk! And meanwhile if that maniac's, that's to say Karali's, party would only break up! Now her resolve is firm.

Suchand will mock—so let her mock. Bonwari has ruled—so let him rule. She won't obey anyone's rules. She'll go running and dive into his arms.

At today's meeting Bonwari had said—If ye wanna go do yer own thing then that's just great; everyone do what they want; some's got duties, some ain't; we don't look to oo's died or oo's livin', nuff said, s'all just great; I'm all right, don't wanna do 'eadman stuff, won't do it. An' if it ain't so, if someone wants ta lay the duties on me, well then my word's gotta be obeyed. Carryin' on like that Karali—it won't do. As he was talking he looked several times in Pakhi's direction. Let him talk.

Neem-oil Panu—with that emaciated face, sly, darting eyes—it's he who's Bonwari's main partner in that mischief. Whatever the trouble, he's the root. He's been on and on badmouthing Karali. He's been talking trash nonstop to one person about everything Karali said to him that day they went to take the snake to Channanpur. He'd brought Pakhi into it.

He was speaking sarcastically—Ask Bashan and Pakhi. They'll obey what ya say, but there's a trap laid for Pakhi in Karali's yard. He giggled.

Pakhi, bird, would have turned on Panu with beak and claw, wings flapping, but Bashanta stopped her before she could. Pakhi has that single weakness. She can't hurt her mother. How could she? Ma's not just her ma—she's her soulmate. No one has such a ma. Pakhi tells her mother everything straight out. Bashan never reproves her daughter. She ties her hair, wipes her face. Mockingly says—Ask Karali if it's nice or not. Can she can disgrace this ma, or make her unhappy?

She knows that if she goes to Karali's home no one will be able to touch them. But everyone will jibe at her ma, Bashan. For ages she's done nothing for fear of this. But today, no more. She'll go this very day; today it's as if her mind's saying, gotta go.

Ugh! What a wet-weather tale old sis, that's to say Suchand, is putting together; still not over. This story bit by bit—Pakhi's been hearing the entire life of this eighty-year-old forever. She's losing her taste for that story, especially today, right now.

Suchand is laughing aloud—the laughter probably won't stop at all tonight. Karali's father's father had been born on a tree branch during the flood, that's what the old woman's laughing about. Why laugh so much about that? The old witch hag, can't see Karali for what he is.

But Suchand doesn't laugh because of that. In flood's bad times, when people had the problem of saving their lives by living on tree branches, Kahar men and women's mindcrazing loveheat played even then! Can Suchand not laugh when she talks about this? O my my! No rest for heat's play in Kahar-clan minds. What a mind Babathakur's given them! Suchand clasps her hands in obeisance as she talks. Folks sitting starving up on the tree branches, shivering in cold, rainy wind howling, ocean of flood beneath, roaring in Kopai's breast; if that Neem-oil Panu's granddad's third wife doesn't get the hots for Atpoure Porom's granddad at a time like that! This lot was on one tree, the other lot was on another tree. Who knows how they made eyes at each other or when they took a fancy! In those bad times—no one's a bit concerned with that sort of thing! Porom's granddad was a young lad then; what's more, they were plantation office sahebs' Atpoures: while there's respect, on call they're kept. And the lass was a young one, old husband—a swarm of squealing kids from his other wives, why'd she stay with him? She wouldn't have stayed anyway. It's an amazing thing, eh; she couldn't hang on for a couple days, sat up on that tree making the eyes of heat's game! Come dawn, everyone's nodding; there was a sound—*plop*. That's it. Only Bonwari's grandma—no sleep "mournin" for her son; she cried out. Everyone woke up—Look, look, who fell! Old Neem-oil started crying—Oi headman, me missus fell in. —She's fallen, fallen, whoever's gone, let 'em go. —What'm I supposed to do? —What else *can* ya do? The oldie started to cry. Oh no! When morning came folks saw: sitting on the Atpoure tree next to Porom's granddad, there was that girl.

Suchand began to laugh again.

Roton's wife said—So it was a fun "fammin" then?

Suchand stopped laughing in an instant and looked up, widening her alcohol-reddened eyes; a sacred fire of sticks and leaves burned in the center of the yard, casting its glow on her face; how blankly serious and strange the old woman's face became. She said—Fun! Yeah, better not be fun like that ever again. Was fun after. Flood went down. Soggy walls began ta rumble an' crumble in wind an' sun. Village earth wet an' squelchin', four inches o' silt laid down, not a spot ta stand on. Cows dyin', calves dyin', goats dyin', pigs dyin', people dyin'; stink o' rot all 'round; paddy an' rice washed away; all our cloth soakin' in wet. Servants an' bearers to the plantation office sahebs were left, Saheb an' Missus'd died, plantation office washed away. No tellin' oo's lord, oo's master. No bosses. No bosses, oo's gonna puttekt? Before when it used ta flood, Kaharpara would go under, sahebs were left—they'd get a load o' big planks an' make a raft an' carry the Kahars to the plantation buildins. They'd give rice, give lentils, give orders—Cook rice stew, eat. If yer 'ouse fell they'd give the price o' repairs, give food money. The Kahars were in the shelter of a mountain. Come storm, come blast, come flood, the Kahars 'ad no worries. An' now the world o' the Kahars was cast inta darkness. Saheb died, Missus died, plantation was sold off. On toppa that, what "dussease" then! A pestilence it was. Burnin' fevers, belly cramps; if ya gi' someone water—ye come down wi' it yerself. A few families were totally wiped out. Then a bunch of 'em began ta flee wi' barely their lives. Some went ta marriage kin, some went 'ere an' there ta beg. No tellin' 'ow many folks died in strange lands. Then lands, riversides dried out; around time o' Ten Hands Mother Durga's festival, one by one the survivors started comin' back ta the village. But if ye came back—still one more danger. Flood danger was nothin' besides that danger! Sahebs' plantation offices shut down; Chaudhury bought the estates lock, stock, an' barrel. That demon's treasure what Lord'd given, wi' that same money Chaudhury bought all the sahebs' stuff up then. No 'omes, no gates, no "puttekshun," no work, "midsnight" fell on the Kahars; the world went dark to the eyes. What'll 'appen? Where to go? Oo'll give work?

Twere two palanquins in the sahebs' days; used ta hafta be on call twenty-four hours a day at plantation offices, sixteen Beharas were stationed there. The sahebs'd given land to each Behara, three acres an' a spot to build on. Farm the land, eat, an' carry Saheb and Missus around on yer shoulders. On toppa that there was "gratooties," bookins for weddins, marriages, 'ere an' there. An' there was yer indigo farmin'. Everyone did a few acres o' that 'ere and there. Then when yer sahebs'd cause a ruckus—get this, they'd smash down some gentymens' paddy fields an' plant indigo there instead, or cut their new paddy an' take it; 'twas then Kahars were sahebs' right 'and. The sahebs' stickfighters'd go, and wi' them'd go the Atpoures, takin' their fightsticks. They'd stand guard, an' Behara Kahars'd take a steer an' plow and break up the soil, mashin' an' smashin', an' sow indigo there; if ripe paddy was there they'd go choppin' an' loppin', an' bring it back 'ome. Whatever paddy ye'd take ye could keep. An' beside that there were "gratooties" in cash money. That was the Kahars' golden age. Sahebs left, the Kahars' fortunes were smashed. Don't Kahars see darkness comin'? How times changed. Now Chaudhury takin' on the 'ole land grant as 'is own farmland. Said—I won't be needing a palanquin carried all year round, the Beharas needn't be kept on call twenty-four hours a day either—why should I grant lands in exchange for work? Grabbed Mother Land. Land, 'ome, cottage all gone. Darkness, a cosmos o' darkness, oh. Kahars weepin' an' beatin' their chests. Me ma used ta say—Ma was a real ripe grown-up girl then; year after that I'm in 'er belly. Ma would say—The Kahars were weepin' an' beatin' their chests, cryin' so loud it'd drown out drums on a festival day. Kahars quit the village an' went beggin' from burnin' 'unger; Ma was bent double at marriage kin's 'ouse so long those stomach pangs were forgot. Nothin' ta put on the stove; cookin's outa the question, leftovers from offerins—no one went ta beg fer them neither. Then whaddappened to Ma, finally, on the ninth festival day, whatta gobsmackin' scene! Chaudhury suddenly said—Go, I released your homesteads, I won't let you up sticks from them, I kept them up. That little bit of grant land's left, you must carry the palanquins whenever needed. But you're not getting any farmland. Yes, do farmwork, herding—that's it. Yet the Kahars 'eaved a sigh of relief. Forefathers' 'omesteads 'ad remained durin' the "fammin," this really is luck. They blessed Chaudhury wi' raised 'ands, and after the final rites o' Bijoya-Doshomi began rebuildin' on the deserted 'omesteads. That was yer good Lord's mercy, too. E'd given Chaudhury a dream on eighth night o' the festival—Don't make people leave their homesteads, if ye let the Kahars leave, my "wraths" will be upon you. It's 'cos o' that Chaudhury got up a'mornin' on the ninth day an' released the 'omesteads.

Suchand stopped. Hearing the tale of Hansuli Turn, the whole party sits there as if frozen in speechless awe; the past whirling around the brain in the heightened intensity of drunkenness. Intoxication coursing through the head like the Kopai's flash flood. In the imagination, the past's boat is floating by on that flood. The Chaudhury house comes floating out like that floating demon's boat. All sorts of sounds ringing out, light glittering like wave on bobbing wave. Everyone sitting overcome. Some are nodding off, someone seems to be snoring. Various kinds of noises coming out, make you laugh to hear.

Bashan is very cool by nature; she hadn't drunk much liquor either—she said to Roton's wife, Kusum, with a faint smile—Damn, oo's that snorin' then?

Kusum too looked around and asked—Oi, oo is it? Oo's done gotta pig up their nose? Oo's snortin' away, eh?

Seeing them moving their heads, Suchand jutted her face forward and questioned—Eh?

Now Pakhi jumped up, annoyed. No, they'll slumber no more! Meantime, at Karali's place the party's barely started! She got up and said to her mother—I'm gone to lay down, ma.

—Ave a drink an' then lay. Stay a bit longer!

—No.

Kusum pinched Bashan's leg. Kusum is Bashanta's friend, she knows all the inside stuff. Smiling lightly, Bashanta said—Awright, go. Make sure ya sleep though.

A slightly annoyed Suchand said—Whatcha sayin' then? Eh?

Bashanta yelled—Pakhi's gone ta lie down. So I says—make sure ya sleep.

Rocking her whole body, waving her arms, Suchand was about to cut a little rhyme, but just at that moment a loud call rose up from somewhere. The dark of Hansuli Turn was shocked into alertness; oh! Patrolman's calling. Suchand too was shocked—she didn't say her say to Pakhi and instead said in surprise—Oh my God! Policeman's callin'? Out there? My word Bashan, when did the train cross the bridge? Say, 'ow comes there weren't that musical-like sound?

In truth the noise of the train passing hadn't yet sounded.

As she left, Pakhi stopped sharp and said—There ain't no limits to yer drunken fun. Remember today's Sundee? That daybreak train today.

Of course, no one had noticed this. The train doesn't run on a Sunday evening. It goes in dawn's small hours.

—What?

—Today's Sundee.

—Yeah, Suchand remembered. Then, frowning, she said—That jackal callin' out the watch? Hear it?

—Speak, then. That story you were tellin'!

Right at this moment the sound of someone's very deep voice was heard some way off—Porom! Porom! Porom Atpoure! Immediately, a long, powerful flashlight beam cut through Atpoure Para's darkness. Everyone was reassured. No, not too late at night. Some gents from the police station coming to check up on the "marked man," the known criminal. The police gents come from time to time, once a week. They come around early like this. Porom Atpoure's a marked man. A few years ago there'd been some robberies from these Sadgop homes in Jangol. Porom certainly wasn't in the bandit gang, but he really behaved suspiciously. Goods had also emerged from his house. Porom was jailed. Porom marked, accused.

Everyone sat back feeling better. At the men's party, song, music, and uproar died down. The party music at Karali's house stopped completely. Station Chief will pay a visit to this hamlet. If he comes to Atpoure Para he also takes a turn around this one. There aren't any marked men in this hamlet now, but there were once. If you said that once upon a time every single person in Kaharpara was a marked criminal, it would be the truth. That's certainly why he's coming; and besides—they're a "backward" caste, who knows when one of them'll go off the rails? So the gents are likely to come and see. Bonwari says—I'm glad it's them's comin'. They'll see our conduct wi' their own eyes, an' those among us oo are still a bit "waysward" o' mind, let 'em cool it, be "honnable," mind it.

Should discipline for those arrogant, ignorant lads like Karali come from headman alone? Bonwari has decided that today he'll tell them—be it Police Inspector or Deputy Inspector, whoever comes, he'll tell them about Karali. He said to Roton—Tie up yer big poultry's legs an' bring it, will ya?

As tribute, on the day the gents come, the Kahars always give poultry, which is to say chicken and duck; and if there are none, then a few eggs. Bonwari decided that today a large chicken must be given. Heaving a deep sigh, Roton got up. No option, headman's say-so; and besides, his son Lota's mixing in that vile Karali's group. Lota's out of control; control's getting torn away from his dad, then! And yet and yet, his dad's very life! Who knows when he'll fall into disfavor with the gentry! It'd be better to get a word in before that.

Bonwari yelled—Getta move on. Sire's comin'.

The glow of light is illuminating the urnlike heads of palm trees all along the northwest corner of the indigo embankment. Two owls screech, caught in light as they flew off. Sire is climbing out of the field onto the boundary. A sound of shoes ringing out like stone on hard ground. And now the flashlight beam's coming right up ahead. Sire has arrived.

He came to a standstill. Everyone paid obeisance. Neem-oil Panu came running with a woven stool. Sire didn't sit on that, he stood with his foot on it. With a smile, he spoke—Well well, quite a show today I see!

Bowing in acknowledgment, Bonwari stood stooping and replied, covering his mouth with his left hand. He had an abscess in his mouth so he was being careful about the smell; he said—By yer leave, master. Today we gave an offerin' at Lord's shrine, so we did.

Sire said—All right, good.

Roton brought the large chicken and set it down before him. Sire shone the flashlight on it and, satisfied, said—That's a big sort, isn't it, eh?

—By yer leave, yes. Gave an offerin' to Lord today; 'ow could we give you just any old "fing"?

—Good, good. And which one of you is called Karali?

Everyone was shaken up inside. Bonwari was taken aback by Babathakur's strange magnanimity. Oh! So now he's made Inspector aware of Karali's ugly, nasty character! Bonwari paid silent obeisance to Father and said—Yes, by yer leave. The lad's a giant now, by yer leave—too much, by yer leave—

Bonwari couldn't think of a reason Karali would be charged.

But Inspector said the opposite—Yes, a worthy young lad. Send the lad to the station. He'll get a little reward. All of five rupees or so.

—Get a reward?

—Yes. We'd noted the whistling business in the diary, report went up too. Now, when the snake was whistling and then that lad killed the snake—I sent that report off as well. He'll get a five-rupee reward.

Sire left. Patrolman took the chicken away.

Kaharpara was struck dumb with amazement. In their dazed mind's eye it's as if Karali's standing there in a new form, laughing. His rounded chest's thrown out, dimples twinkling in his cheeks; in his sweet, lovely smile, beautiful white teeth are sparkling.

There was sudden uproar in the women's gathering.

There'd been talk of Karali's reward, when all at once, who went running right past them?

A sound of bangles jingling.

—Who? Who?

—Pakhi! Pakhi! Someone replied—Pakhi's run off.

—Pakhi! Pakhi! O Pakhi! Bashanta called loudly.

Pakhi had been getting up to go lie down, and right then Deputy Inspector came. She'd been going in the door and stopped sharp the moment Deputy Inspector called Karali's name! Hearing the matter, she too stood speechless for a while. The she swiftly leaped down from the terrace, cut past the party, and fled outside, white cloth slightly flashing through darkness as it rippled in air.

Bashanta went out, calling—Pakhi, listen! Pakhi!

From far inside darkness came a reply—Nah, I'm gone.

Pakhi said—I've gone to the 'ome o' the one I'm feelin' for.

In the tale of Hansuli Turn young wives plunge into tornado and flood, go running to the one they're feeling for, climb his tree, and live in his leafy domain. When Pakhi's ma, Bashanta, was a young woman, she'd get all dressed up every night and go alone to a garden at the edge of the Chaudhurys' village; some days she'd return at dead of night, some days at dawn. Now Pakhi's also gone running, off to Karali's place.

An ugly fight coming after this. Then perhaps sticks—beatings— breakings of heads! Karali's no hasty groom!

Suchand took the opportunity of starting the fight. In a loud voice, a harsh voice, she began the abuse. Karali has no mother, aunt, sister; no female relations. But Nasu-sis is there. Nasu-sis had been dancing for a long time, and he tied up his anklets and came out to fight. He tightened his waistband like the young women, gestured with his thumbs, swung his limbs, and joined in the fight with language as ripe as Suchand's.

Everyone got excited. Especially Neem-oil Panu. Suddenly everyone was alarmed. A skeletal human tottering to a standstill in front of the gathering. Still wobbling. Who? Who?—O, Noyan's arrived. Wheezing, sick Noyan. It's that same Noyan who Pakhi was married to when they were children. Of course, back then Noyan wasn't sick with asthma, and back then Noyan was the hamlet's most eligible groom. Back in the old days Noyan's paternal grandfather was headman of Kaharpara. From that time forth the Noyan clan were Chaudhury's sharecroppers. Over half an acre of their own land to boot. Seeing all this, Suchand allowed the marriage. Noyan was suddenly stricken with pneumonia in early adolescence. He survived, but the asthma took hold. Pakhi says—What a stink on 'is "breff," an' 'is chest rattles so. She can't stand it, becomes afraid. She'll never ever go to his house. Until now this estrangement's ongoing for two whole years, but even till today there hasn't been a final split. Today it's happened. Death's-door Noyan couldn't not come out in such circumstances. He staggered forward and sat down; then, wheezing and gasping, he slapped the earth and said to Bonwari—You be judge o' this. You decide.

But Bonwari just sat there like a clay manikin. It was as if he wasn't all there. He recalls again and again what happened between Karali and Pakhi, the evening's events; he's remembering Kaloshoshi. He has no enthusiasm. It's as if he can't lift his head.

In tears, Noyan screamed—Headman!

Bonwari replied like a zombie—Whatta say?

Roton said—No, no. This ain't right at all. Ya can't just sit there silent, Bonwari. The boy's gone ta ruin along wi' the village 'cos o' that bastard.

Yet Bonwari was frozen.

Meanwhile, the tone of the fight in the women's gathering had suddenly changed. Suchand suddenly began to moan—a deathly moaning. What happened? Did Nasu hit her, or maybe grab her? Prohlad, Roton, Neem-oil Panu went running. What happened?

Suchand is moaning and hopping about. Nothing but a fearful sound from her mouth. A terrible shadow in her gaze. It's as if she's staring death in the face.

There was nothing left for anyone to understand.

Suchand's seen a frog. Suchand fears frogs like heralds of death. What happened was this—Suchand was screaming abuse in a huge voice. Suddenly Karali appeared and threatened her—Shut yer mouth or I'll let it loose.

In other words, he'll let the frog loose.

Suchand ignores it. That someone could actually throw a frog on her—it was beyond belief. Sometimes sons of Channanpur gentry still say they'll do it for a joke; but in this village who'd have the guts, who'd be so heartless? She didn't know that Karali had the guts, that he was so heartless. But Karali really had brought a frog. Seeing that Suchand was not going to leave off, he threw it on her, grabbed Nasu, and made for home.

At Karali's place Pakhi is shrieking with laughter.

Back at the gathering Bashanta clasped her mother in both arms. Yet Suchand keeps hopping. All the women are laughing into their veils. Prohlad threw the frog away and held a cup of liquor up to Suchand's mouth—Drink, auntie. Eyes closed, Suchand drank like one with a great thirst; then, with her hand to her chest, she let herself collapse right into Prohlad's lap.—Aaaah! Aaaah! Then she began to howl with tears.

Prohlad said—No fear, I chucked it, chucked the frog away.

Meanwhile, Karali's setting off from Bansbadi with Pakhi. In this dark of night they'll go to Channanpur. Nasu-sis left too. They didn't have the nerve to stay after breaking with Bonwari and making enemies of everyone in Kaharpara.

Way off on the rail line the signal's red light is burning. That's Channanpur. Karali's stronghold is there. The Kahars don't dare go there. Nasubala broke into song. Karali rebuked him—Shut up. He thinks and thinks as he's moving, how's Bonwari going to get his payback? He's got to get his payback.

Meanwhile, the terrifying form of Bonwari contemplated Karali's house. Karali's gone. The house is eerie, desolate.

Part

One

Some days later.

In accordance with the laws of the world, night turns to dawn at Hansuli Turn. No transgression there. Birds call from trees; on grass tips, night's dewdrops tremble like grains of pearl. From the tops of bamboo, from the tops of rain tree, neem, mango, berry, jackfruit, acacia, banyan, and fig, dewdrops drip down onto earth's breast. To each season its own flowers in bloom. Eastward, open fields that run down to the river's edge yonder—sun rises over branches on the far side of the Kopai where Gopgram village is ringed with trees. But the Kahars awaken long before the sun rises. When merest hint of light touches eastern sky, morning star twinkling in the southeastern corner. That's how early the Kahars rise. After their own morning ablutions, women rinse down rooms and passages, stick circular cow-dung cakes to yard walls, and wash up whatever pots and utensils are left over from the night before. They take out cows and goats and and rope them in their places. They let ducks out, which rush squawking down to the waters of the indigo levee; and as soon as they're down there the ducks make for the bankside, where they plunge their heads, hunting food to eat from washing up's leftovers. The women let chickens out, which make straight for garbage heap, for dungheap. Once the men have done their ablutions, this morning's field work for each household is yet to be done; they finish up that work with a shovel. Stonelike earth—men and women fill a pitcher of water the evening before and moisten the earth; in the morning the Kahar farmhand takes a spade to it. There's always some field task or other. Old walls get repaired at a leisurely pace. If someone's building a new cottage, work moves slowly over time. If there's no such work, then they do some digging in the tiny vegetable patches beside each cottage. Greens for the home, helpful as a child in the belly for a householder. Same routine, all winter.

When all this is done the Kahars go out to work.

Suchand rises at dawn. She's spitting abuse at the top of her voice as she sweeps the yard with a broom. Her language isn't obscene today—it's heartrending sharp curses; and miserable reproaches between the curses, a systematic laying out of the stages of destiny's ingenious prescriptions.

—The one oo's gettin' so much pep in 'is blood, that blood o' yours'll turn to water. Ye'll get sick wi' the shits, ye'll fall ferrever sick, that stone-like chest'll cave in, yer ribs'll snap an' crackle. The one oo comes back wi' a strong voice shoutin' an' yellin', that voice'll come out yer nose, *squee-squee* like a bird. Yer 'ands that threw a frog on me, yer 'ands that set fire ta the bamboo groves, yer 'and that murdered Ma Monosha's daughter by burnin', those 'ands o' yours'll drop off, they'll dry up like sticks. If I keep up me offerins ta God, if I serve strangers, then me word'll be fulfilled—fulfilled—fulfilled. O Father, Master, O Mother Monosha, O Father "Kalaruddu" o' the Brushland, O Mother Chandi o' Channanpur, O ancient Mother Kali o' the Bokul Tree, O Dharmaraja o' the Wood-Apple tree, you judge—you judge.

Methinks Suchand suddenly remembered about eyes—she hadn't cursed eyes even once! She immediately began to heap curses upon eyes—These, yer big eyes, ye'll lose these eyes. Let floods pour out of 'em onta yer chest day an' night. Ye'll go blind—ye'll go blind—ye'll go blind. These, yer big eyes, they'll pop out of their 'oles like lumps o' red blood clots, it'll be so terrible, it will.

This is a specialty of Hansuli Turn's Kaharpara. If there's a fight it's not settled in a day. Day after day scores are settled, and right after getting up in the morning they reopen the abuse accounts. Soon after, they run out of steam and stop. Then, after a rest, when the chance comes, they'll stand on the threshold of their home, look toward the enemy's place, and fling a few more taunts. And this continuity of the Kahars' fights goes from generation to generation—this is what's called a brawl culture. Yet just as the skill to recite a mantra effectively is divided among ascetics, so, following this truth, is Suchand still the best cusser even at this old age. Meanwhile, someone else is insulting Karali—that's Noyan's Ma. She's not insulting Karali alone, but cursing Pakhi over and over.

Sickly, asthmatic Noyan got up quickly, coughing and wheezing. Tears rolling from his eyes. On his chest hangs a large amulet of King Dharmaraja of the Dead—the asthmatic boy's skin-covered ribs rose and fell convulsively with resentment. Right next to his house, on the other side of the same yard, is Roton's house. Roton had finished his spadework and was sitting sucking on his pipe and listening to the insults.

Noyan paused and grasped the bamboo doorpost to relieve the wheezing a bit. His inhumanly keen eyesight sharpening. The eyes of this longtime invalid have perhaps become whiter. Or else Noyan's two eyes look whiter because of his emaciated body and black color.

Roton said—Ya goddup then?

—Yeh.

—Where ya goin'?

—I'm goin' right to 'eadman.

—Ya can't. Sit.

—Nah. E's gotta sort it—

—Eadman's gone out.

—Gone out! He stared hard at Roton as if it were Roton's fault. Next Noyan asked—What carrion pit's 'e gone to "issmoornin"? No one's gone yet?

Roton said—This mornin' Maito Ghosh's goin' someplace by "tain"; Ghosh's servant came, tons o' luggage—gotta carry it ta Channanpur station.

—So . . . ? Now Noyan was disappointed.

—So nothin' ye can do, is there? Go 'ome and siddown. First make beetle stew wi' 'ot water. Relieve yer pantin'.—Though Roton's aged, as old as the headman, he's a friendly one; even though he's not the actual headman, he's wise like that. He gave advice out of a deep concern.

Noyan's Ma had been spouting abuse as she scrubbed the dishes; suddenly she came forward and shook her ash-smeared hands in Roton's face, saying—Ye're 'eadman's right 'and, though. All that whisperin' an' conspiration! I tell ya, what kinda judgment's this? What sorta leadership's this, I'd like ta know. Fer yer 'eadman ta say nothin' when this kinda wrong's done? Did 'e geddup inna mornin' an' run off 'cos 'e's scared o' makin' a call?

Roton said—What am I s'posed ta say? You two talk to 'im.

—Course I'll talk, I'll really let 'im know. Am I gonna leddit go? I'll go ta the lan'lord, get police in.

—Ye can do whatever ya like. But ta get up in the mornin' an' expect 'eadman ta be sittin' in the judgment seat—well, that's just a right ridiculous demand.

Noyan's Ma said—Eadman's yer close "reelayshun." You speak, I'm listenin'.

An irritated Roton stashed his pipe, pulled his cloth around his body like a shawl, and walked out. Sun's rising above the trees of Gopgram village. Sunlight falling on the thatched roofs of Bansbadi's cottages; it's as if liquid gold is pouring onto the new straw of Bonwari's freshly thatched roof.

Roton is not alone, all the village men have set out—from the north side of the indigo levee they're coming down the narrow, winding trail for the fieldpath to Jangol.

All the women will come out after this too. The seven o'clock train is their signal.

This life at Hansuli Turn is a natural life. Theirs is the slow-paced life of a foot soldier walking the fieldpaths. That's not a bit exaggerated. There's not even a wagon road to Hansuli Turn. The wagon road stops when it reaches Jangol village. An age ago, all these trails were used for bringing cows to pasture. By "for bringing," I mean to say: from that Chandanpur—the ancient gentry masters' village—cows were at that time brought to graze on this Hansuli Turn sandbank. Road—cowpath went as far as Jangol; after that, like a flat disk, it was pastureland inside the Hansuli curve. Then indigo plantation sahebs came and set up a plantation on the upland, broke up the cow pastures for farmland, dug irrigation ponds, set up indigo and paddy cultivation in Bansbadi's fields, and created a Kahar settlement around these ponds. The trail on which Chandanpur's cowherds used to come was closed to cattle. That trail was mended and along it began to move the indigo plantation's goods wagons and sahebs' palanquins and horses. The gentry masters of Chandanpur have had farmland in the fields of Jangol forever; their carts and cowherds used to come and go along the trail—they'd take paddy home from the fields; now only that oxcart traffic remained. Even today their carts travel this trail, laden with paddy, molasses, beans. The Bansbadi Kahars have never at any time needed anything more than a decent footpath. They move on foot, they're foot soldiers on account of that, but in those days they were something else besides foot soldiers; they were professional carriers. With a palanquin on their shoulders they bore Saheb and his Lady, bore brides and grooms. From time to time there'd be an order to carry a dying person to live their last conscious moments in the Ganges. Whichever bearer was in the lead would call out the carrying rhyme, and in one voice the others would cry—*Plo-heen—plo-heen—plo-heen*. They'd gallop by, causing a stir all around. Nowadays this profession of theirs has become petty. They're never called for such work except at weddings. Yet carrying work remains, carrying loads up on those palanquin-bearing shoulders. Twenty miles with two hundred pounds on their backs. Forty miles too, but a night's rest is needed on the way. These days loads are more often carried on the head. Besides carrying, there's also the pleasurable pride of being a driver; they drive the steer plow as well as the oxcart. The pace is therefore slower, so they don't feel the need for anything more than a footpath.

As they move along the trails they suck on their pipes, switch arms from time to time, and tell stories. The mundane stuff of this unhurried life is exchanged. Discussed ruminatively. But today everyone's a little agitated. Today's topic—the events of the past few days. Foremost is discussion of how Bonwari's handled things. Bonwari's been unjust—everyone's agreeing on this point. Neem-oil Panu can summarize and digest these things very well. It was he who was saying—If 'eadman's "scairt" ta punish, an' if some scoundrel does a wrong, then 'ow's 'e gonna get punished? When the king's feeble 'is kingdom goes to 'ell. Such a big wrong an' not a word outa chief's mouth!

—"Thassright," said Prohlad. —But say this 'orrible thing 'appens; I run off wi' your missus. Let my missus up an' move in wi' Roton.

From behind them, Roton began to protest—Oi, don't take me name in vain. I told 'eadman afore anyone yesterday, a wrong's bein' done, 'eadman. But each don't watch over o' 'is own wives an' daughters, is it the 'eadman's job ta do it? Is 'eadman s'posed ta sit on guard?

Prohlad yelled back—I can't believe it, jerk; ain't 'eadman failed ta punish Karali?

From up on the bank of the indigo levee behind them all someone shouted—Who's gotten big for 'is britches, what's the name o' the one that'll punish Karali?

They were all startled to notice the sound, and looked to see; the speaker was Karali himself.

Karali's climbing up the northeast corner path to the bankside of the indigo levee. He must be coming from Chandanpur. The very one who fled with Pakhi that night is returning this morning. Perhaps he's come to collect some belongings. He stops and laughs. His Pakhi and Nasu-sis with him.

Roton, Prohlad, Panu, and all the rest had turned and stopped when Karali spoke.

And still Karali's laughing scornfully. Panu said to the others—Look, everyone. Take one good look a' this. If ye can't sort this, ye'll be puttin' the noose round yer own necks.

Prohlad roared—I'll smash yer teeth in, so I will.

Karali laughed out loud and said—Come on then, on yer own; we'll see what a man you are!

Following Panu and company's group down from the top of the bank come Mathla and Notbor. Their destination is also Jangol, they too do farmwork there.

Roton said—Let's go, let's go. Can't stand around on t'path any longer bringin' "issgrace" on the village.

He wants to keep the whole thing quiet. After all, his own son's in Karali's group too.

But Karali's fearless, he doesn't want to stay hushed up because of someone else's fear. He yelled out—I saw yer 'eadman that day. If ya wanna see too, then come on.

Bobbing his head, eyebrows dancing, he said—I taught chief a lesson that day.

This statement is like impossible news to everyone. Bonwari's a son of the Kosh-Shoulder clan, his bone frame like strong, thick, seasoned bamboo. And not just in Kaharpara; Kaharpara, Atpoure Para, Jangol, in all three places there's not a farmhand as powerful as he; a medium-size steer's back will arch like a bow, neck stretched, as Bonwari's powerful grip tightens and pulls the plow handle. Can *that* be taught a lesson by Karali? Is he some satanic outlaw? Not merely that, in the derisiveness of satanic posturing there's a hint of such results, a thing that can never happen—or can it? But the loud and clear declaration of a truth remains staring them all in the face, they can't hold it to be lies. They all stared at each other, speechless.

Karali demon wouldn't leave off; with another round of laughter he said—Yer 'eadman's an 'eadman fer sure. Took 'im ta see the burnin' o' yer Lord—

Straightaway Pakhi thumped his back reproachfully and said—Again! Again! Again!

Karali began to shriek with amusement. Nasu-sis laughed till he fell over. To Pakhi he said—Go on, Buno, go on. Slap again. I whacked 'im ta teach a lesson—whacked I did. Now look, Buno. Smash 'im one, I've told ya to.

It's visibly obvious that this extremely rash statement of Karali's is true. Everyone saw with their own eyes the death of Lord's familiar, in other words the chain viper. But all shrink terribly from admitting the thing could have been this much more sharply daring.

Yet Karali, Pakhi, and Nasu moved off in jubilation. Without a word Mathla and Notbor also came down to the fields, passed by, and overtook the others. They moved on in silence. Notbor was puffing his pipe; seeing his father, he glanced at him with a touch of respect and lowered the pipe as he passed. As soon as they left, the spell on Roton's crowd broke. He was first—he started to move and everyone's feet started to move with him. But they moved in silence. It's as if everyone was robbed of speech after hearing the news.

Suddenly a call came from up in front. Jangol's mango orchard lies directly ahead. The footpath leads through that orchard. Hedo Morol is standing on the path calling in his very loud voice—Oi! Oi you scum, Roton! Bastard! Hey there, shit-eating scum!

Roton started walking fast. Prohlad said—Uh oh, Morol's gettin' 'is ire up!

Roton said—Mud I was puttin' on a wall went bad, went yes'day ta put it on t'wall.

Panu spoke up—Oo knows what'n my boss's done now? Spuds gotta be dug, need a battleaxe fer that. Work left undone fer Lord's offerin'. I tells 'im an' 'e says—Don't know anything about all that. If the spuds go bad I'm gonna pay a hired hand. I'll cut it out of your share.

Prohlad replied to Panu—Aye aye Pana, tell me, 'ow many teeth's yer master's calf got?

—Two teeth.

—Gonna yoke it yet?

—If ye leave it fer a bit wi'out yokin', till s'got four teeth, d'jya think it'll still take the yoke on its shoulder?

—Realize 'ow strong it'll be?

—O, real strong! Ta touch 'is backside would be a feat! Even a bitta spice dust ticklin' its back'll get it buckin' an' jumpin' around. Boss'd give a proper thrashin' if it were sold.

Prohlad said—I was tellin' me boss 'bout the calf.

—Yer boss buyin' a noo cow then?

—Yeh. E'll buy this time. Been tellin' 'im three years, this year got 'im to agree.

—Me boss'll want a loada dough. Yer boss'll 'ave ta dig money out the ground.

—No chance. Me boss don't plant an' dig in soil no more; 'e'll let go 'alf the paddy "grainary." Won' even need ta let the paddy go, don't need to, 'e can do it from spud money. Two acres o' spuds, man! Straight up! On each rod o' land eighteen pounds o' tree bark been put, "salpeet aloomini" been put down. Each rod's yield—six 'undred pounds, real 'appy—yeh, it was a lot.

They call ammonia—"alumini"; aluminum's called—"enamili."

—Ow's uncle Roton's boss's spuds, then? Lovely shoots comin' up.

Roton had no chance to reply. He walked off very fast. He wished he could be before the boss in a single bound. Boss has really been hurt. The state of the soil's very important. Besides, is it some small toil? The earth's been dug and moistened with water for a whole day; next day again at noon or third watch there'd been another round of watering; next day more digging, watering, and treading down, heavy on the feet—on top of this yet more watering. After the earth's sucked up that water and been moistened by it, then it's ready. No good if it's too soft; if it gets too hard then "work's gone fer nowt." It'll have to be started again from scratch. When it's your own work things are different; this was for Boss. Why should Boss accept garbage? And besides, his boss, what a piece of work! Just like a "feeurious" buffalo. If he gets mad he can't control himself. He's like a colossus cut from stone, thick neck, flat nose, wavy hair, plumstone eyes—and red to boot; thick, stubby fingers, tigerlike paws, mustache like a wild boar's. If he gets enraged he'll start roaring and snarling, raining pounding blows. Just like Ma Durga's demon.

Roton's a tough farmhand, for sure. A long, wiry, steel-built man. No longer young, he's past forty—maybe already fifty years old. But you still can't pinch an inch's loose skin on the man. From morning onward he grips the plow handle; at noon he trades it for the spade—when the three-thirty train crosses the Kopai bridge he stops work. At paddy planting time, he puts shovel aside and goes down to the seed-planting plots. Works till dusk planting seed and comes up. He can go nonstop along a few miles of pathway, up and down, swinging his straight shoulders with a four-hundred-pound load of paddy seed. This same Roton is frightened of his boss's fists. Boss gets angry, screams, and beats. He keeps raining blows until his screams become coughs or his voice cracks. Roton's tasted those blows. With one punch his back doubles up, his breath chokes. But the cure for this is for him to hold that breath and stay quiet. He has to hold his breath from even before the beating begins. If he does this he doesn't choke and needs less air. The sons of Mister Ghosh have a *ball* that they inflate with a brass pump; the ball gets hard as brick and if you hit it nothing seems to happen to the ball, it just flies up—isn't he just like that! The more he stays quiet while the punches come, the more boss will scream in rage. So boss's voice will soon crack, he'll begin coughing; if boss coughs he'll quit, put his hand to his throat, and begin to splutter.

As soon as Roton got near, boss man Mister Hedo Mondol said— Aha, scumbag shithead Kahar, what time ya call this, eh scum? Giving offerings to Lord, guzzling booze, you buncha bastards with yer crazy dancing—and ain't me damp sod drying up like tinder?

Roton stooped and began tugging his ear. This is the attitude adopted by the Kahars when they wish humbly to admit a wrongdoing. You also need to smile a bit when doing this—a silent simper. That was undoubt-edly on Roton's face. The meaning of that little smile was this: he's able to perceive the implicit wisdom and tenderness in master's reprimand.

Of course mister bosses have "tendiness." They do. Bosses do a lot in times of crisis. The Kahars will freely admit it—loads, loads they do. In times of affliction and distress they look out for you; if something hap-pens they'll even come visit, make small loans, give such things as aged fine-grain rice, preserves, dried fruit for the convalescent; if there's an ac-cident, they'll come and inquire about what happened. The mister Hedo Mondols themselves weep at the misfortunes of the Rotons, offer advice, stroke head and back; this truly comforts the Rotons. What's more, if some other gentleman tries, with or without reason, to persecute the Ro-tons then the mister bosses protect their own farmworkers, even, if nec-essary, to the point of conflict with the antagonist. If the antagonists are big men, hard men, in other words gentry from Chandanpur, then the bosses will go to them with the Rotons in tow and patch up the fight. The good masters will say—Surely it doesn't befit a person of your stature to get angry with grass? This scum, grass is just what he is.

Sometimes they say—An ant. Good as dead, really. Is it really fitting for you to cut off an ant's head with your scimitar?

Then they rebuke the Rotons—Get, monkey scum Kahar bumpkin; get, touch, touch feet. Scum, stupid vicious bastard!

As they touch the feet, boss will say—Get, twist yer ears, nose to the dirt.

And then if he—the big, hard gentleman—will not bend, boss himself will clasp his hands and say—I'm begging you with folded hands. His dishonor needs to be forgiven for my sake this time. I won't take "no" for an answer.

To cut a long story short, this is the way that Rotons are got off the hook.

That particular Mister Boss has gotten mad. Today the rage is extreme. It's inevitable. Two days' absence; on top of that, the soil's gone bad and today it's getting late. Roton moved his legs very fast. Across fields, the plantation sahebs' mango orchard—to get to Jangol you must go through that ancient mango orchard. Just as you get inside the orchard, countless insects fly down from among tree leaves above and assail face and head. The mango trees are now covered in blossom, a smell of nectar infuses everything, and there's an amazing variety of insects.

Hedo Morol came along, screaming and shouting—Bastard, back-stabbing's a crime of your base caste—what else you done wrong?

Panu said to Prohlad—Uncle Oton really got out of it this time—I mean, coulda got a real nasty beatin'!

Prohlad said—Roton's got used ta takin' the punches. Even if 'e got a beatin' nothin'd 'appen.

The settlement of Jangol begins on the other side of the mango orchard. There's a track, mainly gravel. When the monsoon rains are pouring and the road fills with water it's a gutter. The water flows away within a few hours and then it's a track. The track comes from the plantation uplands on the northwest edge. Prohlad halted in surprise. Panu said—Whatcha stopped for?

Prohlad said—Oo're they then? Don't 'e just look like Porom?

Far off up on the Saheb Tracts, two people are walking—Prohlad pointed.

—Looks like, aye.

—Oo's wi' 'im then?

—Ain't it that big gent, Farmer Mochal? Yeh, 'im wi' the curly 'air—suckin' up.

Prohlad said—Porom's lyin' in wait for us, that land, that money—

—Land?

—Di'n'tcha 'ear 'eadman that day? Big gentry at Channanpur bought up the plantation uplands. Gonna make farmland. Gonna lease some of it an' all. Porom's goin' around it in secret.

Laughing, Panu said sardonically—Let the bastard sneak around other folks' stoops; meantime, dog's gone in the bastard's 'ouse—

Panu began to laugh a laugh with many meanings, and the Kahars know the meaning just as "the snake charmer knows the sneeze of a snake."

—Oo? Gents' Mister Footman came? That's old news.

Panu shook his head—I'm not talkin' 'bout Singh. That's ancient 'istory. Don'tcha know oo else? Bhup Singh's a Chotri Brahmind, 'ow can 'e be a dog? E was a tiger. Oo can chase a tiger out a paddy field? Uh uh, different person. Yess'day at dusk—. It's a funny story.

He started to laugh.

Wiggling his eyebrows questioningly, Prohlad asks—Who? Who? Who then?

Panu laughed even more.

—Who then?

—Swear Mary I'll tell when the time comes. It'll need a lotta time.

Yesterday evening, beneath Atpoure Para's banyan tree, even in the midst of that darkness Panu had discovered headman and Kalobou together. He'd also been going that way to Atpoure Para just then, in search of one of his lovers.

In Bansbadi's bamboo groves an ancient darkness gathers even today. That darkness advances at night and covers Bansbadi's Kaharpara. Yet even in the midst of that darkness the Kahars' vision works fine. In their eyes that primeval epoch's stare lights up; that's to say the darkness-piercing forest-animal stare of humans from the age before the discovery of fire!

Seeing the game of headman's heat, Panu felt insatiably curious. He's really got a little too much curiosity. If it had been anyone else, that curiosity wouldn't have been so great. But Bonwari's headman; besides that, he's like a different order of human. Wonder awoke along with curiosity. So he kept the whole thing secret. He didn't dare reveal it. And as that drama with Karali and Pakhi suddenly blew up yesterday, it didn't occur to him to speak of this other episode. It suddenly came back to him today on seeing Porom. Even today he daren't actually speak of it, despite nearly having done so. Besides, Panu is still thinking about whether to say anything. If he keeps it to himself, he might be able to cash in and get a bit of something from the headman.

Panu left the group and went off down a lane. At the other end of the lane is his boss's house.

But the others, especially Prohlad, were left in a state of suspense.

How amusing! How hilarious! Who was at Porom's place?

The Kahars' entire day's work was lightened by speculating on this topic.

Prohlad, Bhuto, and the rest threshed wheat. They beat the ears and made piles of grain. The women will bring food and drink; the ears will be beaten with a winnowing fan and the wheat grains will separate from chaff.

Food and drink—at least four pounds of puffed rice, a bit of molasses, onion, chilies, and a pitcher of water.

Pana dug potatoes. The potatoes of Pana's boss are really big. Pana's wife will bring food and drink; she'll dig potatoes too. He's stashed four fat potatoes in a hole in the ground marked with a sign. He'll tell his wife to hide them in the folds of her wrap and take them away. It's boss who always gets the fattest potatoes. Large potatoes to be eaten with rice; he'll get this little extra in his own share. The real pleasure is in getting this bit more. And he must show Prohlad. Prohlad says his boss had eighteen pounds of tree bark and some "aloomini" fertilizer spread on each half acre, spuds were this fat. Prohlad's nature to tell stories. Perhaps Prohlad's boss will buy Panu's boss's calf. Wouldn't money for it come from potato money? So show him spuds of his worked land—boss's wealth.

Panu said to his boss—Boss, sir, Pellad were inquirin' about the calf from our 'erd. Said—'ow much? Is boss'll buy a cow now.

Panu's boss is Mister Logondo, that's to say Logendra, Mondol; a shrewd and calculating man. Nose, mouth, eyes are built slender and sharp; the man himself all lean angularity; the impression is of a proper gentleman. Master didn't reply to Pana's question, but got up and entered the plot. He went to the exact spot where Pana had buried the four po-tatoes, dug them out of the earth, wrapped them in his cloth, and said—Look well and dig, scum, look and dig; what I'm taking out now, that's your loss. My spuds'll stay in my ground, if I move the earth I get 'em. Yep, you'll not get a single share of these spuds, understand? A fine for yer greedy eyes.—So saying, he went up out of the plot, sat on the raised fieldpath again, and unconcernedly resumed puffing on his pipe. It was as if nothing had happened. Pana's chest pounded violently. His mouth was dry.

That food and drink's coming. The ten o'clock train went noisily across the Kopai bridge. Quite a sound. Rhythmic metallic booming!

He wished everyone would take their lunch, gather in the mango or-chard outside the village, and tell stories. Everyone's eager to hear about Bonwari and Kaloshoshi. He really wants this too. But all of Panu's en-thusiasm was extinguished by his being caught out by the boss. He sat in the field and began to drink water. Suddenly his rage was directed at his wife. Panu suspects that his wife keeps peeking Karali's way from behind her veil. He began to abuse her with harsh words.

Two

Bonwari had gone to Chandanpur station with Boss.

Middle Ghosh boarded the train. Giving Bonwari a four-anna tip, he said—Caught the train well. Ah, still so strong at your age! He was full of praise.

Bonwari stooped forward to pay obeisance and began to smile. He said—By yer leave, could do a few more miles ta see ye off, by yer leave.

Ghosh said—Well I'll be, you've made me run for it!

—What else'd I do, by yer leave! Ya got late drinkin' yer tea. If ye'd not come quick ye'd not have caught it. E don't wait. When it's time ta go, 'e goes.

Ghosh laughed. Bonwari mopped sweat from his forehead and body with his cloth. His body, like a rough-hewn stone statue, was wet with sweat. Sweat rolled past his ears and down his sideburns like water on a freshly bathed polished blackstone statue.

The train set off; making another obeisance, Bonwari said—Me little request then—

—You'll get it. I've spoken to my elder brother, sign off a few mango trees and five stands of bamboo.

—I'll give o' course, by yer leave.

—Fine.

The train departed. Bonwari took a couple of the bricks scattered beneath the station's neem tree, piled them one upon the other, and sat slightly raised up. No more rush. After a break there's a little job to do; when that job's done he'll go back. There's a gentle breeze blowing; a sweet smell on the breeze—scent of forest tree flowers. Many flowering forest trees along the fieldpaths of this place and beside the roads. Open land south of the station, all the way to Jangol and Bansbadi. Chandanpur's fields completely empty—beside the stubble of cut paddy there's nothing at all. The gentry's village seems abandoned, eerie. Now no more crops in this village's fields. Well, there are, but gentry sires don't pay attention to that. Beside paddy, every single thing they eat is bought. Loads of cash, piles of money—why would they go to all this trouble of farming! These same great Chandanpur gentry have now bought Jangol's plantation uplands; have they bought there so that *they* can farm it all? The

Chaudhurys are in a tight spot—Ma Lakshmi of Wealth has left, they're selling everything, even sold the fallow uplands. Middle Ghosh himself had said—Ghoshes wanted to buy that. But Chaudhurys didn't want to sell to no Ghoshes. It's a caste thing, after all. Finally, they offered it to the Chandanpur gentry; now the gents will plow up the good parts for farmland, the lowlands, which means the parts that get silted up but where the crop isn't destroyed. The rest they'll parcel out; a few allotments for their subjects, for which they'll take tribute or rental revenue. All these allotments will be taken by the Mister Morols of Jangol. Whatever remains will be gotten by Porom, Bonwari, the low-caste Haris of Jangol, the Muslim Sheiks of Chandanpur. Different terms for their settlement—a conditional rent agreement. They won't give tribute. However, the fallow land worked by the tenants will revert to the landholder after ten years. Rental conditions are as follows—rent won't be paid for the first two or three years; the next year, quarter rent; the year after, half rent will be paid; and thereafter, full rent. In the eleventh year, the land will become the landowner's. Because if a tenant occupies land for twelve years, the land title is his. After the eleventh year another settlement will be made for the next ten years. Tenant can't sell; if he does, it won't stand up in law and the landowner will come and snatch it back. So go do your farming without selling, pay rent, get along with your gentleman landowner, be devoted and respectful, and no one'll say a thing—enjoy as long as you like. That's it. That's the very reason the "anchesters" said—puttekt the wealthy, Ma Lakshmi'll enter boss's home, Mother'll leave her footprints in boss's yard for sure, so bring the gleanings on your heads so's your "ownclan" can fill their gizzards. This little saying of the ancestors is no lie. Take heed of the story of Bonwari's family! Lakshmi of Wealth came to the Ghosh house. Bonwari's dad gave puttekshun to the Ghoshes—it's for that assistance Bonwari's father became headman of Kaharpara. Bonwari's dad's position was enhanced by Lakshmi's footprints in the Ghosh house. Otherwise the father of that sick, asthmatic Noyan would've been headman then. Noyan's Granddad had his own acre of land, lived under the "puttekshun" of the Chaudhury house, shared in their land's golden harvest. Noyan's paternal grandfather was a fine figure of a man, very powerful too. Those days the "Broke-Homes" were headmen. Back then the name of Noyan's line was "Broke-Home Clan." In a previous era their cottage had been on the south edge of the indigo levee, at the lowest spot. An amazing thing: they never got to live in a finished home; the rains broke it down every single year. Sometimes the whole cottage

was smashed, sometimes a wall, sometimes half a wall broke; just had
to break. Since then their house's name has been—Broke-Home house.
Later, when Noyan's grandfather had come under the "puttekshun" of
Jangol's sire Chaudhury—when he'd gathered the dust left by Ma Lakshmi's feet at the Chaudhury house and built a new cottage, Mother's
mercy kept the home unbroken. So Noyan's Granddad followed what the
forefathers said. He completed the house, but left at the top of the wall an
unfinished section a few feet wide and long with a strong bamboo fence
there. "Puttekshun" of the fortunate—what else can it be but mercy of
Ma Lakshmi's dusty footprints from the Chaudhury house? The house
of Chaudhury fell, and right with it went the Broke-Homes' headmanship of the Kahars. Bonwari's father became headman. Bonwari became
headman after father. They lived in the "puttekshun" of the Ghoshes,
the Ghoshes who are so prosperous; Bonwari's in no doubt that he'll be
prosperous too. Just the other day he'd heard from Kalobou about those
settlements being made on the Saheb Heights, and he intends to get a bit
of that land; thinking on all this, something else occurs to him. The great
gentry of Channanpur are now the flourishing men of this region; if he
can just get a little of their "puttekshun," if he can just get a tiny bit of
their Ma Lakshmi's foot dust on the very tip of his fingers, then his home
too will overflow with Mother's bounty.

This is Bonwari's inner secret. He can't speak of this to anyone. It would
be disastrous if the Ghosh sires were to know. Yet it seems that fortune is
kind. Maito Ghosh doesn't usually summon him for a trip to the station.
He doesn't usually have too much luggage. What was it called, a *bag*, or
suitcase, and a bedroll tied in a thick, tarpaulinlike cloth cover. This time
he took a lot of luggage. So the summons came for Bonwari of the Kosh-
Shoulder house. It's turned out well, he can visit the great gentry's estate
office at the same time as coming to Channanpur. Bonwari rose. Middle
Ghosh had given him a cigarette, which he now took from behind his ear
and lit on the smoldering cord hanging from the stall selling betel chews,
cheap smokes, and tea outside the station. He set off from Channanpur
on the village road. First through the station quarter. Hitting his stride, he
suddenly paused. He'd remembered his cousin Sidhu. He turned around.

The station quarter is quite large.

When the branch line came, what happened was that Channanpur
station's bounds expanded hugely. Those days the line was built—Bonwari saw with his own eyes. So many women left home to work construction on this line—Panchi, Khuki, Bele, Chitto, Nimmla. Khuki and

Bele left the locality—with two Muslim stonecutters. Chitto and Panchi went off with a Hindusthani line mechanic. And Nimmla took off with another mechanic. Karali was that Nimmla's son. The bitch even went off leaving little five-year-old Karali. Ah, heat's fix is a terrible thing, even children get forgotten! Sidhu and "Jogdhatti" both left home, but their lovers left without taking them. They still live in Channanpur, in this very station quarter. They do a maid's drudging in the masters' houses, pick up burned coal at the station, haul coal and lime at the depot. Then at night they take on another shape. Bonwari still won't let them back in the village. Sidhu's his own cousin; Sidhu whom he once loved. He still feels some inner hurt for this Sidhu. His own uncle's daughter, brought up at his knee. Suddenly arrived today, he wants to see Sidhu once again. He'll also get news of Karali and Pakhi from Sidhu.

Bonwari turned around. He entered the station quarter. Extensive—row on row of houses going from here to there. Brick houses, brick floors, yards in front of some of them; family nicely set up in each house. Why wouldn't you stay? Sahebs' workshops, they've "puttekshun"; but really cramped and dingy. Despite the brick roofs, brick walls, brick floors, it'd choke Bonwari to have to live here. The Kahars' cottages are much worse than these, but their yards are open. And besides, there's a strange smell coming from these people's quarters. It gets right up your nose. In Kahar homes the smells are of cowshit and earth, bodies of cattle, paddy; the smell of wood and dried cowdung burning, smell of the dungheap, smell of fermenting liquor; the sweet smell of the sacred basil plant beside the house is deeply soothing. And the smells of this place are different, a sharp, acrid stench; a powerful steamy smell of mixed coal and water spat from engines gets up your nose. Other than a pharmaceutical works, no place smells as strong as this.

At this hour of the morning Sidhu's combing out her hair. Day or night, rotting food always has the same stink. Bonwari smiled a sad smile to himself. Sitting to doll herself up at this hour of the morning! Seeing Bonwari, Sidhu quickly finished combing her hair and said with a smile—Come in bro, come in, how lucky I am!

—Just dropped by. Brought Maito Ghosh's baggage. Said to meself, I'll drop in an' see Sidhu.

Sidhu rose, quickly fetched a piece of sacking, and gave it to him—Sit.

Sidhu's learned manners, living in Chandanpur. You have to lay a seat down—she's aware of this civilized custom. Back in their hamlet visitors will themselves whisk away the dust and chaff with a puff of breath or a flick of scarf cloth, and sit right down on the ground. If somebody important comes—Police Inspector, for example, or one of the bosses from Jangol—there are two woven stools at Bonwari's house, and these are put out. Bonwari sat on the piece of sacking. He said—So, all right then?

—Good and bad! Sidhu began to laugh—Days I can work I can eat; days I can't work I tighten my cloth round my waist and do nothing. If Jogadatti or someone comes with a handful, then I'll eat. Who of my own folks can I ask, eh?

Bonwari remained silent. There's a hidden accusation in Sidhu's question, the weight of which falls on Bonwari.

Sidhu now said—But yer lad Karali began asking after me since he started working on the line. Comes around, calls me auntie. I hear all about you lot from him.

At last Bonwari spoke—An' you can sometimes go thattaway too, like.

Sidhu replied—Who knows, dad? Not scared of none, scared of you.

Bonwari smiled a sad smile and hung his head. Smiling, Sidhu said—You're a real scary one, dad.

Bonwari said—Did I smack ya round so when ye was a little un?

Still smiling, Sidhu said—Did you! Then, more gravely—Not 'cos of that. You're a real stern dad. Who knows what you'll say? Probably say—No one's to let Sidhu in their house.

Tears suddenly came to Bonwari's eyes. He looked at the ground with head bowed and then, somehow pulling himself together, stood up. He gave Sidhu two of the four annas tip that Ghosh had given him and said—Keep it, get yerself some candy.

Sidhu said—Wait. She went into her room and came back with a bottle of prime liquor. —There's a bit left, drink.

Bonwari thought for a moment, then took the bottle and had a swig.

Sidhu said—Karali killed that snake that day, then came here on a spree. Brought a couple of bottles, we all drank together. This was one of 'em. A juicy topic then suddenly occurred to her; she said in a voice of curious excitement—Hey look, forgot to ask you about the real business—Karali and Pakhi's heat!

—Yeah, that was a right mess. Couldn't leave the lad unpunished.

Sidhu said—After they fled here they did all right. Karali works on the line, got a room, staying there. Gonna punish more? He was saying—Ain't gonna go back to where you are.

Bonwari was astounded.

Sidhu continued—They're staying in that place right down the end. She then pulled her cloth across her face to cover her laugh and said—I saw them really having the hots for each other. Karali says—I'm not goin' back ta the village. I'll work the line, I'll stay 'ere, I don't answer to no one, me. He got a new iron bangle for Pakhi to wear. They've set up home, gettin' it really really fancy.

Sidhu's really changed in Chandanpur. She does not say "eat" for "heat," she does not say "noo" for "new." She wears her hair loose.

—Gimme a smoke, one smoke, said Sidhu.

—Enough. Bonwari suddenly got up.

Bonwari abruptly paused outside. All of a sudden he's very troubled about the Karali and Pakhi business. It's not good what he said, won't even go back to the village—not a good plan. Let him be a villain, a wrongdoer, an evildoer—the lad hasn't yet done anything so bad that he needs to be thrown out of the village. The likes of what he's getting up to with Pakhi have been going on since the dawn of time. If this heat's a true heat, then let Pakhi be separated from Noyan, let there be a companion rite for her and Karali. Let them make a home in the village. Here it'll be ruin. Pakhi and Karali don't know, they can't understand, but they have eyes to see— look at that Sidhu, look at Jogodhatri.

***

They were sitting tight together. Pakhi, Karali, Nasu-sis, Jogodhatri, and two friends from Karali's line gang. In the middle a pile of oil-smeared rice puffs, chilies, and onions, some eggplant fritters, and a liquor bottle. Very heated talking. Pakhi's making most noise. Bonwari could hear from outside the door. Pakhi was saying to Jogo—"With oosoever link my mind, that's the one that will be mine"—what, now can this be punished or given 'eadman's rulin'! I won't stay in that breathless sickie's place, been ran off six months today. Now me mind's taken to 'eat wi' another an' I've come to 'is place. What's so noo 'bout that wi' Kahars? Whatcha say, auntie Jogo?

Jogo replied—What more can I say to that?

Karali said—If there's any grief, it's mine agin' that creep Noyan. So let 'im come, Noyan, let's come to agreement. Bring clubs, bring fightin' sticks, snatch Pakhi back from me.

Pakhi leaped up with a jingle—Drop dead, monster; would I go wi' 'im even if 'e did beat ya down wi' a stick an' tried ta take me?

Nasu-sis broke in—Hey, don't say that, don't say it; it's "blows rain down, friend—blows rain down, sweetie." If 'e 'ad the strenth ta beat wi' a stick 'e'd be able ta drag you off by yer 'air. Ye'd go, thrashin' yer arms an' legs, screechin' at toppa yer voice but "innyend" ye'll calm down, wipe yer eyes on yer cloth, an' sit ta cook rice in 'is "kishchin." Ubby's fists'll make ya ferget, t'was just a sweetheart.

Pakhi said—Nope, no way. If yer 'eat is lastin' then loved one's best in the world.

Nasu-sis burst out giggling.

What's this lasting love 'eat painted on my heart—O lover!

At this moment Bonwari entered the room. The party froze in an instant. Even Karali looked stricken. Only Pakhi kept shaking her head and said—I'm not goin', I'm not goin'. She jumped straight up, flew across the room, and slammed the door shut with a bang.

Bonwari addressed Karali—Listen.

After a long pause Karali breathed a deep breath, puffed out his chest, got up, and said haughtily—What?

Bonwari said—When ya get a break, go 'ome an' take Pakhi. S'not a good plan stayin' 'ere. Leave all that. Go 'ome; we'll set up the companion rites. Got it?

Karali nodded his assent just like a good little boy.

When he'd left the house, Bonwari called Karali outside again; something else had occurred to him. —Ya been ta the police 'ouse? Collected 'eeward?

—Nah.

—Come wi' me. I'll vouch for ya wi' Police Inspector.

—Vouch?

—Yeh, course. Ow's Inspector gonna know ye're the right Karali? Vouch for ya like that. Then ya take 'eeward when 'e gives it. Come.

Three

After vouching for Karali with Police Inspector, Bonwari returned home via the land office of the great gentry. It was then around noon. From the two annas remaining of Ghosh's tip he spent six paisa on puffed rice and two paisa on molasses chews. These he wrapped in his scarf, moistened in the water of the gentry's Krishna Pond, and ate sitting in the shade of a mango tree; he drank water from his cupped hands. There was more than a little left in Sidhu's bottle of prime liquor, good clean stuff too—Bonwari's still feeling a little hit from the treat. Besides, he's very pleased. Has to be said that today's a good day. He thinks Lord must have been contented with the offering the other day. He's brought all the Karali business to a satisfactory conclusion. He'd been filled with enormous anxiety. He really had been in a rage. Held it back through Guru's holy powers. Otherwise maybe the thing would've been a "dessaster." The lad's body's gotten strong, yep, sure has, Bonwari must admit it. He slipped down before Karali in the bamboo forest—that's not why he's saying it; that was an awkward spot where he fell, slipping on the fallen bamboo leaves as they moved beneath his feet. But it was when Karali came and knelt on Bonwari's chest that he really felt the fire of his might. The lad'll become a "crushin' champ." Yet with alcohol—with bad will, doesn't it all go to ruin! That's why Bonwari won't allow him to destroy himself. How many times over the past few days has he thought of pinning the lad down? If he'd come down on Karali, maybe he would've killed him. From that, from that Guru and Lord saved us. Seeing that Sidhu today, his mind wept for Pakhi. He knew it was his "issponsibility" to bring Karali and Pakhi back. Is it really fitting for a man such as himself to get angry with these boys and girls? My my, how could he show his face? Forget it, the lad got the message in the end anyway, said he'd return with Pakhi. At the police house the lad even paid obeisance, hands to feet. Unblest, vile nobody! Bonwari's delighted that the unblest has finally understood. Neem-oil Panu, Prohlad, Noyan will all shake their heads, so let there be public discussion. Must be explained. This headman's work is very troublesome. I'm sitting comfy up there on top of ten men's heads—that's what they all think. Oh Lord, I'm not sitting on their ten heads—it's the stabbing points of ten spikes in the nail-barbed board of Shiva's Gajon festival. O God!

Keep it straight, sonny; one slip and those ten spikes will push and jab. When anger and disquiet rise in your chest you must understand—spikes are stabbing. It was those very nails stabbing when his mind got anxious thinking about the Karali affair. It's sorted—forget it. Really happy.

Things turned out well over there with the Chandanpur gentry too. Victory Babathakur! Sire listened to him—the son of Mister Dashji from the cowherders' hamlet on the other side of the Kopai—administrator of the gentry's record office—he's sung Bonwari's praises to Sire. Badmouthed Porom. He said—Here's the real headman in Kaharpara. Porom's just Atpoure Para's man. Atpoures make up just six, seven homes. And they don't even all follow Porom. Besides, Porom's not a good man. Went to jail for being a bandit. And he's as drunk as he's idle. Bonwari's an excellent, sound character.

Sire listened attentively to all of it. Said—All right, I'm giving you the land.

The great sire of Chandanpur has a four-winged mansion, horse carriage and retinue, all of which is called "foursquare" luck. Mother Lakshmi of his house—"Sovverin Lakshmi" incarnate. If Bonwari can only get that Mother's dusty footprints then he'll have seen it all! And that kind of boss, what a boss! If he were to become servant of that boss his chest would swell ten times its size. How happy would he be telling people that? What precious things all around, besides? The pleasure of being a servant in that palace would be precisely this: to sit all night under the lamp amid tumult and glitter and feast his eyes. Bonwari's imagination was afire.

Bonwari suddenly paused. Jangol to the right—Bansbadi up ahead. Left, eastward, the young herdsmen have released cows, goats, sheep onto Ma Kopai's "selltyful," that's to say silty, grazing land. They're all happily and unconcernedly playing the cowrie shell game under a tree. This way, on the side of that fieldpath, a jackal's poking its face out for a peep; goats scatter, bleating; they've seen it. But the sheep are huddling together and standing in one spot. Excellent species! Stood together with their eyes closed. It's probably taken one. Bonwari screamed—Took! Took! Oi there, lads!

The shepherd boys left their game in surprise and caught sight of the jackal as soon as they stood up; immediately they desperately raced forward.—Go—go—go—go. Bonwari was utterly infuriated. Idiot rabble! They all ran the same way. A bunch of Kahar boys, and the morons don't even realize what the crafty jackal's evil scheme is! My oh my! They're at that stage when they spend night and day hanging out at Karali's talk sessions, spinning yarns day and night about foreign lands, kings and sultans. Never discuss this kind of clanwork, how'll they learn? That's a jackal that's running off. Which means the real hunter's certainly hanging back behind somewhere. It'll take this chance and make off with a lamb. Real sneaky species! If the shepherds are there, one of the tricksters will go one way and show itself like this—the other way one or two more stay hidden. The shepherds will go racing off just like this after the sneak they see; the others'll jump out from behind, snatch whichever goat or sheep is there, and quickly drag it away. It's not for nothing the jackal's called "Learned Sir"! But where's our other smartypants? Where? Let him stay there. Bonwari began to run toward the flock of sheep.

There was a ditch up ahead. Bonwari noisily cleared it with a gigantic leap. This was immediately followed by a scrabbling sound, and a jackal flashed out from ditch bank undergrowth and fled. Run—run—jackal running panting. Well well, Learned Sir, it's here that you were, sneaking up on the sheep from behind through the ditchside bushes! Bonwari had landed but a couple of feet away. Would've been great to come down on its neck. Ah-ha—ah-ha—now our smarty's running off! Gettim—gettim—gettim, grab the sneak! Grab the smartypants!

Laughing much too much, Bowari told the young lads about the smart ones' sneaky, clever trickery.—Be careful, ye never all run together, one o' ya stays wi' the goats an' sheep—someone big-lookin' stays. Otherwides ye'll get the smarty comin' up snarlin' an' showin' 'is fangs and scarin' off yer little man so 'e can finish the job an' run away. Bonwari added—Got fire in yer 'baccy pipe? He pulled out a leaf-rolled smoke from his waistband. Took a puff.

That Lord's shrine coming into view! Bonwari paid obeisance. As he arrived at the edge of the village on his way home, he thought—I've forgot something real important. Wife said—bring back four paisa worth o' poppyseed. Totally forgot. Should've got it from Pana's boss's shop up in Jangol. But no, forget it. He won't take it on credit. He's eaten up two annas of the four himself, and given the other two to Sidhu. That he's happy about—giving money to Sidhu makes him very happy. Pity the "unfortinnate girl"! Sidhu's now the equivalent of garbage. Once a morsel's been tossed on the shitheap there's no way it can be picked back up. But that morsel too is dear as Lakshmi! So how can he not weep inside?

***

A few days later music was playing once again in Hansuli Turn, Kaharpara, in Bansbadi. This time drum, gong, and shanai ring out—*kurutak-*

kurutak-karoom-karoom. A group of minstrels had come, drum, gong, and oboe. Now the women are ululating, *uluu—uluu—uluu—lu—lu—lu.* Drummer's beating along—*kurur—kurur—kurur—tak—tak—tak.* The gong sounded—*kaing—kaing—kaing.* A voice joined the shanai—Ah—ah me, ah me, ah me, O, ah me! Krishna with young Radha beside thee. A restless flock of birds flew up from one of Bansbadi's bamboo groves to another; some hares burst out from among the ancient rotting and dried leaves below and fled toward the scrubland on the riverside. Jackals are not so timid; at first restless, they then became still. Over in the Saheb Tracts a few grunts came from the assembly of wild pigs. There's a hint of winter still; still the snakes are taking their "six-monther" hibernation under the earth, withdrawn in insensible sleep—they tried to lift their heads but could not. Marriage of Pakhi and Karali.

Kaharpara was frenzystruck. Crazed celebration with oil, turmeric, powder paints. Karali's companion rite with Pakhi, which means a second marriage. Nasuram—Karali's Nasu-sis—has tied up his cloth around his waist, smeared on the oil and turmeric, bundled powder paint in a cloth, and is laughing aloud and singing—"Me own weddin' was so-so—Bro's weddin' is so fine—Come along an' down some wine."

Gallons of liquor; someone's ladling out cupfuls of it from enormous jars; they're all getting up to their necks in drink. Karali's laying out openhandedly. Who's his like in Kaharpara? He doesn't drive cattle with a huphup and plow the fields; he doesn't cry *heem-plo* and live by palanquin bearing; he works for the "rayil" company for cash "earnage." He wants to use this chance to show it, to make them understand. He's spent thirty rupees cash. He's bought goat meat and chickpea stew—he isn't going to feed his own folks on sour small fry and green bean soup on rice. He'll give many things to Pakhi, many ornaments besides her conch bracelet, sari, rouge, iron wristlet; silver necklaces, not silver-plated. Eight bracelets, four on each arm, a cord necklet at her throat; beside this a set of gilt ornaments on the waist—sutahar, Parsi earrings, an armlet, endless bangles. Maids and wives of the hamlet blessed Karali again and again. Young men and boys too singing his praises. They're secretly resolving that they too will try to find work in those strange rail company workshops when this is over. Next moment pulling themselves together. What with this headman, he'd let any of them go off thataway? They don't have Karali's bravado, they aren't able to disobey Bonwari and go to work for the rail company. Immediately the image of Bonwari floats before their mind's eye. His eyes bulge, his hand is raised, he's saying, Forefathers' ban. Watch out!

But now headman Bonwari's straightened Karali out too, perhaps. He made him promise again and again, he's not to disobey the orders of the village council. Lord God must be obeyed, he won't behave badly or against dharma. If you don't want to listen to a grey-haired old man then fine, but never "dissgace" the venerable chief; Karali made that promise.

Bonwari had also spoken to him about the cost of the wedding—So much ain't good, Karali. What ye got in yer 'and, to spend ye can stand. Where'd ya get so much ta spend?

Any other time Karali would have said—Where do kings find rubies? He would have said this for sure, and would have said it with the hint of a smile twisting his lips. But this time he clasped his hands and replied to Bonwari—Oh uncle, I'm beggin' ye this time not ta say anythin', just this once. It's me weddin' wi' Pakhi.

With a delighted smile Bonwari said—All right, all right. Then suddenly becoming serious, he called Karali aside and asked—But lookit son, tell me one thing, where'd ya get so much dough? Didn't nab it from the company now, did ya? See? Won't be no trouble after, will there?

Karali placed his hand on Bonwari and said—I'm tellin' ya wimme 'and on yer body. Don' worry 'bout any of it. Swear by Mary.

Bonwari went off toward Bashan's house. He's Karali's uncle, Pakhi's uncle, the village headman; what duties he has!

Karali smeared on oil and turmeric, bathed, and began to part his hair. He'd bought a new mirror and comb. He'll put on a rose pink vest with flowers embroidered on the chest. He's had a fine new dhoti dyed yellow; with Nasu-sis there, he'd folded and put them aside. He had also set aside a splendid new "thoilo," or towel; Karali says—"toila," Nasu says—"thoila." In the tale of Kaharpara, all these fancy trappings of the groom signify—that Karali's brought in the Infernal Age; and although the youths, the maids, the young wives of the Infernal Age are all transfixed by all this, the elders cannot bear it. They're all steering clear of it with a frown. Saying among themselves, So much isn't good. They're not getting especially tempted by the whiff of liquor either. Of course they're all having a cup or two; but they don't feel like losing themselves in drunken frenzy as the boys and girls do. Yet Karali's looking amazingly lovely. His vitality, his beauty, his attire all equally matched. As if a new Krishna has come to Kaharpara in this bewitching guise!

***

Prohlad was the person Bonwari respected most. He was the most upset of all. He said so frankly—Ye didn't do right, Bonwari-bro. 'Tain't work worthy of an 'eadman. No good's gonna come o' givin' Karali this indulgence wi'out a tellin' off, wi'out punishment. An' wreckin' someone's marriage too—

Gupi heaved a deep sigh and said—Eh bro, think 'ow mighty that Noyan's dad was. "Ten ages does a man come by. Sometimes an elephant, sometimes a fly." This judgment of 'eadman's was no good.

Roton—Lotbor's dad; unruly boy Lotbor, blood-loyal devotee of Karali. For the unruly boy's sake, Roton must acknowledge the pull of Karali's, which is to say Lotbor's, gang. He said—Lad's a bold 'un, that's fer sure. Done a lot.

In spite of his young age, Neem-oil Panu hangs around with the group of elders; his capacity for sarcasm is second to none. He said—Rob—rob—know it's robbed cash, right? Folk like us coulda put on all this flash through farmwork sweatin' 'ead to toe, so I sees it. Ya geddit, 'e's sellin' old railway sleeper timber off to a buncha folks in Channanpur, that I know.

Bonwari's thinking in silence. Remembering the flaming heat beneath the bamboo grove, remembering being with Kaloshoshi beneath the banyan tree.

Karali came and stood before them. Under his arm two bottles of prime liquor. He placed them down in front of Prohlad and Roton—Take, uncle; get started, there's more.

Meanwhile Noyan's Ma is cursing.

Noyan is sitting silently on his terrace. Chest pounding, ribs rising and falling; in his black, skeletal, hollowed face, two white eyes stare in the direction of Babathakur's shrine at the top of Hansuli Turn—steady and unmoving. He's mentally entreating Lord. And imagining terrible things.

Noyan's Ma is pouring out a loud torrent of abuse, cursing Karali and Pakhi. She's calling on Babathakur, on Kalorudra, to do justice. Aiming to make the elders of their entire community protest Bonwari's conduct, she's saying—No succor, no succor, where'ere there's such an 'eadman. Between times, when she recalls the former glory of their clan, the Broke-Homes that is, she's lamenting—Eadman Bonwari! Is this 'eadman's justice? Where'ere there's such an 'eadman there ain't no succor. Ta let one build up 'is own 'ouse by smashin' down another's, can ya call that bein' 'eadman? Those Kosh-Shoulders, enemies, ferrever enemies o' this Broke-Ome 'ouse. This 'ouse, this were once the 'eadman's 'ouse; in the yard o' this 'ouse they used ta squat, folks' dads an' granddads, get corns on knees an' backsides. Then came the time o' the orphan boy an' the usurpation. Up rose Ghosh an' took the tiller, in 'is arrogance not reccanizin' the great no more, it was "village don't recognize you no more, chief." God'll judge that.

Sitting there, it's as if Noyan is seeing Babathakur in his mind's eye—that shaven head, beaded neck, pristine holy thread, ochre robes, clog-clad feet. He's standing at the base of the wood-apple tree—looking sharply askance. Gazing in the direction of Karali's house. Lying at his feet it's that gigantic chain viper—the one Karali so heroically killed. Is it dead? It's Father's snake! Lord's familiar. It's come back. Its tongue flickering in and out. That snake will enter the bridal chamber.

***

At Bashan's house there is also a lot of liquor, a lot of drunkenness, a lot of dancing, a lot of song. Suchand says—Eyes gonna go red as rouge, well, it's ecstasy o' marriage. All around day an' night gonna be blood union.

It's Suchand's eyes that have taken on that color.

At first she took a sip of liquor, sat down, and heaved a deep sigh; then took a cup of liquor, wrapped some puffed rice and chili in her waistcloth, and went to the edge of the bamboo groves to sit and weep. She wept for her dead father, wept for her dead son-in-law—for Pakhi's father, that is. —Ah, they didn' live ta see such a day. Now and then she stopped crying and wiped her eyes, munched on some puffed rice, and, feeling the bite of chili on her tongue, took a drink of liquor.

Bashan called her back. Suchand was at that point weeping for her dead son-in-law. Bashan wept too. Not only for her dead husband, but also for the dead son of the Chaudhury house. If only "He" had lived till now. Pakhi's face is identical to his. Her color is just as light. How wonderfully the fair child Pakhi suited the lap of black Bashan! As if a golden marigold flower had bloomed in dark green foliage. The Chaudhury boy used to say this himself. How resplendent Bashan would have been if he were still here.

Suchand stood up, had another drink, then sat in the yard and suddenly began weeping. The young women were singing. Song of love. When they heard the crying they all froze. Suchand's now invoking a terrible name and weeping. She invokes Lord's name.

—O my dear Kattababa, my dear Kattathakur! Gripped in madness. They've all gone mad, Father; taken no counterpesscriptions for killin' yer familiar, Father. Make judgiment by yer own grace, Father. Save yer familiar, Father.

Father's familiar! That chain viper. Bashan began to shake violently. Pakhi was stunned.

On his way back from Bashan's house, Bonwari was standing under a tree listening in amazement to Noyan's mother's curses. When he heard the sound of Suchand's lament beside this, he turned around, eyes bulging. Karali killed the snake. That great python had first made its existence known from Father's shrine. There's no doubt at all that it was Father's familiar. Bonwari too began to shake violently.

O Father! O Kottathakur! O Parent of the Kahars! Cleanse Father, cleanse. Cleanse that Karali, first among idiots. Cleanse Bonwari. We'll give an offering, Father, give another offering.

Evening gloom is thickening now. Beneath bamboo groves, the dreadful twilight of the demigods' touch is gathering. In that darkness Bonwari stole to Father's shrine. He went down on his knees beneath the wood-apple tree, folded his hands, and with closed eyes silently began praying to Father. Bonwari's a man of extraordinary courage. He has felt the presence of so many demigods on so many occasions, but he's never afraid. He remembers one time—it was after dark. He'd been bringing some fish back from the marshy Buffalo Pit on the far side of the river. Two beings in the form of jackals passed him on either side. This side, that side, circling and turning, such traps they laid for him. Bonwari felt amused. The number of evenings he's been to worship at Father's shrine. He's even been in the middle of the night. He did not tremble. Today he thinks to keep his eyes closed in case Father's angry! Karali killed Father's familiar; Bonwari's brought that very Karali back and given him a warm and hearty welcome. The image of a wrathful Father floats before Bonwari's closed eyes. In a flash, that mottled, whistling chain viper swells up, lifts its head, and stands straight—snake's head rises to the top of palm trees, its eyes spit fire, its mottled markings grow and multiply, its tongue flickers—it's glowing like a piece of forged steel in a blacksmith's shop; in his clogs, in his ochre robe, with his shaven head, Babathakur floats above the python's head. The beads around Father's neck are severed heads; the shining white holy thread around his body is a thread of milk-sucking cobras.

Bonwari contines to tremble violently.

A long while later he somehow manages to calm down and say in thought—Father, I'll gi' an offerin'; you cleanse. Then he says—Father, if ye won't cleanse let me know. Make a fruit fall from yer tree, jus' make one fall. I'm countin' five twenties in me 'ead.

He keeps counting. One, two three four . . . one twenty. Once more, one, two, three, four, five, six, seven, eight—

He finished the five twenties.

The fruit did not fall. Now Bonwari left that place.

The hamlet was by then completely drunk. The elders are reeling, bellies filled with prime liquor. Women are dancing. In nighttime gloom it's as if a bloody twilight hangs all around. Suchand's upper body is uncovered. She's dancing. Cloth wrap rolling in the dust. That too will dance.

Bashan and Karali have also decided they'll make an offering. Bonwari was pleased. He took a whole bottle of prime liquor and sat. As he was drinking he suddenly got up. The musicians' playing isn't right. Keeping time with his hands, he said—Play lads, play—"The groom has come, the groom has come, O bride raise yourself. Yes yes, the groom's got down, the bride's got down, O groom raise the bride's veil."

The cymbal-playing lads were themselves saying—*Kai-kai kai—kiti—kiti—kai-kai.*

Bonwari applauded this—Great, great! But whose hidden laughter can suddenly be heard? Who is it? Who? Which girl? Who's got such nerve? Bonwari looked up and circled his gaze around. But when he looked up, his rage dissipated.—Oh my my my! When'd you get 'ere? How lucky we are, how lucky! Wife of the Atopoure headman—Kalobou! Kaloshoshi! It's as if Kalobou's eyes are the river Kopai's whirling deeps. Something seems to play in their depths; on the surface they're glittering, but nothing clear can be understood.

Kalobou is glancing; in which direction? Bonwari looked all around, mad drunkenness all around.

Madness ceased at night's end. On that day's dawn Kaharpara was in bottomless sleep. Someone kicked Bonwari awake. He got quickly up. He's awoken beneath the banyan tree. Out front, the sunlight's sparkle seems to be smiling. Bonwari smiled too. Kalobou's gone.

Four

If day fades in the tale of Hansuli Turn, the night that comes down is a night very different than Jangol and Chandanpur's night. Their bamboo groves add to the night darkness their own secret, ancient darkness beneath. Crickets chirrup in darkness, all sorts of insects call, geckos call with a a tocking sound, owls screech, now in depths of night a humming bird call sounds. In bamboo groves, kicking up leaves as it dances, goes a "spookshape," that's to say a demigod. Along riverbanks wanders a "glowifyin' kittywick," that's a will-o'-the-wisp, flashing with light. Now and then a bansheelike cry can be heard from the tops of the saora and silk-cotton trees. A cracking, tapping comes from the bamboo groves; the Kahars see it clearly in their minds' eyes—a tree sylph or some impish spirit bending bamboo shaft tip over to the ground and then releasing it—the shaft springing straight up again. That's their sport.

Meanwhile, the Kahars of Hansuli Turn huddle together, light the kerosene lamp, and invoke Babathakur's name. Boys and young men play drums, sometimes singing the song of King Dharma, sometimes singing the hymn of Monosha of the Snakes. In the month of Bhadra it is seed-ritual songs of Bhadu-Bhanjo; in the month of Ashwin festival ballads of Mother Durga of Ten Hands are sung; from Kartik through to Magh and Phalgun it is winter—the musical gatherings of those months come slow, it's time to cut and gather the paddy harvest. In Chaitra get-togethers start up again—Ghentu spring festival songs; at the turn of the month it's time for the hymns of the Gajon festival, songs of salutation.

In between come the twenty or so nights unlike any other night. Wedding nights; and for each of the twelve months one of the twelve full-moon nights, or "fourteen-dayers," with the exception of the "dauries" or rain-drenched "fourteen-dayer" full moons in the monsoon months of Asharh, Shrabon, and Bhadra. Moonlight gleams bright at the remaining full moons. There is rejoicing on these few nights; on one side light, on the other darkness—on these few nights the ancient darkness of the bamboo groves remains slumbering among the tangled roots of the forest floor, on an age-old bed of fallen leaves.

During Karali and Pakhi's wedding, the bamboo grove darkness slumbered a few days in the reddish glow of light from kerosene-soaked cow dung. Crickets, owls, geckos, bugs and spiders, even demigods admitted defeat before noise from drum, cymbal, shanai, and songs sung in high female voices.

The wedding was done. Even the ashes of kerosene-soaked-dung lamps had been swept up and thrown on compost heaps; several cauldrons had been returned to the distiller's store; a few empties remained cast beside the yard. A smeared mix of yellow pigment and oil remaining on the bodies of Kaharpara people—now they rubbed field dirt on their limbs, rubbed their heads with straw stalks. Only on their clothing does some red and yellow colored tint remain among dirt stains. The musicians departed promptly; Kaharpara's almost soundless. Only Noyan's Ma hasn't yet stopped; she's still pouring out abuse. Her wrath seems mostly to fall on Bonwari. She curses—Im oo wiped out the "Broke-Omes" rule, 'im oo snatched their wife an' gave 'er to another, breakin' up an 'ome, 'is 'ome too will break—break—break. O Babathakur! O Father Goshain! Do justice, will ye do this justice.

Now and then she says—Don't remember! Don't remember all them days! Saying this, Noyan's Ma begins to weep. Tears stream from her eyes. She wipes away the tears and says in a voice that blazes firelike—Got up like a saint so's 'e can destroy me today!

Let it go. The Kahars never listen to ancient curses. What's more, now it's work. Daylong work. Wheat and mustard cutting has begun. Meanwhile in Jangol the cane work is commencing. Preparations for grinding cut sugarcane and making molasses. It's the Jangol Sadgop masters' Kahar cultivators who are working the sugarcane.

This work was previously tied to Roton Kahar's household. Cane being cut night and day, being peeled, loaded up, carried on the head, and set down before the grinding machine. Pellad sitting by the machine—himself feeding cane into it. The job needs focus—just one little lapse and the machine will grab your fingers; in the time it takes to stop the cattle driving the treadmill, the finger will be squashed and ripped right down to the root until it's chopped off. Roton's father was nicknamed "Stumpy": the machine had cut off four of his fingers. His thumb was the only survivor. Roton's dad was a salty type. He'd say—Ah, thumb survived so's I could sign "zilch" wi' it! Four fingers gone, right 'and crippled—the thumb survived. O Kottathakur! This is what ye did at last, Father!

And yet the boss masters are kindly; if anyone besides that Kottathakur has worldly power over life and death, it's those boss masters. They're beneficent indeed, and they punish too. The boss of Roton's father had taken pity, by way of care had given Roton's father a monthly five measures of paddy, that's two hundred pounds, and a rupee's pension in perpetuity for looking after cows and calves and for the job of overseeing the farming. Of course, Roton's dad slowly gained strength in his thumb and skillfully used to wield a sickle for hay cutting; he was able to use a hoe for short periods as well. He can take the tiller of a plow left-handed, but the right hand is needed for driving the cow; and he'd cleverly drive while giving that thumbs-up zilch gesture. Boss had also kept Roton on as a cowherd; as Roton eventually got bigger, he did farm work for that same household. Roton's father took him to the maw of the machine and "ferbad" him; hadn't Kottathakur come to him in a dream and prohibited his clan from going near the machine? The Universe Builder is the God of Iron and Tools—Roton's father did something wrong at his shrine; for that evil, this punishment. Long ago he went to the forge dizzy with drink to get his plow repaired, disrespecting the Universe Builder's rules. There's no escaping the punishment—the curse has also fallen on his descendants.

Roton's there at the making of molasses. Bonwari is better than anyone at making molasses; in Jangol, Bansbadi, the villages on the other side of the Kopai, Goyalpara, Ranipara, Ghoshgram, Nandipur, Karmamath, in all these seven villages Bonwari has no equal in the making of molasses—except Hedo Mondol. Bonwari's "handmade" molasses keep thickening up as they cool—a blob is like sugar candy, the grains are fat, the taste so sugary sweet you just have to eat. It's of highest quality—doesn't taint even if kept for a year.

A fire burning fiercely in a great stove; overhead a structure of bamboo and palm leaf has been built as a covering. Bonwari sitting on a mound in front of the stove. Roton's son Lotbor feeding sugarcane husks into the furnace mouth to fuel the fire. Boiling sugarcane juice bubbles and rises inside a gigantic cauldron. Bonwari straining out the "gunk," that's to say the scum, with a sieve and depositing it in a tin bucket. The cows will eat it. Roton's right beside Bonwari. Roton sitting in Bonwari's place when he occasionally gets up to stir. The Mister Mondols sitting over to the side. Hedo Mondol's there, as are a few other people. Mondols keeping a hard eye on the molasses. War's broken out across the world. Saheb masters—waging war with each other. Won't the value of goods go up! Paddy, rice, molasses, beans, the value of all these things will rise. Thus the Mondols are "viggilint," not a single thimbleful of molasses must be swiped. Who'd swipe? Kahars would. Privately Bonwari feels a little "urt" about this. Sure, Kahars aren't saints; sure, not everyone is Bonwari, Oton, Pellad; everyone else nabs a "lickle bit" now and then. But as long as Bonwari's there under the works thatch no one's able to steal a single spoonful of molasses. Everybody knows this. Yet to keep Bonwari under such watchful eyes means even he's mistrusted. So let them. Bonwari quietly concentrates on making molasses. He thinks about war.

What a strange workshop is this world! Vishnu-devoted fakirs come to sing; Bonwari's heard it in their songs—What a strange workshop is this world. Fakirs come to Kaharpara too. They say—Allah and all's strange workshop. That it certainly is. Bonwari admits this to himself. Baul singers come, Vishnu devotees come, sannyasis come, all these people say that same thing. The Kahars hear, think. At first, thinking on the unseen, unknown lifebird in the body's cage, they'd accepted it. The workman sits in mother's womb and builds a cage—using the bone shafts he builds the cage and neatly covers it over with skin, in a trice a lifebird hops inside. How that bird dances, chirrups, plays tricks! And then in a trice, one day it flies off again. The Kahar anchesters thought and thought but they could not find a solution—eventually they sought in the blue skies the mark of the coming and going of that lifebird, and the abode of that strange workman; they'd search and search until they were exhausted, until finally, prostrate, they'd beg at the tree shrine of Babathakur, at the court of Kalarudda—Scrub away our wrongs, Father! Darkness in your embrace, folding us into your wings you "puttekt," sheltered in your breast—how we traverse the universes to seek you!

But now with the Company's mechanical wagons, the railway bridge, miles and miles of telegraph cable, aircraft—it's as if they can see the world's strange workshop with their own eyes. What's more, there's this strange calamity, war! Dumbstruck, O Lord! Someone's fighting with whoever else in whatever "counterry" across the Seven Seas and beyond the Thirteen Rivers and here the price of paddy will go up, the price of rice will go up, the price of potatoes, molasses, vegetables will go up! Sadgop gents of Jangol girding their loins—they'll put money away; they're talking—cloth's going to go up. And now isn't the Company sure to levy funds for the war.

Yet in Kaharpara, in the bamboo groves of Hansuli Turn, those who live surrounded by shadow are untroubled.

It's no profit to them if prices of paddy, rice, molasses go up. They eat by working in the masters' fields and receive a one-third share of the harvest; that's enough to eat for six months—for the remaining six months they borrow "one-fifty-percent" paddy from the masters, don't have paddy or rice to sell. Neither sell nor buy. A few greens in the backyard; snails and shellfish in lake, pond, ditch, and river—catch and bring. The price of coal rises; the Kahars never burn a piece of coal in their lives, they gather twigs and sticks in the scrubby brushland on the riverside; cowdung makes fuel cakes that they burn few of themselves—they sell the rest in Chandanpur and Jangol. It's certainly a pain if the price of cloth goes up. Do they never need cloth? For six months the men wear a small handwoven cloth wrap for the part of the day they're doing farmwork. For the rest of the day—they wear a six-foot-wide cloth wrap.

Four pieces a year is "plenty-nuff," that's to say plentiful enough; three will do too. The women love to dress up "a lickle bit"; there's forever some of the Kopai river's waywardness in them, they crave a couple of fine saris with flower-embroidered borders. Two'd be plenty. Worn for going out. A wide, short wrap is fine when at home. Again, there's not much worry about this. The head of household can't meet the cost of a fine, flower-bordered sari; women get them from out of their own earnings—doing odd jobs in Chandanpur and Jangol, from the male gentry. Bonwari has seen another war. Began in nineteen hundred and fourteen time—lasted a few years; Bonwari remembers it well. Cloth six rupees a set. Price of paddy was four rupees. It was at this time that the Mukherjees of Chandanpur saw their coal business expand and they became kings. Bonwari's boss, Maito Ghosh, made more than a little money selling jute and coal. A lot of money. Then four or five of the landlords in Chandanpur went under, sold off their mansions; the Chaudhury house of Jangol fell into a state of utter distress. The time of that war saw the rise of Jangol's Sadgops. Before this, everyone was just a cultivator and would take up the plow handle and the shovel alongside the Kahars, would wear the same short cloth; everyone's become a gentleman by selling paddy, rice, beans, molasses in the war bazaars. Now everyone's girding their loins; who knows what they will become in this war? Yet the Kahars pray for their success. In the increase of their wealth lies the well-being of the Kahars; in the dust they gather from Mother Lakshmi's "footdabs," that's to say footprints, lies the wealth of the Kahars. War makes no difference at all to the Kahars.

Sitting on outspread sacks, the Sadgop gents are discussing the war. Talk's going—must push linseed cultivation. Hasn't it just been announced in the gentry's Chandanpur *gazette*, that's to say the newspaper, that there will be a great need for linseed oil in the war; its value will rise enormously.

Bonwari privately shakes his head in amazement.

Oh aye, it surely is a strange workshop! Paddy, rice, beans, pulses, molasses, potatoes; the value of linseed will rise above all these. Not food for the belly, not "oyyil" to rub on the body, not cotton fiber for clothing; Bonwari knows that a linseed poultice can be given—but its oyyil, what *is* that needed for?

Jhom-jhom—gom-gom—jhom-jhom—gom-gom.

Ten o'clock train crossing the Kopai bridge. Now the mister Mondols will get up and go home to eat. Once they have eaten, Hedo Mondol will come back with the person whose molasses is being prepared and someone else. Hedo Mondol will lie down on his back—will snore like a blacksmith's bellows with his mouth hanging open and a snorting noise coming out.

When these Mondols aren't there then it's break time. They'll swap a few juicy and scurrilous tales, no holding back.

As soon as the Mondols left Bonwari got up. He moved over, sprawled himself on that sack, and said—Lotbor, make us up some 'baccy nicely, will ya. An' Oton, pass us a cuppa "juice." Bring a bitta water, gotta wash me 'ands an' face.

Now drumming will come to an end in Kaharpara. This drum isn't a player's drum. The darkness that descends on Kaharpara is the darkness of dusk mixed with ancient gloom—in order to survive its influence they gather and perform their monotone songs and music; it's the drums of these gatherings that have stopped. In the month of Chaitra it's time for the songs of the Ghentu spring festival. Preparations are being made. One of the drums fell silent. Still two drums playing. In Bansbadi there are three Ghentu troupes. One old troupe in Kaharpara, one in Atpoure Para, and beside these Karali's had a new group for the last two years. Nasu-sis is in Karali's group—he dances twirling his waist, like a girl in a Jhumur dance troupe. Karali has bought a bamboo flute that he plays. That group's really of the moment. They get songs from Mukunda Moyra of Chandanpur. New kinds of songs. Why, hasn't Mister Moyra just composed a song about the war?

Saheb men got in a fight.
In a fight of bulls the reeds will die—
Ah me, we reeds will die.

Bonwari doesn't remember any more. But one day he heard the whole thing. Moyra knows a lot. He is, after all, Moyra of Chandanpur. The *gazette* comes in the Chandanpur mail; what's more, it comes by train. At two o'clock every afternoon boys and young men crowd into the station, the guard brings down bundles of newspapers; Bonwari's seen it with his own eyes. He's also watched Mukunda reading the *gazette*. Mukunda has put a lot of things into the songs. There's even stuff about Gandhi the Raja. Bonwari doesn't disapprove; he likes it. Bonwari's had an objection to Karali and his lads' group for a long time. The lads bring back a lot of bad influences from their work on the railways. But this time they brought a good little song. Folk will hear many things. And the lads are under control this time. He must manage them well. It is Bonwari's belief that if Karali looks out for his dharma, stays honorable, walks the straight path, then he could be a huge benefit to Kaharpara. If not, he's sure to bring its ruin. He'll drag and toss it into that oil-filled machine shop accursed city, place where dharma dies. The men will give up farming, give up palanquin bearing, wash their hands of ancestral custom. The women will follow in their footsteps. Bonwari cannot let this happen. Never. So he needs to make Karali understand, be nice to him, put up with his whims. So, in spite of his pricking conscience, he broke up Noyan's home and allowed Karali to wed Pakhi. There is of course another reason. He alone is aware of this reason, no one else knows. The Kaloshoshi he loves. That love's burning—burning inside him like a shimmering woodfire. Now that's their kind of love.

Roton brought the liquor, the "juice," in a clay cup and sat down nearby. Bonwari said—Call Pehlad.

Prohlad came and sat. Bonwari asked—Ow thick's juice gone?

Prohlad has six fingers on his hand. He said—One 'and. Laughing, he added—Gone ta number six thick.

Oh goodness! You can really see the Ghentu festival decorations in Atpoure Para now. The drumming got really strong in the night. You can understand why Karali's group would put on so much show. But what's the reason for so much sudden excitement in Atpoure Para?

Inevitable. Now Porom's got some land from the gentry of Chandanpur, he's built his body up, imagines he's powerful. Bonwari smiled. He's also taken land. He's taken yet more land than Porom.

With a smile Prohlad said—They're really dressin' it up fer Ghentu in Atpoure Para. Eard their songs?

—Nah. Bonwari smiled.

—Take a listen one day. Prohlad got up. A clattering, grinding noise was coming from the fanged cogwheels of the machine; time to apply some oil.

Songs in Atpoure Para! Now Bonwari added with a laugh—They've got that same old song! Our old song's much better'n theirs. The song that Bonwari himself had composed.

So snap-rap-tap—*the earthen pot rings out—*
Despite sis-in-law's decree—foot's ankle bells don't want to rest.
The heart will not stay home.—O—so—so snap-rap-tap.

Roton remained silent. After a while he said—They're singin' a noo song this time!
—Noo song? Oo made it?
—I dunno. But—
—But what?
—But you an' Karali both get cussed out in the song. Off an' on—
—What off an' on?
In a low voice, Roton said—Dad, there's a gripin' an' whisperin' goin' on, ain't them in that 'amlet 'eard that bastard Pana, summat about Kalo-shoshi—
Bonwari was stunned.
A few moments later he said—You watch this fer a bit. I'm gonna find out what them bastards are singin' about.

Five

In the tale of Hansuli Turn, the bamboo groves' dark realm spreads inside, outside, in all directions—to bamboo roots; under an ancient epoch's rotting, fallen leaves; in thick layers of foliage; in the crevices of banyan roots; from the backyard corners of Kaharpara and Atpoure Para to the inner reaches of the human mind, darkness spreads.

It's really true that Atpoure Para's Ghentu songs are much stronger now. Flowing forth. Bonwari stood and listened.

Alas, th' infernal age, what sights—
God's familiar untimely burned and killed, and by a cowherd too.
O no judgment yet Father, you judge.
Smash down the ones who've grown so big.

Bonwari's chest rose fearfully. The Atpoures hade composed a Ghentu song about that snake. The curse was certainly upon Karali, and yet Bonwari got the feeling that some of it was directed at himself. He began to feel strange all over, and his mind quaked.

No judgment yet, Father, weight of wrong's piled up,
Say who put out vespers' lantern with a breath,
Beneath that banyan tree, Father, beneath the banyan,
What saintly man's eventide caprice is this.
Hey hey, what merry sounds in voices high and low,
What joyousness, what chatter, what intrigue!
He did your rites of vespers in those very clothes, Father,
Alas, in the infernal age—

It was as if Bonwari's hands and feet had gone numb.

It's certain that someone saw him with Kaloshoshi underneath this banyan tree. So he was seen, but it's true the wrong is his. He had changed his clothes afterward. When he went back home to light the lamp and fetch the incense it had occurred to him, but he didn't bathe! He really should have bathed. And something else occurs to him today. He's committed a wrong in not punishing Karali, the one who killed Father's familiar, and in being so nice to him—he's done a hundredfold wrong! But who saw? Certainly not Porom. If Porom had seen he'd never have kept quiet about it. Everyone knows Kaloshoshi's wiles; now and again Bhup Singh still comes by. If she goes to Channanpur, Kaloshoshi still has a lot of people to whom she droopily tells her story; that kind of talk has a double meaning. And in Jangol too, Kaloshoshi will give a sidelong glance and a smirking smile to the middle-aged Sadgops. It's all true and everyone knows it, just as they know that at one time she and he had felt "eat" for each other; but if Porom had seen such a thing with his own eyes he'd never have been able to stand it. He'd have leaped out with a war cry. There would have been a fight with Bonwari. Maybe one of them would have been finished off that very day—right then. There's a rivalry between Kaharpara and Atpoure Para—has ever been, since the "anchesters." The Atpoures say, we don't carry no palkys, we ain't no clan of 'orses. Their clan is not the horse clan; as a joke they call the "carry clan" the horse clan. So let there be a horse clan, a carry clan—that's how God made it, that Babathakur! What are Atpoures? God sent them with fighting sticks on their shoulders, that outlaw bandit clan of theirs. The go-between clan, that's exactly the same as the outlaw bandit clan. The scum are still marked as born criminals in the police station's logbook, gotta be put in the lock-up, Patrolman coming calling in the night, waking folks up. Not a single one of those scum Atpoures has a decently thatched roof on his house, not even enough straw for a cooking pot lid. They've fought with the Kahars forever about this. Admittedly, they once were more powerful. That was the age of theft and banditry on Hansuli Turn. Now everyone's abandoned theft and is doing farming; now it's the time of the Kahars' rise. Before, the Atpoures used to treat the Kahars with contempt and disdain; now they hate them. Some Atpoure scum has composed this song out of hatred. Bonwari must get to the bottom of it.

Only Kaloshoshi will be able to tell. He must get to see Kaloshoshi. But he's afraid. Kaloshoshi is like an addiction; it's not easy to break the spell of that addiction. When he's hungry he can go without food, but he can't go near her without coming away drunk. He doesn't have a way not to drink that liquor. Those days of his are past. He's headman of Kaharpara. If headman's blameworthy then he's no longer a head, people sneer—don't follow his orders. The whole tribe suffers for his evils. He must atone for the evils he's done.

He now came out from beneath the trees and made his way cautiously toward the sugarcane works. He can hear shouting at the works. Mister Mondol has probably come back. Perhaps he saw that Bonwari was absent and started his screaming. Bonwari quickened his steps a little. Now how many insults would he have to hear? If Bonwari wasn't around, whoever else was there would receive a ferocious "thrashin" unseen. No one dares lift a hand against Bonwari. Bonwari's bold enough to restrain the hand of anyone who'd have the courage to beat him. With the exception, of course, of the Mister Mukherjees of Chandanpur. My oh my, what all-round splendor! They for whom it's an everyday thing to go out covered in jewelry like Goddess-Queen Lakshmi of the Eight Limbs, wearing a rich Benares sari, like a bridal maiden with her necklaces jangling, tinkling, a rustling Benares sari. Kahar Bonwari has grown old carrying the palanquin; to how many great mansions of the county has he carried wedded maidens to their parents-in-law? Bonwari says—I've brung Nakshmi ta Vishlu's paradise. He's seen many necklaces and saris, smelled many sweet perfumes, heard the music of many trinkets. But he has never seen anything like these flashing diamantine ornaments, these "makes" of clothes belonging to the gentry of Chandanpur.

As he rushed onward, it was suddenly as if Bonwari made himself stop. As if his feet got stuck. To the west, on the left side, Babathakur's shrine. Far off on the right, Kahars cutting cane in the stony field, a chopping, scrunching sound rising. He's hearing clamor of a discussion. Ahead in Jangol's mango orchard the works is running, lights are glowing. But has Bonwari forgotten everything? He inched his way toward Babathakur's shrine. Wrong—Bonwari's done a wrong. O Babathakur have mercy, scrub me clean. Ah! What a blunder Karali's made! Ay, ay, ay! Karali dharma killer. To slaughter and burn Father's familiar? So "mottiley," so glorious, such a whistle, so "youugely" big. On top of this, what is he doing at such an "owd" age making such a blunder with Kalobou! O Lord, O Master of Punishments, take away this fault of Bonwari's. Forgive Karali too, Father. And forgive one more little fault of Bonwari's. Don't condemn this thing with that Kaloshoshi. His youthful "eat" with Kalobou. So many years later, at this age, that hot spark touching the gunpowder of his mind is producing flashing fireworks. Fire's caught hold and there is no means of quenching it. Kalobou—if Kaloshoshi had not been the wife of Porom, Atpoure Para headman, then perhaps his heart wouldn't have burned so; perhaps the fire wouldn't have ignited the explosive in his mind.

Bonwari paused at the boundary of Father's shrine. Suddenly there, he cannot enter that place in this "rustly nightentime." It's now Father plays his games, sometimes does the rites, sometimes stomps around in his clogs, sometimes stands there holding a branch of the banyan tree and gazing toward Father "Kalaruddu"'s court.

Bonwari moved a little farther forward, announcing his arrival to Father with a handclap. They'd cleaned Father's shrine just a few days earlier for the offering. Winter cold is now retreating from the stony earth of Hansuli Turn; parchtime, that's to say summer sun's cruel heat, is gradually making itself felt. No rain, so Father's shrine, once cleaned, has stayed clean. Bonwari laid himself prostrate there. Silently he swore an oath—Father, have mercy. I'll build at the base of your banyan tree.

At that very moment a fight broke out in Kaharpara.

Six

Fights always break out in the rustling night at Hansuli Turn's Kaharpara. This is the hour when old grudges surface anew. Everyone's asleep; right then someone will wake, go outside, and in the absolutely silent darkness begin to scream curses until they're satisfied. If the opponent should happen to wake up at that time then a terrible fight ensues. Beside that, Kaharpara explodes into a shouting match at the person's reply. It's at that very moment that youths of Jangol and Chandanpur give a whistle, let out a hiss, throw a pebble tap-tapping into the yard to summon the sociable Kahar-Bauri girls. If mothers, aunties, in-laws hear, they don't make a fuss; fathers don't say much either; but if brothers-in-law, husbands, or younger brothers hear there'll be uproar. Thieves don't come to Kaharpara; what's to take if they did? Besides, a crow doesn't eat crow's meat; the Kahars themselves once were thieves; even though these days they've given up thieving they're still called thieves, haven't forgotten the codes of thievery. Straining his ears, Bonwari tried to listen out for the "nouds," meaning the sounds, of whose voices were in the fight. This is a funny thing about Hansuli Turn. The uproar of Bansbadi's Kaharpara hits the bamboo groves on the Kopai banks and bounces back clearly.

Nasubala's voice is audible. Ugh! If a man acts in a womanly way, woman's excess comes out in argument. Nothing more to be done with Nasu. Karali's roaring. Who's screaming in a sharp female voice?—O please, please 'elp, lemme go please!

Karali's certainly giving a beating. To who? Auntie Suchand? Suchand does not look kindly on Karali, in spite of his marriage to Pakhi. But Suchand's voice is a rough voice; if you stuck your face in a big pot and spoke in a female voice, the sound that came out would be just like her—this isn't that voice at all! But can he be thrashing Pakhi? No trusting Karali.

But the screams of pain are gradually getting louder.

There are bamboo groves all around Hansuli Turn, like a "fourist," or forest. Even if a branch falls there and does not become a rice-husking block; if leaves fall and don't become a sweeping brush, when there's a fight, throats are torn out. In the fourist, tiger and bear roar from inside their own territory; in Kaharpara each person hurls curses from their own hearthside. Next a fistfight breaks out at some point. Then A grabs B by the neck, B tries to grab A by the neck. To hell with their headman. To hell with Bonwari. Bonwari ran.

It's Karali indeed! Karali is relentlessly thrashing the ailing Noyan. Women standing all around them. Nasubala clapping his hands and saying—Break 'is nose, break the scabby dog's nose.

Suchand is looking on wide-eyed. The Kahar women always watch the men's fights with this look. A trace of fear is showing in Suchand's eyes.

Suchand will tell this story forever. This exact look will then well up in her eyes. She'll say—O Lord whatta "battil." What a slaughter! What a form Karali took! It's possible that in her mind she is frightened Karali might kill her like this!

Bashan is trying to make Karali leave off—Geddup, Karali; quit, quit. Noyan's a sick un. Karali—Karali!

Pakhi is weeping whimperingly.

Noyan's Ma is crying with pain. She's fallen on the ground in the yard. Her hair's loose, her colored wrap's come undone; dirt marks on breast and back; in the reddish glow of the kerosene lantern you'd take her for a female street crazy. Bastard's certainly given her a beating too; knocked her to the ground, no doubt about it. How pitiless, how brutal!

Bonwari went and grabbed Karali's shoulders, said through bared teeth—Let go.

Bonwari's right there, even in the sound of his voice. Karali looked up in surprise.

—Let go.

Karali let go and stood up. He said—Leggo? I'm gonna kill 'im.

—Gonna kill?

With hands and legs shaking, limbs swinging, Nasu said—Not ta? Why not ta kill, then? If one o' yer own folks were ta bite yer nose off wouldn'tcha go ta kill 'em? Wouldja quit? Wouldja pat 'is back an' feed 'im candy?

Noyan's Ma had come to her son and was trying to lift him up; she spoke up—Oose wife? That ain't Loyan's wedded missus, then? So if a wife sees 'usband sick, leaves, ties the knot wi' another, ye wouldn't cut 'er nose off?

Bonwari understood the situation. Pakhi came and stood before him and he grasped it even more clearly. She showed him her nose and said—Look.

Almost tearing a kerosene lamp from someone's hands, Nasubala held it up close to Pakhi's nose and said—Speak, ya got eyes 'eadman man, got judgment too, I'm tellin' ya take a look. Look what 'e done, bitin' 'er nose. "All the sons are there and it's the grandson's head you pat!" Not the arm, not the finger, not the back, not the shoulder, 'e went an' bit 'er *nose*?

It's true, on the nose a reddish bloody mark has spread from the curved imprint of teeth. Bonwari glared at Noyan. Sick, wheezing wretch, fallen there like something not alive; there's no way to punish him more than he's already been punished. And besides, Bonwari's conscience has been pricking him with a slight sense of injustice about the one who's battered Noyan; now it took this chance to grow. He couldn't obey a single thing; it's reasonable punishment. Bonwari said—Unnerstood, I've unnerstood everythin'. Owwever, it's not right! It's definitely not right! What if the sick man'd died? Ye can speak out instead o' thrashin'—that's what the anchesters said.

Karali spoke up—Company law says ye go ta jail fer bitin' a woman like that.

Bowari roared—*Karali*!

—What? Ave I spoke wrong!

—Look now! Ya ran off ta Channanpur an' village cut you off. I forgave you all that dislike an' brung ya back ta the village. Remember what I said when I brung ya back. Gotta listen to what I say an' do it, don't disobey the elders, no do no wrong an' bad behavior. Didja agree or not?

Karali did not respond to this. Pulling Pakhi away he said—Come on.

They moved away. Wiggling his hips, Nasubala said abruptly—Damn, I'm dyin'! Get, go on, get. Everyone get 'ome. As it's said—

Earth was made soft wi' tears—
I gathered that earth and found me long-lost love!

So saying, he spat and took straight off.

Perhaps Bonwari would have been on the verge of making a big deal of it at that moment. But then Noyan's Ma put her head near his feet, touched his feet with her hands, and was speaking tearfully—Make a rulin', ye make a rulin', ye're the 'eadman, make a rulin'.

Bonwari bowed his head; he's done an injustice. Next he picked Noyan up in both arms and carried him to the porch, where he laid him on a palm-leaf mat and said—Bring some water. Put water in 'is mouth, on 'is fore'ead. Calm the boy down first.

Almost everybody had left. Noyan's Ma had once been headman's wife, mistress of the Broke-Home house, her pride extreme; from the time that pride was broken she's been extraordinarily foulmouthed. So nobody is generous toward her. The folks of Kaharpara don't just know how to mock and snigger; that comes easy; they say—Stars in the sky reflect in water; no chance of that if there's clouds in the sky or weeds in the pond. "No sympathy wi' you, so what's the point of smiling?"

Only Suchand was still sitting there.

She was lamenting—Ah, "Ten ages does man come by; now 'e's an elephant, now 'e's a fly." This state o' them Broke-Omes today.

As she sits she tells the tale of Hansuli Turn in her usual way. The "mightful power of the Broke-Homes"; the rise to greatness of the Chaudhurys of Jangol from the "mercifuls" of Babathakur and the blessings of the demon's boat; proprietors of the Saheb Tracts, indigo sahebs' orchards and plots, farms and landholdings. Those Chaudhurys' tenants— "chiefest" of the lot were the Broke-Homes. What a roar Noyan's granddad had! What curved "andlebars" on his "tasche"! How the points of his red eyes rolled! My, today you lot let Karali snatch Noyan's wife away. Back then Noyan's father used to have the wives and daughters of Kaharpara come to the bedchamber of the Chaudhury boy. My Bashan caught the gent's eye? Noyan's dad would get leftover booze from Chaudhury, would get leftover meat, would get the leftovers from every food offering.

After all this time Noyan had recovered. He opened his eyes and looked. He saw Bonwari and tears began to roll from his eyes. Stroking Noyan's forehead with his hand, Bonwari said—Sleep. Ye'll soon be recovered; I'm gonna gi' you companion rites too. Karali made a companion o' yer wife, whatcha say—that wife Karali threw out, I'll gi' 'er to you in companion rites.

Suchand said—Whattcha sayin', Beano? Eh! What unrightyness I done, then? Ye've become 'eadman now. Ye're takin' offense at the story o' the Broke-Omes' 'eadman, that I know. But I remember you goin' around wi' Loyan's father. Loyan's dad used ta hang round in Master Chaudhury's rooms, 'ad lotsa fun there. You might ferget the way ya used to 'ang around the Broke-Omes' trashpile, but I can't ferget it. Now ye're takin' the side o' that bastard Karali! If Loyan's Ma weren't 'ere now—

Bonwari yelled a loud warning—Aunt!

Suchand was able to hear, and could understand the tone of admonition. She started to shout as well—Why then? S'posed ta be scared o' sayin' it ta you, eh? I know no one's s'posed ta know all about yer little cozycozies wi' Loyan's Ma. I saw ya beggin' er one day down by the river's edge.

Bonwari went and stood before Suchand.

Suchand got up too. She's getting frightened. The Kahar headman is big and scary. She straightaway gave up talk of Bonwari and began to insult Karali. —Brought Karali ta the village, be the ruin o' the village, 'e will. Killed father's familiar, 'im. Works at Channapur's infidel workshops, e's become an infidel. Puts frogs on me body. Ye let Pahki marry *that*?

Suchand moved off, still talking.

Bonwari stood in the yard for a few moments, then began walking toward the molasses works. Whose soft voice called—Listen?

Noyan's Ma was standing on a terrace, her hand on the bamboo post. Bonwari was a little undone.

The insinuation in Nasubala's rhyme was correct, and so was Suchand's story. Today he is embarrassed to show his face in front of Noyan's Ma. Injustice—there's been much injustice done. This injustice of Bonwari's was a deliberate injustice. Business from back in those days, all of it. When that tusker Noyan's dad was headman, Bonwari was the tusker's friend; but he couldn't help envying him. His eyes fell on the headmanship. Bonwari's dad was still alive then. The tusker was going around with Master Chaudhury's boy. That's when Bonwari cheated with Noyan's Ma.

Noyan's Ma came and stood near. Bonwari said—I'm gonna give Loyan companion rites, Bashinibou, I've promised.

Noyan's Ma was crying.

Bonwari said—Let Loyan get better, make a happy family. An'—an' if Loyan don't recover too well, then take someone in an ye'll get by. An'— He went quiet; he could not utter the words. It is not necessary for the headman to utter these words.

A wife's earnings, a daughter's earnings; in Kaharpara the cat barely stays in the bag. Everybody knows. Bonwari had wanted to say this.

He said—I'm off, then. Molasses'll be boilin' at the works.

From behind there was a tug on his clothing. Bonwari turned in surprise. Even in darkness the Kahars' eyesight is acute. Moreover, the Kahar headman knows the workings of the Kahar heart. Kahar women never lose the touch of Kopai river's madness as long as they live.

Noyan's Ma is the birthgiver of a twenty-year-old son. Looking into her eyes, Bonwari became suddenly agitated. Noyan's Ma said—Remember? Like Auntie Suchand said, ya begged me by the riverside.

—Loyan's inside, Bashinibou.

—E's sleepin'. Y'know, back then the Broke-Omes was 'eadman. Back then I was the Broke-Ome missus.

—Bashinibou, I didn't dishonor ya, sis.

Bashinibou clasped his hand tightly. Eyes burning. Bonwari was afraid. Bashinibou has suddenly become scary.

Bonwari silently called Babathakur to mind. He stood facing toward Father's shrine. If in the darkness of bamboo forest he is seized by fear and terror, he can overcome his fright by looking toward Father's shrine. Light glows in Father's shrine in the depths of night.

Auntie Suchand says—Me father's father saw, Broke-Omes' granddad saw, on the night o' the new moon Father's shrine "lumernated" wi' light. That's why every house in Kaharpara lights a lamp and brings it to Father's shrine on the new moon.

If a light is brought to Father's shrine on the new moon, Father gives succor; there will daily be an "evetide" lamp glowing at home; if the path through "fourist" wilderness is lost, it will be found again—this light will flash in the Kahars' eyes. In the City of the Dead you won't have to remain in darkness: you'll receive there as many lamps as you lit at Father's shrine. But if you offer the lamp while wearing dirty "pollutied" clothes or thinking bad thoughts, the results are like this—"like crappy paddy," no pulp in the skin, no rice in the husk—the black oil-stained clay "clod," which is to say the lamp, smolders down on dry, half-burned wick; no flame burns in the lamp.

Shortly before this, Bonwari had prostrated himself at Father's shrine. He'd made a vow. He said that he'd atone for the bad he had done. He is headman—a king's evils ruin the kingdom; a chief's evils ruin the village; a master's evils lay the house to waste; a "faither's," meaning a father's, evils are suffered by the sons. As headman, he will not invite the ruin of the village. To Father, however, he has told the affair of Kaloshoshi and requested "promisshun," or permission, for his past heat games with her. But no more. Besides this, there is calumniation in the "commoonity"; "wimmins," which is to say women, are snickering; men are rumor-mongering; a proud head is bowed; a headman's seat is shaky; in the end Earth Mother will rise up and devour that seat. He looked toward Father's shrine and silently called upon him.

There really was a light flashing. Not in Father's shrine, in the sky. The two of them were taken aback. The surrounding sky had filled with cloud long before. Now these first flashes of lightning. Clouds rumbled.

Now Bonwari was stunned with fear.

The light of Father's shrine is become lightning and is "ferlashin," or flashing, in the sky. Father's roar is ringing around the heavens. But in the next moment he checked himself. Who's that calling—Chief, chief! from over there? He immediately remembered, molasses boiling in the cauldron at the works. If water gets into it, all will be spoiled. He ran. Noyan's Ma gazed steadily at that ominous sky and suddenly yelled—Ride yer familiar's 'ead an' dance, Father. Let yer familiar's tongue flicker, in-out. O Father! O Father!

Bonwari too was saying silently to the Father, O Father, O Merciful One, ye've saved so much. Saved so much.

The works had fallen into frenzy. Roofing straw must be put overhead. Hedo Mondol is screaming loudly. Oton's son Lotbor has climbed up on the roof. From time to time he invokes Father Kalarudra's name.

—O Shiva! Victory Father Kalaruddu! Make clouds flee wi' a stab o' yer trident, Lord. If there's rain molasses'll turn ta dust, Father. Mango blossoms'll perish. "Rain is fire in Phalgun." Make the clouds flee. We've pledged twenty quarts o' molasses sherbet this Gajon festival. Victory ta Father Kalaruddu, gonna gi' five 'undred sesame-oil lamps at Gajon, Father. O Shiva, we'll gi' the best young mangoes for ye to enjoy, Father.

Bonwari was looking steadily skyward.

In lightning flashes he was seeing clouds like molasses boiling up in a cauldron. Black and white, swelling and blooming, spreading slowly in all directions. Rain's inevitable. Doesn't come down if it thunders in the morning, but from an untimely cloud it'll pour. The rainy months are Asharh, Shaon, Bhaddo, Ashwin. All the other months are untimely. Even when clouds thunder during the monsoon, it often doesn't rain. These are untimely clouds, special Magh-Phalgun clouds; if they rumble in response they'll shake their limbs and shed water. Phalgun rain is fire, deadly fire for mangoes. All the blossoms will burn up. There'll be no mangoes. Oh my—"In mangoes see paddy." If there are no mangoes there'll be no paddy. Yet if it rains there'll be work in the Saheb Tracts. When the gravelly soil gets wet it becomes soft. They'll get a "breath," that's to say time, to prepare the soil. Bonwari has received a lot of land in the Saheb Tracts.

Rain poured down hard. Father Kalaruddu did not listen to their prayers. Roton said to his boss, Mister Hedo Mondol—Mister Boss, Father took no notice o' twenny quarts o' molasses pledge. Pledge forty.

Hedo Mondol is an old-fashioned man, he's not a Kahar. He leaned his body on the trunk of the ancient banyan tree in order to avoid the splashing rain, puffed away on his pipe, and said—Get out, bumpkin Kahar scum; thinks rain'll stop if I pledge!

—But molasses'll go ta dust, boss!

From the tree trunk some fat drops of water fell into the embers of Mister Mondol's pipe bowl, extinguishing them with a hiss. Mondol glared angrily upward—Ah-h-h-h!

—Mister Boss! said Roton.

—Bastard Kahar's ruined it—Mister Boss, Mister Boss! Throwing the pipe aside, Hedo Mondol suddenly grabbed Roton by the hair and punched him with a few sharp jabs. When he got free, Roton said—Give, give the pipe bowl, I'll light it.

***

Meanwhile at the works, Bonwari is standing helplessly next to the cauldron. Water is breaking through the straw and palm-leaf roof and pouring into the liquid boiling in the cauldron. Ah! What care he had taken to prepare the molasses, now all turned to dust. It'll stink, the flavor will be ruined. Ay! Ay! Ay!

Panu is sitting a way off, under a tree out of the rain. He's gathered a few folk into a tight little party for the telling of juicy stories. It's getting more luscious with his sense of pleasure at the ruin of Hedo Mondol's molasses.—Goin' good, nice goin', pour Father, chuck it down. Let the bastard's molasses turn ta crap. A right bastard scum. Ma Durga's demon!

Suddenly Mathla arrived. Prohlad with him. They were soaked to the skin. Prohlad sat down and without explanation said—Ye'd better watch yerself, Pana!

—Why?

—Why? Ya know where Bonwari's been gone so long?

—Where?

—Ta listen ta Ghentu songs in Atpoure Para.

Prankrishna's face fell. Bonwari's revenge is a terrible thing. The headman is not one given to rage, but there's no escape if his rage comes on.

Prohlad said—I know ya done their Ghentu song this time.

Panu had protected himself so far. Now with his characteristic craftiness he said—Nope, I swear by Mary; by Mary, I say, I can swear on my son, I don't know a thing. Then, with enormous surprise, he asked—So, 'ave them Atpoures made up a noo song fer Ghentu then? What song? Jokin' song, or what? So saying, he inexplicably burst out laughing.

Prohlad said—Ye'll get the joke, now ye'll geddit. Chief takin' Kaloshoshi in 'is arms song! Ye'll get what a kick is, an' all!

Panu replied—Chief took Kaloshoshi in 'is arms? Well then s'gotta be that Karali lot's mess. That bastard bitch Nasubala—

—Oo then? Oo? What mess o' Karali's? Speaking these words, someone came up from behind and stood there. His body was shrouded in a cloak and on his head was a gigantic load. Nor could his face be seen. Only by the sound of his voice could they tell it was Karali. What's that on his head?

Prohlad asked—Karali? Wassat on yer 'ead?

—S'a tarp, uncle.

—Tarp?

—Yeh. Brought one from the station. Saw the rain an' I thought yer molasses' gonna get ruined. So I brought it. Puddit tight over the roof. Not a drop'll fall. He's brought the tarp on his head wearing a tarpaulin suit. Looks strange. Just like a saheb. Prohlad leaped up—Bonwari! Beano!

Almost dragging Karali, he took him to the stove at the works. Everyone stood gazing hopelessly up at the roof. A couple of young farmhands holding shovels, building a little levee all around the stove mouth so that water doesn't flow in, so the stove doesn't go out. Hedo Mondol wailing, crying out—Get an umbrella, get it and hold it over the pot. Boss Mondol's sense has completely "gorn," meaning vanished. You couldn't even keep your own head dry with an umbrella in this rain, let alone the works' cauldron!

Prohlad hollered—S'alright Bonwari, s'alright. Karali's found a way, 'e's bringin' a tarp. Spread it on the roof.

Tarp! The railway station's tarp! Spread it over rice and paddy sacks in the rains; not a drop of water gets through—that same tarp?

Hedo Mondol heaved a sigh of relief. He cannot stand for any further delay.

—Put, put, spread it out. Up. Geddup there.

Bonwari sighed deeply—S'goin' good—yeh, goin' good. Put it, spread it out.

Karali said—Cos it's in your care though, chief. Brought it 'cos you're 'ere, otherwise coulda given 'undred thou' rupees an' I still wouldn'ta given—wouldn'ta cared if it were a king nor a minister, yeh.

Hearing this, Hedo Mondol smiled faintly, and looking at him said—Oh marvelous, how very nice! How ye're talking! Eh? Smiling again, Mondol looked Bonwari's way and said—Scum's gotta be called hero now—yep, scum's a real hero.

Karali frowned. If it had been Mister Ghosh, Karali perhaps would have hung his head, frowned, and gone away; but Hedo Mondol is not Middle Ghosh. He replied immediately—What? Whatcha sayin' scummy-scum for? What kinda talk's tha' fer a gentyman?

In a second all the Kahars at the works were agape. Bonwari was worried. Hedo Mondol is Mother Durga's demon incarnate; now he'll leap on Karali with a scream. But it's strange, Mondol does not seem quite right; he stands there mute and stares at the tarpaulin-clad Karali. After remaining silent for a while, Hedo Mondol merely said—Why, what'd I say that was wrong? What is it, Bonwari, what'd I say that was wrong, tell me?

Before Bonwari replied, Karali said—All that don't seem wrong ta chief, though; they've got used t'all a that. I'm sayin'—scum, what's that for, Mister; scum? So saying, he walked off quickly. Talking as he went— Scum jerk bastard shit-eating louse, right on the tip—right on tippa gentymens' tongues. Gentymen! Under their thumb! Ah—

He went and stood under the tree where Panu's group was—Where, where's Pana? Where's 'e "geen"? That's to say, gone.

The others sitting there had watched the scene made by Karali and were dumbstruck. They're thinking, What's Karali done? And is it even possible? Karali's made them speechless. The lad's got guts for sure! And straightaway it occurred to them that what Karali said was right too. Those phrases *are* always on the tip of Boss Mondol's tongue, on the tongues of the gentry sires. They won't say it if they're angry; it'll be fondly. They'll say—Oh very nice, scum. They will ask "How's it going?" affectionately by saying—Hey there bastard, how you doing? What Karali's saying is right. Yet—. Yet he ought not have spoken in such a high and mighty way. You have to respect the difference between great and small. In God's, in Father Kalarudda's precepts, it's all written down: the foot is not equal to the head.

Karali asked again—I'm sayin', wheer'sat creep got to then? Why so quiet? Eh!

Mathla said—Runnin' off somewhere.

—Runnin' off! Jackal creep. Creep's gotta be found. Karali waited no longer. Dressed in his tarpaulin clothes, he made off with great strides as if he'd seen a five-legged snake!

Not a drop of water falls beneath the tarp. The making of molasses is proceeding smoothly. Bonwari was thinking about this Karali business as he stood beside the stove skimming off the crud, that's to say the scum, with a long-handled bamboo and coconut-shell ladle. The lad's pulled off an impossible thing. Just doing whatever he wants. Not following any precepts, going out of control, fights all over the place, making every step a misstep.

If the tarp hadn't been absolutely necessary today, Hedo Mondol wouldn't have let it drop. There would have been a real scene. Nope, Bonwari really doesn't like this at all. Thorn bush—Karali's a sapling thorn bush; you go to take him in a fond embrace and end up covered in stab wounds. Yet all those bastard-scum phrases *are* awful, for sure.

Bonwari heaved a deep sigh. Ah, if only the lad behaved himself and followed wise counsel. He's rotted his brains at that Channanpur workshop.

Rain came down harder. Gusts of wind with it. Rainwater flowing down, out from the village toward the fields. My, without the tarp everything would've turned to dust. All would've gone bad. Ah, pounding rain! In Kaharpara children are hollering. Month of Phalgun, new thatch has not yet gone on the roofs; old thatch rotted away, flying off; God's water pours into every little cottage today. Alas, not a wink of sleep to be had tonight.

Leave off, Father. Hey God, Kalaruddo, stop it now Father. Don't be beating on the Kahars no more. Maito Ghosh says—Comes a soak, Bauris croak. If there's a big rain it really is death for Kahars.

Treetops swaying in the wind. Bansbadi's bamboo groves in a frenzy. Rain clattering on bamboo leaves; a clanging, tapping sound coming from swaying, colliding bamboo shafts. A smell of wet earth wafting in from the fields.

Prohlad suddenly got up and grabbed a shovel.

—Where ya goin'?

—Take a look. Prohlad indicated; on one side of the flow coming down from the village was a stream of water like a blackstone Kali. Someone's manure pile is floating along. It's the dark color of sewage water, that stream. Some of the stuff has dissolved and moves along to one side in its own stream. And if you put a foot in it you'll see that it's hot as boiling water. If you put a foot into the earth-colored water right beside, you'll see it's cold.

Prohlad said—S'right by me bitta paddy land, gonna cut it in there, be medicine fer the soil.

—Do it, go an' do it. Bonwari's land is a way off. And now a shovel will work on the Saheb Tracts.

Ah, the wild pigs are squealing on the Saheb Tracts. The buggers have gone out to dig in wet earth for roots to eat. The soil on the Saheb Tracts has softened.

Seven

Saheb Tracts; some call it—Plantation Tracts.

A slope of stony ground—a short rise, a short fall, then another short rise—full of red gravel; it's as if the slope is plunging wavelike from Santal Pargana hill country. Moving from west to east in delta form. All around this slope, soil of Bengal. It's there the place's farmlands are; in all those fields different crops ripen. At Hansuli Turn—a strip of this red earth comes to an end at Hansuli Turn's northwest tip. It's here that the indigo-making sahebs had founded their plantation. Eight months of the year grass does not grow in this soil; from Asharh to Ashwin a muddy-green grass sprouts, like thin new wisps on the head of one who's been so sick their hair's fallen out. From the upper Saheb Tracts, the slope goes slowly downward and becomes one with the Kopai sandbank. For fear of Kopai floods, of course; and in forest and brushland there is no mud—surely it's because it is so sparkling and nice that the sahebs set up their plantation in this place. In the sahebs' days these uplands were a royal city.

Suchand says—Our fathers used ta say, those yoouge big 'orses, this fringe-bordered vehicle, palanquin that is. All these bungalows, flower gardens, paved pleasure areas, wooden furniture; ya couldn' begin ta describe all them riches. One side estate office was a-bustlin', footman Atpoures standin' guard wi' rifles—turbans tied on, fightsticks on the ready, they'd guard. Them honest, simple farmers sat there wi' clasped 'ands—faces pale wi' fear. Ole buncha folks kept tied up. Somma them just wi' a rope round their wrists, somma them bound 'and an' foot. Saheb Man, whatta red face, yeller-brown eyes, 'air like red earth, great bootshoes on 'is feet—'e'd come stompin' out, kick backs an' bellies wi' shoes ta get down, 'arsh Indi words in 'is mouth—"Beat him down, apply the lash, show the bastard the white man's tricks." Sometimes the order was—"Lock him up." Sometimes the order was—"Destroy the scum's paddy field." Or else, "Cut down the rice field of this scum." Ye weren't no Brahmin, no Kayastha, no Sadgop—all in the same boat. Nighttime row on row o' candles burned—*tung-tang—kang-kong—bang-po bang-po* the instuments sounded, Saheb an' Missus drank English booze, they'd dance 'oldin 'ands; in the lock-up everyone'd roar an' shout like tigers—screamed so meself. Late at night the soldiers would fire rifles—*boom-*

boom-boom-boom. They'd yell—O—ho—i. Clear out—clear out—robber, outlaw take care! Don't matter if ye're a robber or a saint, wouldn't have lived if ye'd walked thattaway; they'd fire bullets wi' a boom.

Those same uplands are now desolate. The only remaining sign of the indigo plantation is the mango orchard planted by the sahebs. The smashed indigo tanks are in there, and a few fragments of the bungalow's foundations. All around them, dense woody overgrowth has sprung up. By fertilizing, digging, watering this little area of stony, gravelly land on the uplands, the sahebs had made it strangely fruitful. Then it was orchard, now it's scrub. That remaining ageless red earth is desolate.

Standing on the edge of the uplands, Suchand occasionally wipes her eyes sorrowfully with the edge of her wrap. She truly weeps. At Hansuli Turn, in Bansbadi's Kaharpara, human beings have a nature but no moral character. They laugh easily, weep easily; weep at their own sorrow and weep at the sorrow of others. If they hear report of a great elephant fallen in the vast forest they'll go see, gripped by curiosity; and, seeing such a large body lying lifeless, they're overcome by sympathy, embrace the elephant's neck, and weep. Yet they have no store of good karma; the dead do not arise into life at the touch of their tears. Everyone wipes their eyes on hearing the stories of the Saheb Tracts from Suchand's mouth, but none can cry like Suchand can. Suchand, she's the human of the tale's end of days!

Suchand wipes her eyes and says—Aah, aah, s'what that fable says, city ate by demons, this is. 'S lonesome, empty.

It really is lonesome. Not a human soul goes there. Tusky pigs' assembly, brush-clotted, ruined indigo plantation. They form a herd and come out at night, swarm to the river's edge, tear up earth with their tusks, dig up various plant roots and eat. At paddy time they descend on the fields. The Kahars build a platform in the field and bang on tin sheets to chase them off. Little bamboo slivers scattered around the fields; hooks baited with liquor mash and banana bound to them with strong cord; the pigs come to eat paddy, get hooks stuck in their mouths, get their feet caught on cords, and stand waiting; at morning, the Kahars catch and kill. If there's too much trouble, they come and kill in a posse.

A shovel's blows are falling on those very plantation uplands.

Rain and storm had ended two days before. Rainfall had been quite plentiful. The great gentry of Chandanpur have set almost a hundred and fifty Santal laborers to work. This red gravelly earth has a peculiarity of its own. This earth is hard as rock, a spade won't cut it, if you strike a blow a bit of red dust rises, fine grit flies in mouth and eyes; if rain falls on this same earth, it stays as soft as raw sugar for days. In this condition it's called "ready" earth. With this readiness comes the chance to dig the earth of the place. If the opportunity passes, earth cutting will once again become difficult. That slope of the Saheb Tracts descending toward the Kopai is being turned into farmland. The Santals are working the Chandanpur gentry's own lands at the far end of the slope.

Some of the nearby Sadgop masters of Jangol have paid a tribute fee and taken revenue-settlement lands right alongside this. They're sitting there themselves; a group of hired laborers is working with the farm servants. Bonwari has taken the worst three-acre spot. A nonfee plot, sure to be unwatered. Anyway, how could Kahars ever be destined to better land? He'll break the earth himself; Bonwari's wife and Auntie Suchand will put that earth into baskets, carry it on their heads, and build a boundary ridgepath. Bonwari will certainly give Auntie Suchand a working wage. Nine hours' work, she'll get fourteen paisa cash and puffed rice meals too. There's another thing—in the afternoon cool, after midday break, he'll bring in Prohlad, Roton, Panu, and a few others to dig earth with their spades. Next day Bonwari will employ a few of the hamlet's women to carry and pile that earth. Bonwari knelt and made homage to "unplowed soil"—meaning to the earth of the place. Silently he said—I don't strike yer body, Ma, I'm cleansin' yer body. I'm servin' ya. You gi' a yield. Stay as creation in my 'ome. Then he opened his waistband and laid down flowers from Babathakur's offering. Victory Father, you puttekt. Make sure no rocks come up. No animal nor beast comes in. Lifting his hands, he said—Bugs an' worms, snakeholes, take care, move yerselves. I've taken land from King, orders from God—gonna cut this land. He began to dig. The Sadgop masters are smoking pipes of tobacco, sometimes offering them to their farmhand lackeys. The Santals are chewing "diced": tobacco and lime. Bonwari has bought two paisas' worth of local betel smokes. He smokes some himself and gives the remainder to his wife; to Suchand he gives a whole smoke. She's auntie, of course; anyway, if she doesn't get a whole smoke Suchand's craving won't be satisfied. But Suchand really doesn't want to smoke betel cigarettes, her true favorite is tobacco. Suchand abruptly went up to Hedo Mondol and said—Gimme a turn on the pipe will ya please!

Without a word, Mondol passed down the pipe bowl. Suchand squatted right before Mondol; obviously embarrassed, she turned her back to sit and, thereby maintaining the decorum of womanhood, began to smoke the tobacco. All at once forgetting her embarrassment, she turned around and said—An' yet ya gave me the pipe bowl, bossman; f'it adda been Pana's boss 'e woulda come ta smack me one. An' yet when 'e got 'ot fer me girl 'e comes an' falls at me feet.

Hedo Mondol yelled a reproof—Shut up, don't blather on now. The sound of Hedo Mondol's voice is very loud; besides that, he screamed his words knowing Suchand was deaf, so Suchand could clearly hear what he said. Because of this she's always very pleased with Hedo Mondol.

—Don't blather on?

—No.

After looking steadily into Hedo Mondol's face for some moments, Suchand said—All jackals got the same bark! That's fine. She began smoking the tobacco again. Then said—Y'all don' lift a shovel no more, right?

Hedo Mondol burst out—Ah-ha-ha! I see this slut's a real pain.

—Why? Wha've I done t'annoy? I'm sayin', wha've I done t'annoy? I've seen yer dad wi' a shovel in 'is 'ands fer cuttin' that long strip o' land. Puffin' away, what blows o' the shovel! Y'all gotta cut the earth wi' yer own 'ands. Me, I'm just an ancient crow—I've seen it all.

It's true; some time ago, that's about twenty, twenty-five years ago, all these Mister Mondols were farmers through and through. From the digging of land to the cultivation of crops, they'd take part themselves in all the jobs alongside peasants, farmhands, and laborers; they felt no disgrace in this. In these last twenty to twenty-five years there's been such a turnaround that the Mister Sadgops have now risen to being semigentrified. Hedo Mondol can understand this well himself; his body's still incredibly strong, and he feels a deep affinity for farm work. He even wants to do all the work himself as before, but he can't. Can't because it would be an embarrassment before his own caste kin. Alas! What a wave of English gentrification has swept the land! He feels an inner regret because of this. And yet behind the closed doors of his home, he does a lot of work. But he can't admit to that in front of Suchand. Annoyed, he said—Don't gab on so much. You gave up disposing of peoples' dead cats and dogs; now you're hollering you won't take away a dead cow by carrying it on your own backs, saying you won't clean out household sewers. I mean, how'd you ever get to be such posh folk? You're getting posh; we're getting posh too. How'll our pride remain otherwise?

Suchand pointed her finger at Bonwari. She said—That—that—middleman, geddit Mondol—that's all from Bonwari's 'eadmanning. Im it was raised the refrain, we won't be disposers o' no dead dogs an' cats. Then everyone all whisperin' together got to insistin'—when we take away a dead cow we don't carry it on no shoulders, we need a cart; we'll make exception fer water drains, but we won't put our 'ands in no leftovers-bones-shitty rottin' cesspits. I says, been doin' it since dad's, granddad's time; why shouldn't we do it? Bonwari shrugs 'is shoulders and says—Uh-uh, why should we do the work o' gravediggers an' swabbers?

Now Hedo Mondol got annoyed—Bonwari's fault? But yes, of course, you slut; that grandson of yours, Karali, the one who said to me the other day—Don't call me scum an' stuff, mister; that's Bonwari's fault too?

Suchand put her hand to her cheek—E's lost! Then said—I can see 'im wimme own two eyes. E'll be ruin o' the village—you see, 'e'll bring ruin.

This entire discussion was being overheard by Bonwari. Deaf Auntie Suchand, Hedo Mondol screaming his words. So not only Bonwari, everyone around here can hear. He yelled with extreme impatience—Ey, 'ow much longer ya gonna smoke 'baccy for?

Suchand rose hurriedly. She doesn't respect Bonwari, but today he is virtually in the place of her boss; he'll give fourteen paisa cash and puffed rice meals. She got up and stood. But with a sudden impulse of grief, she wiped her eyes with the hem of her wrap, then said to Hedo Mondol—Jus' look at the fate on me brow, Mister Mondol! Toilin' away at this old age. I've been split from me granddaughter, from me Bashan 'cos 'e got that Karali married.

She sat down again. With a breaking voice said to Mondol—I said ta Bashan, ta that bitch Pakhi—Noyan's got the asthma, s'all right; lettim stay 'usband, 'usband in name. Pakhi's such a young 'un, let 'er make a few earnins an' such. After, let 'er get a bit older—twenty or thirty, leave 'im an' I'll allow a companion rite. Whatcha say, Mondol? Suchand began to cry again—Daughter o' me womb, Bashan; daughter o' Bashan's womb, Pakhi—

Now Bonwari came and stood close by. Suchand immediately got up and said—Come on son, let's move. I've told Mister Mondol these two pains o' me life. She began limping toward the place she was working. As Bonwari lifted the earth-laden basket to her head, Suchand looked into Bonwari's face with intense entreaty, saying—Gotten angry, then? Bonwari?

Without answering, Bonwari turned his back, picked up his shovel, and began to hew the earth. With great thick hands and an angry head he kept digging. A while later he paused, loosened his waistcloth, and wiped the sweat from his forehead with a stroke of his dust-streaked finger. The pounding of two hundred and fifty Santal shovels is advancing the gentry's work like a Kopai flood. And his work's moving like drizzle water gathering in a cattle wallowing pit in a paddy field. So be it. The work's gone on like this for all time. The gentry's work will go on for a few days—so long as the earth remains ready; his work will last a twelve-month. He'll go every morning and dig a bit. Now he'll only prepare one section of land. In Bhadra month he'll till the rest of the land and sow some "threeway" beans, that's types of pulses, and a few pigeon peas and kidney beans. Then Magh month's coming, it will rain; if indeed it does, he'll drive the plow and harrow through, clearing the earth, and try to make a barrier ridge; then he'll cut some earth and level it; the barrier ridge will harden straightaway too. This way it's also easy to make land; little by little, step by step, advancing onto the adjoining fallow no matter how haphazardly. No one will notice. Bonwari has taken three acres—it must be made into three and a half.

When the first crop comes he'll have to offer it at Babathakur's shrine. Boiled pigeon peas, boiled kidney beans, and a bottle of prime liquor. All the beans will be given through Kalaruddu's venerable priest. Father eats through Brahmin priest's mouth. Then he'll give to the great mansion at Channanpur, the new proprietor's house. At the Mukherjee house Lakshmi Queen of Wealth will need to be fed; it'll rise into the King's mouth. And he must give to the Ghosh house, Jangol's bosses for two generations. Can this not be given? If all this giving is done, then a handful must be given to the hamlet; after that maybe something will remain—in any case, by doing this Bonwari's line will no longer be "lowborn." Farming's stuffs—"Gift o' Mother Earth," must be eaten through all these folk. Especially the first year's harvest. God-Brahmin-king, master-kinsman-clan: if there's something left after giving to them, then you yourself can eat—if not, then wash your hands and feet and go home with a smile. What you give will remain—next year the return will be doubled; it has even been credited to your name in the accounts ledger of the City of Death.

With joy in his mind, Bonwari happily continued digging. Bonwari's wife is scurrying along carrying earth-filled baskets. She's clearing two or three baskets while Auntie Suchand limps back from emptying one. Her commitment is second to none! She's really going to make this plot her own.

Oh! That's done it! Hit rock. A clanging is coming from under the shovel. Bonwari cleared earth and looked. Several feet under the earth—rock shards.

Bonwari sat with head in hands. Not just any old rock shards, but a thing like a laid floor; great big shards, there's a layer collected about three feet thick. Strike them with shovel or hoe and the blade will break, the tool will blunt, but the rocks will not come out. He rose and stood straight. Leaning his hand on the shovel handle he began to ponder—How?

The gentry's Santal laborers have also reached the layer of rock. They've put aside their shovels and taken up pickaxes. The gentry sires have a different way of doing business; having "figgered," that's to say figured, this earlier, they'd brought a cart loaded with pickaxes. Hedo Mondol had understood the situation. He too is thinking, if they hit rock there'll be trouble. Hedo Mondol said—Hit it, then? He meant rock.

With a deep sigh, Bonwari inclined his head and confirmed—Yup, hit it.

—I knew it. Hedo Mondol got right up and went over to the gentry sires' farm manager. They began to mutter and whisper. Bonwari shook his head and smiled, which means—"What need to hide a cough when wedding drums are being pounded?" Mondol will give the farm manager a little something and rent pickaxes. Lord, what other whispering words does he say!

Bonwari's wife squatted down in disappointment at his side. She looked him in the face and said—What now?

With bulging eyes Suchand said—Give it up, geddit sonny—give it up. In them rocks there's a God somewhere, a demon heap; strikin' a blow won't do no good—give it up.

She picked up a round stone. Around the center of the black stone body was a circular white mark just like a holy thread. —Look, she said. Then she held up a piece of the demon heap. Its shape was exactly like that of a tree stump; this is what Suchand calls—demon heap. Which means a collection of demon bones turned to stone. The very bones of the demons slain by the gods. The Kahars' forefathers have told all this. But in the epoch of the Bonwaris, all these beliefs have disappeared. There's fear of Suchand's fancies. Bonwari's a lifelong land digger; he's seen thousands upon thousands of stones with marks like a holy thread. Do gods keep scattering all these thousands about? Rocks have that kind of mark. Sure, that's a demon heap. But the sole concern is how to cut through this rock. Without a pickaxe it's "improssable," meaning impossible. But the Kahars don't have pickaxes. They've never had these pointy tools; the white men's "trimportation," which is to say importation, brought in these stakelike instruments. Is it right to pierce the breast of Mother Earth with such things! Anyway, where would you get one! Where's he going to get the kind of money that can bribe the gentry sires' farm manager?

The thought of Karali suddenly occurred to him. Karali can. The pick-axes are loaded at the Channanpur rail shop's warehouse. He can give. But—

Hedo Mondol came and said—What's up, you seem a bit stumped! Bash it and see!

That's right. Need to strike a blow and see how many rocks there are. With a mental gesture of reverence he began to strike. *Clang—clang—clang.* The sound of iron hitting stone rang out. The layer of rocks is a couple of feet deep; soft, black earth below. Oh yes, great. Earth of ab-solutely the finest type. A pickaxe must be got. No other way. The lathe mouth straightens crooked wood; the hammer tames iron upon the anvil; the pickaxe head masters earth and rock. He's seen it—seen it from afar of course—on the Channanpur line; rocks smashed to pieces by blows from the pickaxes in the hands of upcountry workers. The Kahars strike no less forceful a blow than they.

—Aah! Oooh, ouch, ouch, ow!

Bonwari let go his shovel and clutched his brow. A rock had suddenly shattered and a shard of it struck him on the forehead. Ouch. Fast as a ball of iron shot, but worse. Shot is round, no edges; this is a sharp broken stone.

What's this firelike "wairm," or warmth, touching the palm of his hand? Hah, so she's taken! Mother Earth's taken blood.

Bonwari's wife came running—Let's see, let's see! Ow the blood's spillin'! Ooh my! What next! Auntie—hey auntie!

Seeing the pipe bowl in Hedo Mondol's hand, Suchand longed again for a puff. She did not hear what Bonwari's wife said.

Hedo Mondol had seen it; he did not get up, but merely said—She take, then?

Bonwari replied with a smile—Yes.

Hedo said—It's a well-known thing. She'll take. If not, she won't open up. Press it on, press earth on.

Bonwari took a handful of earth and pressed it hard against the fore-head wound. Suchand watched all the while, squatting before him.

Yes, yes sonny! Mother Earth!

Mother Earth gives just as she takes. She'll feed you with rice from autumn harvest paddy, but she'll take your body at last; if you're burned, then at least a handful of ashes must be given to her. Must give nails and hair as long as you live. Sometimes a few drops of blood. "She whose belly bore a son, will it take little to fill her tum?" Mother of so many humans, so many beasts, birds, bugs; gives crops from her torn breast; can her thirst be slaked merely by rain from the clouds? If you injure Mother's breast you must make her an offering of blood. If you don't give, Mother will certainly extract a few drops of blood. Mother's taken what she's owed. Bonwari made a handful out of the blood-smeared earth and planted it in a corner of the plot.

Yet this sign is good; when Mother's taken blood then will she give— will fill his hands.

Da-doom-ba-boom! Ba-boom-da-doom! The earth is trembling underfoot; on the iron-wrought bridge ten train cars are crossing the breast of madwoman Kopai, raising a sound like a random mass of instruments from one bend to the other of Hansuli Turn.

Sire Mukherjee's Santal workers suddenly cast their pickaxes, hoes, baskets aside. Time for the ten o' clock break.

Sun has risen on the twelfth of Boishakh at Hansuli Turn.

In the summer here, work time runs from six until ten in the morning. Then from three until six in the afternoon.

Bonwari picked up his shovel and basket too. He won't do the afternoon work shift. His second shift will begin in the evening. Moonlight tonight, a gentle "blows," which is to say a breeze, will blow, he'll feel the heady touch of liquor, he'll get hold of a few neighbors; then Bonwari will begin work again. The sires' money game; the Sadgop masters of Jangol have some part in it too—something of a power play, of course; they exact labor by force. The toil of Bonwari's own body, and the work of hamlet neighbors given out of love and "revvince," that's to say reverence. Bonwari's land will be dug at night; the Jangol bosses will come in the morning, see it, and say—No chance to get it with these bastards.

As they approached Jangol, Suchand spoke—Bonwari, 'ow much money ya gonna gi' now?

From the moneybag at his waist, Bonwari took out a two-anna bit and put it in her hand, saying—This one time I'm givin' ya pay fer a workshift. Don't need ta come back later.

—Don't need ta come back? Why?—Suchand's chest began to thud. She understood that it wasn't just for this afternoon: he won't take her back to work at all.

Bonwari said—Ye're an old woman, think I can bear ta get ya workin'? An' can ye cope wi' workin' yerself?

Suchand was silent a moment, then she said—All right then. Gimme then, gimme. Your dharma, your place. When yer own belly's child turns away, why expect support from others? Any case, there's work I can still do that yer wife can't.

Bonwari didn't say any more. He took his wife and went back toward the village. It is mealtime, they will eat and drink. Cows must be milked before that; they have to be fetched from the fields. Lots of work. It's getting a bit late today. Bonwari's build is huge; what's more, right from the time he was a strong young man he carried the palanquin at a slant and his left shoulder is higher than his right. He also moves on a slant. The right foot comes down with great force. He moved quickly. He's leaving footprints on the right side of the sodden fieldpath. He sat down, suddenly breathless. Bonwari turned and gazed back. —Huh, he said. Immediately he bent forward.

—What? said his wife.

—Ants.

Numberless ants swarming around a hole. Most of them are carrying eggs.

Wife said—Aha, gotta come see! See 'ow they're runnin' round so nervous-like with eggs!

—Ye're clueless. Bonwari looked this way and that and pointed to a column of ants moving through the field.—Looka that. They've been fleein' this place a long time. Then he looked at the sky and said—Youuge rainstorm comin' in.

—Be a rainstorm?

—Youuge.

—Youuge?

—Yeh. Ants can tell. Ain'tcha never seen 'em get off the ground an' live in a wall during the rains? Wait.

Saying this, he approached Lord's shrine. Rarely, not in a twelve-month, does a human hand enter the wood-apple tree's roots there. Because of this shelter, the roots of wood-apple and silk-cotton tree are filled with ant nests. In vast numbers, they raise up amazing little cone-shaped homes from granules of sandy soil. But at the slightest hint of rain the ants take their eggs and climb trees. There are holes in the decayed old tree knots; they clean out those holes and nest there. If he wants to look for signs of rains or drought, Bonwari comes to stand at the base of that tree; ants are either coming down or climbing up.

He didn't have to go far; he got to the mouth of Lord's shrine and caught sight of some crows descending. A flock of black drongos is perched on the branches of the wood-apple. They dive down now and then and hop about, pecking and eating beside the crows. Eating ants, no mistaking that. The ants have swarmed out and are climbing up. The birds have descended and are feasting on them. No doubt there'll be a gigantic rainstorm. Hamlet folk need to be warned. What if no one was alert like this! Bonwari felt regret; even though he's told them, he's been unable to pass that wisdom on to the Kahars.

Bonwari returned home. Wife went on ahead. She said—Ye've messed up nicely, love! Shabi an' Benoda's sat there. Sun's come up—when they gonna go?

—Don' shout, I'm tellin' ya bitch, don' shout; Shabi an' Benoda ain't gonna melt in the sun like cheesedolls if we're a few minutes late. I know me duties. Go untie the calf, gimme the milk pail.

The cows were lowing for their young. Bonwari went and stroked their foreheads and necks with his hand, saying—S'comin', s'comin'. All ye mothers, 'ave a bitta patience. He began to smile.

As he set down the milk pail after milking the cows, Shabi said—Customers sayin' ye're puttin' too much water in the milk. Putta bit less water in, uncle.

Shabi and Benoda both go to Channanpur at midday. They ingeniously set up piles of dungcakes in giant baskets and place the milk pot on top of them. They take milk to the Channanpur gentlefolk's homes every day. Milk four paisa a quart. Bonwari's place produces four quarts of milk. Bonwari's wife makes it five quarts by mixing that milk with clear water from the Kopai's sandy hollows. Five annas a day. From this, Shabi and Benoda reckon five paisa a day.

Bonwari's wife is a good person. She shook her head and said—Hey, I just gi' that one measure o' water. I don't gi' too much.

Bonwari looked at Shabi and said—So tell us 'ow much ye water it down on the way wi' water from the spring?

Benoda said—Whoa, what's that! Us?

—Yeah yeah, you. Ye're real crafty, ain'tcha. Bonwari began laughing.

Benoda and Shabi began laughing too; after this they didn't deny the charge any longer. Now Bonwari said—Water it down a little less, bit by bit—don't water it down more than ye did before. Then the gentry won't kick up a fuss.

It's true; Shabi and Benoda—and not just them alone—pull that little trick, as do all the young women of Kaharpara who deliver others' milk to Channanpur. They pour in a little water along the way, dilute the milk, and make an extra few paisa a day.

Bonwari said to his wife—Gi' the eggies.

Wife said—Sayin' gi' to the boss-'ouse, then?

—Gi', gi'. Tight fer money right now, need money ta pay people workin' the land.

Boss! In his mind Bonwari spins imaginings, who knows who'll become boss now! If he could only get to the feet of Great Sire at Channanpur, then—

A slight smile appeared on his mouth. With that smiling face he moved toward Karali's house. Karali certainly isn't there. Speak to Pakhi and he'll come. —Tell Karali I'm needin' a few pickaxes. He took a turn around the hamlet. He was checking what condition people's straw roofs were in. Within a few days the rainfall will be heavier; month of Boishakh coming up—when it rains it'll pour.

"Stones," meaning a hailstorm, are not unlikely. Everyone must be put on alert.

Kaharpara's cottages. Drown in flood, fly in storm. Not stonework, not brickwork, no bricks, no timber; earthen walls, bamboo from Bansbadi, sago-fiber cord from the riverside of Hansuli Turn, and straw from the paddy fields—this makes a cottage. Not allowed to build in brick— Babathakur's injunction. Moreover, the gentry and the Sadgop masters will sleep inside brickwork. Can the Kahars do as they do? Or become like them?

Bonwari frowned. No, he could do no more. The Kahars won't learn in this life. He just won't have the strength for it. Everybody's thatch is fluttering. Nobody's thatch is very good. Nobody's aware now. All seems fine now. Moonlight comes through holes in the thatch when you're lying down in the room "anight"; "aday" in comes the sun, it's nice. Unacceptable. It will be accepted, and if the rainclouds thicken the illusion will be punctured. The only cottage whose thatch is in good condition is his. He's put new straw on the roof. Looking really lovely! There's that one other cottage whose thatch has new straw. And that's Karali's cottage! Yes indeed, Karali's cottage. Worthy boy! He proceeded, checking this cottage, then that. He paused abruptly, amazed, before Karali's cottage. This isn't his route. He doesn't walk this way often. He's village headman, he doesn't go to anyone's house without reason. He hasn't been back to Karali's house since their wedding.

Lordy lordy lordy! My oh my! So they've painted up the house all in colors? Hasn't the lad taken his soulmate and made up a home! The upper front of the cottage is painted with thick red ochre, and the lower part's been painted with coal tar. They've put coal tar on the door. On either side of the door they've painted two lotus flowers in red, blue, green, many colors. Very nice!

No one home. Pakhi's probably gone off to cut grass. Karali went off early in the morning to work on the Channanpur line. Nasu went off too, to work with the laborers in Channanpur. He stood and looked a long time. He felt extremely happy.

—Oo's that? Oo's waitin'? Pakhi entered the compound with a load of grass on her head. She can't see the person properly because of grass strands from the load hanging over her eyes.

—S'just me, Pakhi. Came ta see yer 'ouse, girl. Well well well! Whatta lovely palace Karali's made of it!

Pakhi threw the load down in the yard, quickly opened up the cottage, and got a square wooden stool out.—Sit, uncle.

Well well well! A stool, eh! Lordy lordy! Karali's started doin' a right gentyman's business!

From inside Pakhi brought out a new hurricane lantern, an inexpensive new rug, and a colorful palm-leaf fan. She put them before him and said—Now look, if I tell 'im no 'e don't listen; wastin' money on this trash.

Bonwari laughed out loud and said—Oh well now, s'a new weddin' o'course! Besides, when wife's caught 'is fancy, say no more. You're one o' those fanciable ones, yep—an' ye're each other's soulmate.

Hearing uncle's words, Pakhi began to laugh into her hem.

Bonwari got up and said—Well, I was comin' 'ome. Took a turn round the 'amlet on the way too, checked all the thatches. Ain't there a massive rainstorm comin'! So I comes ta your place an' stopped, had ta stop seein' such a sparkly place. I'm off now ta see—oose thatch got straw, oose thatch ain't. Lotta bother bein' 'eadman, girl.

Pakhi said—Bother if ya take on bother; if you didn't, oo would? That Atpoures' 'eadman Porom—'e take on bother? Do all this lookin' out? Oose thatch not got straw, oose 'ouse got no food—would 'e go look? Judge oose done good an' bad? You lemme set up this 'ere 'ouse, else I

woulda gone off ta Channapur with 'im. Then oo knows what woulda
been written in me destiny! Maybe woulda gone off again wi' someone
ta strange lands. Me all's due ta your kindness. Ye're a dharmic man, Ma
Lakshmi's kindness is on ya. Ya gi' incense, ya gi' lamps at Kottathakur's
shrine; if you ain't got wisdom o' dharma, then oo does? Pakhi suddenly
knelt and touched his feet.

Bonwari really liked Pakhi today. Really great girl, Pakhi. Bashan's
daughter, blood mixed with the blood of master Chaudhury, what a great
thing! His mind was filled with joy and contentment, his heart overflowed like a red earthen pitcher of Ma Kopai's chill water in the sum-
mertime. He paid obeisance to Kottathakur in his mind, saying—Babathakur, this is all your kindness. You've created a headman, it's you
who's granted such mind, such attitude. You'll puttekt Kahar house and
home from storm blasts. Bonwari's your devoted servant; at your command he's checking Kaharpara thatches. The cow pulls the plow; does it
have intelligence, or know which way to turn when it must go back? The
farmer's behind, holding the plow grip; the cow can't see him. But at a
signal from the plow grip's pressure the cow goes the right way. Bonwari's
that cow! Babathakur, Kottababa, it's you's that farmer.

And Karali's bad ways have turned around! He's quit the brick-floor
quarter of Channanpur and come back to a painted house in Kaharpara!
Converses sweetly! No, Karali's really straightened up. Look at that day he
brought the tarpaulin to the molasses works by himself. He'll somehow
have to be housetrained, made to quit Channanpur, and set to work in
the ways of Kahar kin; he must be set on the path of dharma. That won't
happen in a day. It'll have to be done "lickle by lickle," "bits by bits," just
as you'd apply force and heat to straighten out a bent piece of bamboo.
Hamlet folk have gotten angry with Karali. But it won't do for him to get
hot-headed like others! He must work with a cool head.

One of the lad's faults is his "swankery." That hair parting, those
clothes, that flashlight beam, a flute; as if some gentry fop is growing up
into a gentleman. Who'd say he was a Kahar boy! Bragging coming out his
mouth. People can't stand all this. And besides, he's done a lot more—a
lot. Seems to be going around that these days the lad's making booze with
an illegal still in Channanpur. Even bringing it to Kaharpara. Nighttime
parties where they drink this booze. Must caution him. Must discipline
him.

In Bonwari's mind there is a desire. Desire concerning Karali. He
knows, he well understands, that Kaharpara will either be destroyed or

profoundly benefited by this lad. If he inclines to the path of destruction, then all of Kaharpara will be behind him—they'll stick with him. If Karali goes that route Bonwari will not forgive him. Hence the wish to take him under his wing; he has no son. God has deprived him of a right hand. That which Providence has not given him—as a result of his own karma—Bonwari wishes to earn on this earth.

He's done good. He's remained devoted at Father's feet, prostrates himself twice daily, keeps watch over Father's shrine. In the two dark, no-moon weeks he offers lamps at evening. He judges in an informed, intelligent, and just way. He did do a small injustice giving Noyan's wife, Pakhi, to Karali; Noyan's Ma weeping—cursing him. Let her; Bonwari will do his own duty. He'll give Noyan a companion rite; he's already picked out the girl. The girl's got a bit of a spirited way about her, something of a bad name in her father's village community. So what? He's chosen such a girl thinking of Noyan's Ma's future. If Noyan never recovers then that girl can earn money and feed Noyan's Ma.

People talk without thinking. Gents talk most. They say—That's what low castes are like. Then there's moneyed people, landholders, regal castes. They're different. "A king's mother need only worry about luxuries," that's their thing. If Noyan had been one of their caste, then even if he'd died his money and land would have been left; so on the one hand Noyan's Ma would have wept, on the other hand she would have eaten. And the Kahar caste? Neither land nor money; if Noyan dies the only resource Noyan's Ma has is her body; if her body goes, it's begging. Compared to that, this bad is a good. It's not that Bonwari doesn't understand good and bad karma; he can understand the value of women's chasteness. But it's divine prescription, all the shit and spit of the clean castes above will fall onto their bodies. The Methar clears up the clean castes' excrement. Hari, Dom, Bauri, Kahar are footservants. Chandals at the cremation grounds. It's all divine prescript. If the Kahar women stayed modest, who'd soak up the gentry's evils, where would they go? Thus do the Kahar-born have to accept their karmic function.

But Pakhi was trilling away like a bird, like a dawn bird. Such praises she has heaped. Bonwari had paid his respects at Lord's feet and was thinking about Kahar life. An abrupt change in the tone of Pakhi's voice gave him a little jolt.

Lowering her voice, Pakhi said—Ya know, uncle, what that scrawny, nasty, lyin' Neem-oil Pana was sayin' the other day—Well look at 'eadman's dharma, it'll come out 'fore year's turn. Crack apart. Someone's done bad an' touched Babathakur's shrine, but Father ain't gonna fergive 'im. Didn'tcha—? Pakhi was silent.

—What? Didn't I—? What'd I do?

—Oo knows, dad! My booze distillin' from before, Kalobou from Atpoure Para—'e was tellin' different stories 'bout all these various folks; think 'e seen somethin'.

Bonwari's chest suddenly swelled with rage. The story's been heard, it's not lies then.

Pakhi said—Ya know oo made up the song fer Atpoure Para's Ghentu festival? That Pana.

—Pana?

—Yeh. Nasu-sis got no lack of pals. Some lad from that Atpoure Para band told 'im.

—Huh. Bonwari stared at the ground a minute, thinking. —Right.

Now Pakhi said—Me man's blind wi' rage. Says—I'll smash the bastard. If it ain't Pana's been creepin' and snitchin' against 'is name at the police 'ouse. Tells ow 'e's sellin' stillery booze in Channanpur, sellin' 'ailway sleepers in secret. Then there's a party wi' all the lads at our 'ouse one evenin', yeh, singin' an' dancin' all secret-like away under the awnin'; ain't it become a counsel o' robbers an' bandits. Thieves' gang's gathered.

Disaster! Bonwari was shaken. Pana, bastard Pana, homewrecker Pana, Kaharpara's evil Pana! It would be such easy work to knock Pana to the ground and crush him. Sticklike figure, birdlike nose; Pana's face is long and thin like a muskrat's. But the bastard's saying he saw something with his own eyes. Saw what?

Bonwari suddenly remembered something Pana's boss, Paku Mondol, said. Paku Mondol had said—Pana sold him a bamboo stand. Paku Mondol surely suspects that Pana's meantime cooking up some scheme. Seeing the bamboo stand, he'd thought, not one stand, two stands. He'd asked Bonwari to tell him the boundary one day. He must go to Paku Mondol. He'll go right now.

Bonwari jumped up. He rushed out of Karali's house and, in the noonday sun, went to Paku Mondol.

He stopped suddenly on the way. Damn, didn't mention the real business to Pakhi; he'd come to ask for pickaxes, but hearing about Pana's chicanery had turned his head. He'd forgotten the real business.

He sighed deeply. For every pleasure a pain when you're headman. The wooden board of the Charak ritual rests on human heads. Nails are embedded in that board, and upon it must lie the chief devotee in the Gajon festival. That's being headman. Lying on a spiked bed above human heads. O God! Pana will destroy him. Of course it is his evil, his wrong. But he's only human! Kalobou—

It was as if his head was suddenly struck by lightning—the Charak board! Next Gajon festival! He'll lie on Father Kalarudda's Charak board, atone for his evil, prove before all the extent of his good karma.

Eight

O Shiva! Oldest among ancients, greatest God among Gods—age-old Father Shiva, Father Kalaruddu! Babathakur of the Wood-Apple, God of the Kahars. His God too is Father Kalaruddu. Dhamma Ranja—Yama, King of Dharma—even his Great Father is Kalorudra.

Now, at Father Kalorudra's Gajon festival, upon the nail tips of the Charak rite's whirling, spiked board, he will earn the good karma of lying there. He must.

Father Kalaruddu—Kartathakur's overseer—Babathakur's Father. Just as sage "Larada" came forth from "Larayan," Vishnu, so did shaven-headed, ochre-wearing, clog-clad, staff-in-hand Babathakur come from Kalaruddu. Karma at Lord's wish, by Kalorudra's decree. Last time, exactly fifteen days after Gajon, Father Kalaruddu's chief devotee dropped dead. The chief devotee lies on the Charak bed's nail spikes; it's *he* who mounts Father's head with petals of flame in "cuppy," which is to say cupped, hands; *he* who dances over petals of flame. It is *he* who must make play with a dead human head. Lots of good karma himself—and no one can become Kalorudra's chief devotee without a great deal of God's benevolence. Now Bonwari will lie in the empty place of the chief devotee. He's made a firm pledge. Father Kalaruddu's chief devotee is always a person of low caste. Right from the ancient times of Ban Goshain. Auntie Suchand tells the legend of Ban Goshain. Ban Goshain was a low-caste king, but a devotee of Great God Shiva Kalaruddu. He drank liquor, he ate flesh, but he laid flowers at Father's feet and never forgot renunciation at Gajon. Practicing his renunciation, he would sit atop the fiery coals and call Father, lie upon the bed of iron spikes, cast aside gold silver diamond ruby necklaces and don a garland of human bones. Day and night he would drum his cheeks, *bom-bom*, would sing Father's name. "O Shiva—O Shiva—O Shiva!" Father's looked upon him kindly. From earthly kings and princes to gods, none was a match for Ban Goshain. Goshain had a hundred wives. One single offspring—and a girl at that; the girl's name was "Rusha," that's to say Usha. Larayan's grandson saw this same Rusha and was shaken to the core. One day Larayan's grandson secretly entered Rusha's room in Ban Goshain's house. Ban Goshain came to know and says—I'll chop up Larayan's grandson. Larayan's throne trembled, his crown slipped. Larayan said—Larada, why does my throne tremble and my crown slip, will you divine and see? Larada inscribed upon the ground, divined, and gave account. Larayan flew off, attacked Goshain's abode. The battle started there. Earth began to shake. Waters caught fire, earth's breast split and water came forth, stars in the sky came loose and fell, a cry went up, "End, end o' the world." Larayan chopped off Ban Goshain's arms and legs with his discus. Yet Goshain was not beaten, did not die; died—but lives on. Then Father Kalaruddu came. Kalaruddu and Larayan, Shiva and Vishnu; Shiva-Vishnu merged. Father Kalaruddu arranged the marriage of Larayan's grandson and Rusha. Vishnu said to Ban Goshain—I'll grant you a boon. Take a boon. I'll fix your chopped arms and legs back on, I'll make you king of the earth. Ban Goshain said—No. I don't want my chopped arms and legs. Won't become king either. If you're going to give a boon, make it that I have to be worshipped along with Kalaruddu. Without a good subject from my caste group, there won't be any devotee allowed at Father's Gajon. Shiva-Vishnu both said—So be it. And that's why Goshain has no arms and legs, just a trunk, which is to say body and head. Which means that's the reason today Ban Goshai is Kalaruddu's devotee-god. Ban Goshain's offering will happen first, yet Father will take the offering. This Father Kalaruddu's compassion is their support. Confident in this, they can come forward fearlessly to do the rites at the offering; else, how little will their good karma be?

He has to obtain Father Kalaruddu and Larayan's blessing, and the affection of Kottathakur, master of Kahar life and death. As the chief devotee this time, Bonwari will get onto the Charak bed. Bonwari decided, what happens will happen. He'll get onto the Charak bed. What evil there is will be dispelled in the good karma of this "riteual," or ritual. With the compassion of Kartathakur, with the offering-remains of Kalaruddu, if he can stand to lie on the Gajon board, the muckraker's mouth will be shut. If he cannot stand it, if he bursts and dies on the Charak board in the fires of evil, will that be his fault too? "Shame you say to him done wrong, what's the point his living on?" He is yet of incalculable worth among the mass, he's first and foremost of this hamlet; he's headman.

But Pana needs to be punished. Punishment could certainly be meted out. One day, on any pretext, Bonwari could grab him by the neck and at once thrash him from head to toe. If he grabs his neck, Prankeshto's life will slip away like a lizard through cage bars. Yet he won't do it. You have to seek out the real wrong and expose it. He found the real Keshto and went to Paku Mondol!

Tangled renown—"Bless'd Pankeshto 'as a tangled renown."

Panu's boss, Paku Mondol, is an incredibly sharp-eyed, calculating type. The web of his accounts is very tangled—even if opened, the knots tangle; that's why people have changed his actual name to Paku, Twisty. Because of his stout figure, Roton's boss's name has become "Hedo Mondol": Mammoth Mondol. But these names are given only by the Kahars. In this they have a pre-Puranic rootedness. Noticing the appearance or nature of a thing or person, they follow their own linguistic knowledge to make the most appropriate naming. Forget all that! Prankrishna is Paku Mondol's farmhand. He's farmed for seven years. Each year, from Boishakh until Ashwin, the farmhands take loans of paddy for food from the bosses. At year's end in Poush, with the paddy harvested and threshed, the accounts are balanced. Interest rate fifty percent, meaning that on a loan of eighty pounds of paddy, a hundred twenty pounds must be given. If repayment is not made within the year, it has forever been the rule that the hundred twenty pounds loan and interest become the next year's principal, with sixty pounds' interest due. Beside this, in hard times they always take loans of fertilizer from the boss. Certain people sell the bosses' fertilizer. Say to the boss—Gentry of Channanpur took it by force. That stands as credit. Interest two paisa on the rupee. Whatever. Now, settling up three years' accounts, Paku Mondol has finalized Panu's debts and squeezed him hard for repayment. So Panu has done this deed. Coughing sickie Noyan is at death's door—maybe he'll drop dead within a few days. Wife Pakhi ran off. If his eyes close for good, who'll sort out credits and debits on Noyan's behalf? So, denying his act, Panu sold that bamboo stand. Then, of course, Bonwari has surely tried to arrange Noyan's companion wedding, but it looks like that won't happen. They have no deeds and documents of sale and purchase; calling a few local men, they say aloud—"I've sold. These five witnesses were there." But Paku Mondol is a careful man. He wrote on legal paper and took Panu's thumbprint. Marked the boundaries; took the signatures of five witnesses from his own locality. He said right to Pana's face—Ye're not a straight fella, ya bastard! Bastard's face, crooked as it's scrawny. With Paku Mondol in possession of a boundary plan, Bonwari understood everything. But he didn't spill everything in front of Mondol. He's not the kind of headman to do that. First he must safeguard the hamlet folk. He'll just pick up a weapon with which to get Panu. He needs a weapon with which to slay Panu.

For all these reasons he did not tell Paku Mondol the true story but said—Yeh, there's one bamboo stand o' Pana's up there. I'll show it ya an' talk later. S'like there's a bit of a problem with this.

Paku Mondol listened and smiled, mustache spreading wide. Crafty man. Bonwari thought, it's Pana's fault for sure. But Mister Mondol also knew the situation. He heaved a deep sigh. The Mister Mondols get many such things done through them. Don't tell them.

Paku Mondol did not tell Bonwari. Panu's mouth had gone dry when he was putting his fingerprint on the deed; he'd then admitted the truth. He'd also said—Nah, let's ferget it, boss sir. Paku Mondol did not listen. He just lowered the ten-rupee price by five rupees, put Panu's thumbprint on the deed, and said—The burden of ownership's mine. You needn't worry. I won't let on. You stay calm. But now he needed to crush Pana too, so he let on to Bonwari.

Bonwari stopped in surprise coming along the path. What's that throng in Atpoure Para? Throng, what—? How his chest rose. Has Pana whipped up a fight with the Atpoures on that pretext, or what?

The sound of Porom's voice can be heard—Ei! Ei! Ei!

Who is laughing aloud? Who is laughing such a powerful, free laugh? No feeble bellows for a chest, him! Who? Now Bonwari heard the sound of his voice—Ei—Ei—Ei!

At the same time a thwacking, cracking sound. Two hard objects striking each other. It didn't take a moment for Bonwari to understand: a match is going on in Atpoure Para. Porom has set up a training ground with students. But such a powerful student—who in Atpoure Para is such a brute male? Laughing so, up against Porom with a fighting stick!

Porom laughing out loud.

A clod suddenly struck his torso. Bonwari was startled. Who? Now his chest heaved in alarm. The clod says something—Bonwari understands it. Yes, right. There's Kaloshoshi waiting inside the bamboo groves, beckoning him with her finger. Ah, this is risky! Won't quit if I warn her off? O Babathakur save me! He shook his head and signed to Kaloshoshi—no. Pointed to indicate the fightstick training ground.

Kaloshoshi smiled. Strange woman! Witch incarnate! Like a lust-formed sorceress, audacious as she's enchanting. Kaloshoshi's coming out toward him because Bonwari didn't go. Two trembling eyes. Bonwari was afraid. Kaloshoshi has probably been drinking. He has no confidence in her now. With no other option, he signed to her not to come out and moved forward himself.—What's up?

Kaloshoshi clutched his hand and said—Ain't seen you in a while!

With a deep sigh, Bonwari said—Ain'tcha 'eard Atpoure Para's Ghentu song?

—Eard it. Kaloshoshi spat. She said—E make ya scared, then? Meaning Porom.

—Scared? Bonwari laughed.—S'only one I'm scared of. Babathakur. I've gotten Babathakur's orders, sis; gotta get onto Father Kalaruddu's Charak board.

Kaloshoshi let his hand go with a shiver.—No bro, now I ain't gonna touch ya. Clapping her hand to her forehead, she paid homage to God.

Victory Babathakur, victory Kalaruddo! The evildoer's evil dissolves in your compassion, Shiva's heralds snatch the being's lifebreath from the herald of death and take it to Mount Kailash. In blindness, sight; in lameness, movement; human inclinations turn around. Kaloshoshi's sense is coming back.

Kaloshoshi said smilingly—But ye'll hafta share the good karma.

Then she said—Let Gajon be, but then we'll get crazy drunk one day. She raised her index finger as if laying fierce claim to her dues. Yes, dues for sure!

Bonwari paid mental obeisance to God. Kaloshoshi said—Oo's gone quiet then? Perhaps she knew what Bonwari was thinking. She frowned. Bonwari smiled and, to change the subject, said—I'm laughin' ta see this farce o' Porom's. Laughin' at someone 'is ripe age gettin' excited 'bout 'oldin' a fightstick. But oo's such a big man in Atpoure Para, takin' on Porom's stick an' laughin' loud?

Kaloshoshi said—Your lot's Karali.

Bonwari was shocked.—Karali?

—Yeh, Karali. Atpoures 'avin' a few days' debate, gonna bring Karali over. There was that scrap down the junction wi' two gangs o' loaders, Karali was really strong wi' the fightstick in it.

—Karali! Bonwari was amazed. And he hadn't heard about that!

—Yeh. So they're bringin' 'im in. Anyway, if they get 'im s'much easier ta do raids on the rail line; s'why they called 'im.

Bonwari was silent a moment and said—So hatchin' plans, eh? Porom's sproutin' wings then?

—E oo 'as wings that grow, no 'e never lets 'em go. Wings disappear, sprout again. Kaloshoshi smiled.

Bonwari turned and stared toward the distant training ground through the gaps in the bamboo. A thwacking sound can still be heard. But Karali, finally—? O God!

—I'm gone. People. Hearing these softly spoken words, Bonwari turned to see Kaloshohi stealthily moving off through the dense woods. Bonwari called—One thing. Which gang's Karali joined? Ya know?

Kaloshoshi paused. Thought a little and said—Don't know that. Ain't yet decided ta join a gang. But bait's been laid. If bait's taken, the blow'll be struck. I know what the plans are!

Kalobou moved off. Bonwari stood in silence. The snake charmer knows the snake's sneeze. Kalobou knows Porom well. O God, now Police Inspector will come to Kaharpara. He'll yell—Hey Karali Kahar! Chief Constable will yell—Karaliya! Hey, cur!

No no no. Bonwari cannot let that happen. As long as he lives, in the time of his headmanship, he'll never allow anyone's "bod," or body, to get a mark like that. Each mark of hate is a mark of sad suffering. At Charak people really mark them down as thieves! Though he thought this, Bonwari trembled. Bonwari is not alone. All the elders of this hamlet will tremble.

When Bonwari thinks about that mark in the tale of Kaharpara, he shivers. Recollection of a monsoon tale, black new moon "nightstime," sky splitting pounding on earth, Kopai's water coursing the Hansuli turns, there love's 'eat grips and burns; those days its glow awoke in Kahar eyes. A jackal would call from a far field. The Kahars would come sneaking out. Head wraps bound, faces smeared with blacklime, clubs in hand, they'd come out.

O Babathakur, "puttekt."

Bonwari, Prohlad, Roton, Gupi—in childhood each one of them saw a little of all this. Suchand saw with her own eyes, still tells the story with widened eyes and heavy voice. —When the Kopai drowned in the "desaster" flood, the land was a funeral pyre! Factory gone! Saheb gents gone. Kaharpara orphaned. Boss gone; nay, dad gone. Ye better not think about yer stomach; if sixteen Kahars turned up at the factory office a mornin', they got laid off. One by one the sixteen Kahars went away. That time Kaharpara was forty, fifty farmhands. Great broad shoulders like this, like oxen. Factory gone, 'ouses smashed down in flood, plague struck, then folk took what they could—ran off ta this village, that village. Some died in their villages, some died in other villages, some died on the road, rotted and blew up round like a drum—didn't even get goin'. Then everyone came back ta villages again. Came back an' saw wanderin' beggars! Chaudhurys snatched up the service land. Outa mercy, just gave a bit fer buildin' on. Kahars got up in the mornin' an' went ta do "beisance" fer Chaudhury 'ouse's Ma Durga an' that Kotta. If them gods 'adn't appeared in a dream then Sire Chaudury wouldn't've even given that much. Then t'was 'unger. Sire Chaudhury says ta go do farmin', do shepherdin'. Sadgop masters won't take on no Kahars. In the saheb masters' days Kahars'd plant "lindijoe," or indigo, by force on Sadgop masters' land. Sides that, what's the Kahars know about farmin'? S'true, Kahars din't know "farm-work" well at all. Yet at Sire Chaudhury's word, boys an' lads was kept on as "herduns" an' "skinkers"; that's cowherds and servants. Great strong young men became wretched. In Atpoure Para was a robbers' gang then. With the midnight jackal call they'd come creepin' out, thievin' an' pinchin' from this village, that village. Cos of stomach pangs at first, o' course, an' 'cos of bad ways too—Kahars went down that road.

In the night blackness the Kahars had to look even blacker; voices would sound like animals, two eyes would burn like coals. They'd silent-ly sneak to a respectable home, drill through the walls, smash the door locks; gold and trinkets, rice and paddy, pots and dishes, clothes and fab-rics, they took what they found. Got up in the morning with pounding chests; on the far side, names would be written down in Death King's ledger of dharma. On this side, police would come and search cottages. Even went through the women's clothes. Abused men's mothers and sis-ters, applied fists, slap, stick in the police lockup in town.

That story's happening even today in Atpoure Para. But they have no shame. That shameless group of Atpoures! The Kahars got out of it with great difficulty. Suchand speaks—

One generation passed in two generations everyone was marked criminal. Then Kahars set their minds to farmin'; still did the thievin' an' pinchin', but not like before. But what'll become o' the risks o' bein' marked criminal? If there was thievin', police came ta Kaharpara, grabbed, an' carted off—took when there was crime an' took when there wasn't crime too. Sometimes the whole clan got dragged inta prosecutions. Then me elder bro—that Bonwari's dad—real honest man o' the village, got put-tekshun of the Ghosh 'ouse—Ghosh masters made a lotta requests an' got our name taken outa the police station record book. Then bro said—Ev-eryone promise, none'll steal. Noyan's dad—young 'un, was one o' master Chaudhury 'ouse's folks, 'e didn't agree. The Broke-Ome lot got putteks-hun from police 'ands through Master Chaudhury's mercy. Then village became two groups. One group listened to my bro. One group took off laughin'. Then after Noyan's father died young, me bro became 'eadman. Wi' yoouge effort bro cleared Kaharpara's criminal name. Still a few of 'em didn't obey, didn't listen; this Gupi's bro Kelo always did thievin'. No gang in the village, so 'e'd go thievin' wi' the Doms. No matter 'ow many beatins Bonwari gave, Kalachand didn't listen. Got taken away by police. E'd go laughin', sayin'—Fix me bod, back in a few days. When 'e'd come

back from jail 'e'd be "lumpygirth," or big and fleshy. With this final statement Suchand laughs.

Suchand is sometimes regretful. Wiping her eyes with the corner of
her hem, she says—Ah! What times they were, 'ow it was! All real men.
These great chests, this darin'—got the women wearin' golden necklaces,
wearin' shiny cloth a' night. Din't matter if t'were nightdark, still got 'em
wearin'. Men today; no, jackals an' dogs.

Talk, let Suchand say what she says. Let the crazies among the Kahars
talk their talk in secret. Bonwari won't let that evil come into the hamlet
again. Today he saw a threat in Karali. The lad Karali's body's "efty," he's
got guts and he can use his head. There's the fear. As if you got a bunch
of young lads crazy drunk and they wouldn't end up doing something
bad! "On the road of dharma's right, you'll have rice many a night." If he
who stays on the road of dharma fasts in the day, then dharma itself will
supply him with food for many nights. Bonwari will speak to Karali, give
him good counsel.

His mood became more venomous as he returned home. Pakhi laughing, tee-hee-hee-hee, practically rolling on the floor. What is this laughing? Is so much laughing good in a young woman? Pakhi's laughter did
not lessen when she saw Bonwari. If it had been anyone else she would
at least have hidden her face in her hem. Women laughing so toothily in
front of a man? And not just any man—a man like Bonwari is a respected
person. Only Pakhi could be doing this. She with the "eat" for young
master Karali who became his married wife! Pakhi's vanity has swollen
with Karali's. Kaharpara's young women and wives are an uncontrollable
Kopai flood if they get crazy; but they're normally water in the indigo
levee, calm and peaceful.

—What? Bonwari said with gravity. —What's up? What's all this yam-
merin' laughin'?

Pulling her headcover up to her forehead, Gopalibala said with a faint
smile—Those "mockerings" Pakhi can do.

"Mockerings," meaning jeering imitations of people; Pakhi had been
doing mockerings of the rail company sahebs' wives. In a high voice she's
caught English speech perfectly—Good-mooning-bood-tingtong; by using
the "-ong" she's getting a fluent pronunciation of the consonants. She's
been impersonating the way the station master's dangling gut moves.
And she's been laughing a lot more than Gopalibala. Bonwari was just
about to utter some harsh words when he suddenly noticed—four new

pickaxes on his terrace, painted shiny red as if some machine has coated them with oily vermilion. These pickaxes belong to the rail company and are brand new. Karali has brought so many pickaxes from the junction; and it must be Pakhi, who came laughing at this strange hour, Pakhi herself who brought them from Karali's home to his. The harsh words of rebuke got stuck in Bonwari's throat. He went silently to the terrace and tried out the pickaxes. Excellent things. Saheb Company's devices. He isn't what the sahebs are: white color, tawny eyes, what can't they do? Machines go rumbling along the line. Airplanes tear through teeming skies. War's breaking out. Many airplanes arriving, even to this place. Bonwari's seen three airplanes.

Pakhi said—E 'eard from someone ye needed pickaxes. So says ta me, go, get 'em right now. So I brung 'em.

Blessing glowed spontaneously from Bonwari's face.—Live long, girl, live long. Ah, what a gift this is! He took up a pickaxe and tried it. Then said—Karali's shown many a thing. Real champ!

—Today's gear, uncle—today's gear! No place ta keep 'em—'e's piled 'em up. If ye forbid 'e don' listen.

—Gave pickaxes ta Porom, then?

—Oo? Ta uncle Porom? Nah. I didn't see 'im wi' me own eyes. Now look, 'e comes around at a bad time, grabs an' goes off—We'll play stickfight! Went off leapin' an' dancin'. Karali says—Let's go. Wi' me there Kaharpara's not gonna lose face to the Atpoures.

Bonwari was rather pleased at what Karali had said—he sure said what should be said! But he's a kid, can't understand crooked schemes. O Father, it's the way of the world to bait a trap with food. Karali has to be warned. He said—S'good. Did good ta go today—don't lettim go again. After all, Porom's marked criminal. S'not good ta do stickfight wi' 'im, girl. Unnerstood?

With wide eyes Pakhi said—Didn't think o' that, uncle. Whatcha said's right. I'll go, right now, I'll go.

—No. E'll come right now, come a bit later, then tell 'im no. And— with a pause he gravely said—Send 'im to the evenin' meetin'. I'll explain.

Suddenly he remembered about the fight at the junction. Bonwari turned and said with interest to Pakhi—Did Karali get inta some kinda fight at the junction, Pakhi?

—O Lord! Ya don't know? Indu loaders one side, Muchlims the other. One o' the Muchlim loaders dragged an Indu workwoman off. That was the argument. Then beatin' on each other. Speed of a floodrush—'e went takin' a stick. Gave a good thrashin'.

Bonwari was not surprised, he was frozen. Kahars are not less tough than Muslims, but until now they've respected the Muslims as equals. Muslims have gone off with a few Kahar women too, but no one's dared kick up a fuss about it. They're "Shaikhs," "Pathans." If the lad had only been Bonwari's son! Bonwari heaved a deep sigh.

Karali came to the evening meeting.

Bonwari explained to him. Today the youths were all around; where were they when Karali came? Everybody listened to Bonwari's words in silence.

Quiet meeting in the usual, slow life of Hansuli Turn. Everyone has drunk some liquor, but a moderate amount. The amount that, after a whole day's toil, will bring a good night's sleep, will ensure that limbs and bodies do not ache in the morning. The meeting sits up above the banks of the indigo levee, beneath the six-layered banyan tree. This is the usual spot. The meeting has sat here since those first days. With the crumbling of the indigo works the Kahars brought up a few blocks of broken brick-work that, for the longest time, have served as seats. On those blocks sit the elders. On the block exactly in the middle at the base of the tree sits headman. Bonwari sits on that block wagging his finger in a lecturing gesture; he slowly says—Blessed son, faithful Karali, 'ave y'understood what I'm sayin' to ya?

—To me? Karali was stunned. Hadn't he complied with Bonwari this very day! An inner urge to establish an amity with him is starting to grow. Bonwari's accepting him, treating him with a degree of esteem—this he can understand. Pana, Pehlad, and Roton there may be, but he's held in greater esteem than them all—this is being shown by Bonwari's behavior. He too is inwardly rather coming to love Bonwari as a fatherly figure. That's why, on his own account, he carried the tarpaulin on his shoulders and brought it to the molasses workshop that day. As soon as he got the news today, he loaded four pickaxes onto Pakhi's shoulders and delivered them. Getting a talking-to after doing all this! He frowned and said—Speak. He sat down at the front. He made a silent resolution—if Bonwari's words are unjust he'll give a harsh reply.

Bonwari said the words he had thought about earlier. Said—Blessed son, if ya stay on the road of dharma's right then many nights—I mean, fer example—at second, third watch o' night, Babathakur'll bring food 'isself an' 'e'll say—Take, son, ya didn't collect any food on dharma's road today; take, eat!

The words are good. All the elders of Kaharpara were moved with spiritual accord; someone said—O Lord, O Lord. Someone said—O Shiva. Someone said—In this world, it's death that is truth. Clapping their hands to their foreheads, they paid obeisance to God. But it made Karali laugh. Not because he believed in some opposite truth; it was seeing the way they said those things that made him laugh. He's been to meetings in Channanpur. How the gentry deliver their tirades! Ouch, how your "bod" smarts from hearing that. But he suppressed his laughter, and with just a little smile said—What ya sayin's right, s'a good point too.

Bonwari looked toward the elders and said—Whatcha say, 'eadmen? Is my argument just or unjust? Say what? It's not good the youth makin' a separate gatherin'.

Roton's son Mathla is a central member of Karali's group and doesn't listen to Roton, but Roton can't stop worrying about him; Roton immediately spoke up—What else ta say, Bonwari? Are you someone oo speaks unjustly?

Prohlad was smoking tobacco. With great indifference he said—Take, smoke. Handing the pipe to Bonwari, he answered the main question— Yeh, ya said right. Let's see what the youth are sayin'.

—All right, everyone, whatcha say? Give all that up. Do gatherins all in one place. Or what?

All the other elders are with Prohlad. They just can't understand the need for so much impassioned discussion. If the youths' group meets separately, plays music and songs, talks of "lusty-heat," drinks a little booze—why so much fuss about that? Bonwari has daubed devotional marks on his forehead. And yet they said—S'a very good point. Oo could say it's unjust?

Now Bonwari got up and said—So, ya gotta listen ta this, Karali. I'll 'ave a word wi' ya in private.

—In private? All right, come on. I'm listenin'.

Drawing aside some way, Bonwari said—Goin' to Atopure Para ta play stickfight on Porom's practice ground, it's no good, son!

—Why?

—E's marked criminal, a bandit, son. Right folks stay wi' right, thieves wi' thieves, whores wi' whores. That's why Kaharpara don't mix wi' Atpoures. Understood?

Karali said—Porom was mockin'. That's why I went—said, now see a man o' Kaharpara.

Bonwari said—That, son, that's the way a seasoned bandit draws a young lad into 'is gang! Unnerstood? First, just stickfights, fun an' jokes, booze an' meat; then the mantra in yer ear'ole. Go wi' 'em once, never letcha go. Dharma's got seven twists, evil has fifty-seven, unnerstood? Can't get out of 'em, can't shake 'em off. If ya say y'ain't goin' in the gang, 'e'll reveal 'isself.

Karali stared at him with startled eyes. He really had not thought of this. Yet what Uncle Bonwari's saying is just right. After a few moments he ungrudgingly declared—I din't think of all this stuff, uncle.

—Well! Don't know 'im! Come along, don't go again. Don't 'ang out there. Taking Karali's arm, he returned to the meeting.

Back at the meeting Nasubala, with arms and legs shaking and body rocking, had "kricked up," that's to say kicked up, a fuss. The reason for this was skinny Neem-oil Prankrishna. As soon as Bonwari took Karali away, he took on Bonwari's role as if by habit and started playing headman. With chieftainly tone and poise, he said—There are no better words to express what Uncle Bonwari's saying. The antics of the youth are no good. Ya know that some are givin' up the clan karma an' pridefully gettin' way above themselves. Ain't it?

Each of his words an invisible arrow fired at Karali. There was nothing left for anyone to figure out.

Nasubala was sat avoiding contact with the men. Now he got up and approached, wagging his finger in Panu's face, swinging his body, and said—Ooh, I'm dyin', I slurp up yer insults wi' molasses! O my "ancient evil oldie"! E's sayin'—We youths! Tell ya, your schemin's real good! Oh yeah, mangy-face dried-up vulture, what've we done? Gonna say? I'm listenin'. My 'eadman's number two! Fawnin' jackal—pipsqueak!

Karali came up, took Nasu's hand, and drew him aside, saying—Shut-tup, you. Sit. Then he went right into that meeting and, before all, touched his hands to Bonwari's feet and said—I'm sayin' this wi' me 'ands on yer feet, I won't ever do like that.

Bonwari had not imagined such a thing, and nor could he think of the right response to offer. He softened with affection for Karali.

The crowd applauded Karali—Bravo-bravo-bravo!

—Oh yes, son. Move on the road, avoid the nonroad, the bad road, the ditch, an' the swamp.

But Panu got up and said—Well, ya can touch feet an' talk! But what about liquor brewin'? That's not illegal?

Now Karali gave him a sharp slap on the cheek. Panu is a person of weak character; with a slap from Karali he said, "Well," and sat down. Karali said—Can ya show 'em, bastard? Can ya prove it?

Bonwari was pleased. Very pleased. But the next moment he yelled—Karali, ye've done wrong.

—Me?

—Yeh. Siddown.

—All right, I'm sittin'. Needs a rulin', this. You allowed me ta set up my 'ome, I obey you. Obey you 'undred, thousand times over. Ye're a dharmic man, ye're 'eadman, I can listen ta what ye say. So I gotta listen ta that scrawny weasel?

—Siddown, siddown.

Everyone sat. Only Prankrishna did not sit. He marched out of the meeting. Even though Bonwari has disciplined Karali, he can well perceive—the measure of affection for Karali is greater. Not only that, he understands quite well that Bonwari's now going to destroy him. He'd noticed more than one of Bonwari's cruel, sidelong glances his way. He doesn't quite understand why, but—he's been insulted too. He left.

—Are y'off then, Pana? asked Mathla.

Pana did not reply.

—What's wi' 'im not answerin'?

Now Pana said—Pankeshto don't answer to the flea on a rat's back.

Words to make Karali leap up, and he leaped up and there would have been a scene, but before that Bonwari yelled—*Pankeshto*! in a severe tone.

Prankrishna's response was heard from near the neem tree in his own yard. He cried—Saintly man, worships under Atpoure Para's banyan tree of an evenin'. Thought to meself—Don't, won't say, honn'able fella—but he could't finish the statement. He was paralyzed with fear; Bonwari had come and was gripping his arms.

Pana fell prostrate to the ground. —I'm not goin'. I ain't got no support from you caste kin. Preachin' dharma to a weaklin'! I don't obey no one.

Bonwari grabbed his shoulders and pulled him upright. Then pushed him to the meeting. Upright again, Panu didn't have the chance to fall back down. Bonwari shoved Panu right into the middle of the meeting and said—Why'dja say that Loyan's bamboo grove was yours an' sell it ta Paku Morol?

Panu's sharp yelps ceased in a flash.

—Speak! Speak in the meetin'!

Now Panu stared at Bonwari in confusion and said—Heeyoo said? In other words, who said?

—Yer boss 'isself, Paku Morol, told me. Read out the boundary deed—East of Hedo Mondol's bamboo stand purchased on Oton's behalf; south of Bonwari's—i.e., my, bamboo stand to the north of the Kopai levee; west of the rain tree and the Ghoshes' bamboo stand purchased on behalf of Gupi. Therein, I, Neem-oil Pankeshto Kahar have sold at the price of eight rupees one large bamboo stand of fifty stalks, planted by myself.

Panu got right up and said—Yeh, I sold that. It was me own bamboo stand, though. Sown it wi' me own 'ands.

—Yeah, yeah—sown! Don't say "no," me. East o' my bamboo grove's a bamboo stand sown by Loyan's dad. East o' that in the empty ground middle o' Master Ghoshes' bamboo stand ya sowed a stand o' bamboo couple years back. Ain't even eight bamboos grown up there yet. Ya sowed up next ta Loyan's stand, that's 'ow ye could easily sell the 'ole stand o' fifty bamboos ta yer boss. Tell, why'dja sell others' fortune sayin' it was yer own?

The meeting exploded into uproar.

—Wrong, youuge wrong, oh Lord! They all cried out in one voice.

Nasubala mockingly put his hand to his cheek—Ooh deary my! Saying this, he stared fixedly in shocked surprise for a moment, then shook his head and said—Dark Infernal Age, Ma! Sellin' Rama's wealth ta Krishna!

Panu spoke contritely—What am I gonna do? It's Boss told me ta write that down!

—Told! Karali spoke up—Wouldja write down Channanpur gentry's brick mansions if 'e told ya?

Bonwari said—Karali, shut up.

Panu began to weep. His tears started as soon as Bonwari told Karali to shut up.

Bonwari said—No snivelin', got it, no snivelin'. That won't fool anyone.

Panu said—Y'all listen ta me explanation wi' fergiveness—or am I gettin' washed away in the flood? S'me fault, I'm ready ta take punishment.

Bonwari sat down on his rock and said—Speak, whatcha sayin'?

Panu's explanation is nothing new; no logical reasoning for the fors and againsts of his wrong, a chronicle of his own terrible ill luck and the heartrending cruelty of his master. This is the ready cunning of Panu's cowardly, twisted mind. Panu said—Boss is killin' me; you lot make the counterpesscription. "Get beaten up, gotta take it." Boss grabbed me an' made me write it—what'm I s'posed ta do? Master, din't reckon accounts fer three years, this year does accounts an' says—Yer owin' twenty-five rupees. Give it. I say—Year after year you ain't done the accounts—'ow am I s'posed ta get such a big amount straightaway after yer not doin' 'em? E says—Ow do I know? Do you bastards earn nothin'? You bastards takin' paddy from the fields. Geddit from yer 'ouse an' pay back. What ta do, master; I says—There's a public cowpath goes by me land which I've cut into t'expand me land a little, that bit's mine now—'e said 'e'll gimme ten rupees fer that, take that an' take one bamboo stand, take that an' let me off. Ow 'e abused me! Panu started to weep grievously.

Panu is smart, undoubtedly intelligent. In a moment, the mood of the meeting has turned around. Everyone shares more or less the same story as the one Panu has told. Even a well-off headman such as Bonwari shares it. With the Sadgop bosses there is usually no accounting. At the Ghosh house this time, Bonwari couldn't get an account reckoned up either. After two, three years the account comes; in most cases the farmworkers are in debt. The bosses don't make out unfair accounts, of course. You cannot speak of injustice, it would be a wrong to do so. Being in debt; half the year—from Boishakh to Ashwin—you borrow from the bosses so as to eat; the other six months, take from them the same way. When boss's dues aren't paid, something is taken from the one-third share of the harvest due to the farmworker; there's no interest on this—it must be said that it's out of sympathy that the bosses do not take it. Then wheat, chickpeas, molasses, potatoes, mustard, linseed—boss doesn't take a cut from these shares. There is therefore no doubt that there are debts not paid off. Yet if accounts were made from year to year, paying off would be easy. If boss sits down to do accounts at the end of two, three years, your chest constricts with fear. On the bright side, when Mother Kopai's sandbank has really been eaten away and there's no lack of bamboo stubble, which means sprouting bamboo stumps, then every year the Kahars plant a few bamboo stands and a few banyan and fig shoots. The bosses take the trees and bamboo stands and forgive the debts. Say there's a little bit of common wasteland beside every boss' land—be it fallow upland, marsh, drainage ditch, or cowpath—they'll cut into it or fill it in, make a ridgepath and farm it with boss's land. The bosses take these too, and forgive debts.

Everyone remained silent, unable to find a response to Panu's statement. Some sighed deeply. Even Bonwari heaved a deep sigh. Bonwari too has broken up the odd ditch like this and turned it into farmland. The Ghoshes haven't made out his accounts for a few years either.

Only Karali sat tapping his feet. He's not one worried about these things, works in Chandanpur, earns cash; he declared—Blow off this farmin'.

Bonwari said—Oi, Karali!

Karali said—Do the counterpesscription, though. What Pana's sayin' isn't lies.

—Speak, Karali-bro, speak.

Nobody had to say anything. Meanwhile, the women have started talking. The meeting's wave had gone home and crashed down. An utterly modern politics blowing up in the fight.

Mutual enemies Noyan's Ma and Karali's Nasu-sis had united in a fight with Prankeshto's wife. Noyan's Ma is raining fire down.

Panu's wife is rocking back and forth insulting Nasu—Ooh childkiller bitch, black widow, barren slut—burn yer face off, I will—. It's forgotten that Nasubala is no one's daughter; he's a man, has no husband, no son.

Now Nasubala's hopping and hurling abuse—I'll dance this coupla bastards buried under a ditch. Yer old man'll die—not sickness, not accident, 'e'll die palpitatin', I'll dance Shiva's killin' dance.

An aggravated Bonwari said to Roton and Prohlad—Off ye go then lads, grab the women by the scruffs of their necks an' send 'em 'ome.

This is the way Kahars close women's fights down if they become unbearable. If they don't obey, it's a beating.

In order further to win over the mind of the whole meeting, Panu said—Gi' a good 'ard thumpin', geddit uncle Prohlad; I'm sayin'—gi' that wife o' mine a good slappin' too.

Karali got straight up, pulled Nasubala away, and went to shut him up in the house.

***

The women's fight ended. Everyone returned to the meeting and sat down again. Bonwari staring steadily at Pana. Pana raising, then lowering, his eyes. He noticed that Bonwari's gaze did not once stray from his direction. He's smart, understands all. Now, pulling on his ear, he's saying—This, this, an' if I—. Then a few tears fall. A smile is playing at the edge of Bonwari's lips.

—Eadman! Pana pleaded with folded hands.

—Ye gonna do that kinda thing again? Bonwari knows that Pana understands the real meaning of the thing.

—I've pulled me ear ten times. Pullin' again.

—All right, go. I'm sortin' it out. I'll find Mondol. I'll say there's been a mistake—ye did it on purpose through Pana. If not, I'll 'ave Loyan's bamboo stand written down in the name o' me boss from Loyan. Then it'll be bull fightin' bull.

Prohlad said—All right, that'll work, y'know Beano-bro, all right! Ghosh'll soon unravel Mondol's twists an' tear through 'em. Ha ha, man, Ghosh is a Bhagalpur bull.

Everyone had a good laugh.

—But what about the accounts? asked Roton. He has been caught in the binds of such an unpaid account with Hedo Mondol. Hedo does not leave off with mere words, he rains down blows.

—Be sorted. Account'll be sorted. Come, we'll all go together one day.

—Tomorrow we'll all go, said Roton.

—Tomorrow won't work, bro. Tomorrow's the day ta wear the Gajon scarf.

—That's fer the one up on the Gajon bed.

—I'll get up this time. Bonwari spoke.

—You?

—Yeh.

—No, no. Won't do, Bonwari. Could do 'arm. Won't do.

—Uh uh. Babathakur's given the order; no way out.

—Babathakur! The assembly shuddered with astonishment.

Bonwari said—Come tomorrow at dawn, soon as yer dreams stop an' the birds start singin'.

Dawn dreams are unfailingly vivid. They all folded their hands and paid obeisance to God.

—On toppa that, continued Bonwari—with all our mistakes we've turned what Babathakur gets to ash. The bad's gotta be undone, so I made a vow ta get up at Charak. Suddenly smiling, he said—I'm gettin' on a bit now. Else I'll burst an' die!

***

At dawn Bonwari went and immersed himself in the Kopai's waters. Ganges—Ganges—Ganges. Tomorrow he'll go to Katoya to bathe in the Ganges and bring some Ganges water back to anoint Kalorudra's head. He'll go by train. He'll come back striding the road for twenty miles with a load on his shoulders, calling, "O Shiva, O Shiva" with joy in his soul. How little twenty miles is for Bonwari of the Kosh-Shoulders!

Drums playing at Kalaruddu's shrine; from today, daylong festivities have begun.

Dadang dadang—dang—dara dang—dadang—
Br-rr-rr—dadang

Bonwari will whirl on the Charak bed spiked with iron nails. Will look to the sky and call—O Shiva, O Shiva, O Shiva!

If it kills him it kills him; no regrets.

He has risen to being God for Kaharpara today. All are sprinkling purifying cow-dung water where he walks.

Pakhi came and said—Ya need Ganges water? E's gone ta Sudhi.

—Oo? Karali?

Pakhi smiled.

—I'm goin' ta Katoya mesself. Goin' by train. Comin' back on foot.

—But don't buy a ticket on the train. E'll fix it for ya.

Part

One

Dadang-dang—dada-dang—dadang. Drarrrrrrrr—dada-dang. Drarr—
dadang—drarr—dadang.

On the backs of great drums, crow, kite, heron feather decorations;
yaktail plumes on rounded handle ends dance up and down with the
beat. Gongs play, horns play, sweet incense smoke floats at Babathakur's
shrine; devotees dance in the "jutebit," that's to say the jute yard, cane
sticks in hand, "scarfies," or scarves, on their necks, wearing ochre wraps,
rouge marks on foreheads, Ganges-mud "marksigns," unoiled hair, faces
drawn with fasting, yet dancing wildly the glory of Father. Hari, Dom,
Bauri, Kahar: whoever wishes can take part as Father's devotee. This time,
the head devotee is Bonwari. That's the foremost devotee. So all Kaharpara's wearing the Gajon "scarfie." O Shiva, O Shiva! Victory Shiva—Kalaruddu—! *Bom bom bom! Bom bom bom*! Drums beat—*dada-dang—*
dada-dang-dang!

Bonwari, head devotee, is lying on the nailstudded Charak bed.
Charak moving upon "ends," which means bamboo rods, on the shoulders of sixteen devotees—whirling around-around around-around
around-around!

The last day of Chaitra is over. Last night of the year. "Fustlight,"
that's to say first light, has come; Kalaruddu's devotees danced all night.
O Shiva, O Kalaruddu, *bom bom bom—bom bobom bom bobom bom*.
The Charak board has been whirled, round and round, like a turning
"wheelie"—meaning a wheel. In the forests and bamboo jungles of Hansuli Turn, the ancient darkness jumped up "started," that's to say startled.
Worms, bugs, beasts, birds sounded the alarm. Snakes in their holes
coiled and raised their hoods. Animal bodies trembled. They knew too—
the year has ended. They too paid obeisance—O Shiva, O Kalaruddu!

First day of the year, Gajon is over. Shiva has gone to his watery repose
under the Kali Deeps; he'll spend the whole year there, will rise again at
year's end, at Gajon, one month before on next Chaitra's auspicious day;
the first, that is. He'll say—O Sun, O Moon, I have risen—end the year.
Shiva's going to his watery repose. That very procession is moving—from
the forest Kalaruddu shrine through Bansbadi's Kaharpara to Hansuli

Turn's Kali Deeps. Drums, gongs, horns, instruments leading the way; then masqueraders. The masqueraders are—Father's gang of ghosts and spirits, demons and monsters. Humans dressing as Nandi, Bhringi, "Tijot," "Dontobokko"—and how many other spirits whose names nobody knows! They who are dressing up don't even know. This time most of the masqueraders are Kaharpara people. And why not; this time it's Bonwari, Kaharpara headman, who is head devotee. The devotees' group moving behind the masqueraders' group. Moving in dancing lines—making their cane sticks dance the beat above their heads, feet falling in time. Behind them, the Charak disc. Turning around-around. Bonwari lies upon the Charak disc's spiked nails, facing the sky. Behind him, Ban Goshain; behind him, Father's litter, that is, a four-person litter—actually a small cradle. Incense and guggul resin burn beside the cradle. And the Sadgop masters are in attendance too. Even ancient Chaudhury had to come out today. Hedo Mondol, Paku Mondol, Naku Pal, even Maito Ghosh has gone along.

How could you *not* go! First God among gods—Kalaruddu! Whether day or night, month or year, origin or end—he is Master of All. O Shiva! O Shiva! Lying on the Charak bed, Bonwari calls these things to mind and pays obeisance to Father. Take my life, Father, preserve honor; punish me, but give succor to the Kahars—O Shiva, let me be born into a higher caste in the coming life. Babathakur's your disciple, Father, I've offered to him too, lain down on the iron spikes of your Charak disc; I make supplication at your feet, Father, tell him to look favorably, tell your disciple—the "slayin" of his familiar, that's to say the crime of burning that chain viper, if he could just forgive, if only misfortune would not come to Hansuli Turn. Fill fields with paddy, save us from storm blast, forbid that minx Kopai from raging up with floods.

What great splendor at Kaharpara today!

Bonwari is chief devotee this time; he's climbed onto the Charak disc—now, on the way to the Kali Deeps, the litter and the Charak disc will descend to Kaharpara. It's descending a second time. Once it came down a long time ago, in indigo plantation days—then the Kahar headman was Gondar Kahar. Because of his immense, "youuge" figure, he was given the name by Chaudhury, rent collector for the indigo plantation— Gondar Kahar, Rhino Kahar. Gondar Kahar had no descendants. It was Gondar who got on the Charak disc back then. Babathakur put an end to his line because he got up on the disc after drinking liquor. It was then that Kalaruddu's litter had come down into Kaharpara. It had been so splendid then. Saheb masters made lots of "gratooties." Really splendid this time too. It's now the second time Father's litter will come down to Kaharpara.

The litter will come down to where that meeting sits, right there. The place has been cleansed by swabbing it with cowdung water, a platform has been set up, Kaharpara is completely spick and span. Black, tainted pots have been put away; ducks and chickens are today shut indoors; children have been cautioned; wives, daughters, housewives young and old are all waiting wearing fresh clothes, bathed, hair loose, with folded hands. Father will come.

Karali is going around hollering and cheering.

Bonwari has mounted the Charak. Karali circles the hamlet like a pinwheel. It's he who has decked out the whole hamlet, yes, really decked it out, decked it out, wowee. Kahars have no other language for expressing praise than this. In a single voice everyone is saying—Oh yeah lad, champion lad! There's no lack of bamboo in Bansbadi, no lack of vegetation; Karali took his gang and made four bamboo-leaf gates. At four corners of the meeting place they planted posts and hung that tarpaulin from the shorn tops; he bought colored paper with his own money and made a pile of chainlike wreaths from it. He wound them together and strung them diagonally from post to post; put up red, blue, green, white colors. Bought cigarettes from Channanpur in honor of the Sadgop masters. What more can you do for honor's sake! They wouldn't consume anything else that had been touched by a Kahar—not even betel chews. He's still going around, puffing on a cigarette. Pakhi is circulating restlessly; she's wearing a fantastically splendid striped sari. Wives and daughters are gazing at her and Karali. Pakhi's aware of it all. Smiling.

Bonwari's wife, Gopalibala, is waiting with folded hands before the dais at the meeting place. Occasionally waving her incense burner. A tranquil, good person, quietly waiting. Suchand sitting beside her. With great round eyes she's loudly telling a story—telling the story of Gajon. She tells the Gajon story every time; is telling it now. If she has to sit quietly and not tell the story, Suchand thinks she's become a miserable vagabond, that people are neglecting her. So, if people listen or not, she tells the story. She says—You, listen an' keep it; if ye get ta be an old woman ye'll tell it. Gajon's always there; story hasn't been. It happens, I tell it so it's there, if I don' tell it, won't be there.

Pakhi says—But whatcha said, weren't no creation then. No moon, no sun, no world, no people, no animals, no birds—

—Oh yes, yes. There was nothin', nothin' at all. Nothin'—not a thing. Then, in order to drive home the momentousness and extent of there being nothing, she stretched out her words—Not a thi-i-i-i-i-ng, and waved her arms as she spoke.

—Not a thi-i-i-i-i-ng?

—Not a thi-i-i-i-i-ng. Da-a-arkne-e-e-s-s-s, glo-o-o-om, deep an' dreadful. Her eyes bulged. Body hair bristled, her voice became deep and sinister; she said—Only Kalaruddu's Charak whirled in darkness, around-around, around-around, around-around. So saying, she held up her hands. She froze in this gesture, as if making visible the ancient time. She made her fingers' gesture extend to the ancient time of creation.

They don't have the power to count or measure with accuracy how long it's been from the ancient time to now; perhaps they don't need to; but in the stunned indifference of powerless minds, the vague shadow of a conjecture is rising in their hearts. So, relying on Father Kalaruddu, they're waiting to greet him with folded hands.

Karali came running—They're 'ere, they're 'ere.

Father descended on the edge of Kaharpara's indigo levee, to the newly consecrated earthen dais set up at the headmen's meeting place.

Suchand drew Pakhi and Karali to her and said—Pay 'beisance, pay 'beisance.

Lying on the plank, Bonwari smiled faintly. Auntie's all right. You belong to the folks you're tethered beside. Auntie's made up with Karali and Pakhi; now, besides them, there's no one else Auntie knows.

***

On this day, the first of Gajon, Suchand has made up with Karali and Pakhi. Bonwari mused upon these things as he lay upon the Charak plank.

That day Suchand's weeping had begun right in the morning. Weeping for Father's familiar. Gajon's on the way, Father's familiar has come to mind. Bonwari couldn't say anything even though he was annoyed. He was lying down fasting—he really didn't like to be scolding the old woman; let her cry. No one dies of crying in misery.

Old woman of ancient times, she. Like the old woman in the tale, it's "I'll weep I'll weep decides my mind; but weeping will not respite find"; which is to say that the soul is not satisfied. They weep if there's a reason and if there's no reason.

Suddenly the old woman stopped weeping for the familiar and began weeping for her father. Began an elaborate weeping—Oh father, make me be wi' you! Where ye gone to! Where'm I gonna go! Ah, what'll become o' me! Utterly deathly weeping.

Bonwari could stand it no longer. He got up. The old woman was weeping at the banks of the indigo levee; he waved his hand in front of her face and yelled—Hey, why cryin' like this since mornin'?

Suchand wiped her eyes and looked at him, repeating his question in her usual way—Why cryin'?

—Yeh, yeh. Why cryin'?

—It's me mind.

—Can't just say that.

—I'm not allowed ta cry?

—No.

—But where'll I go?

—Oo said anythin' 'bout goin'?

—Then?

—Can't cry wi' no reason.

—Can't cry wi' no reason?

—Yeh.

—Can't?

—No no no.

Suchand suddenly got up. Got up, tightened her waistcloth, and went off like a bomb from the Channanpur gentry's arsenal exploding on the Radha-Krishna festival.

—Wi'out reason? Wi'out reason? Wi'out reason?

Screaming, she went to the middle of the meeting place and sat down cross-legged on the ground, sending up a pile of dust. She said—Eadman! Council! I say let council judge! Where'm I gonna live? Oo'll feed me?

The fasting Bonwari was on his way back home. Anyway, he's Kalaruddu's chief devotee; at this time of renunciation it's forbidden for him to sweat over these worldly fights in dust and dirt. In his absence Prohlad got the meeting together. Prohlad was not surprised by Suchand's bluster as that's Auntie's style. Auntie is like a "fourist," or forest; if a twig falls in that forest it's a husking beam, if a leaf falls it's a winnowing tray; if the forest is drunk it's a tempest, if it weeps there's a downpour. Such is Aunt; she makes mudballs of painted forehead dots, mountains of anthills; if she weeps, her cries rend the heavens; if she laughs she dances like a maniac. Prohlad smiled.

Suchand became enraged and started beating her forehead—Oo'll feed me? Oo'll feed me? Laughin'? Ya laughin'?

Prohlad then said in a grave voice—Why, yer daughter's still around.

—Won't eat it. Won't eat me daughter's food.

—But ya can work yerself an' eat.

—Work an' eat?

—Yeh, ya can still work.

—Course I can. Very well. Better than all yer wives, I can. Much better than that floury-faced missus o' Bonwari's. Can so. Can so.

She struck a pose that demonstrated how much work she was capable of doing.

Prohlad smiled and said—That's just what we're sayin', sweetie!

—Well? Other day I went ta Bonwari ta work, Bonwari keeps me 'alf the day, gives nine paisa, an' dismisses me. Spent the rest o' the day goin' all 'round the ponds an' ditches an' got one shellfish; oo'll cook that up for me?

Now Bonwari spoke—Don't shout, stop. Bonwari had turned back from going home.

—Eh! She was a little surprised to see Bonwari.

—Stop. Please stop.

—I'll stop?

—Yeh, stop.

—Gonna stop. Speak, answer what I've said!

Bonwari said—Ye'll go ta work an' sit down wi' Hedo Mondol ta smoke 'baccy, tell stories—

Not letting him finish what he was saying, Suchand said with as much humility as she could muster—Won't do it again, won't smoke 'baccy again.

Bonwari said gravely—Besides, didn't ya tell that Mondol everythin'?

—What'd I say? Notta thing!

—Not a thing? Didn't say nothin'? Not throwin' out dead dogs an' cats or cleanin' sewers, ya din't say all that's from Bonwari's bein' 'eadman?

Suchand stared speechless and bewildered at Bonwari's face.

Bonwari said—Come on, speak, ya didn't tell Hedo Mondol?

Now Suchand spoke in a calm voice—Yeh, told 'im, son. All that the anchesters used ta do, told 'im that too. All ta your credit, son.

—Yes dear. Sure it's to me credit. So where's the wrong? Are we shit-swabbers or corpse-keepers?

Suchand stayed quiet. But nor did she understand where the wrong was in being disposers of dead dogs and cats, in hauling off dead cows on your own back.

Now Prohlad said—Sadgop gents of Jangol've learned ta wear fancy frock coats; they used ta carry the Brahmin dead ta the Ganges banks; given that up now. Why should it be us does all that stuff?

Putting all this aside, Suchand now said her own piece—Tell me where I'm s'posed ta go. Bashan, daughter o' me own womb, she won't feed me. Felt like eatin' a couple o' shellfish, an'—

Now Bashanta came forward from her yard. She's a calm person; in a calm voice she protested—Well—really! Tell me when I said I wouldn't feed ya? I came an' brought food—ya threw it out!

Looking into her face, Suchand said—Threw it out?

—Will ya put yer 'and on my 'ead an' say whether ya threw it out or not?

Suchand screamed—Done well, done a lot. Won't give? Why'd ya let Karali get hitched wi' Pakhi? E's such a pain—put a frog on me body—

Bonwari yelled—Karali'll clasp yer feet fer doin' that.

—Clasp me feet?

—Yes. Hey, Karali? Call Karali. Must have got back from Channapur by now.

Suchand shook her head and said—No. Why just let 'im clasp me feet? Me grandson got hitched an' did 'e even gimme one good new bitta cloth? Drinks bottle after bottle o' prime booze, did 'e gimme any?

Karali arrived and said—Give, I'll give.

—Gi', gi' right now. I'll drink booze, put on me new gear, an' dance.

Pakhi came forward. She tugged Suchand's hand and said—Come, come on now. Right now.

With her other hand, Suchand gestured to her feet and said—Lettim clasp, let Karali clasp me feet, then I'll go.

Karali did not just clasp her feet; he lifted her in his arms and said—Come, I'll take you away in me lap. Come.

Karali's gang all rushed toward Karali's house.

From that day on Suchand often started a party at Pakhi's house. It's there she stays, drinks prime liquor, smokes cigarettes, takes turns dancing with Nasubala, and only goes to Bashan's at mealtimes. She cannot eat at Karali's place. First, she eats food from the daughter of her womb, and even then says in embarrassment—I could die, me tum's got no shame, I eat me daughter's food, that's embarrassment. But grandson's food! Lying on the Charak disc, Bonwari remembered all of this and smiled a little.

Kalaruddu was installed in Kaharpara—with incense smoke, lamp-light, oil, and rouge he received offerings at Kaharpara. Men, women, children lay together face down on the ground and showed their reverence. Only Noyan and Noyan's Ma did not come. Noyan said—What's it mean fer me ta pay 'beisance? Nothin' worse than wishin' someone dead. I'm on the verge o' dyin'. Go an' tell 'em ta worship Karali. He began to curse the world obscenely, then broke into a coughing fit.

Noyan's Ma stroked the boy's chest with her hand. She did not respond to his words. Her voice was heard in the evening. She came back to the hamlet after bathing at the Kali Deeps, in a soaked wrap and with tousled hair, with hawkish voice shrilly cursing—E's ruined yer glory, 'im oo did evil an' then got on the Charak disc; crack 'im apart, Father. E oo burned Babathakur's familiar ta death, destroy 'im, Father. Make the Kopai flood flow, Father, drive out the evil; whip up storm, Father. O Babathakur's dead familiar, raise yer 'ead in the sky, come hissin' an' swayin', lamentin'.

On this blessed day, the whole hamlet was anxious and alarmed.

Bonwari heaved a deep sigh.

Two

Let Noyan's Ma curse; Bonwari could not be hard on her. He's headman, that's not his duty. Rather, he kept himself busy making up for the prejudice he'd shown Noyan. He began searching for a girl to tie the knot with Noyan. Yet opportunities are so few. So much work. Boishakh month, days passing for Jangol's Sadgop masters to have their homes re-thatched. Kahars are experienced thatch weavers: Bonwari, Prohlad, Roton—the most renowned thatch weavers of this area. Also a lot of labor in thatching. This is one of their earning seasons. They must go as far as Channanpur. No rest night or day now. Daytime thatching cottages, nighttime left to work the land. It's fortnight of the waxing moon, so Bonwari brings the Kahars and is working the land. Pickaxes cutting. Rocks being defeated. Fortune is kind: the "stay," or layer, of rock is not too thick; earth below the rock is also good. The Kahars do not take wages from Bonwari, they take the fee of a day's drink. Every day they bring two jars of liquor on their backs from the Channanpur brew store, drink, and then, at the end of the evening, when evening lamps are glowing in cottages, each one takes his handtools, that's hoe, shovel, pickaxe, basket, and the group heads off toward the Saheb Tracts. On the way they pay obeisance to Babathakur. Unafraid, despite their dusty heads—Enough, let's go now.

Sometimes Karali also comes to work the land with them. Karali's become much more compliant. Realizing this a few days before, Bonwari said—Now good'll come to ya, Karali. Yer good will's comin' back.

Karali smiled, flicked his head to move back his hanging hair, and said—People make mistakes.

Bonwari then worked on for a while in silence. All are silent. Only iron tools, earth, and rocks make clanging, scrunching sounds; at the same time, on four sides, earth falls from baskets with a flop. Bonwari's plot is growing fast.

Porom's plot next door has gone to ruin. Just the same old dry upland. After some robbery or holdup where he didn't get money, Porom's land will not be dug.

A little later, Bonwari spoke again. Regretfully, and with a deep sigh, he said—Ah, if only you 'adn't done that killin', Karali!

—What? Karali snapped his head up and stood straight. What's he done? His brow furrowed.

—That familiar o' Babathakur's—. Bonwari again sighed deeply. He can't forget a single bit of this fear. Noyan's Ma isn't letting him forget. She's constantly abusing him. Whenever he hears it he's shocked. He feels bad.

There is no anxiety or doubt about this in Karali's mind, though. He works on the rail line where so many snakes pop out when earth is dug. Sees a snake, kills it. Besides, a few days before he killed that snake their saheb had shot and killed exactly the same kind of chain viper right before his eyes. So as far as he is concerned, the snake's nothing more than a snake. If any of his friends raise this with him he says—Go ta hell. He could not answer Bonwari like this, but said with a sneer—That's yer one point. Now the snake—

—Don't say it, sonny, don't say it.

Karali was silent. The tone of Bonwari's voice resounded sternly. He put his spade aside and folded his hands in reverence.

A little later Bonwari said—Quit Channapur, Karali. When ya go there ya get all this attitude. Buy a bitta land—

—Land?

—Yeh. Buy land, buy steers, farm.

—I'll do that when I'm old. Karali began to laugh. Then said—I mean, really! Can I quit rail work now? War's really on now. Rail work's gonna be part of the war. Unnerstan'? Wages gonna double. They're cryin' out fer people now.

War conditions. Kalarudda's mind, glory. It's he who started the war. Great things happen in the turn of his Charak wheel. Bad times come, slaughter comes. War is here.

War, terrible war's broken out. Even here many things will happen because of that war. The line will extend. Airplanes will gather someplace. The whole rail line's been snatched up by the war Company. They'll take on many new people. Lots of labor, lots of wagework. Bombs falling at home, abroad, Rangoon or someplace! The "Japoonese" or somesuch are coming! People fleeing Calcutta. Calcutta folk supposedly even coming to Channanpur. Channanpur's getting noisy and chaotic.

Airplanes are even flying over Bansbadi's Hansuli Turn now and then. Birds noisily take to air; in far-off sky, soaring, dotlike hawks spy the planes and fall fluttering downward in fright. Kaharpara's men and women stare speechless. Little boys dash unthinkingly from field to field, keeping the airplanes company. If skies are cloudy they fly through clouds, now hidden, now suddenly breaking out of cloud; whining they go, from one kingdom to another.

Bonwari still remembers the first day airplanes flew over. Nighttime, Noyan's Ma hurling abuse, Bonwari sitting alone. Suddenly shaking Bansbadi's darkness, this tremendous noise from a corner of the sky.

A whining sound coming from a far corner of the sky. The sound slowly approached.

Bonwari's arms and legs began to shake.

Father's mount must have reared up its hood, returning in a new form! All Kaharpara stood in suspense, staring anxiously toward the dark sky.

As if rushing forward, two stars, red, blue. That sound with them.

Karali's followers Mathla and Notbor said—Airplane sound. Airplane. They're gatherin' someplace ta side o' Channanpur.

O God! Ill-omened airplanes have flown right over Hansuli Turn!

Now there's no more fear. But there's no doubt that this is a bad omen. Price of paddy's starting to rise. Cloth going up too. Prices of other "fings," or things, rising, but the Kahars only have food and clothing—no great matter if prices of other things go up.

***

As soon as the nine o'clock train rolls with its rattling music across the Kopai bridge, the Kahars finish work and return home.

Toil done, no more get-togethers. Everyone takes his lie-down. Only at Karali's house is there gathering a while longer. The group of youths is not tired after work, and because of their age they won't be able to sleep without a bit more fun. Suchand, wise old woman of Hansuli Turn's ancient days, sits at the center of their gathering nowadays. Sitting beside, so close he is touching, is Nasubala; Pakhi on the other side. The lads sit all around. Many of the young girls come and sit as long as the lads are not yet back from working headman's land. They go home as soon as the men return. A new hurricane lantern burns in the center. In those days clay oil lamps were burned at Hansuli Turn. They burned neem or castor oil. They'd gather neem flowers, collect castor flowers, and bring the pressing from the mill. Once "kerachini," or kerosene, arrived, there were "lomps," meaning kerosene-burning lights. The Kahars still do not buy hurricane lanterns. There's one at Bonwari's home, an old one donated from the Ghosh house at that. There's also one at Pana's cottage, that's old too—stolen from boss's house. Prankeshto smeared it with pitch to cover up its old paint. There's an old, broken lantern lying in Noyan's house, left from the days of the Chaudhurys. The bottom's split, the top's missing, the glass is broken; now it's held with wire all around. None of these lights is lit very often. Lit for festival and fair, emergency and crisis. Four kerosene lamps can be lit with the oil of one hurricane lantern. So why would the Kahars light them? But Karali really needs lantern light because of his job in the Channanpur workshops—. Suchand now wants it right before her face. Wants it shining as bright as it can go. Stares into it and smiles. Sometimes she winds up the wick a little, and if in doing so she turns it too much she cries out—Ah, s'gone, s'gone, oh no! O Pakhi, O Nasu—! When they turn it down she calmly says—Uh—huh, whitey contraption!

Pakhi says—Damn, old woman's fallen in love wi' a lantern!

Suchand pinched two tufts of hair with her fingertips and stretched them out from the roots, saying to Nasu—Eh sis, look, ain't it 'orns?

Nasu says—Oooh lords, them 'orns! Just like a steer! Saying this, he puts the hair over his left thumb and pinches with the nails of his right hand—there's a "pot" sound. Immediately Nasu's mouth makes a sound—Unh! Without that sound, the lice do not depart this world.

Pakhi says—Get them golden wisps cut. They've become the king-dom o' lice.

—Whatcha say? Get 'em cut?

—Yeh.

—Hairs?

—Yeh.

—Me 'air's golden wisps?

—It's not? Wanna look in the mirror?

The old woman hollered—Mirror at night? No. No use my lookin'.

—Why?

—It'd be a disgrace at my age.

Now all the women burst out laughing. Nasubala breaks into song—

What's to fear from an unchaste moon, friend; in my black hair
disgrace—
Disgraced Radhika—name spread far and wide.

Coming from the outer perimeter of the house, some exceedingly beautiful male voice suddenly mingles with this—

Bearing evil disgrace for Krishna—
I'll leap into those black deeps, friend,
Finally lose myself in blacksnake's love coils!

Everyone was amazed—Oo's that, eh?

Suchand now smiled and lounged back—Come at last! she said.

Nasu leaped up and went out, saying—Where's that wreck come in from? Corpse ain't dead yet, then?

Pakhi shrieked with laughter.

Then the singer entered the house and stood in the lantern light. Strange attire. A head of dreadlocks, a trident in hand—but not Shiva; the Gajon masquerade outfit of Nandi, Shiva's attendant.

Pakhi rose, clapping her hands—Pagol-bro!

Pagol Kahar—completely crazy, neither in anyone's good books nor bad books. No home, no family, no "missus," no son; Pagol, strange, colorful person. He has a single daughter from a marriage in another village. If he spends ten days here, Pagol will spend a couple of weeks there and the remaining week here, there, elsewhere. In cases of extreme need he turns his mind to work, does day labor for cash, eats. No shortage of work; the man is very skilled. He's a master of roof thatching, an experienced builder of clay walls, has a beautiful hand for plastering cottages; if you cut some bamboo and give it to him, he'll make baskets and birdcages as well as an expert Dom craftsman can. His hands are good for everything. His chief skill is song; he composes and sings his own songs, which are also marvelous. Nowadays it's Pagol who always composes the Ghentu songs of this place. Bonwari's best friend. Whose isn't he? Pagol's everyone's friend. There's gossip and scandal. Why wouldn't there be? Aunt Suchand says—Pagol's Ma got the 'ots wi' the stonemason Rakhal Raja Das Bostom. Weren't in Channanpur; when Kalaruddu's brick shrine was bein' built in Jangol, Jangol Chaudhurys searched all round an' brought stonemason Bostom from Katoya. That Bostom's blood runs in Pagol's veins. At one time it was Pagol who'd bring all the news from Channanpur. Back then he'd go to Channanpur daily. He formed an elder-sisterly relation with Lalthakrun, a Brahmin wife of Channanpur. She had no son and was a widow; what devotion Pagol had, obsessed with calling her "elder sister," he'd go every day to sister's house with a pot of milk. He'd milk the cow with his own hands, change his clothes, and bring the undiluted milk. Pagol's elder sister Lalthakrun would wait upon him at nighttime; she'd break her fast following the eleventh day of the moon and give Pagol the remains of the food offerings. If in Channanpur there was any preparation for a feast, Lalthakrun would take her platter and say—There is a man at my house, so give me some food to take, I'll take it and feed my Kahar brother. She would feed him. Lalthakrun passed away. Pagol quit Channanpur too, wandered here and there. Now his passion has alighted on his daughter's daughter, his five-year-old granddaughter. He's making up rhymes about her—composing songs—"At this old age, O you're me noo passion."

He left home absorbed in this passion, and the joys of Hansuli Turn faded. Ghentu was no good this time. Bonwari had inner regrets; if Pagol had been there he would have given a response to Atpoure Para's Ghentu song. If Pagol had been there Gajon would have been even more splendid. Everyone had given up any hope of Pagol. Suddenly he turns up today after a few years. Arrived in this strange and colorful garb.

Suchand said—So ya came? Sit, sit. So why this getup? Gajon's been.

Pagol said—I'd set out in this gear, tell ya—set straight off ta Gajon masquerade, I'm gonna dance. On the way, seein' all the show at Katoya, I stopped off right there. Gajon went off. Din't take the gear off again, I wore this stuff an' came along singin' an' beggin' fer alms. There's a saying—If ye're not a renouncer ye won't collect alms, ya know! Saw yours, unnerstan', got a great haul, ye did.

He displayed his large shoulder bag. Said—Loads 'ere. Got rice, sold it fer cash. He began to smile.

Suchand said—Great show 'ere too.

—Eard so. Beano got on the Charak!

—Yeh. Father descended at Kaharpara this time.

—Yeh, 'eard that too. Eard a lot o' Karali. Eard of 'is 'eat with Pakhi, 'eard about the snake-killin'. S'good, s'good. Saying this, he gave Suchand a sudden pinch, and with a wink said in a loud voice—Now, set me up this time. No?

Nasu was surprised and straightaway began to mock—Damn, damn, troublemaker.

A jesting comment. So as to annoy Nasu because of his female clothing, Pagol says—I'll marry. Nasu is totally enraged. Runs off.

Amidst this laughing and jesting the nine o'clock train crossed the Kopai bridge. The young women there left. Karali's gang returned. Pagol embraced Karali and said—Oh wow, I'll be darned!

—Pagol-bro?

Pagol broke into song—

I've gone mad wi' love, love's fix didn't flee—
Ah, sweetheart dear—it's evening, yet the pumpkin flower hasn't
opened!

Karali did not applaud the song; he laid out the mat, but did not sit. Rather, pulling on Pagol's arm from behind he said—Found a right feller.

—Now look, what kinda feller?

—One ta talk right. Speak, you speak!

—What?

—Sit, Nasu-sis; get the bottle out.

Nasu shrugged dismissively—Can't. Thass a very bad youman. Youman, which is to say human—meaning this Pagol.

Karali laughed long at this. Said—Damn, monster, damn. See 'er in old age, puttin' on an act.

Looking hard at their faces, Suchand was listening to the conversation. She didn't have much trouble understanding if she listened and watched the faces. Now Suchand said—Now look, look at oo says—see 'er in old age, puttin' on an act!

Nasu grumblingly brought the bottle and handed it to Karali from a distance.

Karali said—Where's the wrong, then?

The issue was this—on the way home Bonwari had warned, reprimanded, Karali and his inner circle. War's breaking out—they need a lot of people in the Channanpur workshops, wages have doubled. Many have said privately to Karali that they want to go. But Bonwari's saying—Caution! Watch it! Don't cross the limits of Hansuli Turn, boys. Channanpur is north of Hansuli Turn. But that's really Dakshinpuri, Southern City. It's in the tale—Look around all ways, mind wants to walk to the other side, but don't look toward the south; don't walk that way, on that road.

Finally he said with grave voice—Watch it! Caution!

Karali wants to say—Why caution? Tell me Pagol-bro, ye're a decent person, you say, why caution?

Pagol said—Hmm, what ye're sayin' ain't wrong, bro; what Bonwari's sayin' ain't wrong either.

Taking this opportunity, Nasu spoke with waving hand—What you're sayin' yerself ain't wrong either, bro. You're good, I'm good too—tied in one spot, ye're wanderin' free. What ye're sayin' ain't wrong—what Bonwari's sayin' ain't wrong either. Lots been said there.

Everybody burst out laughing. But Pagol was neither angry nor put out. He also began to laugh.

Karali said—Now anyone can get a wage job. Else won'tcha just farm forever? If I'd farmed woulda been just like this. Would've 'ad a life o' takin' beatins from those Jangol Sadgops. Ya know what Mathla got for farmin' this time? Eight hundred pounds o' paddy. Think! Gi' farmin' the brush-off!

Everyone agrees, but silently. The meeting was quiet for a while. Suddenly Suchand said—War war! What a war, laddie! Oo knows?

Karali said—Dammit! S' the saheb man's war. English, Germany, Japanese—

Suchand said—You don't understand a thing! Was a war back then. Marathas came. Boys slept, Marathas took over the place, Marathas came ta this land! Dad 'eard it in granddad's day. Them Marathas came. Orses gallopin', *tabum tabum*, wavin' swords—choppin', burnin', smashin' 'omes—choppin' peoples noses, choppin' ears, choppin' arms, choppin' 'eads—*crunch-scrunch—crunch-scrunch*, off it goes! For fear folks would 'ide their 'eads in upside-down pots an' sit in a pond up to their necks in water.

Pagol says—Yeah, sis, the Santal Revolt—tell that one?

The old woman's eyes widen.—Faces painted red, all like black death 'imself—ooh Lord! Village quakin' in fear.

The old woman tells that story. Pakhi got irritated and said—Sing a song, Pagol-bro.

—Song?

—Yeh. War upon war; there's war on now—an' there was war back then. Rather ye told the ballad o' Rama-Ravana.

Pagol began. Karali got up from the gathering. He took Mathla and company outside and began to counsel them. Karali had become upset with Bonwari. And besides, what *is* all this stuff anyway? Caution upon caution! Don't youths have caution? He said—Come on, you come—come, then whatever 'appens'll 'appen.

Mathla said—Look 'ere, didn't tell anyone, didn't show, see this.

He took Karali's hand in his own and stuck it under his hair to show a place on his head.

Karali shivered—Ow'dja cut it?

—Boss whacked me wi' a cattle crop.

—Why?

—I said I'm gonna give up farmwork. E says—I get five rupees; give it. When you've given, go where ya like. I said, sire, if you get rupees, 'ow come I got eight hundred pounds o' paddy back? You did the accounts yerself an' gave! Then in a flash 'e grabbed the crop from me 'and an' gave me a whack. Me 'ead got cut. Then 'e feels sorry an' rips up some rags an' wraps a strip on an' says—If ya play smart one more time I'll thrash again!

Karali said—Wait. He quickly entered the cottage and came back out with something. He put a five-rupee note into Mathla's hand and said— Gi' that tomorrow an' come—unnerstan'? Then we'll go straight ta Channanpur. Mathla'll go wi' me. I'll be waitin' right beside the station signals, unnerstan'?

Pagol's ballad was still going on. War of Rama and Ravana. —Rama took Sita into the forest. All the land's people wept. Rama went, Sita went, Lakshman went trailing behind. On the way they made friends with a Chandal hermit. They wandered through forest upon forest, and finally met with the demoness "Shuponokha." Lakshman cut off her nose. Brother Ravana arrived in rage. He took on the illusory shape of a golden deer and carried Sita off. Rama and Lakshman searched and searched, wept and wept, took up with the forest monkeys, became their friends. The monkeys cry victory to Rama. They crossed the ocean, came to Lanka. War began. Arrows of fire are extinguished by ocean arrows. Ocean arrows fly away in wind arrows. Serpent arrows are cut down by half-moon arrows. The Brahma weapon's fire erupts in a blaze. The wicked demon's chest quakes. The earth shakes violently. Birds and beasts howl. River water freezes. Trees are scorched.

Pakhi and the audience listen, dumbstruck. In olden days at Hansuli Turn, the Kahars' ancestors trembled. Birds and beasts of Hansuli Turn howled; Kopai's water froze. The leaves of bamboo groves were singed. Whatever the age, Hansuli Turn was ever in that age. The age of that Rama-Ravana war.

Pakhi suddenly glanced at the sky, startled. From the corner of the sky comes a noise, a whining, droning noise.

Three

"Fry a neem leaf up in ghee, it still won't quit its family."

Karali was the neem and Bonwari's solicitous care was the ghee. The saying was uttered by Neem-oil Panu. This morning's trip is to the Ghosh house at Jangol—to thatch the roof of Bonwari's boss's house. The name of the Ghoshes' other house is bungalow house; Mister Ghosh has built a long, single-story house after the *fashion* of the sahebs' dak bungalows; had it whitewashed, got floors put down, put green British paint on doors and windows, had the inner pair of rooms roofed with a canopy—so the thatch frame is not visible; even had a pulley fan installed. A glorious home. That's where friends and marriage kin who come to Jangol are put up. Marriage kin of the house install one of their cowherds or errand boys or farmhand's sons on the veranda of that Kahar paradise; he works the pulley fan. Actually, everything about the house is beyond the Kahars' wildest dreams. This is not really the time to be re-thatching the house, but a celibate monkey group has suddenly declared war, leaped onto the roof, and completely torn up the straw.

It's a terrifying thing if a bachelor monkey troop gets angry. There are usually twenty to twenty-five female monkeys in a monkey troop; their general is a giant male, what Kahars call a Marigold Hanuman. He's the tall one whose white teeth constantly make a tapping sound, chattering clackety-clack. Now and then he'll let out a deep whoop, leaping from one branch to the next, from this tree to that, leaping from tree to nearby roof, landing with a bang. This group's second generation is not male. Each female delivers her offspring. He keeps a sharp watch. If there's a birth, he'll check carefully—is the infant female or male? If it's female it lives, if it's male he'll straightaway tear the infant to pieces with sharp claws and cast the parts away.

If the females deliver a male, they flee—hiding here and there, they bring up their offspring for a time, give him away to an all-male bachelor troop, and return to their own troop. The bachelor troop's general will from time to time begin war with the regular troop's general. Terrible war. Biting-bruising slapping-punching—it's a bloody business! This one tries to bite out that one's neck, that one digs its claws into this one's chest and tries to bite and tear out its heart. Sky and wind shudder with whooping;

every roof in the village gets shredded; with a thump they leap from one roof to the next, this monkey pursuing that one, that one pursuing this. The bachelor troop suddenly jumps in from all sides full of exhilaration and hatred. The female troop leaps from roof to roof too, leaps with excitement and dread. War doesn't stop until someone admits defeat. War continues for three, four days at a time.

There is no recourse, no remedy. Maito Ghosh owns a rifle; in rage he'd wanted to shoot bullets but folk of home and village wouldn't let him. Hanuman—hero Hanuman—Rama's bearer; Rama gave them sovereignty over tree branch and house thatch; gave shares in humanity's harvest too. They are Sons of the Wind; if you kill them the Wind Lord will not bring rainclouds to the region, there'd surely be drought. Bonwari too pleaded with Maito Ghosh. If there were no rain Jangol's Sadgops would still survive; paddy and money in their homes. But what ruin for the Kahars! What would they eat? Entire families, clans would wither away! He promised Ghosh, all Kaharpara will together re-thatch the house in three days. Two days later Ghosh pressed his claim hard. One of his friends is coming from Calcutta with his children; coming from Calcutta for fear of bombs and will stay as long as war continues; therefore the house really must be done. He'd said work should have already started yesterday; but they'd been doing another Mondol house—the house was left half thatched. So Bonwari had taken a break yesterday. Today he'll do it—Bonwari had promised. In the morning all the Kahars, young and old, were gathered; Mathla, Notbor, Phoring, Hebo did not come. Karali's thing is different. He works in Channanpur, a Kahar of Kaharpara, but not a Kahar—a fruit off the tree, all right, but he's cut the stalk himself. But four big strong lads, why didn't they come?

And why? All four of them have gone to Channanpur with Karali. They'll get work on the railway. Karali's taken them. The whole group shook their heads, sighed deeply. Bonwari sat still and silent a while. Realizing his opportunity, Neem-oil Pana said—Fry a neem leaf up in ghee, it still won't quit its family!

Bonwari could not reply to the saying; there certainly can't be any delay in thatching Sire Ghosh's house, but what's gone wrong? After so much petting and stroking Karali has not come around, he's broken Bonwari's interdiction and taken the lads away! He's started the breakup of Kaharpara, walking the lads to Channanpur—on that road to Dakshinpuri!

Pagol has come after all this time. He'd spent the night lying in Karali's yard. Hot days; in the open yard he put his head on his own shoulder bag and lay on a mat. There are no large mats in a Kahar home; they weave rough floor covers from date palm or palmyra leaves, such are their resources; but Karali had given him a mat—a new mat. He got up in the morning and went to where Bonwari was. Boishakh month—house thatching time, it's there he'll see everyone. Smiling and singing, he came and stood—

I've gone and lost my mind on the banks of the Kopai, O—
Who's found it, O friends, give it back to me, O!

But the assembled folk merely looked up with small, thin smiles and became solemn again. Bonwari, Prohlad, Roton, they who should have embraced him, remained silent too. A moment later Bonwari spoke— When'dja come?

—Last night. But what's up?

—A lot. S'good ya came. Come on.

—Where?

—Gotta finish Sire Ghosh's bungalow in three days.

—Hey, look, why I gotta? Leave me out.

—Why?

—I've, bro—. Pagol smiled and said—I've gotten the taste fer singin' an' beggin'. Not all that toil an' sweat.

—Nope, won' 'appen. Hup. Go beggin'? Not ashamed?

Pagol began to laugh—neither wife nor son, 'usker nor winnower, 'arth nor 'ome, night nor day, month nor year; life nor death—what kinda shame could I 'ave?

Bonwari suddenly became agitated and said—If you 'ad any shame ye'd a come ta my place last night instead o' Karali's. I'm telling ya, telling Karali too, you tell the lad. Tellin' ya—got nothin', got caste dharma? Or that neither?

Pagol was rather offended and said—Whatcha sayin' that for, bro?

—I'm sayin' 'cos I want to! Cos I'm very upset. E's gone off ta Chan-nanpur takin' 'ow many lads. Casteless wicked depots—. Bonwari became silent, he couldn't find any more words. After remaining silent for a few moments, he said—Sayin' ye'll beg alms? Got yer body an' ye'll beg alms? I mean—dear me, gotta ask ya somethin'. If someone's gotta destroy their caste so's you can eat, would ya let 'em?

Pagol said—Come on, no need fer this. Come on, I'm goin'.

On the way Bonwari said—Friends after that!

—Speak, friend.

—Ow old's yer girl? Doin' all right?

—Oh, she's hit five. Gettin' more grown up by the day. Now to get 'er married somehow. Pagol began smiling. He broke into song—At this old age, O she's me new passion!

—Sing that song, will ya.

—Which?

—That "Sahebs Laid a Road."

The railroad-line Ghentu song Pagol composed. When the railroad line was first put down at Channanpur, Pagol had composed this Ghentu song; he'd become highly renowned singing this song. Kahars sometimes still sing it today.

Up on Sire Ghosh's roof Pagol began to sing—

O, sahebs laid a road!
Alas, in th' Infernal Age!
As time passed, the sahebs came and laid a road—

The youths sang the refrain—

For a sixmonth wagonmachines kept moving by.
O saheb road—

Up goes straw with a whoosh, thrown from below. Amazing technique—sat up on the roof, the thatchers catch it in their left hands with uncanny dexterity. Piling it up beside them. They're binding it to split bamboo with cords, hammering, and then, taking a chopper or a sickle from their waists, cutting the cord and sliding the tool back onto the waist.

Standing on the "nib," that's the top, of Ghosh's roof, Bonwari is occasionally calling out orders. In the intervals looking now northward at Channanpur, now toward Bansbadi's Kaharpara, bounded by Hansuli Turn.

The people of Hansuli Turn have looked toward that Channanpur a long time as they linger in bamboo shade. Jangol lies north of Hansuli Turn's Bansbadi and Kaharpara. North of that, half a league distant, which is to say one and a half miles, lies Channanpur. Kahars say—Could be a little bit more or a little bit less. Channanpur has forever been a place of terror. The Kahars have slaved for the sahebs; they fear Channanpur exactly as they fear the sahebs' "ruddyface," tawny eyes, red hair. The settlement of Channanpur's lords and masters, settlement of shopkeepers and merchants—settlement of "Almighties," which is to say of gods and goddesses. Lords had sunlike power, Kahars would quake with fear to walk upon that road; man, who knows what detritus you might get swept up with. Fear of merchant sires is fear of their accounts. Slow, painstaking writing, black ink letters in great fat huge ledgers, moving from one ledger to another, interest upon interest the dues rise; if you take credit from their stores the dues weigh down like a rock upon your chest. Yet more fear of god and goddess. They are not Babathakur, they are not Kalorudra; what glory, what rites for their worship. You have to stay far away from their court, from their place of worship—Kahars can't even enter the temple porch, they must watch from afar; if the Kahars' gaze falls on the items offered for the gods' consumption, the feast is ruined. The Kahars wouldn't willingly walk that road with all these terrors.

A bundle of cord whooshed up from below and fell in front of him. Bonwari grabbed it in a flash. Sat down and began to bind. The work's going well. Pagol's entertaining well. A singer is as good as his voice. The biggest pleasure is to carry the palanquin with him. How he'll call out rhymes!

Pagol continued singing the Ghentu song—

Redface sahebs came, tawny pale eyes—
From many lands came crowd on crowd of folk—
—O saheb road—
O the sahebs laid a road—Kahar clan's living lost
So many good folk quit the palanquin to ride the rails.
—O saheb road—

In those days, they had occasionally been called to carry the palanquin for a local wedding party. Garuda the bird carries Lakshmi and Narayan; the milk-colored Oxen Lord carries Shiva and Durga; the "horse-clan" Kahars are there to carry earthly bride and groom—lords and gentry, merchants, Mondols and Sheiks and Sayyids—brides and grooms of every kind. It is virtuous if the Kahars carry the palanquin on their shoulders. Lords do not bathe when they climb into the palanquin. Their fortune is in that good karma. Those Channapur workshops are destroying that karma.

In every age times turn. Who keeps count of how many years have come and gone in the turning of Kalaruddu's Charak board! In night gloom Suchand tells Gajon's story. Those who are headmen like Bonwari ponder and stare detachedly into the deep, darkness-filled bamboo groves, losing their bearings. The Kopai lass, she knows how times turn in every age. Tarry at the Kopai bank. You'll notice that where today there are deeps, tomorrow a sandbank can be seen; deeps appear where hard stone's crumbled from river's edge.

Something is known by Babathakur's "sanctarry," that's to say the silk-cotton tree that stands above the Kali Deeps. Of how many crevices filled, how many branches broken, how many branches newly grown, how many leaves fallen, how many flowers opened, how many fruits ripened, how many seeds scattered here and there, how many shoots sprouted, how many seeds wasted—of all this it knows a little. Yet it won't talk to just anyone. It talks to ascetics, to renouncers, and to people upon whom Babathakur at least looks favorably. Says to them—Seen many ages, sonny! Saw the Rama-Ravana war, saw Lord Krishna kill Kangsha, saw Maratha invasions, saw sahebs' offices, saw the era of the Chaudhurys, saw the lords and masters of Channanpur become proper gentlemen; the call came from Channanpur for the Kahars—well, that was an affair of the old days, lad! The lords of Channanpur became gentlefolk and started wearing frock coats, put creaking new shoes on their feet, practiced untouchability rules a little less strictly. How could they not, eh!

They bought land, began loaning money, learned English. Many also bought up landlord's rights. Began to travel far afield for work. The Kirtan choir at Channanpur broke up and became a traveling actor's troupe. Bonwari himself had heard the troupe's songs when he was young. Then it became a theater. It was at this time Kahars were often summoned to Channanpur. To work on the gentry's fields; to do construction, meaning—carrying house bricks; it just wouldn't work without Kahars to crush bricks. Women were summoned to do manual labor. Then at this time the sahebs' offices disappeared, Saheb and his Missus drowned in the rage of Kottathakur, the Kahars turn to robbery and banditry and now also farm.

But even though Channanpur is north of Hansuli Turn, it is really Dakshinipuri, Southern City; whoever goes there does not do well. Back then there was fear of curses; nowadays, other fears. Women began to disappear. Almost all stonemasons were Mister Sheiks; they'd get the "ots" on with the women, have them recite the Islamic articles of faith, make them into Muslim ladies, and take them home. The gentry's foot-men also began ruining the women. Even the young gentry pulled at Kahar women's hems. "Bruhmin" boys; how can Kahar girls stand their touch, it's the girls who've exploded with evil. The headman exercised his leadership and made a ban; he stood stretching out his arms, guarding the path—Don' go. As little as ya can. If ya can't not go, don't walk that path more than ye must.

Times turned again. Mechanical wagons came to Channanpur. Iron lines laid, dirt highways built; earthen bridge construction elsewhere. Channanpur became a river wharf. Every wave of the crumbling of the world's time crashes onto the ground of that Channanpur. The gentry masters of Channanpur can take that wave in the chest. They're "Brahm-bins," they know "readwritin," God has placed blessed bounty in their homes; in his kindness the wavecrest will bring a little good into their home—just as the Kopai flood deposits gold-yielding silt onto the lands of the lucky ones. If the wave hits the Kahars full on it's ruin, just as when the Kopai flood hits the lands of the luckless leaving only sand, sand, and sand. The rail line arrived at Channanpur, and with it the value of the gentry's land rose; trade and business expanded, and the Kahars were ruined. A whole group of women left together. Karali's Ma went with that group. Alas, shameless brazen Karali! Now a new wave coming—war's wave. War's wave has crashed down on Channanpur wharf. At Chan-nanpur the rail line will grow. It sends a beckoning sign through Karali's hand to the stupid and foolish of Kaharpara. Don't go wrong, don't go wrong, y'all.

At this point, Pagol finished his song—his song also has the same tenor. Bonwari purposely told him to sing this song. Let them hear, all those lads with itchy feet who can't yet take off, who aren't yet foolhardy--let them hear, let them wise up. There is another aim too. Let Pagol first sing—

Caste lost, dharma lost, infidel foreign workshop
Don't go that way son, Kottababa's ban.

Sing, go on an' sing, Pagol—

If girls take that road, they never come back home—
Caste lost through the outcaste in a far-off place.

Karali's Ma went off. Who knows what stage Pakhi's reached! Bonwari heaved a deep sigh.

Pagol finishes the song, sings—

The luckless workshop troubles fortune's Lakshmi
Don't walk that road, precious; Kottababa's ban.

Bonwari said—Well? Pagol me buddy, well?

—Well what?

—Eard ye were givin' Karali a real pat on the back las' night. Sing Karali that song.

Pagol went quiet. He'd been outwitted. Soon after he smiled and said—Yer a real sly 'un, Bonwari!

Bonwari said—Won't say anything about Pakhi, not fer me ta say, I'm uncle. But ask 'er, will she destroy caste fer money, will that be good?

***

Boishakh month. Terrible heat. On top of that, no breeze today. The Kahars were worn out, streaming with sweat. But they continued working with pleasure, singing songs. Pagol suddenly said—Beano, what's done is done. Let's some'ow cover up the rest wi' loose straw, bro, s'lookin' bad. Bonwari looked up at the sky. Yep, sure lookin' bad. Sky's took on the exact "you," or hue, o' steel. Not like shadder's fallin', but like the light's gone "iskily," that's to say sickly. You can't see due west. One-story house, low thatch roof, far horizons are hidden by treetops all around. But you'd say a storm was coming. Bonwari silently called out to Babathakur. —Hold storm back a couple days, Father, couple days. He spoke an order— You lot work, move yer arms an' work. Those on top bundle up the loose straw. Chuck, chuck straw! Hoi, lads! Hoi!

Suddenly a cry went up—Ho——!

Oh my Lord! Fine voice! Who? The voice's sound extending to the corners of the sky!

Pagol stood up terrified. —Beano?

—What?

—Look look!

—What then?

—Karali.

—Karali?

—Karali's got up on Babathakur's silk-cotton tree branch yellin'.

Bonwari stood up on the roof. Disaster! The age-old silk-cotton tree is Babathakur's "refooge"; Karali's getting up there! He's gazing to the west and screaming—Ho——! Calling. Calling who?

—Ho—Uncle Beano—! Ho—! Ho—!

Bonwari began to shudder. That tall silk-cotton tree—thorn-filled branch throne. He's climbed up there! If Babathakur could only give a shove! Karali seems like a manikin.

—Ho—storm—storm! Uncle Beano! Youuge storm! Get down off the roof. News came ta Channanpur by wire. Ho—Un-cle Bea-no!

Coming down, now Karali's coming down.

Pana said—Gonna fall. Whoa—

—Fell?

—Nah, saved it. Whoa—whoa! Oop, saved it. Can't see 'im now.

Everyone became anxious because Pakhi's crying could be heard. But Bonwari does not forget the work. —Straw, straw. No one's gettin' down till it's covered. Cover. Cover.

Pagol said—Beano, look now. Take a look at Kottathakur's wood-apple an' the silk-cotton tree.

What is that thing "heavin," or raising, itself up in the sky behind Kottathakur's wood-apple, above the Saheb Heights? Don't you see blackish coils of cloud? Yes, yes. That's lightning "glammering," that's to say like the glow of blown flame. There again. There again. It's coming then, coming this very day. Coming. Thunderclap.

In the "bowl" of the sky, meaning its northwest corner, it's as if a cotton cleaner's bowstick is thrashing the cloud's cottony entrails until they billow, puff, and spread.

—Two more bundles o' straw, gi' quick, now. Gi' two more bundles up top. Bonwari glanced toward the sky again and, sitting firm upon the roof, started to fasten the top thatch down strongly.

—Enough, down, down. Himself abandoning the ladder's support, he jumped from the roof onto the pile of straw below.

—Get—run off now. Ome—go 'ome.

At the head of Kaharpara's indigo levee stands Noyan's Ma, screaming curses like a witch. Oh my, just waving her arms and screaming, as if dancing.

—Come Father, come. Come, me ragin' Father.

It came. Hansuli Turn's nor'wester storm. In black cloud body a reddish "throw," or sheet, of ochre dust flying. As if the blood-red cloth wrap worn by the blackstone Lord Kalorudra is billowing upward. It comes screaming, *whaa-whaa*. Two arms swinging, chest-shoving, snatching up whatever stands in its way and dashing it to the ground, it races like a mad elephant, like a wild bent-horned buffalo; it snaps trees in the middle, breaks branches, tears up the very roots, rips away leaves and flowers one after another. Thatch straw flies up and floats off like wisps in a flood. Palm trees go to war. Treetops fling to the ground and spring upright, then down again. Lightning play scrawls shapes, clouds crash with thunder; in that light, human eyes see darkness, noise deafens ears; minds shrunken with fear, thinking the world will be no longer. Yet Bonwari's wife Gopalibala has courage in the middle of all this, and sets out a wooden stool for Storm Lord to sit on, fills a pitcher of water to wash his feet; she says—Lord, sit quietly. Bonwari sits inside the room, eyes staring fixedly. Oh, not been a storm like this in so long! Oh man! What a "terrble" thing, maybe it'll be the "annilation"!

Everything was dazzling in the light. Earth quaked with the sound of rumbling. Lightning struck. Where? Oh my Lord, top of that palm tree in the field's caught fire!

What's that! Whose house is it? Whose thatch has come away from the wall by force of the storm and is flapping up and down? A roof thatched with new straw! Not Karali's house! Yes, it *is* Karali's house. Storm's bearing from the northwest corner, roof's northwest corner rising and falling. It's as if a wild buffalo is stabbing its horns up into the roof. It's gone, no doubt of that. A larger break is slowly opening, as if the wall's peeling away. There—there, ruin! The entire roof left the wall and soared into the sky; took off, soared swift as an arrow—toward the fields, into the mouth of the storm wind. Suddenly it tilted a little, then tilted right over—whirled around a few times, tumbled downward. It fell into Hansuli Turn's middle field.

Bonwari went out of the house.

Pagol immediately came out. —Oose place, Beano?

—Think it's Karali's.

—Karali's?

—Yeah.

There's no more doubt about it. Even in the middle of the storm, the voice of Noyan's Ma can be heard. Karali's home flew away; it is as if Noyan's Ma, in the joy of rage's fulfillment, yelling into this very storm, is adding her cursing voice to its voice.

Bonwari shivered hearing the curses of Noyan's Ma.

The curses and imprecations of the tale of Hansuli Turn don't exempt anything—there's neither mercy nor guilt in them. Blast eyes, blast body, feed husband and son into death's jaws, call on God to burn home and world to dust. Hair falls loose, cloth falls open, she'll completely ignore this; maddened with rage and fury, Kahar women dance as they curse, clap their hands, sometimes rock to and fro. Bonwari knows all that. The cursing sounds bitter, though nothing comes of it—this much he has experience of too. They've been born low-caste from the "bad karmies" of previous births; in this life there is not enough good karma to make words do what they say. Fear of "Brahmbin"—Vaidya upper-caste gentry tongues—no difference between those tongues' pronouncements and the pronouncements of Shiva. Bonwari doesn't shiver to hear the curses of Noyan's Ma. He's shivering to hear of what she saw in the storm. Noyan's Ma is laughing aloud, clapping her hands, and saying—Father's familiar raisin' its 'ood in the cloud banks. Tongue "grabbin" flashes, that's to say flickering out. Givin' a hissy roar. In its body's burnin' rage glowin' wi' fire it struck sky's roof an' raised storm. Seen wi' me eyes, seen wi' me eyes, made the killer burner's 'ouse fly off. O Kottababa, O Babathakur, fly into fury Father. Go up an' stand atop the familiar. Throw thunderbolts upon the wicked caste corrupter, Father. Roar yer roar, throw yer thunderbolts wi' a shout. Let 'im be blasted an' burned at once. O Father! O Father! O Father!

Bonwari began to shake violently. The vision of the burning death of that terrifying, "mottley" snake had come to mind. It was Auntie Suchand who'd first said it. He had, to some extent, come to believe those words. What's this Noyan's Ma is saying today? Seen with her eyes its hood, its tongue in the clouds?

Pagol was shocked to see his frightened look. He knows nothing of that incident. He's just gotten a mere hint. Nevertheless, he's a Bansbadi Kahar. He can take a guess at Bonwari's fear. Now fear's creeping on him. In a terrified voice he called—Beano!

—Hmm.

—What is it?

Bonwari pointed toward the sky.—Looka that.

Bonwari continued to stare at the sky. Big fat drops of water are falling into his eyes, but he's staring toward the sky's northwest corner. Sky dust has been rinsed and fallen to earth in the torrent of water. The cloud-mass is clearly visible, rapidly whirling in strong wind. Black and white clouds have made a mottled formation there. In the tale of Hansuli Turn many demigods appear to humans; they apprehend "elephant descent" in monsoon skies; see the coming of the demon's boat in the Kopai flood, great torches burning. And today too Noyan's Ma has seen Kottathakur's familiar in the midst of cloud and storm. Bonwari seems to be seeing it, yes, yes, right in the cloud shape, that's a daughter of Ma Monosha of the Snakes—you can clearly see that the black-and-white colored cloud formation is one with the mottled chain viper's body, Kottathakur's familiar.

Even though he was trying, Pagol could not properly comprehend what Bonwari had seen. Yet he too is a Kahar and was able to see yet another probability from this state of cloud and nature. Fearfully he put his hand on Bonwari to bring him around and shouted—Beano—Beano! Stones, stones gonna fall! Beano!

—Stones?

—Yeh, stones.

The rain was getting very light. A few small hailstones now beginning to fall.

—Get inside. Pagol's grabbed Bonwari's arm and is pulling. Bonwari freed his arm. —Evil Karali! Let go Pagol, let go me arm. O great Babathakur—take pity. Purge.

Pagol pulled Bonwari into the house. Immediately hailstones began to fall heavily. With their hands over their heads little boys went down into the yards, collected hailstone fragments, and began to eat; elders scolded and picked them up. Women ran to the indigo levee banks. The ducks are in the levee water. They'll die. They'll likely die. They'll dive under water, that way they can certainly survive. But for how long?

—Aaah—aah—ooh—ooh—ooh! Aah—ooh—ooh—ooh! Eee—ee—ee! Bonwari was alarmed by a voice. Kalobou! Kalobou was rushing along with two ducks under her arms and glancing sidelong around her. Let her go. Bonwari doesn't have time to worry about that.

Pagol said—We're in luck, goats've gone indoors. Beano's four goats are standing next to Pagol, shaking off water now and then. Fur stands on end. Calmly ruminating.

Innumerable hailstones falling, gradually increasing in size. Falling with a thundering sound. A plushing sound in the thatch. A splashing coming up from the water. The levee's lotus leaves have been ripped and shredded to pieces.

The Kahars are dumbstruck. Watching the hailstorm. Even the voice of Noyan's Ma has stopped. Field, riverside, cottage roof, everything has been covered with pieces of hail and turned white.

***

The sky cleared a few hours after the chaos of rainstorm and hail shower. The nor'wester dropped. The sun appeared, on the verge of setting. The sky reddened.

After the rainstorm the girls and boys of Kaharpara dashed off to search in the woods. Where have branches broken, shoots broken, palm trees' dry leaves fallen. They must be gathered and fetched. The elders began to clean up their homes. The straw of yard thatches is patched up with fresh leaves torn down by storm and hail.

Nasubala and Suchand are shrilly weeping. A custom of Hansuli Turn. Bashan is sitting with her head in her hands.

Meanwhile, Noyan's Ma is still dancing wildly. Half the roof of her cottage has also flown off. She doesn't even notice.

Pakhi is saying to Karali—Listen, listen ta what the bitch is sayin'! Noyan's Ma, that is.

Karali kept looking steadily at the roofless cottage. Occasionally saying—Scum! Scum! Scum, ya took ya took, ya took me 'ouse?

Pagol came up.

Karali said—Look.

—Seen.

—Scum brought that storm upon me!

—Stones di'n't strike ya then?

Karali laughed well. He said—That's a thing. Like cows under the cot in the middle o' the room—. Karali burst out laughing. He said—Pakhi won't go under. Pulled 'er, unnerstan', 'eaved 'er under. Then whack-whack, bam-bam—wow!

Mathla and Notbor came. Mathla said—Ah, you've done yer place up real nice—

—Get lost, scum. I'll redo it. I'll fix the bastard's roof up wi' iron wires this time. Just see.

Then their meeting sat. Karali's meeting.

Pagol gradually explained a lot to Karali. Bonwari's words came to mind.

Finally he said—Bonwari's sayin' a valuable thing. Said, if someone says—Give up yer caste fer money, would'ja give it?

Karali burst out laughing. He said—Caste? Oo takes caste? Where's 'e live? I'm sayin', oo destroys caste?

—Oo destroys caste! Pagol was speechless.

—Yeh, yeh. Oo destroys caste? Caste! Caste goes away by eatin', pickin' up, others' leftovers. It ain't lost through touchin'. Their caste's lost, not mine. Unnerstan'? Oo'll destroy my caste?

Pagol shrugged his shoulders, trying to understand. The statement has no meaning, yet it's surely a statement worthy of the name. Daredevil statement, imperious declaration. A fine statement.

Someone came and called from outside.—Pagol-bro, 'eadman's callin'.

—Why's that? I'm 'ere though.

—People's arrived at Master Mitra's place in Mitra-Gopalpur. Weddin'. Need Kahars fer two palanquins. Need a stickfight dance group.

Four

The call has come for "horseclan" Kahars. They must carry bride and groom's palanquin. Tips, gratuities—cloths, old clothing, liquor, belly-filling fries and sweets. Of course they have to go. They'll go. The Atpoures have a stickfight dance group; they'll take them too. Even though they're separate, both groups are Kahar. Let Porom be told. A glimpse of Kaloshoshi at Porom's house too.

A little before this, during the hailstorm, Kaloshoshi had come from the indigo levee to pick up the ducks. She'd made sidelong glances as she went. It's possible she was angry. An enraging thing. Bonwari is sometimes even angry with himself. It seems to him that the position of headman is like being the attendant of a flaming hot oven. If he'd not been headman he would, even at this age, have taken Kaloshoshi and run off to a Kahar community in distant parts. He would have performed companion rites and set up home, if only it weren't for the headmanship. As he ponders, Bonwari shivers involuntarily. Although he has received a hugely fortunate human birth, he's been born into a lowly race because of bad karma in a previous birth. Horseclan Kahar; though he's human, like a horse, he must carry humans of higher breed, get shoulder sores from carrying palanquin poles. Gotta stoop and carry. At one time they'd had to dispose of dead cows, buffaloes, dogs, cats from bosses' houses—in the temper of the times, with great difficulty, they'd managed to free themselves of this in the era of Bonwari's headmanship. But they'll have to remain at foot level for eternity. All fruit of prior births. Now if they act badly in this birth, will they be born in a clan lower than even the Kahars? He ascended Kalaruddu's Charak disc this time. He lay on the iron spikes of the Charak board and gazed into the sky at Father. Father's forgiven him, will he do evil again? Again? No. No. Have pity Lord, have pity.

But to look, to take a look, where's the fault in that? That's not evil, is it? He'll get a look at Kaloshoshi. He will explain to her—Din't 'appen in this birth, sis; the birth's comin' where you'll get me, I'll get you—go ta Father's shrine an' pay 'beisance at two o'clock ta make it 'appen. Fix up fallen clods at Kalarudda's banyan tree shrine. That I'll do too. An' burn yer mind's fire, I'll burn too, burn burn an' purify, let it blaze. Let the fire o' love smolder like eternal wood embers. Through this good karma we two will find each other.

Roton, Prohlad, and even the lads are getting very excited. After a long time, a large overdue payment has come in. Huge storm and hail shower are immediately forgotten in the excitement. The "waft," or weather, is turning nice. The day following this rain and hailstorm will be cool. Anyway, the fields have turned to mud, can't work there. The bosses' thatched roofs are dripping, can't climb those roofs for a few days; everyone's restless and "carefee," that's to say carefree.

The Mitra-Gopalpurs hold the position of developed upper-caste Kayastha gentry. Much greater than the Ghosh gentry of Jangol. Their son's wedding. Extravagant wedding. "Yinglish" instruments, military band, drum, shanai, pipe, the hip-swinging Khenta dance, stickfight dances—a real show. The Kahars' luck is good—the wedding is not on the railroad but along the village track. Two by eight, sixteen bearers and two palanquins will go. Fries, sweets, pilaf, fish, meat, a bellyful of eats—despite wet weather, feet are kept in line. Then leaf-rolled smokes and cigarettes, good Kastogarh tobacco—a honeyed aroma such as Kahars would never get even if they died and went to paradise. On top of this, everyone gets a red scarf as gratuity from the bridal home.

Gifts from the groom's home! Can it go off without this? And why would the Mitra masters listen if the Kahars quit? There's the mechanical cart after all—having imported motor cars, they lay the Kahars off, call them only if there is unpaved road. How could it go on if they did not? It's because of this road they need the palanquin Kahars, otherwise the Mitra masters would have hired a motor, a motorbus.

Sixteen miles, makes a thirty-two-mile road. Some paved, then about twelve miles unpaved cowpath—fieldpaths in between.

No way without a palanquin. Kahars' good luck.

Slapping Pagol's back to get him to come, Bonwari said—Gotta go, buddy. Got it?

Pagol really didn't want to, but he said—Come on. This morning Bonwari had said so much to him about the karma of their clan's work that to say "no" could cause a rift.

—Dance a bit, dance.

Pagol did not dance. He sat down on the terrace. His mind still spinning with Karali's declaration. The lad's saying a very forceful thing—Who destroys caste? Where's he live? Certainly a correct statement, certainly. If you're right, then who destroys caste? Though Bonwari's statement is not negligible either; forefathers' declaration. He's thinking.

Bonwari was surprised to see Pagol's thoughtfulness. He said—Tell whaddappened ta you then?

—I'll tell. Tell in secret. Difficult thing. Unnerstan? Yer 'ead'll spin.

Bonwari's spirit is feeling the touch of joy. He was not especially worried about Pagol's statement; it's Pagol! What's more, after Karali's cottage went flying up he can no longer worry about Karali's bragging words. Even though he's miserable about Karali's cottage flying off, he's also cheerful. So he's both miserable and cheerful. Misery—a cottage, such a cottage gone! Cheer—peril avoided, the punishment for the wrongful fault has been taken out on the cottage roof. He saw with his eyes the form of Father's familiar in the clouds. Done, peril avoided. And he's formed the idea that Karalicharan understands in his own mind. This very day the blessed boy climbed up Babathakur's ancient silk-cotton tree. Thought he was so high and mighty climbing so high. In a single stroke Father taught him a little lesson; and it's also certain that if Bonwari had not appeased Babathakur, Karali would not have gotten off so lightly. Perhaps there would even have been a lightning bolt today.

He went off toward Atpoure Para. Called a summons into Porom's yard—Porom! Y'there Porom?

Kaloshoshi came out. She spat, pouted, and said—Ooh my! The pious 'eadman! What, then?

Bonwari gestured a question by wiggling his eyebrows—Where? Where is he? Meaning Porom.

Smiling a strange smile, Kalobou replied—Oo knows? Maybe Penoyini's place. An' you? Whatcha think? Lost yer way?

Something from a few days before came to Bonwari. He said—Was somethin' about sharin' a bitta the good karma, sis, so I've brought the share.

Kaloshoshi pulled up her head covering and did not give a flirtatious reply. —S'comin', she said in a strangled voice.

—Porom? Bonwari turned and looked. Porom has drunk a lot of alcohol. He comes staggering.

—Ooh? Oohzat? Which jackass?

Bonwari said in a grave voice—It's me, Porom.

—An' oo're you? Me, I'm me.

—I'm Bonwari.

—Bonwari?

—Yeh. Orders fer Mitti-Gopalpur's marriage've come. Want Kahars, stickfight dancers. So I came ta let ya know.

—Huh. Mitti-Gopalpur? Real fancy! Eh?

—Yeh. So ya gonna go?

—I'll go. But—

—What?

—Wi' you, gotta—d'jy unnerstan', I've gotta bit o' business.

—What business?

—Goddit. Goddit. D'jy unnerstan', real urgent business. 'S—.

—Won'tcha tell?

—Uh-huh. Tell ya, tell ya one day. Goddit? I'll mek y'unnerstan' well. S'not today. Get weddin' over, then, un'stan? What say?

—Fine, tell me then.

Bonwari went back. He doesn't get along with these repulsive drunken types. He'll drink alcohol—alcohol is the sustenance of the Kahars, so you drink; but why'd you stagger around? Gross drunkard! But now who's this up ahead?

He called—Who?

—Me?

—Oo is it?

—It's Panu—Pankeshto.

—Pana? Bonwari's blood rushed from his feet to his head.—You, 'ere?

—Been ta boss's 'ouse. Goin' 'ome.

—Huh. Bonwari understood. Pana still twisting threads. Let him, then. Bonwari is not afraid.

Panu said—You? Come ta Porom's place, then?

—Yeh. There's an order fer a stickdance group. At the Mitti-Ouse.

—Smoke a little cigarette. Me boss's boy studies in school, smokes cigarettes. Today 'e got 'em out 'is pocket an' put 'em in an alcove, I got a chance, unnerstan'—. Pana started to grin. Then said—Nabbed it an' stashed it. Weren't more'n two in the box. I'll smoke one, you smoke one.

Neem-oil Panu is bitter on the inside, sweet on the outside. Bonwari has heard about the English neem; Panu is that English neem. Panu said, smiling—Dharma's machine turns wi' the wind. Retribution's been taken.

Bonwari gave no reply.

Panu said—Karali's cottage flew up. Why put up wi' such? Nooly thatched cottage. Babathakur's rage. Rather quietly he said—Babathakur's gonna tek 'im, unnerstan'? I've said fer sure. I've gotten proof.

Someone responded from a short way off in the midst of the darkness—An' now ye won't get it? You, thought so virtuous, you wi' all yer prayer an' meditation, not gonna get proof now? They say that in the glow o' that virtue a pomegranate'll light up. Yer past-present-future in yer thumbnail, kill a bird wi' one glance, jimmy-bar in yer shoulder bag—still ain't gonna get proof?

Nasubala. No delay in recognizing Nasubala from the voice and the tone of the statement. Bonwari said—Nasu?

—Yeh? I'm Nasubala indeed.

—Where ya goin'?

—Off ta the Mitti 'ouse. I've found their person, I'm goin'.

Nasubala is going with the person who comes bringing the dowry gift to the Mitra home. In these parts Nasubala has a standing invitation to wedding houses. He even invites himself. Goes and puts in an appearance. A woman's fine outfit, nose ring, hair in a bun, body ornamented, basket on the shoulder. He arrives, stows the basket, pays obeisance, says—Let 'em be blessed. I came, ma'am, miladies. I'll chuck yer leftovers, I'll tidy up, sing songs, dance. When I leave I'll take a sari, take food, make eulogy an' dance me way 'ome.

Thus Nasu's going. Bonwari smiled. Pana's fleeing fast. This didn't escape Nasubala's notice. He saw the moving glow of Pana's cigarette and understood. He said—Cottage flew off today, be fixed tomorrer. Sayin' now 'e'll build in iron. Got that, scrawny shanks!

∗∗∗

The very next day Karali began preparations for house repair. He rose at dawn, went to Channanpur and took two days' holiday, went from there by train to Katoya and returned in the afternoon. And if he didn't come back bringing a carpenter and a stonemason with him. His sole regret was that Bonwari was not home. If he'd been home he would have been shown the productive power of Channapur's workshops. The others had all eaten and set off to carry the wedding palanquins of the Gopalpur Mittis. Suchand said—Is 'e just yer any old geezer! Huge employer. Sahebs were boss. Those days the plantation office's sahebs were boss. My Karali's as lucky as the Kahars o' that time.

Karali was annoyed by this statement. —Don't blather so. I don't carry sahebs' palkies.

Suchand does not understand; what's with Karali getting so enraged over this! A fight could have broken out about it, but Karali let it go. Karali couldn't find the force of his own logic. Though he did not carry the palanquin, he'd had to carry ten sahebs on his back across the banks of a small canal that other day. Many sahebs coming because of war.

The necessaries for construction were all in place. He'd bought everything and brought it in the day before. But with Karali all is amazing! Having cut the new bamboo, bought the rope, bought the straw, and set everything up to make the thatch anew, he suddenly announced—Uh uh, stop.

—What stop? An' why? Pakhi said—Damn damn damn, killin' me with this act!

—No act, cottage roof flew—'s'a good thing, I'll make a new brick 'un.

—Brick?

—Yeh. We'll sleep up top. Cookin' below, pots an' pans there.

Pakhi gaped dumbly in pleasure and surprise, staring into Karali's face. As soon as the others left she ran and embraced Karali's neck with both arms, kicking her legs with great delight.

Karali thought a lot, did research, said—I'll gi' cottage east-facin' doors, stairs'll be in the west way. South' facin' an' east' facin'll be two "windies." I'll bring iron wire from the station. Gonna do it like they do wi' the tin shacks at the station, wire holdin' each corner an' drive a pin in the ground to pull 'em taut. Let's see, how's the bastard's storm gonna make it fly this time?

It was enough to make Pakhi dance. Pakhi really danced. Nasubala's away, he's gone to the wedding house to dance, to clean up ritual leftovers. If he'd been here he would have cut a rhyme and whirled his hips in dance. It is not in the nature of good and kind Bashan to get excited; she only smiled. At first Suchand smiled and cut a rhyme, then wept in the name of Pakhi's father—Where ya gone dad, don'tcha see, Pakhi's gettin' a brick place!

People were frozen with amazement.

If a Hansuli Turn cottage flies off in storm or burns in fire, folk certainly rebuild walls three or four feet higher and top off with thatch; some make a pot-mouth-sized opening at the top of the new wall so a little air can enter. If a cottage collapses in flood, the new one, built to preference, will have some small windows put in; when the home's finished they say—In a way it's turned out well because of Mother Kopai's mercy.

Those whose homes were not smashed say with regret—Woulda been saved if me cottage had fallen! Still standin' crooked, an' just a bitta wall fell!

That saheb-drowning flood in which Mother Lakshmi of Wealth arrived at the Chaudhury house is the very flood that smashed Kaharpara. That time, Kaharpara was made anew. Before that, no one had been able to stand straight in Kaharpara's cottages. That time new Kaharpara was built and the cottages reached their present size. Now a person can stand comfortably in the center of the cottage, but in four corners you'll still hit your head. Now in Kaharpara you see such large cottages, all built with the blessing of that flooding-smashing Mother Kopai. In their corners you no longer hit your head, and there are also small windows in the upper walls. But now Karali's astounding drama! Cottage roof flew off in the storm, walls remain standing; paying to have those walls demolished and a new home! And a brick-built home at that! Has this ever occurred at Kaharpara?

Bashan summoned Karali and discreetly questioned him—Son, brick cottage costs loads. That's—

Karali calmed her fears—Don'cha worry 'bout it.

Bashan asked Pakhi—Sweetie, 'ow much money ya got, eh?

—Zilch.

—So?

—E's takin' a loan. S'a guy gives loans at station.

—Oh my God! Bashan shivered. —E'll take a loan then?

—Yeh. Pay off interest week by week. An' repay principal bit by bit.

Bashan was speechless. She now went back to Karali. Karali explained smoothly. There's a Marwari at Channanpur station who lends money along the whole of the little line, lends to everyone from the gents to the coolies. He takes one anna on the rupee as interest and each week collects one paisa interest per rupee. At the end of the month he wants something on the principal. If you can give, good; if not, there's no harassment. And in the third month he certainly wants something of the principal. Karali will borrow a hundred rupees from him. Each week he now earns a day wage of eight rupees four annas—he carries a few goods at the station, that's a couple of extra rupees. From this ten rupees four annas he must pay one rupee nine annas interest per week. Eight rupees eleven annas will remain. The Marwari moneylender said that if Karali gives two and a half rupees a week from this as repayment on the principal then it will be paid off in about ten months—he'll give exact accounting later. And he'll have the account checked over by the Master. If she doesn't believe him, his mother-in-law can ask Mathla and see that he too is taking a thirty-rupee loan to build a thatch. She can also ask Notbor. Since giving up farmwork, Mathla and Notbor have begun work on the line.

Bashan was even more lost for words. She's never heard such talk of loans, credits, debits. This accounting, this commerce—it's new to the tale of Hansuli Turn. Their commerce with the Mister Mondols of Jangol is different. Take paddy. If you take eighty pounds you have to give a hundred twenty pounds back; don't make the repayment and the interest becomes part of the principal and more interest accrues. Take money and it's no loan—it's an advance. Advance on manure, advance on milk. Manure is sold at three or four cartloads a rupee; the rate for an advance of four loads of manure—five and a half loads. Milk: sixteen quarts a rupee; if an advance is taken the rate to be paid is twenty-two quarts per rupee. If you take an advance of more than five rupees the rate is twenty-four quarts. There's no advance above ten rupees. In a tight spot, a pitcher, water pot, a couple of silver ornaments must be given as security. That accounting is amazingly complex; they neither can nor want to understand it because it will never be settled. Therefore, such credit-and-debit commerce is an utterly astounding subject for Bashan.

That which is astounding in the world is a matter for fear in Hansuli Turn. They do not have the force of intellect to give the astounding a prod to see its real shape. If they did have it in some ancient epoch, it's died under repeated blows. The hard and sharp power fearlessly to dissect and analyze the astounding proved to be of no use in avoiding the punishments of Saheb and Sadgop. So Bashan was frightened by this proposal. After worrying all day, she could see no way to stop Karali. Finally she remembered Bonwari. She summoned Karali at dusk and said—I'm just tellin' ya son, 'old off a couple days.

Karali is determined to start work today. He has brought a few friends and wants to finish demolishing the old cottage. He said—Why 'old off? What 'oldin' off?

—Bonwari-bro, Oton-bro, Pellad-bro—let 'em come back. Ask 'em all what ye need to ask about it.

Karali laughed in fury—Oo do I need to ask ta build a cottage?

—Gotta ask. Gotta ask 'eadman. Gotta get promission. S'an auspicious job, like a weddin'.

—Huh, I got written promission. He suddenly laughed—Promission? Oose promission, what kinda promission? I'm buildin' a cottage an' 'eadman'll give promission! Huh. Go, go, work those pickaxes. He climbed up on the wall himself and began to chop.

It's amazing, Suchand came rushing up right then; she was panting. She spoke as she puffed—No no no. Ye can't make a brick 'ouse—can't—can't.

—Dammit! Whatcha come clownin' around again for?

—Ooh no, no one's ever done this. If ye build a brick place in Kaharpara ye're dead. Can't take it. Suchand had gone to pick shellfish; searching for shellfish in the pond water, it had occurred to her that you cannot do what the forefathers did not do. Won't bear it. Can't stand it. People will die.

Suchand began to weep. Bashanta thought the same thing. She too trembled.

Karali did not reply to Suchand's pronouncement. He began demolishing the cottage. Ah! When Bonwari comes back!

***

Mouths agape, Mathla and Notbor also blurted out—Yeah bro, ain't gonna at least ask 'eadman once? Won't 'e come back an' get mad?

Karali tossed his head, throwing back his hair, and said—E can blow off 'is rage on a big dinner. Oo's 'eadman? I'm me own 'eadman. Then suddenly said—S'go.

—Where?

—S'go. Gonna climb silk-cotton tree again today. That time storm took me cottage up 'cos I went up the tree. Today I'm climbin' the tree again. Today let 'appen what will.

Off he went. Mathla and friends followed in trepidation. No way not to go. Karali is now their captain. The wretches must work under his command at Channanpur.

Karali said—If ya do good, it's bad! Got news by wire at Channanpur—youuge storm comin'. Couldn't find ya, came rushin' ta village—ta warn village. Got there an' saw village chiefs all gone ta Jangol ta thatch Ghosh's place. What ta do? See sky's gettin' black. Realized they can't see nothin' sat up on the thatch 'idden amidst trees all round. Got up on the rain tree. Could see westward—ah! By Mary, 'ow ta describe the sight! Rain tree's not so tall though, couldn't see enough. Then I got up on the other tree. Marvelous! Fantastic! 'Twas really beautiful!

Notbor said—Was, saw, done well. Now gi' it a rest today. What's the point o' gettin' up on God's tree?

The trunk of the silk-cotton tree is huge; impossible to put your arms around it to climb. Karali began to climb, grasping hollows in the trunk. Up on the first branch, he spat at Notbor, saying—Scram, bastard!

Then he said—Wow, by Mary, so easy ta dive in the deeps from 'ere!

—Oi, oi, crocodile's in the deeps, Babathakur's in the deeps.

—Course they are. Croc can stay there.

Postponing a dive into the deeps, he began climbing higher. Up top today he again began to shout—Ho—

In other words, Look, look you lot, I've climbed the silk-cotton tree again—

All Kaharpara heard the shout and stood staring toward the tree in frightened amazement.

Five

Wedding palanquin-carrying is two days' merrymaking. At some weddings it goes on for three days—when it's been a long trek. The groom sets out on the day his body is anointed with turmeric; inaugural rites take place at the bridal home. Else he sets off on the wedding day. On the wedding day, the groom arrives at the bride's home by evening—feasting and merrymaking! By evening again the next day bride and groom are taken to the groom's home for a return party. Then parting gifts, and the Kahars return home by first watch of night. In some cases it can be the middle of night. Rather tired bodies of course, but they return noisily, totally drunk. Two days' worth of drinking at the wedding, no doubt, but too much drinking is forbidden. You have to keep your footing when shouldering a palanquin—have to walk in step with one another. If someone kicks another's foot, palanquin will shake. If legs stagger, palanquin will lurch. Palanquin timber will knock the heads of bride and groom, that's a pain. Then you must move over road, fieldpath, ditch, muddy track—would it really work if you'd drunk too much? So it's after the return party that the Kahars fill bellies, swill booze, and stagger home. The sharing of earnings takes place at the liquor shop. Each understands what's his before going in; else the headman saves it and distributes to each his share the day after returning home, when the high has gone. It's the rule of Bonwari's group—understand the day after. Roton, Prohlad, the elders say—Understand a human, word is said; understand God, nod the head. That's to say you bow your head down. There's no difference between keeping money with Bonwari and offering it to Lakshmi while smearing rouge on her urn. Bonwari says—Others' wealth is poison in Kalaruddu's throat; there's no way ta chuck stuff that belongs ta yer own folks, no peace in keepin' it; gobble it up an' it's just in this life—be burned to ash in the next life.

The earnings were not bad—sixteen Kahars, two palanquins, sixteen rupees per palanquin—that's a two-rupee award for all; sixteen men, sixteen scarves; from the bride's house five rupees gratuity given, or two-and-a-half rupees per palanquin; the liquor tip for two palanquins is two globes; that's the price of two big round jars of alcohol. Porom's group got plenty too—six men had gone to do the stickfight dance and had taken twelve rupees in gratuities. Beside this, a globe of liquor. In the liquor stakes Porom and company had done better. Bonwari didn't object to anyone about this. Shame! That's a game for small-minded types! Porom and company had performed well. Yes, Porom is indeed a master of the fighting stick—he'd performed what's called the one-piece move. The five followers surrounded him with fighting sticks, Porom beat all five back and broke out with a leap. Two men with cracked heads, one with a finger so badly slammed he'll suffer for days. The Lords of the two wedding parties entreated—Bonwari must engage Porom with the fighting stick. Porom said—Ye'll see stickfight play, so tell Bonwari. Yes, I'm happy to play single-handed; you'll be happy to watch too. Bonwari folded his hands. He performed stickfight play, but all alone. He also played double with Roton and Prohlad. But did not play with Porom. What's the point? Eternal rivalry of two hamlets. Besides, Porom's a bandit, a hoodlum; Bonwari does not trust him. And Kaloshoshi's in the middle. He remembered the subject of Atpoure Para's Ghentu song. He does not like Porom's smile either. So what; by Father's grace the wedding's work has gone off smoothly and merrily. Lots of fun too. A long time since there was such fun. Rivalrous sparks flying between the palanquins.

It didn't happen so much on the way there. In one of the two palanquins was the bride, in the other was the family's "Lord Guru." It began on the way back. In one palanquin the groom, in the other the bride. Rivalry between the two palanquins—who'll get ahead? The fun of this rivalry calls to mind the fun of those first days of the tale of Hansuli Turn. Time when they were bondslaves of the factory court, time when there were great mansions there with pearl-fringed, brocade-covered palanquins, palanquins with silver handles fashioned as leviathan heads, or tiger heads, or lion heads. Rivalry of Lord and Lady's palanquins. Strength would rise up in the bodies of Hansuli Turn's Kahar serfs, would make them run—like horses with passengers on their backs. They would take Saheb and Ma'am, Lord and Lady, on their shoulders, rivalrously shouting a beat of *plo-heen—plo-heen*, raising a hue and cry all around as they went. That time has gone. Now is the age of the broken palanquin. The Kahars no longer have service land on the estate, palanquins have disappeared from the place. The palanquin-riding Lords and Ladies of old are gone. The weight of that Lord's frame was a good hundred and sixty pounds. Same as the Lady's frame, not less than one-sixty, and on top of that the Lady's jewelry at about another twenty pounds. It felt like a cut in the shoulder when the palanquin was lifted on. Some folk would be even heavier than that. To lift the palanquin with them on it would make the head whirl, make the heart pound in your chest. Among other things, the wittier bearers would say—Gent's real hea—vy. People still say that bearer's line today, jokingly intoning—The bearers say, bastard's real hea—vy. Oh dear Lords! Can the Kahars say that? Ages after all this, a rivalry between two palanquins for this wedding. Usually these days the bride and groom come in the same palanquin, so there's no chance for rivalry. The Mitra gentry did it with two palanquins.

They've covered a sixteen-mile road, whipping up road dust. Each palanquin moving on four men's shoulders, the other two pairs of four running alongside. They moved almost as fast as a carriage. Will groom get ahead or bride get ahead? Lord ahead or lady ahead? "Nakshmi" ahead or "Larayan" ahead? *Plo-heen—Plo-heen—Plo-heen—Plo-heen!* Bonwari carries his palanquin and that Pagol Kahar is also there, first on the palanquin's forward pole. He's singing the ancient songs of Hansuli Turn's Kaharpara as he goes. Pagol has no equal in singing songs. Pagol singing—

—On the good straight road—

The rear-carriers shouted—*Plo-heen.*

—We'll go with strong step.
—Plo-heen—Plo-heen.
—With a stronger tread—
—Plo-heen—Plo-heen—Plo-heen—

Pagol now laughingly sang out—Groom's palanquin.—*Plo-heen—Plo-heen!*—Fallen behind—

—Plo-heen—Plo-heen!
—Lakshmi moves ahead—
—Plo-heen—Plo-heen—
—Larayan comes behind.

Roton was in front of the groom's palanquin, and he called—Harder now, harder now—*Plo-heen—Plo-heen.* In the bride's palanquin, the bride grins at the groom; the groom, sat in his own palanquin, smiles too—they know of this.

Bonwari suddenly called loudly—Careful bearers!—*Plo-heen—Plo-heen.*—Gone down fieldpath. Foot on foot—foot on foot. That's to say, do not step to left and right, put one foot in the footprint of the other; one man treading in the other's step, the bearers proceed cautiously. In all these places Bonwari directs with his own voice; he can't trust Pagol. He's the sort of simple man who might be swung by song into speaking not of the footpath but of the bride and groom. The rear bearers will make a misstep. Bonwari yelled—Step carefully, come on bearers. R-i-i-g-h-t, l-e-e-f-t. Stay alert—stay alert. *Plo-heen—Plo-heen*! Lift the front—ditch ridge, bro. *Plo-heen—Plo-heen*! Pullin' in the back! From the back, the word "plo-heen" changed to "shoulder, shoulder." The palanquin stopped. One man will quit the palanquin, one man will change shoulders; in other words, shift weight from the right shoulder to the left.

Straightaway Roton overtook on the right with the groom's palanquin, shouting *whoo hoo*. Running fast, calling the count.

—Heyyo, careful—

—*Plo-heen.*

—Overtake palanquin—

—*Plo-heen.*

—Lord's command—

—*Plo-heen.*

—Lady's palanquin—fallen behind—

—*Plo-heen—Plo-heen—Plo-heen—Plo-heen—*

They passed on by.

Bonwari and Pagol rushed again—Groom's palanquin's gotten ahead, go, go. The bridal palanquin again moved with strong steps. —Step by step, move now bearers. Pagol began to sing loudly again—Lord's gone ahead. *Plo-heen—Plo-heen*. Step it up wretches, catch that palanquin. Harder, harder. Lakshmi will get ahead. Now a smile will grow on Lakshmi's face. Beaten by Lakshmi, "Larayan" will also smile. *Plo-heen—Plo-heen—Plo-heen*. They well understand that bride and groom are smiling at each other. They can actually feel the touch of those smiles as they carry the palanquin shafts!

Much later there was a huge party. The Kahars returned with vast amounts of betel chews, pressed rice, parched sweet rice, fries, sweets.

Lord Mitra clapped Bonwari and Porom on the back—Bravo! I'm well pleased.

Porom removed his skirt, bodice, anklets, and earrings. Tied up his bundle, put it on his head, and set off. He called Bonwari—Come on.

Bonwari smiled and said—S'go, meetin' set up at the boozers' place; we're goin'—still work left to do.

Porom said sarcastically—Huh. Sure, sure. Horses gotta be stabled after pullin' a cart.

The Kahars are the horse clan. Hence the joke. Now Bonwari has to return the two palanquins to the house of Channanpur's great gentry. The two palanquins are theirs. The Mitras had used them for the wedding. An honorarium of two large fish must be given to the great gentry for the palanquins. If you take palanquins for a wedding, fish must be given. If you take a palanquin to carry a dying person to the Ganges, a food offering must be made—offering of ghee and flour. It's Kahars who carry and deliver these things. When this job is finished Bonwari and company can take a break. But the job is for the young lads. They always do it. Two Kahars carry an empty palanquin, one Kahar carries the fishes; sometimes the fishes dangle from the hand of one of the two bearers. An ordinary household gives four pounds of fish, five pounds' weight if it's urgent. Where would they get fish to give weighing more than that? Those who have such cannot give them as tribute. Mister Mitra is a respectable man, he gave two fish weighing twenty pounds. They're going to the home of the great gentry, could he send small ones? Precisely for this reason, Bonwari will not give the lads the responsibility but will go himself. Great gentry watched over by Regal Lakshmi, he'll gain audience, obeisance will be paid. Sire will see the fish and be pleased. He'll say—You? And who are you, pray?

Bonwari will say—By yer leave, honor, I'm Bonwari. Yer servant, just become yer new subject. Takin' land in the Saheb Tracts.

Beside this, there's another little reason. During an interval, Nasubala came and said—Uncle Beano, groom says 'e'll see ya. Better not leave wi'out visitin'. Told me in secret. Bride was laughin'.

Bonwari, Pagol, Roton, Prohlad all looked at each other and grinned. The bride and groom were both very, very happy with the rivalrous game of bringing them in the palanquins. A secret "gratooty" will come from a red-painted hand. He does not want to let Porom know about this either. They'll be silently resentful. Perhaps they'll also go to the groom and make demands. Everyone will find out about it. They may be bride and groom, but they're still children and have received as a blessing a few rupees from various people; it's this money they'll give from. Where would they get enough money to dole it out to all these folk? If they give to Porom then the musicians will come; behind the musicians the lighting man; who can count the crowd who'll be behind him?

Hey there! Standing at the back door sill, Nasubala's calling him over with a wave. Nasubala's clothing is completely "colored up," "bloody-red." Nasu has plastered on a lot of paint. Voice cracking. Singing day and night. Both arms covered in smooth glass bangles.

Bonwari and Pagol approached. Pagol said with a grin—So let's 'ave me weddin' when we get back ta the village, Beano-bro'. Bride's all ready.

Nasubala blasted back—Go die, monster! Don't mind it's a gentyfolks' 'ouse! Shameless, 'ang ya by the neck!

Pagol suddenly widened his eyes and said—Oh man, what's this? Sparklin' on the bride's nose! 'Tain't no brass, di'n't see it when I arrived the other day!

Rocking his body in great delight, Nasu now said—I've got me dues, got me dues. From the bride. These gold "thingies"—all these! Four, five sets o' nose rings. Eight, nine sets o' gold flower earrings. Bundle o' clothes. Bride gave the nose rings. Lady o' the 'ouse'll give a striped sari. I said ta the groom—Big bro, 'cos I'm Kahar means I don't get no sisterly favors? 'Tain't gonna be, not gonna quit, me—yeh. New striped sari—. He suddenly covered his face with his headcloth and modestly stood aside. Master groom had emerged. The groom put a five-rupee note into Bonwari's hand and said—The bride's palanquin bearers get three rupees, my bearers two rupees.

Bonwari was happy indeed. But Nasubala spoke up—Ooh deary me, three rupees? Three's a bad 'un! No, big bro, ya can't 'ave a bad 'un in yer good works. Gi' one more rupee.

Smiling, the groom said—You're a dangerous one! Though he said this, he couldn't fail to give a rupee.

Bonwari said—All best fer yer success, young sir.

Pagol said—One due outstandin', though.

The groom said—Speak, what?

—When there's a baby son, we'll carry wife an' son 'ere; our advance is due.

The groom smiled shyly. Nasu clapped his hands and danced.

So *snap rap tap*—so *snap rap tap*.

***

Bonwari came and sat down in the booze shop. The booze shop is crowded, busy. The drinkers have sat in groups. Jele fisher caste in one spot, Santals in another spot; a group of Doms is sat beneath the mango tree, the Haris nearby, the Channanpur Bauris sitting apart; the Bagdis are sitting there, they don't drink much liquor here but take it back to their own neighborhood and drink. Porom and his entourage have sat near the group of Doms. Bonwari was hoping that at least on this day, having done the wedding tasks together, they could all sit together on the way home. He was disappointed. He said—Porom sittin' over there!

Gupi said—Leave it dad. Whatever one's mind, there 'eaven they'll find; seatin's fine.

Bonwari immediately understood that something had happened on the way. He knows Porom. He smiled and sat. Sat and said—Whaddtap-pened? Scrap over the earnins? A fight, that is.

—I thought it'd be a scrap over the earnins—'ot temper. Scrap 'bout caste, 'bout anchestry.

—Bout caste, 'bout anchestry? The veins on Bonwari's foreheard stood out.

Pagol said—Quit it now. Come on, pour, pour.

—What quit it? All yer bile an' spleen's gone, Pagol.

—Ye're crazy, Beano. What's the fight 'bout caste? Ooever's big is big, 'ooever's small is small. Oo can control 'ow God makes us an' sends us forth? Real caste's about yer 'abits, behavior, deeds an' karma.

Bonwari understood. This is his quality.—All right, all right, ya said right, enough. Come, pour. Called small's not small; standin' tall's not big. Enough.

Pagol sang. Liquor began going down with puffed rice and eggplant fritters. Bonwari suddenly called Pagol and indicated—Looka the bastard showin' 'is caste, look wha' the bastard's doin'.

Everyone looked; Porom was sitting down in the middle of the Dom group. He was also drinking.

Pagol said—Leave it.

—Why leave it? Porom's made 'is caste Dom.

—Indeed. All agreed with one voice.

Only Pagol said—Oh no, caste ain't lost like that. Ooever's caste is lost, it's lost—perishes jus' like that. Oo's ain't lost ain't lost. If ya don' give up yer caste, oo takes it? What's 'is name, where's 'e live?

Bonwari was speechless.

Pagol said—Karali said a priceless thing. Said right. Since then I've thought an' seen. Lad said a true thing.

—Karali! Karali said?

—Yeh. The day I told 'im what you said. You'd said, ask Karali. So Karali says—If I don't give up me caste, oo can take it? Where's 'e live? An' 'e said another thing too—great thing. Said caste ain't lost through touchin', caste's lost through eatin' others' leftovers. My caste ain't gonna be lost, I don't eat no one's leftovers. Kahars gather up Sadgop leftovers an' leave this world.

Everyone froze. Bonwari stared fixedly at the ground.

Only Pana spoke—I ain't sayin' a word, pal. Everythin's my fault. Gottit!

Bonwari grabbed his hand and pushed him aside, saying—If I see yer scraggy face, ya bastard, me 'ole body burns wi' rage. Geddout, geddout from in fronta me.

Roton said—Up, up, get 'ome. No more.

Bonwari said—Take a full jar. Lads an' lasses—. No good wi'out a jar.

They must take liquor for the hamlet. If they drink liquor, have fun— and the hamlet folks don't, what's with that? It's always been usual to bring liquor back for the hamlet.

Porom asked—Goin' or what?

Bonwari replied gravely—Yes.

Porom said to his group—Up. We're leavin' too.

There is a huge meadow between Channanpur and Bansbadi—several miles long. About three-quarters of the way through it, first there's Jangol village on the left-hand side; then Bansbadi. Halfway along there Porom called—Bonwari!

Bonwari was up ahead. He replied—Oo? Oo's callin'?

—It's Porom. Yeh. Wanna word wi' ya.

—Wi' me? What?

—Wait, I'll tell ya.

To the two groups Porom said—Get, get, get on wi' ya. We'll walk an' talk. We got a secret thing ta discuss.

Pagol called everyone away—S'go—s'go. With that, he broke into song—

In secret, let me speak my mind, sweet, in darkness 'neath the tree,
Ah me, this freezing cold eventide.

In a flash Porom grabbed firm hold of Bonwari's arm. He stared hard into Bonwari's face. Bonwari understood. He immediately took a breath and stood with puffed chest. Said—Gonna hit? Which is to say, gonna fight?

Porom said—Whatcha say ta Karali? I'm a bandit, I'm marked?

Bonwari said smiling—Admit to all that, don't ya? Don't you say so yerself?

Grinding his teeth now, Porom said—Pious bastard, what were you worshippin' under our banyan tree?

Porom has no shame. "Why should a naked beggar fear a mugger?" He's covered head to toe in filth, the spit he aims at those above him falls back on his body and he smears it in; how on earth would he have any sense? To start a fight over the affair of the woman of your house and to spit at those above you are the same thing. Neither sense nor guilt; he who has no guilt has no shame. But Bonwari has shame, he has to be afraid of the affair; he is headman of all Kaharpara. The old days were different. These days are different. And the conduct of these days—two generations of Bonwaris, father and son, have established a "Don't Stare at Girls" rule in Kaharpara. Not everyone follows it, and yet some order has returned. In spite of his drunkenness, therefore, Bonwari thinks straight and says—Get yer 'ands off, Porom. That's all trash talkin'.

—Ya bastard, Pana told me. E saw yer triumphs wi' 'is own eyes. Porom spoke low and free without once pausing.

Bonwari remained silent. No, he won't answer. His fault, sure, yet he does have a response. If he gives this response then he'll have to put the blame on Kaloshoshi. It was she who pulled Bonwari onto the path of wrong out of contempt for Porom. Bonwari did not call her. But he will not say this, cannot say it.

Porom suddenly slapped his cheek, gave him a smack and said—Eh bastard, gone quiet! Righteous! Eadman!

Bonwari could restrain himself no longer. He roared—Porom!

The drunken Porom put his hands out to nobody and said—Fightstick? Me fightstick?

In his excitement Porom had thrown his fighting stick aside and grasped Bonwari's arms. Without paying attention. In a second Bonwari leaped onto Porom's shoulders. No fightstick in his hand. If Porom gets his fightstick he's a man-eating tiger. He won't let Porom get his fightstick back.

Then began the war. Soundlessly—in that deserted wasteland they attacked each other like savage beasts. The two men locked together and fell rolling to the earth like the rocks of this place. Now one, now the other on top. Bandit Porom, murderer Porom—him on top, trying furiously, mercilessly, to thrash Bonwari. Bonwari, son of the Kosh-Shoulder house, has a hard body; he defends himself but doesn't want to strike a mortal blow. No, he won't do that.

In the tale of Hansuli Turn's night, tusky wild pigs do battle. In tree-tops monkey troop warriors make war. Suchand says—In those days at Hansuli Turn it'd sometimes be man-on-man fight ta the death, rivers o' blood. This man-on-man killing no longer happens in Kaharpara. Those days it happened all the time. As if two "demonds," that's demons, had gone to war. Battling, goring each other like a pair of tusky boars. Now such battles are a matter of shame. But what to do? If Porom attacks you must defend. You defend, get thumped, get angry. Now he'll strike back—! Porom on his guard! Now Bonwari recovered and glanced toward the road. Porom and Bonwari's companions had left them behind, moving unconcernedly ahead. Bonwari wanted to shout a summons to them. But no, that's a deeply shameful thing. That would be the same as admitting defeat. With his life's strength he tried to stand. He stood with huge effort, taking Porom with him. And immediately took this chance to hurl him to the ground. Porom was knocked nearly unconscious by this throw. Bonwari didn't have much strength left either. But he slammed down upon Porom's chest. Rained down more merciless blows. Then quit. He sat to one side and began to gasp. His whole body seemed wrecked.

Much later he managed somehow to pull himself together and stand up. Porom was also starting to get up. Bonwari grasped his hand and said—Can ya stand?

Porom growled—Get off.

Leaving him, Bonwari staggered off. Porom tried to stand a few more times, then lay back down in that field.

***

Meanwhile, the village was enjoying alcoholic pleasures accompanied by various tasty foods. Bonwari paused in surprise at the village boundary. He had somehow not entered the village and instead gone through the darkness of the thick, dark, ancient thickets adjoining it to Atpoure Para. Today it's as if Kalobou is drawing him with hundredfold magnetism. As if the blood in his body is still burning fire. He's thinking that today, right now, he will take Kalobou home with him. No evil will be done. Porom himself has forestalled that evil. With trembling hands, he picked up a few pebbles and tossed them into Porom's yard as a signal. Tap, tap, tap. Sharp Kaloshoshi understood right. A white form came and stood in the yard's shadowy darkness.

Now he gently cleared his throat. Smart Kalobou turned to hear and tautened like a violin wire in response. In the flash of her alarmed look

she saw Bonwari and slowly approached. With a huge smile she said—
You! I knew it, sure I did!

—Yeh.

—But whassup? Why ya pantin'?

—I've 'ad a fight wi' Porom.

Kalobou touched him and recoiled—What's this! Blood?

—Yeh. E's fallen down in the meadow.

Kalobou was not in the least bit flustered or concerned. She stared
at him for a while entranced, then said—First wash off that bloodiness.

—'Tain't gonna wash off wi' no pitcher water. Bonwari laughed. —
Dust-an'-blood—gotta take a bath.

She took Bonwari's hand and said—Let's go ta the river then. Cleansin' water, bathe an' scrub ya clean.

—Come on. Bonwari was happy. Today Kalobou seems more lovely
than ever. It seems that if Kalobou washes him down, the agony of all the
cuffs and blows will dissipate! Putting his hand on Kalobou's shoulder,
he said—S'go.

At that point the hamlet was blissfully drunk. Drums playing. Everyone mad with drink. Same happening at Atpoure Para. Bonwari staggered down into the river's womb with Kalobou. Moon just rising in the
sky. Huge, slightly waning, red-hued moon. On the other side of Hansuli Turn, sky showing pale behind treetops, leaves on branches rustling
and dancing in the reddish glow of moonlight. It is not light dancing but
leaves in the breeze, though you would think—it was moonlight dancing,
playing, circling like the fluttering wings of a butterfly in flight. Bonwari
immersed himself to the neck in the Kopai's waters. His wounds smarting
at the water's touch, and yet it seemed as if his body was cooled. Kalobou sitting on the river sands with her legs stretched out. The moonlight
straightaway became milky, made the bamboo grove's lines of trees glisten, and came down to the river's breast. The Kopai's water took on the
luster of molten silver. As if the moon shatters scattering in the Kopai's
fast-flowing current, as if it's rolling and swelling with tinkling laughter.
Kalobou is looking so beautiful in that glow. Besides, heat is gripping the
mind; the glow of that heat is showing in Kaloshoshi's face too. Bonwari
said—Will ye sing sweet a verse o' song?

Kalobou smiled. Her teeth glistened and she said—Song?

—Yeh. Good song of 'eat.

—I see ye're real drunk today!

—Bonwari smiled. Kalobou began to sing. Song of the tale of Hansuli Turn. Nobody knows who composed it. Kalobou sang—

The glow of my mind's 'eat
Didn't give you a drop—
Ah, I wept onto a lotus leaf
Leaf didn't take those tears—
Overflowing—overflowing—
Alas, lover, fallen away—
O alas, the glow of unloosed tears does not glisten on the earth's breast.

On the Kopai's north bank a pair of "partiges," or partridges, suddenly squawked; overhead an owl flapped out of a palm tree with clattering wings. Kalobou gave a start, said—O God! Damn, damn the monsters. As she spoke she turned around and glared at the birds of that unlucky moment. As she turned to look she made a faint and frightened moan!— Who's that? Him. In the moonlight Porom can clearly be seen standing on the riverbank. Eyes burning like a beast of prey. Porom's eyes burn in darkness like a wildcat's. But no one has ever seen them burn like this. He is staggering. Kaloshoshi stood up in a flash; she called Bonwari. But where's Bonwari? Where? The whole river stream is shining in the moonlight. But where's Bonwari? Meanwhile Porom has jumped down from the riverbank. Kalobou knows Porom. She has heard from his own mouth—how easy it is to kill a man by stamping on his throat, and how many men he has killed. Kalobou began to shake, then she ran—across the sandy hollows of the Kopai's belly. Porom ran after her. Porom is whining.

Bonwari had floated down quite a way when he resurfaced. He had been floating underwater with the current. He was shaken to see what was happening as he came up. Kalobou is running upward, meaning against the direction of the stream. Behind her comes Porom with a tottering run. Now he quickly got out of the water. He tried to run. But he's tottering too. And it's sandy.

There Kalobou's running! There!

There's Porom!

Disaster! The "Saheb-Drowning Deeps" are up ahead, sometimes called "Demon Deeps"; Kaharpara's folks call them—Lord's Deeps. Lord bathes in those deeps. Kalarudra is at his watery rest in those deeps.

The Kahars come down there four times a year. They take Kalarudra's blackstone figure there at Gajon, put him to his watery rest; and there resides the "pot" of Kalarudra's daughter, Ma Monosha of the Snakes. That pot descends once and is taken away—that pot descends once and is immersed. Beside this, no one goes near the place. A huge, ancient crocodile stands guards there. Comes out for a wander now and again, for sure; but if there's trouble in the deeps it will certainly come rushing, cutting like an arrow through the Kopai's waters. Save us, O Babathakur, save us.

Kaloshoshi is clambering up the edge of those deeps. She could climb it easily; beyond the silk-cotton tree are Kopai's woods. If Kaloshoshi gets into the woods it will be beyond Porom's ability to find her. Kaloshoshi is climbing like a wildcat, grasping at silk-cotton tree roots. Tree roots have come through the earth of the deeps—hanging down so she can hold on and use her feet to climb up. Bravo—bravo! Bravo, Kaloshoshi!

Suddenly at Kaloshoshi's terrified cry it seems the Kopai's frozen wombland is shocked to see a murderess's dagger flashing over its breast. What's that? A crooked head stood shooting up like lightning from under the tree roots, what's that? Kopai's water and sand glittering in moonlight. You can see grass swaying as far as the scrubby banks, grains of sand sparkling on the river beach. But why can't you see Kaloubou? Where is she? Where's Kalobou gone? Bonwari looked everywhere, calling out in a strangled voice—Kaloshoshi!

Porom started to giggle. Grasping the sides of the deeps, Porom is going back down toward the water. Where's Kalobou? What has happened? Only the water of the deeps is rippling. He ran toward the deeps. Water is rippling, wave on wave. The crooked, lightninglike thing that came up from the bottom of the silk-cotton tree, swinging above Kalobou's head and breast, is still standing, head up, rocking. It too is watching the water of the deeps rippling, wave on wave. Bonwari stood frozen in terror. Then with hands clasped he paid obeisance and began to back away. A white cobra.

From behind Porom began to laugh again. Bonwari turned back. Let there be an end to compromise. Porom is standing on the other bank of the Kopai, laughing.

Bonwari called harshly—Porom!

Porom did not reply. His vengeance is spent. He's fleeing.

Bonwari said—Be a man an' come back!

Porom laughed, showing his teeth. Then he vanished into thickets on the river's far side. But Bonwari did not have the courage to go down into Lord's Deeps.

Bonwari began to tremble violently. Has the wrath of Kottababa come down upon him too? Did someone from under the water pull Kalobou down? Who was standing over her head and breast, raising the Rod of Death? Father's familar! Father's familiar! His eyes saw darkness, perhaps he too would have fallen. But someone suddenly grabbed him from behind. Pagol grabbed him, shouting—Bonwari! Bonwari! Bonwari!

Part

One

Pagol brought Bonwari home and laid him down. Bonwari was beside himself. The hamlet folk crowded in. What happened? How did it happen?

Pagol said—Fell down at the edge o' Jangol village gaspin'.

—Edge o' Jangol?

—Yeh. Pagol was saying this after much troubled thought. He saw almost everything that happened at the end. Seeing the moonlight, he'd gone down to the Kopai's banks on a whim. Kalobou had then been singing. With boundless curiosity he climbed a tree so he could watch Bonwari's love play. Then Porom came along and the whole thing was over in the blink of an eye. Porom was on the far side when he got down from the tree; water in the Kali Deeps rippling, Bonwari standing on the edge tottering and shaking. He grabbed Bonwari. He didn't have courage to go down to the deeps either. He knows that Kaloshoshi's body will wash up tomorrow. Police will come. If anyone says that Bonwari was there, they'll drag him in and won't release him. *So why was he there then?* Everyone's mistaken by moonlight, but Inspector is not. Thus, after much troubled thought and in order to save himself and Bonwari, he said—Bonwari was sittin' at the edge o' Jangol village gaspin'. He knows that Porom has fled. If suspicion falls on Porom it will not be an injustice. It's Porom who really killed Kalobou. If Kaloshoshi had not drowned in the deeps, Porom would certainly have killed her. He would have grabbed her by the throat and thrown her into the deeps in a flash. The edge of Jangol is a long way from the Kopai deeps. Jangol village, then fields, then Kaharpara, then the bamboo edges, then scrubland—the Kopai tears her way through the heart of that very scrubland. Kalobou will float up in the Kopai deeps. Mister Inspector will not be able to stretch out his arm and grab Bonwari.

Pagol told of the scene Porom made. At the booze shop Bonwari said—Porom's got no caste, caste's lost, sat with the Doms and drank booze. Porom heard. Called Bonwari on the road. We didn't understand why. Then this tragedy.

Everyone believed it.

Karali rose.—Where's that Porom? Where?

Bonwari is shivering as if unconscious. He's got the shakes. In spite of this he said—No. Pagol, stop it. The lad'll start a riot wi' the Atpoures. An'—

Clenching his teeth, he raised himself. That—that there boy is the root of all mischief. He killed Babathakur's familiar. He climbed Babathakur's silk-cotton tree. He glanced toward Karali and was utterly undone with astonishment. Karali was wearing long pants and a jacket. He continued to stare steadily.

Gopalibala covered Bonwari's eyes with her hand and said to Pagol— O bro, see 'ow 'e's starin', 'ow 'e's shakin' all over. What's 'appenin', dearest!

Pagol knows how to take a pulse. Taking his hand, he said—Fever's comin', fever. Bring a sheet, bring a sheet.

Bonwari said—Take 'way, take far 'way from fronta me—

High fever overcame him as he spoke.

Next morning Kaloshoshi's body floated up in the middle of the Kali Deeps. Loose hair dancing with the rippling swell, Kalobou's body rises and sinks.

No sign of Porom.

**

Everyone felt wretched. Only Noyan's Ma was not upset. She was pleased at Bonwari's distress. She was delighted too by Kalobou's death. Kalobou, the one Bonwari had the "ots" for! She bathed, and with loosened hair went to pay respects to Babathakur. She began to sing a hymn of praise to Babathakur.

But nobody was surprised.

In the history of Hansuli Turn's bamboo grove-encircled Bansbadi such unnatural deaths happen all the time. Snakebites, injuries from the tusks of wild pigs—there's a nominal inquiry; beside this there are drownings, often falls from trees; and then there are hangings, poisonings, and somewhere in the history you can find people cutting their own throats with kitchen choppers. Women die more unnatural deaths. It's in the police station ledger—The women are of poor character; in the majority of cases they commit suicide because they are unhappy. Occasionally there is the suspicion that it's not suicide—murders, it's the men doing murders. A few of them absconding. That's all in the past, though; doesn't happen much nowadays.

Suchand knows more of the tale of Hansuli Turn than anyone. She says—Bonwari's father's father's father an' my father's father were the same man. My granddad beat my first grandma's 'ead in wi' a grindin' stone, sat on 'er chest an' killed 'er wi' the slab. Suchand's eyes bulge as she speaks. She speaks very softly—Didn't granddad see one o' the Atpoures sneakin' out of the 'ouse one night. That's it, blood went to 'is 'ead. Grindin' slab in fronta the 'ouse, took the stone an' smashed 'is wife's 'ead in. Then dragged 'er an' chucked 'er in the middle o' the Kopai; said—She fell an' banged 'er 'ead on a rock. That was in the Saheb masters' day. Sahebs sent police away. But they slashed granddad's back ta ribbons wi' a good whippin'. Nothin' escapes their knowin', kid!

Roton's forefather beat his younger sister to death. Back then there was a huge crocodile in those deeps; that's where he threw her corpse.

Gupi's forefather poisoned his wife.

The feats of Porom's forefather were the greatest of all. He bound his wife's hands and feet, gagged her mouth with a cloth, and strung her up with a rope around the neck. Then he undid the cords on hands and feet, took the gag off her mouth, and raised a hue and cry. Nobody suspected a thing.

As soon as her only son died, Broke-Home Noyan's first paternal grandmother leaped into the deeps and was killed. After that Noyan's grandfather married Noyan's grandmother.

Unable to bear tormenting heartburn, Panu's uncle had put a rope to his neck.

There are many stories in the tale. The story of Kalobou was added to them. Porom himself used to visit a neighborhood in Jangol. He would spend evenings at the house of Nophor Das's sister. Kaloubou's disposition was not good. As soon as Porom was in jail for banditry she went to Chandanpur and did the "skivvying" of a low-caste drudge in gentry homes. Everyone knew she was in love with Mister Bhup Singh, a gentry footman. So she was. Many in Kaharpara have such loves—they do it with Sadgops from Jangol, have a fling for a few days with one of Channanpur's gentry boys—nobody makes a deal out of it. Porom would give the occasional beating, but that's just how he is! But how long before going to this wedding had he started huffing and threatening Kalobou. Even Atpoure Para people said—they heard Kalobou's raised voice saying—I done well, go wherever ya want in Jangol in the evenin', I'll just do whatever I want. I'll get out yer 'ouse. Am I starvin'? People are saying he was threatening Kalobou because she was going to go to Singhji. Last night Porom and Bonwari hung behind to have words on the way back from the wedding at the Mitti house. The Atpoures say they were drinking booze in the hamlet without any attention to the time of night, and when the moon rose they could hear Porom's enraged and venomous tones coming from his yard. He was calling Kalobou—Where ya gone? Where? Where ya goin'? I'm yer lord o' death. So saying, he went out. A couple of people went to look, but neither Porom nor Kalobou was there. Porom's voice could be heard coming from Jangol's bamboo groves. They could tell from the sound that he was going along the riverbank. They don't know anything about what happened after that. Porom didn't come back. The ones who'd gone to the riverbank in the morning saw Kalobou's body floating in the deeps' water. They whispered their suspicions—It's Porom, he bound her feet with her clothing, threw her into the deeps' water, fled. Kalobou's clothing was tangled around her feet. But Pagol Kahar knew the real story. He did not say a single word though. Bonwari's fever had set in during the night. He'd found him unconscious with fever on the edge of Jangol. Kopai's Kali Deeps are a long way from there.

Suchand spoke regretfully—Ah, ah, what a lovely girl that was—that 'air, that bosom, eyes as good as 'er teeth—oo'd say she weren't a lass—she 'ad some years on 'er! Ahh—ahh! Pagol simply made a rhyme and broke into song—"I enter 'eat's game, my oh my! If I must give my life then so be it; but my soulmate I can't quit." Then he lamented—Ahh—ahh! O God! Next he took up his shoulder bag—I'm gone, off fer a few days. I'll 'ear some new songs abroad an' about, an' come back.

He left.

***

Two weeks later. Afternoon.

Bonwari had recently recovered from his illness and was sitting with his head in his hands, listening to an account of Kalobou. Suchand was telling it. Bonwari sat silently staring at the ground. Tears welled in his eyes and fell. Bonwari wanted to weep, screaming. Scream to them all—Don't know, ye don't know, s'my fault. Ah! If he hadn't submerged himself in the water for fear when he saw Porom, if he'd come up and stopped him, then Kalobou would not have run off in such blind panic. She wouldn't have climbed those roots of Babathakur's silk-cotton tree at the edge of the deeps. She fled because of Porom's pursuit; because of Karali's evil she was bitten by Babathakur's familiar, passed out, and fell into the waters of the deeps. The fault is his. He never punished Karali. The fault is his, he did not immediately fall with a splash. In fear of his own life, for fear of a bad name, he fled trembling. He could have died too. The fault is his own!

He is suffering an agonizing inner torment. There is no release from this evil. O God, O Hari, O Kalaruddu, O Dharma, O Father, Kottathakur, purge Bonwari, save him.

All the hamlet's old women are sitting around him. All the men went to work in the morning. Jayastha month's rain falling, time to farm the paddy fields. To scatter seed and till the land. Wind's farming. Which means farming at the right time. To do "wind's farming" on half an acre at this time is the same as putting two carts of manure on the land. This is not an occasion for time off. "A lickle sickie," that's to say illness, in the farmhands will not be tolerated in this season. Besides, the bosses are there. The bosses say—If they're so "sensotive" why would they be doing farmwork? What the bosses say is right. "Wi'out me, threshin' doesn't happen," without its herbal remedy the cow doesn't walk, without a rider the horse doesn't gallop; so it is with a boss—without the likes of those Sadgop gentlemen, peasant Kahar farmhands do not do their work right. It is different with the proper gentry. They have no real mind for farming. Not one of the Sadgop bosses' Kahar peasants is home. The hamlet's old women are surrounding Bonwari. Excepting only Noyan's Ma.

Bashan has also been sitting in the women's group since that morning.

Her problems are with daughter and son-in-law. Karali and Pakhi have built a brick house. She's very scared at the fact that the hamlet's women are looking into this. She herself knew that no one had done this before. Karali is doing it—what's bad about splendor and color? But Karali will not conform. If it had been any other woman there would have been a mother–son-in-law fight. Karali and Pakhi have already fought with Suchand. Karali virtually banished Suchand. Suchand weeping, calling to Babathakur, not cursing Karali and Pakhi this time, but reproaching them and saying to Babathakur—Change 'is mind, give 'im good will. The first day she'd been weeping in pleasure and pride for Pakhi's father, for her own father. But later she had understood the danger. *She* had understood first of all. She had gone to prohibit it. Karali had shown her the door and said —Beat it; in other words, get out.

Noyan's Ma throwing in comments from nearby. —O Father, take as ye've took before. Do it wi' a quick puff o' yer familiar's poison breath. Now crush the walls, Father! Brick 'ouse walls—smash 'em down.

Nasu cracking back with an allusion—Gonna be a pantin' quick puff, dearie! He means Noyan. Those mouthing ill on other folks get creepy-crawlies down their throats!

He's gesturing rudely with his thumbs and swaying like a wave.

The rest of the hamlet is stunned as though by an afternoon storm. They're expecting Bonwari to be better and get up. Karali has caused a huge amount of trouble. He's raising his head higher than Babathakur's silk-cotton tree. Really raising it. He climbed to the top of the silk-cotton tree again the other day. This time he was not satisfied with ascending the branches, but climbed to the very top and yelled to Kaharpara—Look!

So many weird things happening with Karali's crimes; in order to protest this bad name, he'd climbed the tree once more. This time he brought down a lovely little parakeet fledgling from a hole in the silk-cotton tree. He's become many times more unbearable than before. He goes around in a jacket and long pants. Called—War Uniform. Karali has taken war work. He suddenly turned up one day in that uniform and said—Took on war work! It's no longer day labor. Monthly wage. Shoes on feet. Blisters sprouting, corns rubbing, but he'll not give up the shoes. The youths all getting restless. Not even afraid of the elders. But Bashan's problem is the brick house. That imagined house has started to be worked into a reality. House building has begun.

Bonwari got sick on the way back from the marriage home. An uncomfortable Bashan got hold of Roton and Prohlad. It would have been good if Pagol had been there, but he'd left that very morning, saying—I'll be off a couple days an' come back wi' right mind. Two weeks had passed and still he had not returned.

Roton and Prohlad, dumbstruck, said—Brick 'ouse!

—Yeh. You stop it. Mustn't do what the forefathers didn't do.

Roton went and said—Karali?

—What? Karali understood.

—Ya makin' a brick 'ouse?

—Yeh.

—Forefathers never did it—

—So it shouldn't be done? Me dad didn't do war work either.

Now Roton approached.—Look, Karali, listen. Fine, ya don't listen to us, but you'll listen to Bonwari, right?

—An' if I don't listen?

Now Prohlad rebuked—Gotta listen. Everyone listens, 'ow can ya not listen? Let 'im get better, go an' consult wi' 'im, an' do what 'e tells ya.

Karali said—Get! Ye'll nothin' from me! What use 'is counsel, what's 'is advice for? Go, go. If you need advice an' counsel then go to 'eadman once fever's gone down. I don't want no counsel advice.

Prohlad said—If yer buildin' an 'ouse the rule is 'eadman comes an' grips the measurin' cord.

—I don't follow the rule.

—So gettin' too strong fer yerself then? Take the world for a clay plate, do ya?

—Not a plate, a cup. Go, go, stop all this gassin'.

Roton is Mathla's father, Mathla is Karali's follower; Roton spoke to him—Hold on two days, all right, son?

—Uh uh! Cottage's gotta be done before the rains, Uncle Oton. Where's time fer delay? Got war work now. Gotta go wherever they say soon as they give the order.

Roton said—But it's not a good thing, Karali. No one's ever built a brick 'ouse.

—Let 'em not build. I'm gonna do it.

Gupi said—If ya do what no one's done it does injury. Master Chaudhurys baked bricks ta make a buildin', people ferbad it, those days Chaudhury didn't listen; brick kiln was bakin'—meanwhile Master Chaudhury's youngest son got palpitations an' died.

—I ain't got no son yet, Karali answered, laughing.

Bashan is filling with regret. She'll never be happy having taken this son-in-law. All these ways of talking, so nasty! Bashan shrinks aside in fear and shame when Karali talks like this with all these distinguished people. He's saved beating Neem-oil Panu for later. Nor does Neem-oil Panu come near Karali. He does not say anything to his face; sat in his own house, he said to Noyan's Ma—Been three powerful 'eadman clans in this age—Atpoures' Poroms, Broke-Omes, Kosh-Shoulder clan; none o' them took their wives ta lay down in a brick 'ouse, lass.

As soon as this reached Karali's ears he went over to Panu's house, squatted down before him, and said—Hey scum, 'cos 'eadmen don't lay down in bricks, I can't lay there?

Neem-oil Panu is still in terrible fear of Karali after being slapped that day. He did not respond. But Karali did not quit; sitting in exactly the same position as unresponsive Pana, he elaborated softly and with irony right in Pana's face—Hey scum, say 'eadman Bonwari's wife is black an' ugly—does it mean I can't marry a good-lookin' fair girl? Yer own wife's fair colored, so—dump 'er. Scum. I tell ya summat, scum! He edged forward toward Panu.

Poor Panu was terrified and in his terror was trying to edge slowly backward, also sitting. He said—That—whass all that about?

Gradually, Karali edged yet closer to Panu and said—Brickbats instead o' bricks, creep.

—Do whattever ya think! What's it ta me?

Karali moved even closer and asked—Well, creep, I'm inquirin'. What's it ta you? I'm buildin' a brick 'ouse; why you gonna talk about it? Scum creep!

Bashanta couldn't make Karali desist, in spite of her repeated requests. His stubbornness is oxlike. Finally Pakhi came, got him to leave off, and took him away. Pakhi is just like Karali. The girl's spirit is as intense as her glowing color—

Like a heatwave. No fear and dread. She said to Karali—Get up.

Karali did not yield.

—Listenin'?

—No.

The girl went and grasped his hand; Karali took it back. Pakhi grabbed a handful of his hair; enraged, Karali tossed his head to release it and let out a scream—Aaaaii! Pakhi immediately began to slap and punch her own forehead like a lunatic—Tek that—tek that—tek that!

Karali was flabbergasted. Next he went and took her hand and said in a sweet voice that acknowledged his compliance—S'go, s'go, love, s'go. Goin' 'ome, I am. Stop love, stop. On the way over I said ta Noyan's Ma I don't say no words ta the dead. I don't cuss no dead uns. Go on, cuss, as much as ya can.

Pakhi can stop him deciding to raise the brick house. But Pakhi has also gone crazy for the brick house. Girls these days are just like boys these days. Pakhi says—Channanpur's Bauris makin' brick 'ouses. Haru Bauri, Sombhu Bauri, Kanai Bauri.

—That's Channanpur though. An' they're not Kahars.

—So what?

Thus Bashanta has come and sat with Bonwari. If she gets the chance she'll speak with Bonwari. He's the only one who can persuade Karali. Beside this, she also has another dread. The people who Karali's fighting with will no doubt come to Bonwari in a group and act against Karali. She wants to keep him calm by letting him know beforehand. Bashanta dreads to think what will happen to Karali if headman Bonwari gets ugly. But she's not getting the chance to speak in this gathering. Luckily, the chance suddenly came. Bonwari suddenly got up. Gopalibala said—Hey, where ya goin'?

—Babathakur's shrine. Seeing his face, no one could say no.

Just as Bonwari rose, Bashanta said—Come on, I'll go with.

Bonwari said kindly—Wanna come? Come on. One fever ain't made Bonwari weak. I can still do yer two-mile road an' be back by noon. He smiles a little.

On the way he smilingly paused by two steers and several cows and fondly stroked their bodies. Eight Spotside, which is the steer with eight black marks upon white, is very fond of Bonwari. It was his cottage's calf—the steer showed its pleasure in various ways, licking his hand and nodding its head. Bonwari takes a touch of cheer from them. He says to himself—Mother Goddesses, won't ever go wrong in service to you, Mothers; lift this evil with your blessings.

On the way is the foot of that Atpoure Para banyan tree where he used to meet with Kalobou. Bonwari said—Stop a moment, Bashan.

Bashan thought: tired. She said—Shouldn't 'ave come! I shoulda come before an' brought back some soil from the shrine.

Bonwari did not reply. He is thinking. About Kalobou, about his misdeed.

—Bonwari eh? That's to say, aren't you Bonwari?

Bonwari looked around. Atpoure Para's aged Romon Atpoure is standing looking at him. Romon is Porom's relative—brother-in-law; he married Kaloshoshi's elder sister. Bonwari stared at his bowed, broken-down figure. Romon is an ancient person, Suchand's age. Yet Suchand is still strong; Romon is broken, as if he's been crumpled up. At one time Romon was regally tall. The man was seized by sickness. Bonwari was anxious. Has the relative of Porom and Kaloshoshi come to bring him to account? Bonwari forced a smile and said—Yeah, man. Goin' once ta Lord's shrine. What wi' afternoon sun, twelve-fourteen days fastin', body's got no strength; so sat down a bit under the tree.

Bashan was annoyed. She'd missed an excellent opportunity to say her piece.

Romon sat beside Bonwari. Said—Y'eard all 'bout Porom then? Ah, I'm so sorry 'bout Kaloshoshi.

His chest began to pound again. Who knows what the old man will say? Is there anyone in Atpoure Para who does not know, who has not heard, what Porom had learned from Pana? Did Pana—

Romon said—However furtive do yer bad, in time the fruit of bad is had, the bad don't obey its own dad. Get it? Fruit o' Porom's bad. Kaloshoshi's too, no doubt; else an unnatural death! Gave 'er so many warnins. Bhup Singh's Brahmin, 'is touch is a bad—'ow many times I said!

Bonwari heaved a deep sigh.

Romon said—So that night on the way back, what's Porom call ya back ta discuss?

A fluttering started in Bonwari's chest.

—Bonwari!

A made-up story flashed into Bonwari's mind. He said—E was speakin' o' Mister Singh from Channanpur. Says—Bro if ya stick wi' me then one day we can smash that bastard. Said—When we've done 'im in we'll chuck the bastard in the deeps, sink 'im wi' a bucket o' sand 'round 'is neck. I got the point. Finally 'e quarreled wi' me. Said ta me—Why'dja say I'd lost me caste in the booze shop? Suddenly leaped on me. Then a fight. I got weak. Threw me down an' then 'e rushed off. What ta do, pain in every limb, dirt, sand—went in a pond along the way. Then I 'eard Porom goin' along abusin' Kalobou. That's when I got fever—I'm shiverin'. Then Pagol came—. He heaved a deep sigh.

Romon said—Leave it, ye're still so feverish! Everyone was in dread. It's this Kaharpara's fortune that ye survived. No 'ead, no crown. You alone 'ere. So we in this 'amlet say, if only we'd such an 'eadman! So I says the other day, what's the use of there bein' one 'amlet there an' ours stayin' separate? Perhaps they can become one. Make it be, let them wed. Ow many of us Atpoures left now? Sides Bansbadi there's them there—where the old indigo offices was, two, three cottages. None nowhere else. You, son, become 'eadman an' do this. Else Atpoure Para ain't prosperin' no more. I'm become old, my marked criminal name still ain't been wiped clean, son.

Bonwari was speechless.

Is this the caprice of Gods Hari, Kalaruddu, Kottathakur! In his mind he honored the gods. What is this joy amid sorrow, renewal amid ruin!

He said—Feelin' a bit better, Omon-bro. We'll see 'bout all this after.

Romon said—Letcha body get strong; one day take us ta the big gentry's offices in Channanpur. Porom's a fugitive. Ain't never comin' back. Us Atpoures'll share out that two acres o' land Porom took on the Saheb Tracts. We need the gentry's promission though. There ain't no one to ask it on our behalf.

Bonwari rose. He'd understood what Romon said.

***

In the hot months of Boishakh and Jaistha the loveliness of Lord's shrine is a delight. It's filled with innumerable tender wood-apple tree leaves and a show of tender leaves on the bushes; the young wood-apples cannot be seen for the abundance of leaves, though their smell is coming through. But the marvelous glory of the tree is he who lives there, Lord himself. The old leaves of every tree fall as soon as three or four weeks of spring's Chaitra month pass, and then wood-apple trees remain shaven for a while—only wood apples remain hanging. A week or two into Boishakh tender leaves can be seen. But the leaves of the tree Lord inhabits will fall in Chaitra's first week, and leaves will appear before Gajon rites. If they don't, it won't work out. In the Gajon rites this tree's new leaves are first placed upon the head of Jangol's Father Kalorudra. There is no other such leaf-bearing tree in this province in Chaitra. In Father's glory, several saplings have grown up all around this wood-apple tree. In every age this majesty must thus remain. The saora trees also have new leaves. New leaves too on the soyakul bushes. Creepers spread from the treetops, covering the bushes all around like an umbrella. Occasional flower-filled jimson weed and milkweed shrubs; the most beautiful of all is a laburnum tree. The tree is filled with numberless yellow flowers—countless long-stalked flowers. It dips and nods under the flowers' weight. You couldn't describe the blooms as anything but fireworks. An enclosure of palm trees all around. The palms are in clusters. There is yet another glory of Lord's shrine—all-round views. Far to the east—you can see Bansbadi at the edge of the alluvial fields; beside it those very deeps in which Kaloshoshi drowned. Look north and you'll see that Jangol village is visible. To the northeast you'll clearly see Channanpur station. If you glance west the Saheb Tracts come into view. Look to the southwest corner: the first sharp bend of Kopai's Hansuli Turn will come into view. Simply put, the Lord can sit up in the wood-apple tree telling his rosary beads and take the whole of Hansuli Turn in his gaze. In his contented gaze, pleasure and peace fill peoples' houses, crops swell in fields, storm in the westerly sky respectfully bypasses Hansuli Turn; Kopai flood, about to overflow both banks, slowly retreats from this bank and overflows the other bank. And if he now casts an angry glance it's the other way around. Misery in every home, arguments, fistfights, inner despair, disputes between villages, no rain in the sky, crop failure in the fields, storms overhead, Kopai deluge, so powerful at that first sharp bend of Hansuli Turn—where the levee is, it smashes through that levee and inundates Hansuli Turn.

Bonwari prostrated himself before the wood-apple tree. O Merciful One, O Ruler, O Master of Hansuli Turn's succor and misery; O Father Lord safeguard of our people, rescuer of others, safeguard Bonwari, let me trust you'll come to the rescue. You forgive all wrongs. He who's done wrong—he's owning to all those wrongs a hundred-, a thousandfold at your feet. Tears fell from his eyes. After much prayer he rose.

Bashan was speechless to see tears in his eyes. Bonwari-bro is a good person, she knows he follows dharma; but she had not known he was such a dharmic soul. The sun is climbing overhead, Bonwari's body is weak, they must get back quickly; but she did not have the courage to say anything more after all this. She looked over, there in tree shade Bonwari was squatting. At last his mind has found a little peace. The anxiety in his breast is much relieved. The evil will certainly be discharged by Karta-baba's mercy. He has also made a vow in his mind. Then seeing Romon had been a good thing too; his account of the meeting with Porom on the road had been terrific; after this no blame will fall on his shoulders. His offense was surely slight. He could have killed Porom if he'd wanted to, but he did not. And neither did he summon Kalobou. He'd gone to see her. To tell her of Porom's coming. Kalobou had herself taken his hand and led him to the riverside. Porom had gone to murder Kalobou. It was the pull of destiny that made Kalobou tumble into Lord's deeps. You could say that the Lord *had* punished him. His offense—he submerged himself in the water when he saw Porom, he didn't stop him when he came up, and he didn't jump into the water to pull Kalobou out. Thinking on this he shivered. It was his good fortune not to have jumped in; otherwise he would not have come up either. Father's familiar—Father's familiar had drowned her in the deeps. He saw with his own eyes. Kalobou died because of Karali's evils.

In the tale of Hansuli Turn there is wrong—there is right. Rather than wrong and right, it is better to say worldly wisdom and dharmic wisdom. Earthly bamboo groves and living desire were themselves born in an ancient epoch; under the dense shadows of banyan, sacred fig, silk-cotton and rain tree groves, the variously shaped saplings of the knowledge of right and wrong are born—in Hansuli Turn's bamboo and banyan groves their forms are pallid and spindly, like carefully planted mango and jackfruit saplings; even amidst dense shade of banyan, sacred fig, and bamboo grove they get a little taste of light and heat and have deep desires to get more. But no way to get it—it's as if the tracts of Hansuli Turn are giving more sap to banyan and bamboo. The Kahars look at mango and jackfruit trees with a thirsty eye. When will they grow up and escape the bamboo grove darkness! They'll open their leaves beside the banyan! When will they give fruit! But they receive no assurance. In Kaharpara there's a difference of opinion as to whether these trees are dying or on the road to recovery. Suchand's opinion was, dying—definitely dying. The majority of elders thought the same. Suchand says—In them days 'ow devoted folks were. Ome upon 'ome gave goat saccifices. Great youge goats, beards like this. Weren't saccificed till at least a year or two old. Men went out ta rob at night—went out ta worship at Lord's place. Before women got ta feelin' 'eat wi' someone they'd go under Lord's tree an' put some rouge there, only then did they get down to love. Lord'd tell folks what ta do in a dream. Gupi's granddad tapped 'is 'ead on the root o' Kottababa's tree—What do I do wi' this wife, tell me Lord! Gupi's granma got the 'ots fer someone from that place. Lord told in a dream—Kill 'er wi' poison. In the dream, Lord 'anded 'im their cow-killin' poison an' said—Take this. Gupi's granma died o' that poison. Then Suchand says—Rama ain't no more, nor is Ayodhya. People don't 'ave that strength—that devotion; even Father's cut down 'is glory. Go accordin' to the Infernal Age. No dharma in the Infernal Age. That's why people are in such a state. Master Chaudhury of Jangol used ta say—In the Infernal Age dharma's only got one leg. An' it's losin' that too.

Though it's worn away, there's a little left yet. Bonwari certainly does not maintain otherwise, and yet he hopes he won't allow the dharma of Hansuli Turn to lose any more of its single leg. Bonwari went and lay down in Father's shrine. He found solace. Silently said—Forgive, Father, forgive. I'm not responsible for it. Yet I didn't punish Karali, that's me offense, sure. But O Babathakur, ye broke me 'eart by snatchin' Kalobou away. Calm yer rage now.

No matter what anyone says, Bonwari knows that in Babathakur's eyes the offense of his 'eat with Kalobou is not a great wrong. Father does not hold this offense against ignorant Kahars. Babathakur is master of the Kahars' punishments—he understands that besides the play of 'eat, the Kahars don't lose their minds in any other sport. To Babathakur, the main offense has been committed by Karali. It was he who killed and burned the familiar. Who climbed his silk-cotton tree again and again, disturbing his sleep. Karali who has now urged Kaharpara to go to war. In the midst of illness, pondering these troubles, Bonwari has arrived at a new truth. He's understood the meaning of the familiar's whistle. By whistling and whistling it was cautioning the Kahar clan of Hansuli Turn—Watch out! Droning airplanes will fly daily over Hansuli Turn. Caste-wrecking workshops of Channanpur will surround and draw near. War has broken out in the world—watch out! By sheltering Karali, Bonwari suffered the blow of Babathakur's fist; the familiar struck Kalobou's breast so as to smite Bonwari.

Bonwari remained sitting silently beneath the wood-apple tree. Saheb Tracts directly westward. Black-skinned people moving around there. Now and again a hot summer's gust floating across. The sound of new leaves rustling together comes from that banyan tree in Atpoure Para.

In the Saheb Tracts, black-skinned people moving around—gentry having land dug. They're Santals. Bonwari's land is still unworked. He heaved a deep sigh and shook his head.

Bashan is waiting silently beside him. Seeing Bonwari's expression, she does not have the courage to speak to him. If only Bonwari-bro would smile once again!

Bonwari rose abruptly. Bashanta took this chance to speak—Come on, 's gettin' late.

On the way she mustered the courage to say—Bonwari-bro!

—Mmm.

—Ya gotta stop the lad Karali.

—Oo? Karali? His eyes began to burn. Bashan was afraid.

Bonwari said—Eard 'e's makin' a brick 'ouse! E'll come to understand. After a brief silence he smiled and said—Can't I build a brick 'ouse, Bashan?

Bashan shivered. She remembered—did Karali give an answer to this question? Bashanta can't properly understand what's going on in Bonwari's mind. Karali is not trivial. Did they both finally—? Her mind filled with thoughts. Bonwari suddenly stopped. But everything is weird with Bonwari! Bashan said—What's up? Just as she spoke a whirlwind engulfed them from behind. All was filled with dust and leaves—dusty sand in their mouths. Now taking this as a comic role, Bashanta began to laugh—Pthh-pthh, ooh dear! The next moment she said to Bonwari in surprise—What's up, Bonwari-bro? Ya stopped?

Bonwari kept staring with an astonished look. The whirlwind had overtaken them and was moving forward. Atpoure Para's banyan tree was nearby. The whirlwind went forward, whirled furiously around the tree trunk, and then died down. All the tree's leaves leaped into motion.

Bonwari began to shake. Bashan understood what it was. In a fearful voice she asked—Father 'ob? Meaning, ghost?

Bonwari took her hand and said—Come beside me. Taking his hand, Bashanta notices it is sweating, violently trembling. She could not figure out whether Bonwari was trying to give her courage or was trying to draw courage from her.

She cried—Beano-bro!

Bonwari did not reply. Headman Bonwari of Hansuli Turn recognizes it, Bashan cannot recognize it. Kalobou! Kaloshoshi! No one but. Smiling Kalobou! Danced away just like that. She beckoned—Sweetheart, I've made my home in this very tree.

Perhaps she has invited him too. Picking up courage, Bonwari began to move again. When he got home he lay back down in bed. Bashan went away helpless.

Two

Meanwhile there was a huge disturbance on the Kopai riverbanks.

Suchand was sitting weeping at home—O no, no—where ya gone—O go see, Karali's dead!

Bashan began to tremble violently. —Whaddappened? Hey, stop screamin' an' yellin', tell first, whaddappened?

—O, I'm done for! O, Karali's dead!

—I'm beggin' ya, say, whaddappened?

—That Aga Saheb, Bashan, that fightstick—So saying, she pounded her forehead and began screaming again.

There is no one left to ask in the hamlet. Everyone's rushed off to that place. Her feet won't move to go there. Only Noyan remains in the hamlet. He sits panting, white eyes seeming to smolder. It's as if Bashan's tongue gets stuck as she goes to ask him a question.

She herself rushed off. All Kaharpara has gathered at the Kopai jetty. Karali wasn't visible in the crowd, but Bashan could see the turban of Aga Saheb. Aga Saheb means the Kabuli man, the Afghan. Bashan shoved her way into the crowd and was dumbstruck. Karali is not dead. He has grasped Aga Saheb's arm with a champion's strength and is threatening him—We don't 'ave none o' that no more. Yeah. I'll gi' ye a real bangin'. Throw ye in the deeps—crocodile'll eat ya. Those days are gone.

Aga Saheb said with amazement—Hey what, you've come here from Channanpur?

—Yeah. My home's here, my house. Thought there'd be a thrashin' at Channanpur? Here it'll be.

Aga said—Give me my money, brother.

—Why? Why'd ya grab 'is arm? Why? Why'd ya talk filth ta women? Why? Whatcha gonna do if we all get tagether an' pound ya ta dust?

It was about Pagol. Two years ago Pagol had bought a shawl from Aga Saheb. He had promised to give the money for it the following year. But Pagol had left the area. At money collection time Aga had not been able to find him. He went away. And now by the river Aga had suddenly bumped into Pagol. It wasn't that Pagol had no wish to give the money, but he tried to flee across the river in fright because he hadn't given it at the right time previously; Aga gave chase—caught him. —Hand over the

cash! Gave him a few knocks too. Pagol screaming. Just at that time Karali had been returning from work in Channanpur. Hearing the screams,
Karali hastened with his group and confronted Aga head to head—Watch
it! Touch me an' I'll smash yer head in.

Astonishing statement. Aga was stunned.

Aga Saheb is a fearsome man—a terrifying man. The Agas have long
done business in this place by the strength of the fightstick. This the warrior, this the fightstick. If an Aga enters a village, the entire village is pet-
rified. To get their money the Agas have hurled abuse, given beatings,
and even dishonored women if no men were around. Confronting that
Aga—O my!

Pagol said—Karali, I'm givin' the money, bro, leave off.

—Wait or not. I'll leave off. I'll wipe away 'is scowl. So saying, he
said—Get, scram. I'll give yer money tomorrow—tomorrow, go—go—

Astonishingly, Aga slowly went away—Give for sure, give the cash
tomorrow for sure. All right.

—All right, all right. Bring a little hing spice. An' stop all yer bullying.
Else we'll kill ya, right.

Aga really went away. Crept quietly away.

In Kaharpara it is as if Karali is one from a foreign land. So what if he's
the same caste and kind, his way of behaving is different—talk, even the
talk coming from his mouth is other than the kind of talk he learned in
Hansuli Turn's Kaharpara.

One of Channapur's own, a son of Mister Mukherjee, went to England and came back a saheb. He is other among the people of Channanpur. Channanpur's workshops are England compared with Kaharpara;
Karali has become Kaharpara's own England-returnee by coming back
from there. Now he's also been to Katoya; Karali has taken on yet another
form on his return from there.

Karali went home, taking Pagol. Pagol said—'Tain't good ya got so
much guts, Karali. They're a murderous kind.

—We'll kill an' become a murderous kind too. Let 'im know that wi'
a smack that day in Channanpur. This one was alone. There was three of
'em; ten of us together beat 'em up—dropped their fightsticks an' stuff an'
ran off. At last they came back an' settled up through the line mechanic.
Were owed thirty-five rupees, took twenty-five and closed the loan. E
knows me. Unnerstand?

Pagol said—Nah, bro', I'm givin' the right money. In the 'ereafter—.
Nah, bro, won't do it.

Karali shook his head with impatience—Go give it then. But 'e'll come, grab ya in a trice, an' shame ya; if I'm there that won't 'appen. You gi' the money, I'll trim it by five rupees even—you'll see. Why'd 'e drag yer wife inta this?

—Don't 'ave a wife, me; why all this aggro about it?

—Now ya don't, but ya did once. I won't listen ta what you say. So saying, he sat down on a tree stump. He took a box of cigarettes from his pocket, gave one to Pagol and took one himself, gave local leafrolled smokes to all the others. Then he said to the workmen—Ard at it then, boys.

Karali's house is being built. Today's the day to prepare the ground. Tomorrow a new section of wall will be raised. The walls are almost six feet high.

The whole hamlet is standing all around. Looking his way with an annoyed and resentful gaze. They can't bear so much vanity, so much arrogance. Pana isn't there. He's sitting in silence in his cottage with a dazed, blank stare. Noyan is gasping and clawing the earth with his nails. Noyan's Ma is silently cursing: cursing the neem tree in Pana's yard. The tree has grown extremely high and broad-leaved; crows perching, dropping bones, dropping shit; monkeys settling there. The monkey leader sits atop that tree, and with a clattering snarl he threatens the bachelor monkey troop living in the scrubland by the Kopai; and now and again he looks toward the cottages of Kaharpara—in whose yard, on whose roof or tree are there eggplants or bananas or pumpkins or squash or okra? If he sees something, then with a whoop he leaps and crashes onto Noyan's Ma's roof. Jumps down from there—then up on the roof again, tearing it to shreds, he leaps back into this tree. So Noyan's Ma is cursing the tree.

***

Kalobou—Bonwari understands—Kalobou had gestured to him—she's made her home in that tree. Perhaps she has invited him.

Though he had eaten and was feeling better, Bonwari lay silent and still. Amazing thing. Kosh-Shoulder Bonwari never stays laid out once he's gotten over a fever. The fever subsided yesterday, he'd risen that very day; this morning he'd been down to Lord's shrine. That very man, living on rice meal, lying down!

He is thinking about Kalobou. She is standing beneath the banyan tree in Atpoure Para. She is making the branches rock, perhaps swinging on them. In moonlight at dead of night she'll surely come out—toward

Bonwari's cottage. Through Bansbadi's bamboo groves and leafy shade in darkness, body caressed with moonlight's white rose-petal touch, walking with a sound across fallen leaves, she will come and wait behind his cottage. *Tiptap*, she'll signal by throwing a pebble. Deeper in the night, seeing that Bonwari is not getting up, she'll quietly hum a song; then in dawn light, when the morning star rises, she'll return through the bamboo groves, along the banks of the Kopai—descend into Lord's deeps. She will emerge from there and come back to the foot of the banyan tree. If Bonwari passes beneath the banyan he'll toss a few banyan figs in curiosity; if he goes by the Kopai riverbanks he will sprinkle some river water or sand on himself. Someday perhaps the enchantress will appear in her loveliness, wearing a rain tree flower from the Kopai bank twisted in her hair; or with hair loose, shining with water from the deeps, with countless fireflies upon it, a glittering smile of white teeth in a black face. One day she will perhaps appear in terrifying form, will dash her head against the crest of the silk-cotton tree, two eyes burning like smoldering coals, she'll stretch out her long fingers—hands cold as ice, toward Bonwari's cottage. She will cleave Bansbadi darkness with a scream of suppressed rage; or weep with unfulfilled desire, filling darkness with hidden pain.

Bonwari shivered. Kosh-Shoulder Bonwari goes to Channanpur in the middle of night to call a doctor for the Ghoshes. Bonwari crosses the Kopai river in drought years, silently and fearlessly walks along the banks of Ghosh Para's marshes—to see who has built levees to catch the Kopai water and where. If there's a fight in Jangol it's Bonwari who grabs his fightstick first of all, no matter how late at night. One time bandits descended on Jangol; Bonwari went rushing with the hamlet's folks, and he was the one standing ahead of everybody else, confronting the bandits. Today it's that same Bonwari laid out like this? Where's that state of mind of his that can get enraged by anything? How's he going to work up a sweat over Karali's brick house?

In the tale of Hansuli Turn, Kalobou's womanghost is no falsehood. They're in the forefathers' stories, they saw them with their own eyes. In the corner of a room, in bamboo groves, in Hansuli Turn meadows, beside marshes—some stand in silence, some weep, some sing, some sit on cottage roofs dangling their legs, some catch hold of fire and scamper playfully in fields, some wander with the sound of footsteps splashing in water. Besides this there are "Enticers." They'll make you forget the way, lead you astray—likely toward a nasty death. Then there are "Nightwalkers"—if a person is supposed to call on another during the night, the

Nightwalker will take on their form and call in exactly their voice. They'll lead you to that sticky end too. As one generation ends, so the ghost-souls bound to it by obsession or hatred find release; then with each new generation, new dead souls—caught by something, obsession or hatred, they flit in Bansbadi shadows—on Kopai banks, through trees' thick cover, in Hansuli Turn fields. The borderlines of Hansuli Turn's nonhuman world stretch far—from sky to earth, from ghost folk to mortal folk.

Even today Suchand says—The Broke-Omes' forefather, Noyan's father's father's father, died committin' a robbery when the owner threw a plate, stuck right in 'is for'ead. Owner smashed the plates an' chucked 'em whizzin'—plates wi' shattered rims; them plates whirled 'round like Vishnu's discus. No savin' ya once one o' them strikes. Got stuck in 'is for'ead. Died of it when 'e got 'ome. Then 'e became one o' them. O my, day an' night on the pot shelf, else maybe in the garbage pile, sat in a tree branch swingin' 'is legs. Folks were scared stiff! Only one not scared was 'is wife—Noyan's granddad's ma. Son would be lyin' in the cottage— Noyan's granddad. Little boy back then. Boy would cry an' wife would say—Damned old man, even dead ya don't give no peace, come ta piss me off? It don't do for ya just ta sit on the pot shelf swingin' yer legs—shut the boy up. A queer mother; the boy flew up onto the pot shelf. Happy boy rocking to and fro in air. Then ever so quietly it says—A woman wi' a boy was widowed, tender age—so don't remarry; if ye do I'll wring yer neck. But get shelter from a gent an' I won't say a thing. So that's what it was. In these parts an upcountry salesman came ta deal in 'baccy. She caught 'is eye an' got puttektion. E'd come an' go. Didn't say a thing about it. One day no water in the 'ouse, got thirsty in the night. She said—Ow am I gonna get water so late a' night? Just as Ma was speakin', it set down a jug o' water—water from the Kopai sandhole. Once guess what 'appened— Suchand spoke with grave face—it was month o' Kartik, full moon night o' Radha-Krishna's festival, the Kandi kings' mansion was really decked out; the boys and girls craved to eat sweets from Kandi. They said—Oh, we're dyin' to eat sweeties an' candies from the feastin' at the Kandi kings' mansion. That Noyan's father's father's father—name was Omai, speaks 'is name an' says—Eef Omaii can feeed youu then youu'll understaand Omai's power! He spoke then in a nasal drone from the bamboo dump— Coome toomorrow morning. If I tell what 'appened ye won't believe me— folks went in the mornin' an' saw a great basket in the bamboo dump, an' in it frycakes, patties, sweets, candies, confections—all sorta stuff. Even sound o' Noyan's granddad's voice got a nasal drone, that was the touch o' the thing. From then folks gave 'im a name—Droner Kahar. Chaudhurys gave 'im a job under the spell o' the ghost.

That was Hansuli Turn's fable of the olden days' ghostly folk. But like the spiritual life of humans, it seems that this also has changed. Suchand tells this too. Regretfully, because devotion to the gods has declined, she says—These days, if there's a ghost the gentry lads from Channanpur come along wi' rifles ta stand watch, come to investigate. Young Jangol Mondol masters come wi' clubs an' fightsticks. What's their interest? Why'll they go to all that trouble? They'd rather live 'appily far away in Hansuli meadows by the river, play music on bones o' the burnin' grounds; catch fishes in river an' marsh when they feel like it, play catch wi' cremation fires, float whoopin' from top o' one tree to the top o' the next.

A frightened Bonwari had closed his cottage door and even blocked up the two air holes at the top of the wall; he was lying down.

Wife said—Midsummer's 'eat, ye'll be steamin'!

Bonwari screamed back—I'll get cold—I'll get cold!

His wife said—Well, you lie inside, I'll lie outside.

—No.

In depths of night he rose, tied his clothing onto his wife's, and only then felt unworried. A little sleep finally came at the end of night. After sleeping a while he became frightened and began to babble and gibber. In a dream he saw—Kalobou standing and moaning beneath a tree. Her whole body entwined in the grip of that familiar of Father's, the One that made Karali's cottage fly away, the very One that drowned Kalobou—She.

Daylight bloomed forth. Bonwari was heartened. Not merely heartened—with the passing of a night he's become a little better. In his anxious night thoughts he's made a decision—he'll wear the amulet of watchful Mother Kali of the Funeral Pyre; he'll put on the flower talisman of Kartababa. Thus he is untroubled. However merciless ghosts and spirits are—gods are equally merciful. It is in this equilibrium that the days and nights of Hansuli Turn pass. He will go himself. There is no way he can make this known. A summons might come from the police station if it were known. Way too much disgrace hamletwide, villagewide, district-wide. He's headman. Folk will see him and laugh. They'll say all sorts of things in private. Perhaps people will not follow as they do; time is past when the headman's word was put into effect. This is not that time.

His wife came and set down some puffed rice.

Bonwari said—No. I'm goin' ta Ma Kali's shrine.

He got up. He stopped at Karali's new house on the way, astounded. Karali is not there; walls are being set up by Channanpur's experienced "wall-growers," which is to say earthen wall craftsmen; a few local lads are digging the earth. They're working as laborers too.

Furrowed lines appeared on Bonwari's brow. He remembered hearing about Karali's brick house right in the midst of his illness; bastard devil untimely Karali! Strong of body, earning money from war work in Channanpur's caste-wrecking workshops, so he thinks the world's his oyster. Burned and killed Father's familiar. Climbed Father's silk-cotton tree. Father's rage whipped off his new thatch, but still no sense. Don't grow too big, storm will smash you down—forefathers' word. Though the tree grew too big and was smashed by the storm, that tree still has no sense. He'll break the forefathers' rules and build a brick house! Desire to uproot everyone from Kaharpara! He'd heard yesterday about what happened with Aga Saheb. Grown so bigheaded. His weak body and brain became frantic with rage. He'll lie with his wife in a brick house! They'll "hang"; which is to say, laze about. They'll make like big folks! People will pass by, Karali will smile out from his brick "windie," or window, and say—Where y'off to then, Uncle Bonwari?

When the "wall-growing" laborers saw Bonwari, they all stopped work and looked at him. Bonwari is owed respect. When he stops and inspects something carefully then he'll surely offer his opinion; he's certainly an expert; they'd stopped work and were waiting to hear his opinion. The growers, or craftsmen, expectantly asked questions—How's the wall looking then, headman? We measured up, but how's it seem to your eyes—bit crooked, bit uneven, eh?

Bonwari answered with a question—Where is good master Karali?

Everyone was taken aback.

Bonwari answered his own question—Channanpur, I s'pose?

Then he said gravely—Stop the work. Go back 'ome.

In a second everybody's hands were still.

Bonwari said—Let Karali come back, there's things ta discuss. Brick 'ouse ain't ta be built. He admonished those from the village who were working—Ain'tcha listenin' ta this? Get outa here! Put yer shovels aside. Put that can o' water down. Get—get—

Brick house, brick house! The lad's acing the village! Is it so easy to play the ace card? In the game of love's "eat" the jack beats the ace, the nine beats it. Headman of Kaharpara—this is not loveheat's game—here ace is high. Then king. Ace is Babathakur, king is headman. Here knave Karali's game will not work. These are God's rules; Bonwari was made headman by Babathakur's mercy. Really, look at Bonwari's cottage. Couldn't he have made a brick house? The ant has grown wings. Ants grow wings when they're about to die. Flutter off after any glistening thing without understanding good or harm; burn and die, get swatted and die, die lost and homeless. Hansuli Turn's golden meadows. After plowing in the rains, these meadows are as soft and yielding as they are hard in midsummer heat. If you couldn't fill your belly from the paddy, beans and pulses, vegetables and herbs of these meadows, then where in the world could you fill it? If he who plows and digs this land can't fill his own belly, then you have to realize there's an unseen fault, effect of karma from a previous birth; a punishment, taken out on soil or body, for the twisted mind of this birth. An age has passed, the age when the Kahars survived as callus-shouldered carriers; then Kottathakur showed his mercy, looking upon the Kahars in the midst of famine. In a dream he had Master Chaudhury give the homesteads, told him to give sharecropping land to the Kahars. By means of Master Chaudhury, the Lord commanded the Kahars thus. It's through his mercy that part of the whole meadowland of Hansuli Turn is in their hands. There are a few Hari, Dom, Muchi homes in Jangol, and previously it was they who had worked the land of the Sadgop masters. These days they have lost ground. At one time a Kahar would not have known farmwork; today there's no better farm laborer in the district.

Loser Karali—wicked Karali. And why stop there? Ill-fated, untimely Karali; his untimely birth. If you put your ear to the telegraph poles along that rail line at Channanpur you can even now hear of his mother's disgrace. You can hear it in the sound of the wires above the line where traincars go by. Now men and women say—Traincars sayin'—Tamarind-raw—tamarind-ripe—tamarind-raw—tamarind-ripe. Folk used to rhyme—Sidhu-Joga-Pebati, no caste no heredity—Sidhu-Joga-Pebati. Karali's Ma was called Probhati. Can the loser not hear that rhyme amid those sounds? He who goes around with puffed-up chest working on the Channanpur rail line? "Shameyless," or shameless, loser. Now he flaunts the war to everyone, flaunts the greed of war work to Kaharpara by wearing a war uniform!

War! War! What's war to Hansuli Turn? Does Bonwari know nothing of war? Or hear nothing? How many wars do you know about? There was the Ramayana's war of Rama and Ravana; the Mahabharata's Kurukshetra; the war of King Ban and God Hari; Ravana's line was exterminated, Yudhisthira became king and King Duryodhana died; King Ban's daughter was married to Hari's grandson. Did anything happen to the Kahars? The Kahars survive by worshipping Kalaruddu and Babathakur. The Marathas came on raids, the Santals rose up, there was war, don't you know? And then twenty years ago there was another war. What happened to Hansuli Turn then? It wasn't great. It was awful. It was awful. There was scarcity, disease, misery, the good days were wiped out. Now war's broken out again. Let it. It'll be pretty awful again. No more than that. Airplanes fly over Hansuli Turn; let them fly. But the wave of war won't hit Bansbadi full on. Babathakur is here. What do the good and bad of the world have to do with Hansuli Turn?

He closed up the cottage and set off for Kali's shrine.

***

He got an amulet at Mother Kali's shrine and went back.

He took Mother Kali and Babathakur's flowers, filled the two silver amulets he had bought from the silversmith with them, and bathed; he put on fresh, clean clothes, tied on the amulets with red thread, and felt assured. Next, after eating, and feeling much better in mind and body, he made a decision concerning Karali. His mind is now calm, and he thinks it lucky that nothing was settled while he was angry. If Karali had been there, maybe that would have happened. If so, it would have been a hugely embarrassing, appalling scene. Lord has preserved Bonwari, blessings of the forefathers have preserved him. He's a venerable headman; is such anger becoming of him, especially anger over that young lad? Or is it necessary? He has to look out for the hamlet's well-being, for everyone's well-being—has to "sherish," that's to say cherish, each and every person at his knee—else what kind of headman would he be? Besides, there's also the lad's "learnin'," which is to say his talents. He taught Aga Saheb a lesson yesterday; Bonwari will say how good that was. He's able bodied, broad chested. In time he'll be a real man. Bonwari has no son; if Karali remains obedient, he will in the end make him hamlet's headman. For that he's got to get some good sense into the lad's head. One day he will have to summon the lad and tell him this confidentially, speak "wi' an open 'eart."

He lay a while on the outer terrace, calmly smoking tobacco. He can see the crest of Atpoure Para's banyan tree. The crest is swaying. Bonwari is no longer mistaken: the swaying is a sign from his consort; Bonwari is now beyond your reach. Bonwari has in his hand Mother Kali's talisman, Father Kottathakur's talisman. Yet he is sorry for you. Bonwari heaved a deep sigh. A little later he went to the Saheb Heights. Day going by, or water going by. The water flowing by in the Kopai—it doesn't come back. The day that has passed will never return. He still has not finished up the land on the Saheb Tracts. Nonetheless, his mind's impulse made him go up there.

From the Saheb Tracts Bonwari went to Jangol village. He had not been to boss's house in two or three weeks. People from boss's house had come looking and gone away. They'd said there's work coming at the Ghosh house. Maito Ghosh is coming tonight; the rite of first rice will be held for Maito Ghosh's son. Bonwari has a lot of work duties at the Ghosh house. Chopping wood, cleaning the house, setting up the oven, fetching vegetables from market; in other words, Bonwari has to take all the work's weight. He has to spread word in the hamlet too. You'll get work— why should outsiders get that work? Besides, as well as gifts of leftover food, they'll get extra-loaded platters of rice, vegetables, dal to take away. They'll purify the leftover-polluted leaf plates, women will scrub the contaminated crockery—they'll get a measure, that's a couple of pounds, of dry rice and a hemful of puffed rice. Of course, work's still fallen two or three months behind. But this has got to be done. He suddenly sprang into movement. He remembered about Karali. Karali saying—Caste is lost by eatin' leftovers. Kahars eat the Sadgops' leftovers.

**

As Bonwari entered the Ghosh house, Big Ghosh said—What's this! Body still sick then?

Bonwari shook his head and said—Got a throbbin' in me 'ead. That'll pass.

Middle Wife said—What's that now, little Kahar brother-in-law, sick at this time? There's work in the house!

Bonwari is a lot bigger than Big Ghosh, but because he is "small in caste" the wives call him "little Kahar brother-in-law." Smilingly Bonwari said—All better now, ma'am, what further worry? Coupla days an' I'll be right as rain. Gi' the order what needs be done.

Big Wife said—You don't need to do anything today. Go tell the servant's boy he'd better put some palm leaves on the chopped wood. There's lightning in the clouds, sky's flashing. If it rains, dry wood'll get wet.

Big Mistress is an extremely vigilant mistress. There surely does seem to be flashing in the sky. The westerly sun is being covered over. Bonwari stood at the wood-covered wall. Finally he lent a bit of a hand himself.

When it was time to leave he returned with some puffed rice and candies tucked in his waistband. He has accumulated a few other things too—a little broken leg from a wicker bed that'll make a great hoe handle. He also found a glass doll with broken arms and legs—it had been squashed into the ground. It'll be a nice ornament on the cottage shelf. And he also found a few strings of yarn and some strips of packing paper. The yarn will be useful, but he does not have anything specific to do with the paper. He'd found two sparkling metal buttons that he gave to Ma'am; who knows if they're not valuable!

On the way back he paid respects once more at the foot of Kalarudra's tree, Lord's Shrine. Save us from danger, Lord, make the earth fruitful, make sure there's no bad will, see to Kaharpara's succor. When he'd been to Lord's shrine to pay respects, something suddenly occurred to him. He remembered the words of Atpoure Para's "Omon." He made a vow before the Lord—If it works out with Atpoure Para, if the Kahars get up to the same "tier," or level, as the Atpoures, then he will build at the foot of Father's wood-apple arbor, just as the Ghoshes have built at the foot of goddess Shoshti's tree. Kalarudra's tree-base shrine is now fractured and splitting; at one time the Chaudhurys had built there.

Bonwari got up from paying his respects and was dumbstruck. A gorgeous adolescent girl looked right at him and immediately began moving off—girl seems to be swinging her hips.

Bonwari was dumbstruck—Who's the girl? The girl seems to have something of Kaloshoshi about her. She looks exactly like Kaloshoshi.

The girl went and stood under that banyan tree. Bonwari stared fixedly at her. It feels like his chest is being beaten from the inside with a rice pounder. Has Kalobou taken on the shape of a beauty so as to lead him astray? He touched the amulet to his forehead.

—Who? Bonwari?

—Who? Bonwari looked around in surprise. Old Romon Atpoure is approaching from Jangol. Romon said—Ye thought about it? Comin' ta your 'amlet tonight.

—Fine. Come. Bonwari spoke distractedly. He gazed again toward the foot of the tree. No, Kalobou hasn't taken on the guise of a gorgeous beauty. Else she'd certainly have disappeared on seeing Romon. But who is she?

The girl now spoke. Yelled out—Get a move on now, uncle. Ow long I gotta wait?

She's calling Romon "uncle." So she's Kalobou's niece. That's why she looks like her. Reassured, he paid obeisance to Babathakur once more.

Bonwari finished paying obesiance, and at once a disturbance broke out somewhere. No need to look elsewhere to find out the source: he looked toward Kaharpara.

***

Karali—Karali—Karali. Who else? Karali alone provoking Kaharpara's thousand quarrels. Bonwari went and stood in Karali's yard. People gathered all around, and in the middle Karali grasping someone else's arm, chest puffed out, hackles raised, and screaming like a wild animal. Who's that man? Footman of the Chaudhury house, Nobin from Atpoure Para. What's up? What's happened? No one speaks. The man seems too distressed to speak. Bashan standing there pale-faced. Karali screaming—I won't obey. No one gives me orders. There's laws, there's courts, tell me ta give up if ya can. Ya mighta come in force, but I got force too.

Suchand is weeping piercingly.

But what's happened? With regard to the indigo levee, the Kahars are subjects of a land grant on the banks of the Chaudhury house's levee. An age-old custom: when a house is demolished and a new one is to be built, permission must be obtained from the Chaudhurys. Ask verbally and permission is given—a one-rupee fee must be paid. Karali had sent the one-rupee fee through Bashanta. But today one of the Chaudhury house people had come to take Karali away—you can't build a brick house for a one-rupee fee. And there has been no deal with the Kahars about building brick houses. If the Chaudhurys had their former power, their guardsman would have come and dragged Karali off by the cloth scarf around his neck. These days they have lost everything and are a venomless snake; instead of a guardsman they have sent a footman, Atpoure Para's Nobin, to take Karali away. Nobin cannot quite get the measure of Karali. He set out with the order from the salt-encrusted brick terrace of the Chaudhurys' broken-down mansion, the worm-eaten ancestral fighting stick of the Atpoures in his hand, swiftly grabbed Karali's arm, and said—Oi, come on. There's an order fer you ta be brought.

—Order? Oose order?

—Master Chaudhury's.

Karali was already in a bad mood. He had come back from work on the line only to hear that Bonwari had stopped work on his walls. He flared up at a mere word. He grabbed the Atpoure man's fightstick, tossed it aside, tore his arm free, and quickly grabbed hold of the man's arm. He gave the arm a good twist and began to scream. Not inarticulate; raving words about rule of law. He learned them at that Channanpur station. There has been a settlement—he has record of it. It is written there that the homestead is his. He can put whatever kind of home he likes there; there was even no need to give the one rupee that, like a good person, he had; he must give a little compulsory labor as rent—which, according to his wish, he can do himself or get out of by paying a laborer's wages in cash.

When the settlement was made the Chaudhurys wanted to switch from the requirement of palanquin bearing to compulsory labor. Their palanquin had been smashed when the veranda roof caved in. Compulsory labor would be of much more use to them than palanquin bearing—this was the calculation they'd made. Let that be; the neighborhood folk—they don't see Karali's arrogance, they are astounded and dumbstruck by his unprecedented exposition of the law and the power of tenure.

Bonwari moved forward, placed himself between Nobin and Karali, and said—Quit.

Karali looked him in the face and said—Well now! I was sayin', where's 'eadman? Wi' you 'ere it's two birds wi' one stone! Say, why'dja stop work on me 'ouse?

Fire flared in Bonwari's head. He began to shake violently. Suddenly he roared—it was like a thunderclap!

What happened next is a scene in keeping with events in tales and fables, not something befitting our age. But it happened at Hansuli Turn.

Even Karali could not have imagined it. The venerable elders—Prohlad, Roton, Gupi, Pana came along with shovels in hand. Several people restrained Karali. The rest put their shovels to work. They destroyed the foundations of his brick house. Bonwari stood there impassively. Now and again he pointed and gave orders—That there bit left, cut it down.

Hey-yo, hey-ho; hum-hoi; ha-hup—different farmhands making different sounds as they drive in the shovels. Pana is the most enthusiastic of all. He digs—Hey-hey. Someone suddenly yells out in a screeching voice—Mek way, mek way. Everyone was dumbstruck. A skeletal human is staggering forward. He also has a spade in hand. The sickly, wheezing Noyan.

—Mek way, mek way. I'm gonna dig. His heart is visibly pounding beneath his ribs; his two eyes are bulging and seem afire.

Karali is no longer struggling; he's covered head to toe in dust. He too is standing nearby and watching steadily. Pakhi is also watching steadily, her gaze fixed on one person—sickly, wheezing Noyan. That gaze is like a poison gaze.

***

Karali suddenly grabbed Pakhi's hand and said—Come, let's go to Channanpur.

He went off with a swagger. Noyan was delighted at this too.

Then the assembly sat.

Bonwari sat grim-faced. For a long time no one had seen Bonwari looking like this. Bonwari began to speak slowly. For a long time no one had heard Bonwari speak like this, either. What is more, the entire hamlet's mood seemed to have become identical to his. It seemed such grim darkness had not descended for a long time. It was as if the olden nights of Hansuli Turn had returned.

Bonwari spoke—There'll be no place in Kaharpara fer 'ooever goes ta work in Channanpur. What the forefathers didn't do, that ain't ta be done. True fer all the thirty-six castes. If ye're lookin' fer more money, it won't work. That money won't last. Character'll turn bad. Ooever can't fill their belly from the great fields o' Hansuli Turn, their belly's unfillable. Won't be able ta fill that belly anywhere on earth. Work these fields wi' yer strength—'ands fill with food. Remember—God birthed you in Hansuli Turn so this karma would be done. Doesn't birth anyone by the side o' that rail line. Them as goes, they'll be destroyed. This ain't my word, it's Kottathakur's word. Before all that row over Karali's 'ouse blew up s'evenin'—I'm payin' me 'beisance, word came ta mind. Lord put it in me mind.

Right at this moment Atpoure Para's Romon came and stood there. The Atpoures were with him.

—Bonwari!

—Who?

—Me, Omon, came cause o' that thing we said.

—Come, come, come. Sit, everyone sit.

The matter was put to the meeting.

A strange night! In the days of Kaharpara's saheb masters they split into two parts. The Poroms took fightsticks and became Atpoures, the Bonwaris shouldered palanquins and became Kahars. That time is long gone for both hamlets; both groups have farmed for a long time; one group sometimes carries the palanquin, the other sometimes dances the fightstick dance. Yet all this time they were divided. Today this split has gone. Porom's land was discussed and Bonwari will make it over to the Atpoures. And he'll go to the police station, say—take the oath—that the Atpoures are no longer involved in robbery, no longer involved in banditry, do not step in the shadow of evil. Besides, Porom has disappeared, the root of evil has been uprooted, acquit them, Your Highness. The Atpoures will honor the Highnesses for this. Chicken, goat, milk—what's more, betel chews to eat; they'll give these too. Of course this won't all happen in a day, it will take one or two years. Let it. Bonwari himself will stand as guarantor. But Atpoure Para will have to follow his "counsels."

Bonwari said—Let's see 'greement.

Without agreement the Atpoures have no recourse. The Atpoures have entered such deadly straits. Their numbers have forever been fewer than the Kahars; working with the fightstick and haughty as Kulin highcastes even today, they come through with loud mouths and little effort. Even if they farm, Atpoures never do it well. They've no mind for it. They used to be renowned for thieving and robbing. This renown was a matter of honor, and still they certainly don't see it as a dishonor; but now that renown has become terrifying under police pressure, lack of patrons, weakening power to stand the beatings. No more hero Rama, no more Ayodhya city. Those days, the bandits' patrons and caretakers of goods were huge fat lords of great big mansions such as there are no more, don't even have a headman. Porom, headman in name, has fled too without a trace. If a trace were found there would be no saving him; this time police will string him from a gallows for the murder of Kalobou. Meanwhile, things are getting more incredible by the day. War breaking out in England. Prices of paddy and rice rising, prices of salt, oil, cloth aflame. Many wares not available in the bazaar. The Atpoures must survive. Bonwari can do it—this faith they have. If he becomes guarantor, they will get farmwork at Jangol Sadgop masters' homes. If Bonwari goes to the police station, Inspector can believe him or not; at least he'll hear. He'll hear dozens of times, and belief will follow. By repeating the name of Hari, a thief becomes a saint; if a saint is called a thief by all then he becomes a thief to all. Besides, there is the immediate attraction of that land on the Saheb Tracts. That land Porom took. Porom gone, Kalobou dead, no heir. Now the gaze of the Atpoures has fallen on that land. The proprietor is Channanpur big gentry. Need his permission. The Atpoures have no good repute as farmers, nor do they have the courage to go ask big gentry to their face. Porom would have had the courage to go, as does Bonwari. This is why Bonwari must become their chief today.

All Atpoure Para said—"'Greement." Yes, 'greement.

Romon assented in a strong voice—Course 'greement.

Neem-oil Pana, demonically smart and wicked but very calculating. Pana said—You need a big man ta grind yer paddy. Ye might've made Uncle Bonwari yer 'eadman, but will it wash wi' us? An' won't ye be callin' us 'orseclan an' stayin' split off? Tell us. Else ya won't get nothin' from us, no matter yer greed fer Uncle Bonwari as 'eadman. Uh-uh.

At this the Atpoures went silent. Meanwhile, the Kahars all nodded their heads in agreement—Said right Pana, said right. Why should we?

Pana said—Uncle Beano can take Porom's land 'isself. Can gi' it to us.

Romon quickly objected—"No rice in the belly, dharma take a fast." Be a lot better ta go along wi' the Kahars than fer a caste to act outside its caste karma. Atpoures, Kahars—two fingers o' one hand; an' two clans o' one line. What you are, we are too. We don' eat together. Don' swap gifts or marry each other. Except fer yer palanquin carryin', we'll become one wi' ya. What say all?

Now the Atpoures gave their assent. Leave it out, leave out palanquin carrying.

Bonwari shook his head—Uh-uh. That don't work. If ye're called for weddins or last rites, these two ye gotta go to. The two 'ands o' Lakshmi and Larayan become one, their carryin's gotta be done. Go take the dyin' for last rites in the Ganges—good karma, blessed. Journey ta paradise by power o' good karma and the livin' body. Takin' 'em on yer shoulders speeds ta the next world. If yer called for these two things, gotta go. We can't say "no." If ya wanna stay separate 'cos o' this, then stay. Whatever ye like.

After deliberating a little, Romon said—All right—all right.

Pana said—Say Hari Hari, bro! Say—Victory Father Kottathakur!

Two groups, Kahar and Atpoure, sounded in one voice.

To stop the noise Pana said—Great, but propose some exchange ta seal the meetin'. Let it be—the finish of all this.

—Exchange? The Atpoures gulped.

Panu said—Yeah, exchange. I'm sayin'. He came forward and sat in the center of the meeting. Panu is very pleased today—Karali is far, far away from the village. Now he's got the advantage of sitting a hair's breadth from Bonwari. He said—Yer widowed sis-in-law's lass came along, Uncle Omon; let 'er take the companion rite wi' Bonwari. Uncle got no son, 'amlet's 'eadman line's gonna die out—that can't be. What's everyone say then? Pana is crafty, he has correctly noticed that the girl has something of Kaloshoshi about her. Bonwari banished Karali today; today Pana wants to please Bonwari.

Niece of Romon's wife—Kalobou's niece—Bonwari had seen her this afternoon. Something of Kalobou in her every limb. Adolescent girl. Kalobou's color was black—this girl's color shines. The girl had been widowed with one son. The son also died. She'd taken refuge with her mother. Mother wanted a companion rite for her. But mother died before even this. The girl landed on Romon's shoulders.

Romon was thinking. He had to fall right into the trap's net—he didn't think of this. But on the bright side, Shubashi is his sister-in-law's lass; neither his own sister's nor his daughter's, not his niece on brother's side or on his sister's side; he won't lose caste on her account.

Bonwari was sitting in silence. He was thinking about Kalobou. Thinking that the girl would make up for the loss of Kaloshoshi. Thinking that when a girl from a highborn family comes in like this, there is no more need for caste exclusion. And in this context it's first of all necessary for a girl from an Atpoure home to come into his. Besides, Pana also said this dead right—it's never right that a headman line like his own should die out. Father looks kindly upon him. Today in the midst of misery he gave happiness, gave the entire Atpoure hamlet over to Bonwari's rule. What's never happened all these years has happened today, that's Bonwari's fortune. Victory Kartathakur! Victory Lord of All Punishments! Yours a just ruling! You did not punish that Karali who killed your familiar, didn't take it out on him, so you took it out on Bonwari, snatched Kaloshoshi away. Today Bonwari punished Karali, you're happy—you've rewarded Bonwari with the Atpoure headmanship; given back his Kaloshoshi. Just as you adorn your ancient wood-apple tree with new leaves in the month of Boishakh, so you returned Kaloshoshi as a gorgeous young girl. An angry look from Kottathakur and young lives burn to ash, mouthfuls of food vanish, laden boats sink; now if happy Kottathakur smiles a sweet smile, gazes kindly, the dead come back to life, the lost are found, the missing come home, the ordinary becomes extraordinary. Today what Bonwari has heard as tale has literally come to pass.

Romon agreed. Pana explained, calling him secretly aside—There'll be an exchange, ya won' be responsible fer the evil o' breakin' a clan! Sis-in-law's lass an' a reared calf—those two's just the same. Gents buy up cows an' steers an' give 'em ta Kahars ta rear, Kahars feed 'em, bring 'em up, deliver the calves; Kahars get milk an' a half share in that calf. Gents buy the calf for two, three rupees from Kahars. If they don't buy 'em, we call the stock trader, sell the calf, an' split the money wi' the gents. Yer wife's sister's lass landed on yer shoulders; put 'er in Bonwari's 'ands, take the weight off yer back, that'll be the exchange sealin' the joint of Atpoures an' Kahars. When Bonwari shares out Porom's land among the Atpoures on the orders o' Master, won't you get a little extra like the half share fer rearin' a calf? Young Panu spoke to Romon in an absolutely genial, friendly manner, tickling his desires. Romon smiled too, and agreed with pleasure.

The thing was decided.

Roton, Gupi, and all seemed extremely happy. Everyone said—We're happy, very happy.

The young girls began to smile shyly. Suchand wanted to rush up and say—Done great sonny, done great! But it is today that Bonwari had the cottage of Karali and Pakhi smashed down and sent them away from Kaharpara. How's she supposed to feel? How can she say something nice?

It was at this time that Pagol showed up at the meeting. Where he's been all day, only he knows. He sat down and said—What's up?

Pana poured some liquor and gave it to Pagol—Drink. Sit wi' us an' listen.

As he listened Pagol began to hum and then broke into song. Suchand speaks the tale of Hansuli Turn, Pagol sings the rhyming ballad of Hansuli Turn.

Hey bravo—Hansuli Turn's Bonwari
Built a new house, door facing southerly.
Filled the house, sweet breeze of Shubashi, O me, O me!

Bonwari laughingly scolded—Tellin' ya, stop!

Shaking his head, Pagol was starting to sing a new line of song when Noyan's Ma came running, weeping and beating her chest.

—Oh no, what's me Noyan doin'—go an' see! Oh no! Oh no! Oh no!

What's this? He with skeleton body and elephant strength who'd smashed Karali's cottage with a shovel at the beginning of the evening!

***

Noyan was lying on the darkened porch. Covered in sweat. Arms and legs going cold. Pagol sat to examine his arms. He knows how to take a pulse. Bonwari can grasp a lot by looking at his face. He cried—Where's light? Light?

No light. Can't get kerosene. War markets. Pana brought his own lamp from his house. He keeps it extinguished. There is still a little oil inside. Bonwari looked. Hari—Hari—Hari!

Noyan is on his way out. After wielding that shovel he lay down, then gradually became like this. But even in this state Noyan's speaking with a gasp—I'm dyin' smashin' the bastard's 'ouse, I'm glad about that. He set off on the road with that happiness.

Kaharpara sat surrounding Noyan. This is their way. Bonwari stood a little way off arranging for wood and bamboo. Noyan's Ma wept, Noyan's own people wept. Suchand and Bashanta came last of all. They sat and wept too. Young girls silently sitting, wiping their tears; only Nasubala came from Karali's house. No Karali and Pakhi, they're in Channanpur. Nasubala wept too. There was genuine grief in his words—how he's talking! Of Noyan's boyhood, youth, adolescence; he was exactly his age, they played together, grew up together, words of memory. Not a single word of Noyan's faults; all about his virtues.

The light suddenly went out. No more oil. Everyone sat in darkness. Noyan's Ma sits weeping with her hand on his chest. That's how she'll know. When his chest stills she'll let them know with a cry. Maybe they can get a light, but nobody's thinking of that now. Kahars have lived forever without an abundance of light. Born in darkness, live in darkness, die in darkness. Pagol makes a rhyme—what of light?

Why worry about darkness, ah well!
Life's bird goes to that place in darkness, ah well!
No moon, sun, lamp, lantern, none, ah well.
Not here, there's a brother here,
Comes forward and puts out a hand,
Ah, two eyes his two lanterns illuminate the gloom.
Ah well, why worry about light!

Bonwari reckoned the people for the cremation. No lack of people today. Today, the Atpoures too will go.

On such a night no one is alone at Hansuli Turn. In such circumstances everyone from Karapara even goes to Atpoure Para. The Atpoures come to Kaharpara. And more than this, today a new bond has formed between the two hamlets. Today the Atpoures will go to the burning ground as well. In the epoch of Bonwari's headmanship Noyan is the first traveler of the two hamlets' journey together. It's he who'll go first, borne on shoulders of two hamlets. Today, an old headman lineage has become extinct.

Who knows how many Kahar headman lineages have become extinct; who keeps count? Does the tale of Kaharpara have origin or end? Earth was created, the gods created Kahars, the headmen of the Kahars were created with them. Father Kalaruddu's Gajon board turns with a whirling noise; that board turns days nights months years, passing one by one. Years passing, ages passing. So much passing with them—headmen passing, houses of headmen passing; after so long, the Broke-Home house ended with Noyan. Father's board turns; the years turn with that board. This time Noyan was first to go in the turn of that whirling. Who knows who else will pass? Kaloshoshi died around the new year too, but she was an Atpoure. Then the two hamlets were not one.

These things were being discussed among those traveling to the burning grounds. Bonwari going with them too. Ancient headmen's line, after all. Respects must of course be paid. And Noyan was in fact penniless. Bonwari will meet all the expenses. That's custom. Pagol went to support Noyan's Ma. All the curses of Noyan's Ma have today been silenced. The fires of her spirit have all been extinguished.

Bonwari moving with heavy step through the darkness and thinking—please let the year go well. Babathakur's rage is so terrifying. Bonwari shivers the moment he thinks this. Ah, when will the Gajon drum sound again; Kalaruddu's wheel will spin and stop an instant. He will say—Stop moon, stop ocean, stop with me a moment. Let the year end. How many folk will weep then for blessed lost ones! There's been wrong done to Babathakur —Bonwari will keep thinking about this whole year. Despite his good fortune, his worry isn't passing.

Part

5

One

Dadang—dadang—darangdang—dadang—

Gajon festival's drum sounded again. Bonwari lay on the Charak board looking up at the sky and paid obeisance to Kalaruddu. That's it. Year's over, year's over, the Kahars' year has passed very well, by grace of the most kind and angry Father. Bonwari's terrors did not come to pass. Youths, elders, headmen of Kaharpara all made it through. No more "deeth," that's to say death. Well, there was some, but of the regular type, no more than usual. One little accident happened in Atpoure Para—that Kalobou died. And Noyan died suddenly too. Besides this, three or four children died of "mayloyria" fever, four old folks died—Gupi's maternal aunt, Roton's Ma, Prankeshto's uncle Gobardhan—who was mute, and Gopal's paternal aunt. Gopal's aunt was from another village. She showed up and became a weight on Gopal's shoulders; she's not really included in the death accounts. No one's ever kept account of the number of boys who die "tendergreen," or at delivery; only via the village patrolman is it written in the birth and death record book, filed at the police post, and there the record remains. That account is also a poor account—the village patrolman hardly ever comes to Kaharpara to record that account, and then only during the daytime. Nobody can remember the count of dead children, and they get it wrong if they say. The village patrolman recites that wrong number over and over in his mind until he gets to Jangol, has some Sadgop child write it down for him, and deposits it in the Union Board files at the police station.

This time Pagol shows up for Gajon. He's doing a fine masquerade. Done himself out like Shiva, on either side a child dressed up as Durga and Ganga. One grown girl and a teen. Boroki and Chutki, Biggie and Smallie—Gopalibala and Shubashi. They're mocking Bonwari. Go ahead, Pagol-bro, go ahead. Bonwari's even quite enjoying it.

In accordance with the resolution of last year's meeting, Bonwari had performed the companion rite with Kaloshoshi's niece. Now he has a two-wife home. Boroki and Chutki, Biggie and Smallie—Gopalibala and Shubashi. The year has turned, marriage year gone by fast, though you'd think it was still those days. It's as if his pal Pagol's song is still ringing in his ears. It's like he just sang a song! Ah, Pagol-pal, crazy man, great guy, the songs are as good as the voice! Aunt Suchand tells the tale of Hansuli Turn. Pagol-pal composes ballads of Hansuli Turn. Makes songs at weddings, marriages, makes songs at the Bhanjo festival, makes songs at the Ghentu festival, masquerades, dances, and sings songs at Gajon. Now it's the war of Durga and Ganga; that's to say fight between Gopalibala and Shubashi, with the aged Shiva, or Bonwari, between them—one boxes the other's chin; the other wields broom in hand.

***

Pagol Kahar, panchali balladeer of Hansuli Turn, is a humorous man. His mind is like the blue waters of the indigo levee. Sky's clear is their color. When the sun rises in the sky, black waters glisten, and if wind blows, wave on wave ripples like molten silver; if it's a moonlit night, the moon rises in the indigo levee's black, shadow-smudged waters, stars twinkling with the moon. If the sky's cloudy, the indigo levee's waters are deep black; it seems like the sky's weeping and the indigo levee's waters, sharing its grief, are weeping too. Why would they not? Indigo levee's waters are falling from the sky—they're one of its daughters. Pagol Kahar himself says so. Who else could dress up like this and utter such blissful lines! Bonwari smilingly says—Pagol-pal's mind is like indigo levee water. Kaharpara is his sky. If Kaharpara laughs, he laughs; if it weeps he weeps. If, neither laughing nor crying, Kaharpara gets into a languid state like the fog-covered indigo levee's waters between the months of Agrhayan and Phalgun, then Pagol's mind gets just that way; he falls into listlessness.

Pagol had composed a verse as he sat beside Noyan's deathbed—

Brother, alas! Why worry about darkness, ah well!
Life's bird goes to that land in darkness, ah well!

A few months later Bonwari's companion rite was performed with the Atpoure girl Shubashi. There Pagol dizzied Kaharpara with his saucy songs, rhymes, ballads. Only a certain Nasubala would have been able to compete; but Nasubala said—I'm sick. He's not sick, everyone knows the real reason. He wouldn't be in the mood to sing and dance at the wedding of the same Bonwari who's forced his Karali-bro and Missus Pakhi out of the village. Nasu says—Born to Kahar clan, live in Kaharpara, Bonwari's Kaharpara's 'eadman, master o' punishments, better obey 'is orders outside; but the mind ain't no one's slave girl, neither Kahar nor Atpoure, the thing's just 'uman—neither a king's subject nor a moneylender's debtor, why should it obey Beano? So let Nasubala not dance, Pagol's a multitude in one. He carefully prepared liquor. What a taste that liquor has! What power to "blind," or intoxicate! Notorious boozers began to reel. But Pagol remained sober. It's he who cooked food. Went back and forth, poured "glugs" of liquor, drank, set down the cooking pot, dipped the ladle into the frying pan, put wood into the oven, and sang songs the whole time—

> Hey bravo, Hansuli Turn's Bonwari—
> Built a new house, door facing southerly.
> To build that house came (all the) Ostopaharis.
> Sweet-smelling Shubashi-sprig of Ostopahari Para
> Was planted today in Kaharpara.
> Old garland maker Bonwari (tenderly) adorns the arbor.

Prohlad, Roton, and Gupi gave many bravos. The elders had been crazier than anyone about this marriage. Pagol continued to sing—

> Shubashi-sprig flower will be worn at the ear
> Her sweet smell will awaken an old spirit's sap
> Don't take that road, I forbid you—
> (the old one will come chasing,
> cudgel in hand, the old one will come chasing)

At this point Bonwari came to stand beside him and said—Listen Pagol.

—What? Why that face?

—I'll tell why I'm callin'. Call Pellad, Oton, an' Gupi.

Bonwari's first wife, Gopalibala, has been weeping. Weeping and sobbing. So Bonwari had come—Tell me, what ta do now then?

***

Gopalibala weeping? Pagol was taken aback. He didn't think of this. No one in Kaharpara ever thinks of this. If a Kaharpara husband marries when he already has a wife, then the first wife immediately tears off her conch-shell and iron wedding bangles, throws them out, and leaves, hurling abuse at husband as she goes—she goes and sets up with another Kahar man. Kahar women do not make homes with co-wives. Kahar women don't object if their husband is a moneybags, if he's a "mightful," that's to say mighty, headman type who brings another woman home and keeps her without marrying her; but they can't stand it if he marries. The women of Kaharpara are not throwaways, husband doesn't need to feed them, they provide for themselves; besides youth and beauty, there's value in the ability to "body," meaning to work hard; for this value, many blind, lame, aged folk call Kahar women to take the place of mistress of the house with honor, and they willingly occupy this position. Do housework, cook for the invalid man, do the daily chores too. If Gopalibala leaves it will be his disgrace. Besides, Gopalibala is a really wonderful person. There are no Kopai ripples in Gopalibala, her mind is not fickle, she's water in the indigo levee—no noise, no current, quiet, calm, coolness; if you sat chest deep in that water it would not move; it would surround you with stillness. Bonwari loves her just like the indigo levee's waters; but because she isn't wild like the Kopai, he has never been infatuated with her. That's why Bonwari cannot obey his mind's better judgment. Kalobou was like the Kopai, Shubashi is just like Kalobou. She has returned like new year's flood from Kopai's breast. Besides, Shubashi was a girl from an Atpoure home. Because of Bonwari's qualities as headman, the Atpoures have agreed to come along with the Kahars; the Atpoures couldn't give anyone but Bonwari the honor of this first exchange, of bringing an Atpoure maiden home. So, despite the Gopalibala worries, he has agreed to tie the knot with Shubashi. One day, when he had informed Gopalibala, and Prohlad and Roton had also spoken with her, Gopalibala herself said— Do it, tie the knot, I won't leave. But don't drive me out. Ave yer kids, I'll bring 'em up. You two take yer pleasures. I'll watch, laugh. But on the wedding day Gopalibala began to weep.

Pagol stared into Bonwari's face open-mouthed, speechless.

Bonwari said—Tell me what ta do now?

Pagol replied after much thought—If Gopali 'grees, then wi' great honor I'll keep 'er. Unnsertan'—tell 'er.

Bonwari's face became overcast.

Pagol understood—Don' get mad. It's a noo exchange wi' Atpoures, gonna 'appen too, yer gonna 'ave kids an' make a family 'ome, fulfill yer desires; don't hafta make 'ome wi' Gopali as no co-wife.

***

But Gopalibou was astounded. She said—No.

Prankeshto lent a hand; he took Bonwari discreetly aside and suggested a way—Do this one thing, uncle. Gi' ten rupees to auntie. Tell 'er—Keep 'ouse, make an 'ome, lend money in the neighborhood, be a moneylender. *You're* the real mistress o' the 'ouse; ye'll remain what ya were; Atpoure girl's comin' ta live there, there'll be kids, ye'll work a bit an' live. Unnerstan'?

Bonwari is taken by this. He cannot but admire Pana's ingenuity. He has money, but this hadn't occurred to him. Money turns minds, indeed! How many Kahar men have ignored their wives' demands, got into fights, caused riots, and been saved by money in the end? Bonwari is not ignorant of the fact that money does many other things. Put a gaudy toy or a sugary candy into a child's hands and its wailing stops; fill the cupped hands of a grown man with money and he forgets all his sorrows.

Pana said—By money beguiled ye'll forget yer dead child; that's it—. So saying, he spat.

Instead of ten rupees, Bonwari filled Gopalibala's cupped hands with twenty.

Gopalibala stared at her husband in astonishment. As he lies on the Gajon board staring at the sky, it is as if Bonwari is seeing that scene.

Bonwari had laughed and said—Given it all ta you. Ave a necklace made. Or do whatcha want.

Gopalibala's mind boggled. Handfuls of shiny money! She'd looked into her husband's face and said, smiling—Ya gotta get a pair o' golden earrings made an' give 'em too, though.

Bonwari said—Give, sure I'll give. Let gold get a bit cheaper, s'gone up terribly 'cos o' war; let price drop a bit, I'll give.

Pana said—Drink a drop o' booze now, auntie. Ya gotta dance.

And Pana really got Gopalibala drinking liquor. Bonwari couldn't but be pleased with Pana after this.

—Come on, time ta get ready ta go over to Atpoure Para.

The Kahars' journey to Atpoure Para today is not just any old journey; such a journey has never happened until today. Prohlad, Roton, Gupi, Panu—every Kahar had tied a freshly washed scarf around his head; had put on his waistcoat, carefully preserved over the years; held a fightstick in his hand. With moustaches twirled, flaming torches in hand, they all went. Drums playing, pipes playing, cymbals playing. Bonwari had put on a new cloth wrap. He'd had to pay the scorching prices of the wartime bazaar. After putting on the wrap, he sought out Pagol.

—Pagol! Pagol!

He must get everyone under control and go. With good karma, nothing will go wrong. The Kahars are drinking liquor; the girl's being brought to Atpoure Para—heads are whirling with that burning fix. Tonight what has never happened in the tale of Hansuli Turn will happen. The Kahars are not used to making the impossible happen. Pagol is a cautious person; he must be put in charge.

—Pagol! Pagol!

Pagol is not to be found. Not in the whole village.

Laughing away, Pana said—Har, talkin' all lusty—maybe took off fer shame in the end.

Right at this moment lightning flashed.

As if someone's saying—Thunderclouds, s'go, s'go.

Oh, what clouds! Monsoon clouds. Monsoon descending on a wedding night, downpour.

Downpour's clouds, thick black. Lightning flashes. Clouds' instant boom of thunder on all the turns of Hansuli Turn, as if kettledrums are being beaten in Bansbadi's bamboo groves. A breeze blows gently. A trembling of still waters on the indigo levee. From their leaf-covered holes in the bamboo groves, lordly pot frogs make a deep, resonant croaking. They look like little urns—frogs of just that shape, hence the name pot frogs. Tree frogs reply from tree branches with a relatively high call—*Aah-o! Aah-o!* The din of yellow frogs rises from the pond edges. It's as if Hansuli Turn resounds with the throbbing of a thousand frog instruments being played. Sounds of chirruping overhead. Hearing the Cloud King's roar, iora birds begin to sing even at night. Such clouds gathering that day.

When they heard the clouds' call, the groom party's Kahars leaped up with a joyful roar. And what a call! Hurrah! Victory, victory Babathakur! Start of Asharh—two days remain of the month's first three days; what thundering rains accompanied the clouds' roar! Maybe the hard cultivated earth of Hansuli Turn is getting the "tremblins"; that's to say, is trembling.

Roton, Gupi, Prohlad leaped up and said to the drummer—Play bro', play. Play rolls. *Da-rum-dum-dum, tak-tak-tak-tak—*

Panu said—Good sign fer Uncle Bonwari's new missus.

—Course. There'll be benefits, benefits; Kahars an' Atpoures, two 'amlets movin' together, there'll be benefits. Who gets the "wet of Ashir"? Meaning, who gets the plentiful rain, good for farming, of Asharh month?

At first Bonwari was afraid; he looked at the sky and said—Oh Father, let yer familiar not whip, twist an' flash; let its tongue not flicker and 'iss like before! Bonwari's mind was not put at rest. There was no rain at the end of Jayastha month; rain in Asarh is rare. So? At this untimely moment, this untimely roar of thunder and rain pouring on heads coinciding with his wedding; why now? Last time Father's familiar had risen up in the nor'westerly clouds. Its mottled hues spreading black-and-white in the clouds. And today too—?

Bonwari! Beano! Beano!

Bonwari came around at Roton's shout. And he was reassured when he looked at the clouds and knew he could not see Father's familiar in them. A thick black cloud rising to fill the sky. It's a rain cloud. Bonwari said—Come on.

**

From that night forth, in the tale of Hansuli Turn, the instruments of farming played their tune; these rains—they're rains of good fortune. "Asarh's rains. In Asarh who gets the wet? In Shangon paddy gets the wet. In Bhadur shoots get the wet. In Ashwin, what of wet?" What fortunate one gets the soaking waters needed for farming in Asarh? It hardly ever happens. This time the Kahars have got it.

What deep-voiced rumbling and roaring of clouds! Kopai's waters run muddy; from bank to bank clouds' roars sound like kettledrums. In bamboo groves new bamboo sheds its "punnets," or its husk sheaths, and new pale-green leaves come out; old bamboo leaves have a darkening touch in their green. Silk-cotton, banyan, rain tree, peepul leaves form a dreadful darkness; the leaves are thick. Leaves compressed beneath bamboo groves are soaking wet; if you tiptoe through with "oldie" steps, reddish water spurts up. So many new young plants sprout. Reeds, grasses, verbena on the Kopai banks, long tender leaves sprout in clumps and dance wavelike in the breeze. Loveliest of all is the chatim tree above the Kopai jetty. It is shaped like a conical crown in eyebalm green. A Krishna among trees. Grass fills all four directions. It's as if someone has woven a green-colored border all around the yards of Kaharpara, right up to the cottage "piles," that's to say their foundations. Water spreads in fields, grass brightens. Meanwhile, Kahars leap to work—some driving plows, gripping plow handles and driving over fields with crooked backs and heads bent like demons. Some lift seedlings in muddy fields, knee-deep in water; they pull up grass and weeds from the muddy water, twist them, and shove them into the earth. They rush to the fields during night's last watch and return when first watch of the next night is done.

"Who gets the wet in Asharh?" Now it has been gotten, the Kahars are putting it to best use. Their farming's going well this time. Fields have filled with paddy, the masters have received a huge amount, and each of the Kahars has also received his due. War's broken out in the world—hard times don't respect borders or frontiers. The Kahars' sole resource is paddy. The price of paddy was eighteen annas—now it's gone up to five rupees. In the wet of Asharh harvest has been plentiful; this time the Kahars have made it through.

Bonwari got a lot of paddy this time. The sharecropping harvest was plentiful, so how much more he has received! Now paddy from the Saheb Tracts plot is piling up at his cottage. One of the two and a half acres has been cut; got two-and-eighty aris, that's to say two thousand pounds, from there; no share to anyone else, no levy taken. To him, these two thousand pounds are the same as one hundred thousand. If his sold it this very day the merchants would count out fifty rupees in crisp new "lotes." No coins in the land, all "lotes," all "lotes"; else Bonwari would have sold a little, but lotes won't keep if you bury 'em in the ground! And there's something else besides: it doesn't make sense to bury money before knowing Little-Un's, that is new wife Shubashi's, inclinations.

There are huge amounts of paddy on the gentry masters' Saheb Tracts lands too. They had dug the land and then spread pond sludge and fertilizer on it; Bonwari cannot do that. But wherever he and Gopalibala see any cow dung on path and verge they snatch it up and go and spread it into the earth. Gopali's doing another job too, something that no one besides Bonwari knows about. When there was no one in the fields she went down to the gentry's land, gathered up lumps of the sludge, and hurled it onto Bonwari's land. Gopalibala is Lakshmi incarnate. Sure, Bonwari's overcome with hunger for Shubashi's teenage body, but even as he hungers he can understand that this hunger isn't good for the household. The girl is a flawless Kaloshoshi—same sensuality, same attitude, same smile, same languorousness; sometimes Bonwari's mind rages.

Then at the harvest festival there was a scene. It was that scene that made him understand this girl's hands do not hold Lakshmi's bounty. This harvest festival Hansuli Turn's Bansbadi was all decorated. They've always decorated for harvest festival. The Kahars take great pleasure in the splendor of the pure castes, doing one offering after another, attending at the offering place; but with all that fancy decoration, God never steps into their own homes. Their splendor is at year-end's Gajon, Dharam Puja,

Amuti, that is Ambubachi, the fertile earth's three days of menstruation in the month of Asharh; Mother Monosha's Puja, Bhanjo festival in Bhadra, harvest festival in Agrhayan, and Lakshmi Poush. Around seven festivals. Beside these there is Josthi and there is Chandimangal—these are women's "pledgers," which they have to make sat on an edge of the "outyard," or courtyard, of the pure castes' Mother Lakshmi pledge place. Harvest festival is their great celebration. They cut the new paddy, make offerings to Lakshmi and Annapurna, let Kalaruddu and Babathakur feast, "mek ready the five" foods, and give to eat with pleasure. And to Kalaruddu is said—Father!—

We've shook the "la"—we've threshed the "la"
Built a home wi' "la" and old
Fill store wi' noo, we'll eat the old—
In this eating let life unfold—
Noo stuff, old rice—
By your kindness blest our life.

"La" meaning "na"; here they pronounce *n* as *l*—"na" meaning "new." Much excitement for the feasting. Everyone invited to everyone's house. The feasters' afternoon consists of a baitstick, that's bat-stick, competition. The young lads take a two-foot wooden stick and a hand-width wooden slug up to the Saheb Tracts and begin to play; they play till evening and, meal now digested, go back home. By turns they whack the slug with the stick, hup—off it goes, away across the seven worlds. Bari Duri Teri Chal Champa Dhek Lanka—if the slug's distance hits seven times a yard then you've been "yarded," which means your team's lost a round. And the ones who toil don't go infrequently to play; swiftly catching that flying, whirring slug two-handed, they touch the tip to their mouths and say—Ate it, which means the player has caught it. It's a madhouse. Even the elders sometimes cannot hold back, they too will take a couple of turns. The boys come out with their bows and arrows—they make split-bamboo bows and new reed arrows and charge out into the meadows, giving chase to all the flocks of birds that come down into the paddy fields—crows, mynas, sparrows.

Eveningtime is a liquor feast. Drumming, song, dance. This time Bonwari had invited all Atpoure Para. There has been a new alliance with them, marriage kinship too. Bonwari has also had a tremendously favor-

able year, so it's his duty. Everything was finished in the day, at eveningtime the liquor party sat—a great gathering; Pagol struck up a beautiful
song—

On this 'arvest's noo paddy rice cake—
What good's a fish curry today!

Dancing began just like that. Pagol's song continued—

Wives comin' wi' a rustle o' noo cloth—
Ruddy noo babes in their laps!

Immediately the cry went up from all. Do the count, who all is having
a baby. Who all did harvest wi' a noo babe in their lap? Bonwari heaved
a deep sigh. Only Babathakur knows when he will grant him a lineage.
As he pondered, he suddenly noticed that Shubashi was nowhere to be
seen. He looked around carefully, yes, definitely not here. Gone where?
Getting up on a pretext, he went home and did not find her there. Gone
where? He went out to the fields. He began looking all around. Karali
suddenly came to mind. Came to mind because he's getting a slight whiff
of cigarette on the breeze. He began to search, maddened. Suddenly it
seems as if someone's going far, far off—into the heart of Atpoure Para.
He cried out—Who? Straightaway began to run. But no one is there; a
dead, bark-peeling-off paper-tree stump sticking up beside a clump; that
looks just like a person. On the way back from there he paused, suddenly overcome and afraid. He'd stumbled upon the yard of Kaloshoshi's
fallen-down cottage, and whose white shape was standing on the broken
terrace! He stood, speechless. He did not know how long he stood there.
On hearing the white shape's utterance he came to. It said in a very soft,
nasal voice—Fleee—you fleee—I'm gettin' greeedy fer youuu—
    Bonwari's fear of the shape evaporated in a flash. He came to. He
leaped and grabbed the thing. That Shubashi.
    —Bitch—
    Amazing Shubashi, she squealed with laughter. Insane with rage,
Bonwari grabbed her by the throat and said—Say what ya was doin' 'ere?
Was anyone else 'ere?
    With great difficulty Shubashi said—Candies!
    —Candies?

—Was eatin' candies in secret. Ere look. She brought a container of candies out of her clothing.

Bonwari released her throat. You were eatin' candies in secret?

—Yeh. She hung her head and spoke—Sis only gave two out, so—

Now Bonwari began to laugh.—So ya came 'ere to eat in secret! Ya couldn't've gone 'ome to eat?

—What if someone saw!

—So in this broke-down cottage—snakes, or holes—

—Woulda been good 'f I died. Ya coulda made 'ouse wi' old Gopali, Queen o' Bounty.

Bonwari laughed. Said—Come on, shall we see 'ow many candies ye can eat? I'll get candies right now.

—No. Now Shubashi began to cry.

—Don't cry. Come on.

With great difficulty he broke through Shubashi's sulk. But this kind of girl—who gives in to greed, doesn't believe God's word, tricks her husband, steals, and goes to a haunted place to stuff her belly, this is not a good kind of girl. That sweet festival day was a day of giving to God. Bonwari had not even lifted his head until then.

Bonwari was thinking on all this as he lay on the Charak board a second year. Last year's matters. When that year ended, its matters became this year's legends. Music stopped, the board is descending, overhead the silk-cotton tree's huge branches are swaying; the disc is coming down at the edge of Babathakur's deeps. Like the year, Father will go to his watery repose. One year has ended, another year has begun.

As the board came down, Bonwari was struck speechless.

A red-faced saheb and beside him Karali. Both smoking cigarettes. Jangol's Sadgop masters attending, even Maito Ghosh. Karali not even paying them heed. White man blah blah saying something. Maito Ghosh answering in English. Bonwari wished to leap up and smash the lad a huge punch in the chest. Shatter his audacity, demolish him. But he is lying on the Charak board and the saheb is there beside Karali.

Speechless! Karali saying—*Hello man*? Saying this and turning his head. This gesture means—let's go. That's sure. The saheb left with Karali.

***

Karali evil, Karali the incarnate "deemo," that's to say demon. For the Kahar clan's many evils he arrived at Hansuli Turn. Bonwari's age was almost sixty, Auntie Suchand'll be nearly eighty; neither of them has ever witnessed such a "deemo's" coming.

In the tale of Hansuli Turn Auntie Suchand knows, there's no such thing either. There are always the casteless and bad ones; always will be, a hand's five fingers aren't all the same; but this one's a demon incarnate. You hear of demons and fiends in stories of the most ancient times; they'd be born as humans on earth, would wreak chaos in lands of hamlet and village, would themselves do evil, would fill others with evil desires; humanity would cry out for deliverance. Mother Earth's breast heaved, even she wept. Then came the gods, came and slaughtered the humanoid demons. Humans had no ability to slaughter the demons. Bonwari is getting extremely vigilant. He's understanding well. A small issue has opened his eyes.

The issue of that brick-built house of Karali's. He disregarded the prohibition of all Kaharpara, he did not obey headman's ruling. He ignored the word of a mother-in-law like Bashan. He did not listen to the well-meant advice of an ancient elder like Suchand. He built that brick house. Not even the strength of all Kaharpara could hold him back.

Look up above Kaharpara today and you'll see the top of Karali's brick house standing tall. The brick structure firmly planted in Kaharpara is like the raised banner of Karali's obstinacy—at evening they come and light the lamps, play the drums to "porclaim" themselves. Not just the banner of obstinacy, the banner of antidharma—of the Infernal Age. The loser doesn't know what danger's in a raised head! A palm tree is blasted by lightning, a fightstick crashes down on a raised head, a tall house flies up in a storm; if a tall house catches fire it'll never be put out. Thieves and bandits espy the top of a fine, tall house and come back around; hateful people see a fine, tall house and reel off a venomous mantra. Your ghosts, your spirits—them flying around in the skies; they'll install themselves on top of any tall house they find in their way, and if you stop them they'll give the house the evil eye. He who at a bad time does what the forefathers didn't must take the consequences.

Lying on the Charak bed Bonwari recalled the details of that house's making.

The day all Kaharpara gathered together with a hue and cry and razed the beginnings of Karali's house to the ground was the very day Karali took Pakhi off to Channanpur. Noyan died that night, and just as Bonwari and company returned at dawn from the burning ground Gopali said—S' bad. Karali's brought police. Constable had said—You've gotta go to the police station.

—Go to the police station! Bonwari's chest began to pound.

After much thought, he gathered courage. He had neither stolen, taken part in banditry, nor murdered, so why fear? Government has a law, hamlet neighborhood has a rule of caste dharma. How can he, as headman, permit irregularities—let the police officer compute it through law, let there be judgment. He took Prohlad and Roton with him as well as Sire Chaudhury's footman Nobin. The land is Sire Chaudhury's, a house built there because Karali's dad didn't have a place; therefore how can Karali build a house there without permission? And Karali abused Nobin, beat him. This counsel had been given by the Ghoshes. Maito Ghosh said—Say that he broke Chaudhury's orders and laid house foundations.

But Police Inspector said—Uh-uh, all that doesn't count. Understood! It was his house in that spot, that one's smashed and he's making a new one; doesn't matter if the plot's Chaudhury's or whoever's; they're owners of the work-in-lieu and they'll get the work-in-lieu; no one's allowed to stop house building. And hamlet rules don't count either. He can build bricks, put up rotundas, you have to let him do it.

In a final attempt, Bonwari said with folded hands—By yer leave, it's 'armful, somethin' 'appens—

Karali himself answered from the other side—What 'appens is: mine'll 'appen.

Police Inspector laughed. Bonwari stared at Karali in enraged consternation; he could not speak. Finally he conceded and went back. He also had to give Mister Inspector a goat. Mister Inspector ordered compensation to be paid to Karali for damages. When Karali had gone away Constable summoned Bonwari and said—How'll ya pay compensation?

Compensation! Bonwari's eyes watered with shame and bitterness. If he has to pay compensation to Karali he will be utterly disgraced! Better to be "deaded."

It was Mister Constable who finally saved his face and said—All right, I won't put you through that disgrace. I know you. Mister Inspector's a new guy. I'll talk to him. Give the new Master a goat. He'll eat, we'll eat too.

That very afternoon Karali came and laid the foundations of his house. He sat leaning on that dead tree stump pulling on a cigarette and gave the order—Do it.

Then laughter, ha ha ha.

He had brought people, all from Channanpur. Got them to begin work. Kaharpara's people stood some way off, watching speechlessly. Suchand, even Suchand remained speechless. For fear of Inspector she could neither weep in joy at the memory of her father nor weep in terror of imagined future adversities.

Only Mathla and Notbor had come. These few openly joining in with Karali's group. It was they who told Karali about the goat. Told him with great amusement. Said—Properly settin' up! Laughed a lot.

But Karali was taken aback. He said—Why'd 'e give?

—Not give?

—What not give?

—Woulda 'ad ta give ya compensation. Woulda been so disgraced.

—I don't want no compensation.

—Whassit matter if you don't want it? Law—

Looking annoyed, Karali said—Law! Get out, stupid bastard bumpkin! Ripped off. Ripped off 'eadman. Speak—agree an' I'll take it ta the Swadeshi independence fighters. We'll pull the goat outa Inspector's belly.

Bonwari heard the talk. But he said nothing to Karali, nor approached anyone else. Shame! Not merely that, he no longer even looks at Karali's house. Does not take his habitual stroll in that direction; if he finds himself walking that way he turns around and goes another route. When the house has raised its head above the rest of the hamlet there will of course be no way not to see it, but he makes a habit of not looking. But amazing Karali—he built the house and did not fix up the inside. Why should he? Building the house is his obstinacy. A brick house has been built in Kaharpara, age-old norms and customs have been dealt a blow, the work's done. He's living in that brick-built shack quarter of Channanpur. War work, he has to stay. And there's another reason. Bonwari can understand that. He has gotten quite old. Karali's afraid to live here. Now Nasu's living in Karali's house. He stays, lights the evening lamp, rinses the wall with cow dung, sticks up dung cakes, goes off to Channanpur in the morning, comes back in the evening. The days he comes back in the afternoon are days when Karali and Pakhi come too. They leave again before evening.

Daarang—dang—daarang—dang.

***

Dang-dang—dadang.

Kalaruddu's stone form has gone to his watery repose. Bonwari has brought his remembrances of last year to a close and descended from the

Charak-wheel board. The year of fear is over. Passed into fearlessness. Victory Father Kalarudra! Thirteen forty-eight of the Bengali calendar is over, 'forty-nine has come. Nineteen forty-three in the English calendar. Suchand says—Ow many decades, 'ow many years, say. Then, scratching her head and trying to catch a louse with the fingertips of her left hand, she spoke again—That 'air o' God's never goes gray, teeth don't break. An' so? If ye get through the year, release. Since them ancient days—. So saying, she pointed behind her with the index finger of her right hand; her eyes bulged with a strangely amazed look; she remained silent a few moments, and all Kaharpara regards her face in silence. Then Suchand speaks—Oo knows 'ow many years there's been! Ye can count the 'airs on an 'ead—but that ye can't count. She spoke and continued to shake her head.

Two

Forty-nine came in with wind and storm. On the auspicious first day of Boishakh month there was a nor'wester. On the second there was another blast of wind. Nothing on the third and fourth, then again on the fifth a storm blew up, rushing and wailing. There was a storm blast every two or three days, continuing almost constantly. Pagol also returned in 'forty-nine.

Bonwari now recommenced digging the remaining land on the Saheb Tracts. The Kahars wielded their spades after evening, just as long as there was moonlight; now the Atpoures are joining with the Kahars. Porom's land was shared among eight Atpoure households; only Romon, old and childless, didn't take any; he's become the Atpoures' headman; lesser than Bonwari, of course. Romon's now getting by somehow or other. Helping Bonwari. Shubashi's uncle, Bonwari's uncle. Romon takes care of Bonwari's cows and calves—does this and that, whatever's needed. Bonwari is seeking land for the Kahars and went again to the gentry master of Channanpur. Master gave some cause for optimism.

As they dug the Saheb Tracts' land, Bonwari and company discovered this truth. Forty-nine "sets in bringin" winds; which is to say, seems to come bringing winds.

Pagol sits on the edge of the plot smoking tobacco and giving it out to everyone else. He does not lift a shovel. Now and again he goes off dressed as a wandering Baul or Fakir minstrel. He wanders for a few days, fills the belly of his shoulder bag, comes back with enough to eat for a week. Says—This'll do fer a few days. Why lift that shovel? Bonwari does not tell him to take a shovel. Pagol's a fine person. Hearing of the inquiries, Pagol said—An' why shouldn't it come, eh! Forty-nine's Paban's year, year o' the Wind God. Unnerstood! Then he said—Now monkeys are gonna gi' trouble, just see! Paban's son 'e is. Pagol's words are true. Not because they're sons of Paban. If there is a storm, monkeys sit on a tree branch getting wet; the colder they get, the more madly they jump about. As soon as the rainstorm ends they come leaping out like maniacs.

In 'forty-nine there was thus no limit to the Kahars' misery from the "poyer," or power, of Paban and the sons of Paban. Thatch roofs in tatters.

When storms ended they no longer cut palm leaves and laid them on roofs. No more straw left in the thatch. Bonwari's has some left. Everyone in Kaharpara does farm work. Straw's not available as part of a farm-worker's share; you get a one-third share of paddy, that's a custom settled in ancient times. They can get a few scraps of straw by asking the bosses. And there is some straw to be had from paddy-cleared fields. It's even hard to buy straw now. The price of straw is afire. It's exceeded twenty rupees a bundle. War! O times of war!

Go to Channanpur, you'll understand what kind of war is breaking out in the world. The workshops have grown, and it's as if the epic Bhima's half-demon son is now growing into Warrior Ghatotkacha. And what a roar he has! Rows of iron machines booming, clashing, pounding, clattering—as if a great slaughter has begun. Sometimes they scream out with a whooping shriek. A body shudders from head to foot. If you tarry there the noise will turn you deaf. People would be boiled alive just by entering. Three or four injured every single day. One or two getting killed every couple of weeks. Someone being pulled into the engine wheels, another getting smashed on the head by a shard of iron come loose, another killed falling headfirst from above. Of course compensation is paid if you die. Probably a lot of money. No matter how much money, is it worth more than life?

Karali has become a coolie leader inside those very workshops. Wearing a jacket, wearing long pants, shoes on feet, cap on head, he gives orders. Bonwari is astounded; why has Karali still not been punished? Babathakur's judgment and justice, carried out with a blow from the Death Rod! Why has Karali still not received that punishment? Perhaps it'll happen. Maybe there hasn't yet been time for the weight of that loser's evil to fill out. This time nearly everyone's cottage was blown up in the storm, but Karali's house is almost completely fine. Of course he secured the roof with iron wires and earth, fixed a rope net over the straw to cover the thatch; but Babathakur's wrath smashes the tops of palm trees and casts them down to earth, washes away brick railway bridges; what's all that securing compared to this? That evil's weight hasn't come to term yet, that must be it.

A few lads have crowded into Karali's mob. Crowd away. They'll be punished too. Babathakur is there.

Suddenly a servant from the Ghosh house came and stood. —Big Lord summoning Bonwari.

—Big Lord! So late? Tomorrer mornin'—

—No no. Gotta go tonight. Else why'd I come to these Saheb Tracts?

—What, whassup?

—Ye know there's a feast at the 'ouse, right?

—Yeh. All the supplies were got in.

—You go. Ye'll know all about it when ya get there.

The servant left.

There is a feast held at the Ghosh house every year on the last day of Boishakh. Great Mother Ghosh personally installed this tradition of good karma. She had said—So that bad things don't happen, you don't stop doing this.

Brahmin, Kayastha, Sadgop masters all feast. The Kahars get leftovers, clean up polluted waste, wrap food left on leaf plates in their scarves and take it home, eat with pleasure next day.

Pagol said—So, we're done fer today. The 'eavens got a bad attitude up there, yeh. Lightnin' flashin' in the west, wind's dropped. Been four, five days since God's trumpeted forth. Prob'ly gonna come out today then!

Sitting doing nothing, Pagol's seeing rightly. Clouds rising in the west. There was still some light left because the moon was in the middle of the sky.

Big Ghosh was waiting with dark and forbidding face. Bonwari was afraid. Since taking land from the Channanpur gentry he's been somewhat neglecting work on the Ghosh masters' lands, and for this Big Lord will one day get angry with him—Bonwari is arriving having sensed this for a few days. Now he understands that some flaw in feast preparations is bringing it crashing down on his head. He spoke fearfully and humbly—By yer leave?

Big Lord burst out—I'll straighten your Kahars out.

—By yer leave?

—Don't you dare come to me for kerosene. Nor for sugar. Nor for cloth. Nor for quinine. Watch out. I'm not going to give.

Big Lord is a member of the Union Board. He is in charge of the requisition letter for Kaharpara and Jangol. Aren't "kerachini," sugar, cloth coming under *control* because of war! You can't get them by paying money in a bazaar. If you get a requisition letter, show it, then you can get these things. The Kahars get "kerachini" but not much sugar. Rations of two to three and a half ounces a week. He's saying he'll stop that too. No harm if they don't get sugar. They don't eat sugar, their boss masters take their sugar. But how will they go on without a little bit of "kerachini"? The Union Board gives "quinial pills" to members in the malarial season of Bhadra-Aswin-Kartik months—if you don't get quinial at that time you're dead! But what had they done wrong?

Big Lord said—Wear holy thread on your necks you lot, get it? Your women gone to Channanpur—

Big Lord made absolutely explicit the extent of Kahar women's degradation. Big Boss angrily made explicit things about Kahars—Kahars are no longer Kahars; Brahmins! Let Kahars wear holy threads. Finally, in a complete rage, he said—Ye won't eat leftover rice, ye want invitations! If ye don't get a beating ye get all stuck up!

Bonwari was speechless—What's this? Oo said all this to ye?

Big Lord rose and came over. Said—That Karali of yours is saying it. I'll beat the bastard wi' me shoe one day. Fool's getting really obnoxious. Junior—that's his younger brother—got down at Channanpur station today to go to the bazaar. Your lot's Sidhu was there. Sidhu asked about the child's rite of First Rice. Said—Yez gonna give us leftovers then? Junior said—Course you'll get. Come along, y'all. You, Karali, Pakhi come along; all Kaharpara's coming. Karali was standing just nearby. That little whelp said—Karali don't eat no polluted waste. The lads from Kaharpara are saying—they won't go either. He says to Sidhu—If you go, we ain't gonna eat wi' ya.

Bonwari was dumbstruck. He cannot imagine such defiance.

Big Lord said—That bastard Kahar's coming, I'll see him. He's got a meeting together in the hamlet!

***

It is true. That very night a meeting of the Kahar lads was taking place at Karali's house. Karali giving them that word. —Touch another, won't lose caste. Eat leftovers, lose caste. The Kahar that eats others' waste falls into outcaste. Got no caste.

Karali's regret—the elder Kahars don't understand this simple thing. Regret—they don't go to Channanpur and try the workshops just once to see, is it pleasant or horrible there! Good or bad for people there!

The meeting had begun. Bonwari should have been there. But on the way back from Jangol the storm blew back in. Came with a roar. Droning and whistling! Lord has not yet arrived with such force this year; today he's surely coming to snap the head off Karali's palm tree. Surely. He looked to the sky. Moon still visible below clouds. Cloud twisting in coils, black and white. Bonwari was startled. That coloring, that dappling! Such winding twisting turning. Lightning playing, flashing like a tongue. O Babathakur, save us. O Babathakur! Trees shattering, bamboos knocking, clouds booming; joining in today, after so long, the voice of Noyan's Ma answering.

Noyan's Ma directly brings up the topic of Suchand as she speaks in her piercing voice, saying—O Babathakur, destroy, Father, 'e oo killed yer familiar, 'e oo broke up others' 'omes, 'e oo didn't foller village rules, built a tall 'ouse; give one puff an' blow 'is 'ouse up, smash it again. Smash it ta bits. Bite their 'eads off. O Father! Those oo forgave the crime o' killin' yer familiar, bite 'em ta death. Make their eyes bulge wi' blood clots; let their bodies crawl wi' bloody spots. Judge ooever's done a wrong in Kaharpara. Finish it, finish it, finish it. Make 'em all cohorts o' my Noyan. Jus' let me live. Kinless one o' Kaharpara, I'll come out an' dance the empty 'omes— come out weepin' like a banshee.

Bonwari sat silently, watching the clouds. There was a sudden crashing sound.

Fallen? Has Karali's house fallen? Bonwari stood up. The voice of Noyan's Ma has fallen silent.

As soon as the storm finished he went out into the hamlet. –Oose 'ouse fell?

—Noyan's 'ouse, mate.

—Noyan's 'ouse? Bonwari was astonished.

—Bonwari? Beano!

—Oo? Bonwari was irritated—who's that calling behind him?

—Me, Pagol.

—What?

—Been a clamity, bro. Been a disaster.

—What, tell me?

—Karali shouted it out on 'is way ta Channanpur—Babathakur's wood-apple tree's fallen down.

O God! Dear Father! Dear, what have you done! Have you left us at last! Infernal Age! House of antidharma! Karali's fulfilled his evils in Kaharpara. You've gone, can't bear that evil!

Standing in the moonlight, all Kaharpara looked on. The clouds cleared and the moon came out once more. Clear and silvery moonlight. There was also a hurricane lantern in Bonwari's hand. Babathakur's tree is leaning to one side.

Bonwari said—Everyone bathe.

—Bathe?

—Yes, bathe. Come on, pull the tree up. Small tree; wi' all Kaharpara's shoulders it'll go up nicely. Then we'll buttress it. No fear, next-door tree's all right.

All Kaharpara lent a shoulder.

Victory Babathakur! Victory Kalaruddu! Call—Shivo—Dhammaran-ja—! Going up, going up. Call again, bro. Again. Done. Done. Put earth all 'round—buttress it. Build it strong.

Suddenly someone screamed in severe pain. Child's voice. Everyone was startled. Chests began to pound. What's happened to whom at Ba-bathakur's shrine?

—What? What happened?

—Snake! O Father, snake!

—Snake! Oo's child then? Oo? What snake? Pana began to weep and beat his chest—Neem-oil Pana.—O God, it's that, that. It's that very One, man.

A chain viper was moving into the bushes with its natural sluggish pace.

Kaharpara was frozen. Pana's son died in a while, exactly as Karali's dog had died; in just that way his eyes burst and bled, his body came out in circular bloody welts. Blood flowed from nose and mouth. Suchand screamed—Oh my, I said back then I did! Within the year what'll 'appen then? There's no years fer Babathakur, no! O Father!

Noyan's Ma answered from the terrace of the smashed cottage—Ah, oo did the Brahmin-killin', oo lost their life? Pana gave a good goat in place o' the marked goat though! Say, why ain't anythin' 'appened ta that maniac oo killed Father's familiar? In other words, why hasn't anything happened to Karali? She's not upset at the smashing of her own cottage, and even if she were upset she would not be sorry. Her sorrow—the evil-doer has not received the rod.

Pana and his wife were speechless with fright. This penalty is a penalty from Babathakur. No question about it.

On the day of the Josthi offering, the tale of Hansuli Turn's God gives the "writ" of fate's outcome in Kaharpara's "scrip," or record-script. The acts of prior births give a corresponding outcome in fate. Else that chain viper would not have come along. That's enough. Many others are dying by its venom. But this death of Pana's boy, and at this shrine of Ba-bathakur's, on the very day Babathakur's tree fell, this death on that day—

the reason for this act is plain for all to see. The dog-bitten, polluted, leftover goat of Pana's house was used to pay off a fine and was sacrificed by the Chaudhurys at Father's shrine; where will punishment fall? This is surely the rod of Babathakur; no mistake of that, absolutely no mistake. This death is a son's death for a father's wrong.

Bonwari sat head in hand. The year has passed, the time of the rod has not ceased with it. Punishment in the next birth, punishment in the next age; who knows when karma's fruits from Hansuli Turn's ancient times will be punished? Yet punishments will surely come.

Three

The tale of Hansuli Turn's people—a group of people sheltering under a banyan in dark night. This night began in ancient times; when it will end is unknown. Yet the day it ends is the very day Hansuli Turn will also end. Kahar life span equals this night span; Hansuli Turn's span too. Then perhaps Kopai's rage will grow into whirling deeps, or something will happen, but who knows what! In night sky stars fall, rain comes down; Kahars suffer consequences, will it ever end? Bonwari had been mistaken, he'd thought that with the end of the year the dangers had passed. Is that so? Danger did not pass. An hour or so like this contemplating moonlight; there'll be no more rain, stars will no longer fall from the sky, he knows nothing. Bonwari knows and, knowing, made a mistake. Kaharpara has made many more mistakes. This incident has shattered everyone's illusions. But that's a good outcome.

Karali's entire group has departed except for a few. In the end most people secretly inclined toward Karali's group. Bonwari had cautioned everyone again and again but could not get them to obey. Now everyone's shocked. Turned back.

Roton, Prohlad, everyone shook their heads. Pagol sang a song—an old song—

Hey you, leave if you want—I'm not going—
To play 'neath kadam-tree, O people!
If you find a jewel, take it—I won't want it—
Black gem Krishna, O people!

Rightly said. Who else would say all these things if not for Pagol; and without Babathakur's punishment, how would they be put back on the right path? This snakebite on Pana's son—the familiar of Babathakur, that snake; its clan has shocked Kaharpara with a punishing stroke of the rod. It's smeared fear's black shade over all those colors—of Karali's laughter, his assured words, his fancy outfits. One day Babathakur will with a puff extinguish the red and blue lights of the airplanes flying overhead—with this true insight, that old-time, torpid look has come back into their eyes. There was another result. Bonwari saved face at the Ghosh house.

Everyone went to the Ghosh masters' house to pay respects. Ancestral Kahar dharma, how can you quit that! Only some of Karali's people did not go.

He said—Go, go! Ye're fallen outcastes. I've outcasted Kaharpara. He also said—If Lord Ghosh refuses anyone "kerachini," refuses sugar, then I'll see about it. I'll make a request at headquarters. I'll take Man wi' me ta see Magistry Saheb.

"Man" means the red-faced war saheb who sometimes accompanies Karali to Kaharpara.

Bonwari listens and laughs. If a grasshopper lifts its wings it don't become no elephant, sonny! Elephant's a big stretch, don't even become a bird. The buttressing of Babathakur's tree base is proceeding—Bonwari is having it shored up. He sits supervising and watches Karali's constant antics. He swaggers about; regularly goes all around the area taking "Man" saheb with him. The man has a box hanging around his neck with which he takes pictures, *click-click*—"photoks," or photos.

That day Bonwari was gazing at clouds.

There was scorching heat all Jayastha month. As soon as Boishakh came, Paban of the Winds left off. With all arrangements made and with Babathakur's tree put up straight, work on rebuilding the shrine is not quite done yet. Bonwari searched for British cement in all the fourteen worlds. Cement is "contolled." "A'last," or at last, he got two sacks of cement at triple price. Asharh is coming—monsoon month. Sky looking troubled. Sometimes it's threatening in all four corners, sometimes it's clear. Now time for downpour.

> Sun's heat in Chaitra, in Boishakh storm and hail.
> In Joshti earth cracks, but know that monsoon is for sure.

There are all the signs of that happening. But just two more days, Babathakur, two more days—in just two days rebuilding of the place will be finished. British cement will be laid down today. Dry by tomorrow. That British cement's of amazing quality!

Karali came and stood.

—What?

—Came ta say somethin'.

—Got nothin' ta talk about wi' you.

—It's not your businesss, s'mine. Whole 'amlet's.

—What's yer concern wi' the whole 'amlet?

—My concern's same as yours.

—Nah.

—If you say "nah," why should I listen?

—Fine. Say what yer sayin'.

—I'm sayin', 'amlet's 'ouses got no paddy. Bosses blockin' off paddy. You sort somethin' out, else say—they can go ta the workshops.

Bonwari was furious. Karali laughed, said—Don' come out wi' all these threats. I've said what's ta be said. You do what's ta be done.

Karali strode off. Bonwari glared after him in rage. Times of war! Paddy's gone up from five rupees to ten or twelve rupees in two months of wartime. Sadgops busily selling paddy and making money. In the month of Jayastha they stopped paddy supplies on the pretext there was no water. The hamlet folks are certainly lacking. But that hardship must be accepted.

Eyes suddenly dazzled. Cloud thundered with a rumble. Bonwari was reassured. His chest filled. This thunder is monsoon-cloud thunder. In Boishakh month the Wind God's clouds thunder with rhythmic crashing!

Monsoon clouds are clouds of King Indra. These clouds thunder with a rumbling growl. From the west comes a gentle, soft breeze. Clashing and smashing, clouds seem to break and plunge onto Mother Earth's breast.

**

In 'forty-nine Asharh wet came down again. Victory Babathakur! The Kahars rushed down to Hansuli Turn's fields. They hurried with plow and ox. Pagol fled, quit the village. What'll he do staying in the village now? The Kahars have got stuck into their plowing; who'll he spend the days with alone in the village? All Kaharpara is in the fields—cattle, human, woman, man, all.

Flocks of egrets coming down all around plots being plowed; standing there on long legs, suddenly stretching long necks, stabbing long beaks into muddy water, grabbing frogs, bugs, worms, crabs to eat; plow blades turning up insects from under the plot's earth. Flocks of shrike and crows flying overhead. They too are swooping down. Crows and shrike have an eternal rivalry; in greed for food they even forget that. Bonwari says— Such is the belly, no doubt! Belly's need is a big need!

Small Kahar children grabbing crabs from inside fieldpath holes. Kahar women finish up household chores, milk cows, give milk to those people who supply it to Channanpur, and then bring refreshments to the men in the fields. They also have their baskets and sickles; when they've fed the men they'll cut grass on fieldpaths. Load upon load of grass. Some they will feed to their own cattle, some they will send to Channanpur for sale.

The fieldpath to Channanpur has become almost overgrown with grass. It pleases Bonwari most of all to see that overgrown path. Beside Karali's gang, hardly anyone from Kaharpara walks this path.

No one regularly walks and disturbs the grass on that path except to carry supplies of milk, grass, and dung cakes. And that's not even to Channanpur's machineworks district anyway. They go to the gentry masters' quarter. It's women who go. Those among the men who have little field work on some day go to the distiller's liquor shop. They bring a liquor called roshi in a great barrel, the strongest country brew distilled from paddy. This they augment by mixing in a proportion of water, and each gets a share corresponding to what he can pay. Karali has forged a new fieldpath to and from Channanpur. The path has cleft the field's breast in an absolutely straight line.

Mathla and Notbor following behind Karali; behind them, some other folk coming and going on that path. They leave unused the old ancestral path that grazes Jangol, and are beginning a new one. But it's still not a properly raised path yet. Beside Mathla, Notbor, and Gopal, the others have come into line, they've set back to work in the fields. It's Bonwari who's gotten the work. What worry about work? A new field coming at Saheb Tracts. Gentry's plentiful money, land's already been dug a lot, covered over with dried-up-pond silt. Farming moving on apace. But gentry don't farm with their own hands; Kahars do the farming, as do available lowborn clans like the Kahars. This was God's prescript, Babathakur's command. Toil, eat. Toil hard, with chest and arms do strive, in Hansuli fields may Lakshmi's golden bounty rise. Gentry masters' and Sadgop masters' fortune, and your reputation. Pile up paddy in Boss's yard, blow the jeweled conch horn, bring Lakshmi's bounty to the house with a sprinkle of water. Come dust off your hem in the granary, Mother. Dust of Lakshmi's feet. That's plenty for you, could you want more than that? "As the wedding, so the music." When you're born into the Kahar clan this is the prescription for that birth. Steal, rob, won't get to anything more than that. The Kahars stole and robbed and saw for themselves. Look at Porom—a bandit right up to the end. What happened? And this too: do robbery, thieving, and give the stuff up to Mister Fence; theft's bounty piles up in his house, and you come away with the dust off that bountiful Lakshmi's feet. And you also haul away the weight of antidharma. Better than this, with great good fortune Kartathakur has opened the road of farming; walk that road, keep dharma in your head. Morn and eve pay obeisance to God by saying—That was this birth; in the coming birth please bring me into a higher clan, O kind Hari!

Gopalibala came and waited on the fieldpath. She's bringing food and drink. Bonwari is flattening, which is to say leveling, a corner of the share of the Ghoshes' land, wielding the shovel with a scrunching sound. The Sadgop masters' cattle go down this path to graze on the riverbank. The cowpath seems to have wound its way through one of the plot's corners. Bonwari digs the plot outward imperceptibly a little farther each year in order to finish it up with four equal corners, so it's "beholdy," meaning it looks nice. If Jangol's Sadgop masters noticed they would make a terrible scene. If it reached the Ghoshes' ears they'd say—How many times have we warned you, Bonwari. What need of making my bit of land bigger? Middle Ghosh would say—Amazing! I would've understood if it was your plot. Tell me, what do you get out of this? Bonwari cannot answer all this, he scratches his head; but when he goes out to farm, his mind is not happy until he has done a bit of expansion.

Gopalibala sat. Bonwari does not have leisure to look anywhere just now. At this time there is no one around here, not even Kahars. This is a suitable time. The Kahars are loyal to him, sure, but he doesn't trust them on this one. They won't say anything themselves, but whisperingly it will reach the ears of Sadgop bosses. From the ten- to fifteen-yard fieldpath Bonwari chopped and cut earth, half a yard here, three quarters there, and mixed it in with what he has plowed and dug on the plot; he came up and dusted off his head. Water dripped from his bushy hair—dripped from black Bonwari's hair in fat drops falling free. His abdomen is smarting. He can't stand straight. Bonwari stood bent and looked at the sky. It is past time for food and drink. Thick dark clouds in the sky today. No way to tell the time. Hard rain coming down since last night. Ashen-colored clouds enfolding Bansbadi's bamboo groves, banyan, fig, and rain tree treetops; one coming, one going—one swelling, another billowing—successively merging and scattering in the sky, one goes blusteringly on from someplace to another, where, who knows! Gentle coils of smoke from ovens of Kahar houses winding themselves around rooftops of Kaharpara, around trunks of great trees, through dense leaves of bamboo groves; it's as if someone's wrapping mounds of carded silk-cotton around them. The clouds have become so thickly layered in all directions that you can't

tell the right time. Only feeling hunger pangs in the stomach and hearing calves calling can he sense that, yes, it's time for food and drink. But
Bonwari wasn't especially happy to see Gopalibala. Why didn't Shubashi
come? If she'd come he could have gazed at her an hour, could have had
some smiling banter with her; could have satiated mind and spirit along
with his belly. Bonwari heaved a deep sigh. How could he possibly say this
to Gopalibala? Yet Gopalibala is a wonderful person. He had brought that
twenty rupees and said, don't object, don't protest—she's following that
word, does not object or protest. She's in charge of cows, calves, ducks,
chickens; she's sticking up dung cakes, fetching cow dung, husking paddy
to make rice. Shubashi just mops with cowdung, does the dishes, cooks,
does her own toilette, and primps herself up. Tying her hair up, letting it
down, tying it up again. Bonwari cannot see in the night; when he rises at
dawn it's visible—Shubashi's hands are marked with rouge, and Bonwari's
own limbs are daily covered in red smears. It's embarrassing. The lads and
lasses of the hamlet smirk; if Roton, Prohlad, and Gupi catch a sight they
don't hold back. The day Ghosh Ma'am saw, what a ribbing she gave him;
Bonwari was so embarrassed; but at least there's no Pagol. As soon as that
wet started he quit the village for someplace and still hasn't come back. If
he'd been there he would have composed a song.

Bonwari sat on the fieldpath and washed his face and mouth with
muddy field water. Gopali opened a huge pot and set down a pile of
puffed rice, a bit of molasses, two chilies, and two onions before him. She
poured some water from a large pitcher. Bonwari moistened his food and
began to eat with great gulps.

—Ho-ho-ho. Oi-Oi! Tell 'em "no" they don't listen. They've gone,
look; toward someone else's land, gone look! I'll smack ye flyin', Posta;
whack till ya move, Pamba!

Bonwari was scolding the two cows. The two yoked cows were about
to make for another, paddy-seeded plot.

Gopalibala got up and went to stand in front of the yoked pair. Bonwari left some puffed rice aside and stood. This is usual. Wife will eat this
bit. Gopalibala sat with her back to Bonwari and began to eat. Bonwari
said—Go by boss's 'ouse. Ain't been a few days, me. There's some chores,
so you do 'em.

Gopali nodded her head to say, will do.

What an odd person Gopali is becoming, doesn't even speak properly.
Now Bonwari said—I was sayin'. Buy paddy wi' the money I gave an' 'old

on to it! Everyone's sayin' the price o' paddy's goin' up like crazy in war markets. You 'old on to that paddy o' yours, I ain't gonna touch it. Whatever profits ya make are yours.

Gopali nodded again to say, will do.

Now Bonwari spoke jokingly—But if famine an' scarcity come I'm gonna take it away from ya. Ye're mistress o' the 'ouse after all, ye're me wealth o' Lakshmi, everythin's in yer gift. I beg, toil, eat.

This time Gopali spoke—Take it.

Bonwari said—I took Smallie 'cos she's an Atpoure girl, y'unnerstan'?

Now Gopali turned her head and said with a half smile—An' 'cos Kaloshoshi's niece looks an' sounds like Kaloshoshi!

Bonwari was speechless. How did Gopali know about this?

After a long time he pulled himself together and said—What's that nonsense yer sayin'?

—Not nonsense, I'm sayin' right. I've 'eard.

—Eard? Oo—oo said?

Looking at Bonwari, Gopali was a little afraid; she said—Im, 'er, an' t'others (him, her, and the others). Plenty folk sayin'. An' when Kaloshoshi'd see me she'd smirk so. An' women understand these things right, geddit!

Kaloshoshi smirked, of course she smirked, and however dumb Gopali might be, she certainly understood the meaning of that smirk. There's no point in saying anything about it. Who are the plenty folk?

The sound of weeping suddenly reached their ears. Deathly weeping. Who's weeping? Noyan's Ma? At farming time the young Kahar men toil at farmwork; young men would come to mind at this time, of course. You'd remember him constantly. But—but not such memorial weeping. That voice isn't drawn-out weeping like a song!—O no, my golden treasure, O beloved child, O where ya gone? Fallen ta yer watery earth, darlin' child, O where ya gone?—Is it sounding a bit like that sort of thing? This frenzied, distraught weeping, as if something's happening to someone this minute. O my child, O! O Ma, O! O my child, O! O treasure, O! Weeping aloud as if beating her chest.

Gopalibala listened and said—Oh my!

—Whaddappened ta who, then?

—At the Mathlas' place, dearie.

—At the Mathlas' place?

—Yeh, Mathla's wife's voice.

—Whaddappened?

—Don't know that.

—Go, will ya? Bring tidings.

What's happened at Mathla's place? Three people at Mathla's place—wife, boy, self. Mathla is in Channanpur. Wife's crying. But the child—? What disaster! No disease, no pestilence, what's happened suddenly? Something happening means Babathakur's rage. But has Father's rage fallen on Karali this time? Mathla's going to Channanpur workshops with Karali—to the evil city of the Infernal Age. But what—?

Immediately it seemed like someone started pounding his chest with a rice-husking beam. O Father! O Babathakur.

A little boy came running. Pellad's youngest. Something's bitten Mathla's boy. He'd gone to the fields to collect crabs and when he put his hand in fieldpath hole something bit him. Shortly afterward the boy had lost consciousness.

Bonwari ran.

Hamlet headman, he's a skilled person. He knows the medicine for several kinds of snakebite. Has to know. And Pagol would know too. He's a real master.

In monsoon time Kaharpara—in Hansuli Turn—there are always a few such events. Destiny. "Snake's writing, tiger's sighting." If it's not already written on the brow of your destiny you will not get a snakebite; if "tiger" is written there it's meaningless—if a tiger sees you it eats anyway, writing or no. Thus, in the tale of Hansuli Turn, there is as much care about tigers as there is carelessness about snakes. There is caution, of course, but they accept it as written fate. The Kahars have always caught crabs during rainy season; now and again this happens to a few. But not all of them die. It's therefore either "desty," which is destiny, or God rage or Brahmin rage. Everybody brings home a daily bundle of crabs. With a bit of chili and salt they make a great crab curry. It's good just on its own with rice. Bonwari suddenly paused. He has caught sight of a medication. He told the boy to go ahead and began to dig up the root.

He immediately called the boy back. Another necessity has occurred to him. —Go ta Ghosh masters' place—my boss's place. Say ta master Big Ghosh, chief's sent ye fer that medicine from Mihijam village—remedy fer snakebite; if they've got the "Newnain-Bod" medicine then please give.

The Board people have given Mihijam snakebite medication to Union Board member master Big Ghosh. Snakes are a terrible pest in this place of hard earth, especially so in Hansuli Turn. Here in cool comfort of Bansbadi shade, the climate of a primordial age lives on like deep sleep at the brink of dawn. That's where snakes, scorpions, spiders love to live. Here too flies and mosquitoes buzz and hum in the steaminess of those moldering bamboo leaves. They cause various poisons to circulate in human bodies. In times when Kaharpara's humans had the strength of the epic warrior Bhima, they would assimilate the poisons. These days "maloyria" shakes break out even before the month of Srabon. Then you can get "kuneen" pills from master Ghosh, member of the "Newnain-Bod." Bonwari makes the recommendation. But it seems that this year the "Newnain-Bod" will give no more than one or two. War breaking out. The Board's funds have taken a hit because of hard times—from where will they give snake medication, quinine pills? But Bonwari sent the boy—just in case he has "a lickle bit" left in an old bottle.

Bonwari stood and checked the back of his loincloth. The loincloth is tucked in, fine. If it had fallen open the root's medicine would not have worked. All this was expert charmery. Uh-oh! There's been a mistake in one of the charms! He should have slapped and chased off the boy who came with the tidings. If tidings bringer runs off, then sufferer's poisoning also begins to leave the house. Ah, made a huge mistake! But which snake? If it's Babathakur's wrath, then it's certainly a bite of that same familiar's fangs. That'll be it! Started on Pana's boy this time. Nope, no good. No good. No good.

Four

No good, no good. Bonwari shook his head and spoke. All Kaharpara shook their heads right then, just like Bonwari. Good no more.

Mathla's boy died. How the already black child went even blacker, foaming at the mouth; palms of the hands turning black, lips turning black, even his nails turning dark blue. Not the bite of one from the race of Babathakur's familiar; this is likely the bite of a khorish, that's a cobra or a black cobra. Black cobra most likely.

Roton's youngest boy, Teba, is very "percepty," which is to say smart and intelligent; tugging at his waistcord, the naked boy said—Eh up! Blacklike pitchy t'were, thiiis big. He spread his hands indicating a middle-sized shape; and pitchy, which is to say the color of dusky Krishna.

Roton beat his chest and wept. He had cared so deeply for his grandson. In spite of his differences with his boy, meaning Mathla, the child practically lived with him.

Teba said—E shove 'is 'and in 'ole an' got bit on. Nephew says—Ooh uncle, s'a big crab. E's bitin' loads, lettim bite; I ain't lettin the bastard go. Says this an' pulls it out real quick-like an' snake! Blood fallin' out 'is 'and. Lets go an' bastard don't let go. Then falls in water an' whisks off wi' a hiss.

It may not have been the race of Babathakur's familiar. Yet a snakebite. And a snakebite on Mathla's boy—a warning has been given. First Pana's boy, then Mathla's boy. Let who has eyes see, let who has wits understand. Let who has ears hear, Babathakur is speaking—Watch out! Watch out!

Otherwise, fear of snakes at Hansuli Turn is not a great fear. Many snakes here. In Monosha of Snakes's lore it's not possible for "serpn't, ooman," or serpent and human, to live together in one place. But it's possible at Hansuli Turn.

Snakes in garbage heaps, snakes in trash piles, snakes in cottages, snakes in fields, snakes on tree branches—where are there no snakes, when are there no snakes? Suchand says—Forefathers o' Hansuli Turn said, It's everywhere, 'oldin' up Mother Earth on Its 'ead.

Auntie Suchand says—Ferever, ferever they're there. Leaves o' Ma Monosha scattered through the world. In forest, in jungle, in cottage, in trash pile, on bankside, in field, in bush an' clump, land an' water, ever'where. Serpn't an' ooman, this avoids that, that avoids this. Sometimes when they bump into each other this one says—I'm gone; that one says—I'm gone. That's when you 'old it calm, sweetie. Clap yer 'ands an' say—Off ye go, off ye go. An' pay 'beisance. They'll normally do ye no 'arm; step on their 'ead or tail an' they'll call sun an' moon as witness an' strike. An they'll strike on the order o' Time—on the order o' Father; else they're not bad. They 'elp people out, catch mice. When we set up 'ome they bring good to an abode.

Auntie doesn't tell big lies. Otherwise, wouldn't snakes kill as many people as people kill snakes? They don't kill. There's that day Noyan's Ma went to cut grass and cut the head off a baby blacksnake. Called it—"fate's writ." Head hidden in grass; Noyan's Ma grabbed that head right up with a handful of grass. Grass all around, head in the center—so it couldn't bite. Then *swish* she cut the grass and threw it in her basket. Next the chopped-off head fell out, and it was opening its mouth trying to bite; headless body twisting and writhing over there. She survived because she's unlucky, else she'd have died and been acquitted; but why'll that happen?

In Bonwari's own household an ancient khorish snake has practically established itself as marriage kin. It often appears. Comes and goes, catches mice, eats frogs, lies in the middle of the yard with a bloated stomach. Bonwari does not strike it, nor will strike it. He is now even a little careful and has told Gopali and Shubashi to be careful too; better not go into the house without a handclap if it's not outside. Give a handclap, it'll move aside; if it's "noyed" it'll say with a moan—Watch it, I'm gettin' 'noyed. The Kahars have learned this. Their patience is boundless. Everyone in this county knows the story from Bonwari's childhood of the patience of Porom Atpoure's father. Rainy season, there'd been a great flood of the Kopai, "watterfull," or full of water, all around; Porom's father lying on the cottage terrace. In the middle of night he was suddenly awoken by a strange touch of cold. But he did not move. First tried to think—whose cold touch is it? Those who have died and become "hauntblowers," ghosts that is, call those they summon by placing a cold hand on them; or is it some "creepercrawl"? The snake's name is not used at night, so it's called creeper. All that time a fat, icy-cold rope is constantly moving over his waist and stomach up to his shoulders. Porom's father lay there stiff as a board. Slowly it traversed him and moved away. Porom's father heaved a huge sigh and it immediately froze in alarm—then it realized he did not want to harm it and moved off again with a rustling sound. Bonwari himself had stepped right on the head of a "middly," or middle-sized, khorish snake in the doorway of his home. Right away the snake twisted itself around the foot. What a "scrushing," that's to say crushing, twist! Yet Bonwari did not let up his foot's pressure on that head. If he'd let up it would have bitten. He'd finally saved his life by chopping the snake to pieces with a sickle. No fear of snakes; fear of Babathakur's wrath and of the decrees of Time. When these two are upon your head and a snake comes out, then no one can stop it.

It seems that the snakes have taken on Father's wrath. Has Father given a general order? It seems that everyone senses a sign of misfortune.

***

A terror appeared in Kaharpara. Kahars do not fear snakes. But this seems to be Father's rage. Father's rage knows no bounds of time. You're saying the year's turning? But your year and Father's year are not the same.

Prohlad, Roton, Gupi said—Bonwari, ya gotta find a way. Your boss is chief o' the Newnain-Bod; go to 'im an' beg fer gettin' a keracheen lamp. At nighttime—keep it extinguished near yer 'ead, keep matches. Summat bad 'appens an' ye just light up.

Kerosene cannot be obtained because of the war. Even the masters must use coupons. As you pay tax to the "Newnain-Bod"—so you get "kerachini." There are neither "Newnain-Bod" works nor services at Kaharpara, no road or embankment building; the Kahars don't even pay cash taxes, but give one day of free labor as tax by repairing roads and embankments in other villages. No coupons for them either. They can get fuel oil in a hush-hush way, but its price is exorbitant. Stolen and sold. Karali says—Its name is "belack markati." Who knows what name. It's of no use to them to know the name, they have not the wherewithal to buy fuel oil at that price. Karali's giving oil to a couple of folks. He has written his name in the ledger of War, sold his dharma, left his clan function, and he's getting oil. Gets oil, gets sugar, gets flour, gets ghee, gets clothes—gets them cheap—in market's the price of rice has risen to sixteen rupees—Karali gets it for five. He gets; let him get. Don't anyone else stretch your hand out to get, don't harbor any hopes. Watch out! Watch out! Yet Bonwari will do his duty. He will go to Big Ghosh. Kaharpara must be saved, saved from the wrath of Babathakur's familiar—silently call to it mid-evening, keep a "lampy" by yer 'ead. What's more, the rains are starting—"maloyria" will break out, need "kuneen," need sago, need sugar. Can't get sago and sugar in the market. Even if you found it, the price would be aflame. That war market! In this market the "Newnain-Bod" chief's order will be effective.

In the afternoon he left his field work and went to master Ghosh. You can't go to sort all these things out after dusk or after drinking liquor at night.

Big Lord listened and smiled a little. He spoke—Kerosene! If I could get it I would.

Bonwari said sadly—By yer leave, so whatta we ta do? Fear o' snakes an' no more. Coulda been normal fear o' snakes, by yer leave; this is fear o' God rage!

—God rage? Big Lord asked with a little smile. There is pleasure in hearing about the curious superstitions of the Kahar clan.

—By yer leave, Great Sire, think it's 'cos Babathakur's gonna punish. Karali killed Father's familiar; a marked goat was sacrificed to 'im 'cos of Pana; Karali went up Father's silk-cotton tree an' mussed up Father's—

Feigning great empathy and deep understanding, Big Lord nodded again and again—Hmm, that's right, you're not talking rubbish, dear Bonwari—

Tears came to Bonwari's eyes at his vast compassion. He wiped his eyes and said—Great Sire, s'been terrible damage when Father's wood-apple tree fell. Got it up wi' a lotta difficulty, secured the roots, put the trunk right too, but Father sent a sign sayin' I'm gettin' displeased. I'm gone away from yer shrine.

The curious Big Lord doesn't like to talk too long with Bonwari, and what's more Bonwari has started to wipe his eyes; if after that he weeps aloud, it'll be absolutely unbearable! Cautious of the time, he became grave and said—Yes. You lot must be a bit careful.

Then as if a suppressed flash of humor had pushed its way out, he said—Now this time you'd better not steal off with any of the paddy and stuff from the fields. Understood?

—By yer leave, we won't. I'll make all swear at Babathakur's shrine this time.

—Good. Very good. Now go home.

—By yer leave, keracheen?

—Well there's no keracheen, Bonwari. Big Lord spoke with deep sympathy—Gentry boys can't even find where to get fuel oil. Got it now?

Big Sire of Channanpur did his head in and couldn't even get two cans; finally, with huge effort, he got one can. You understand, tell me where I'm going to get?

Bonwari heaved a deep sigh and rose. So what else will happen? War's wave has probably never crashed down on Hansuli Turn like this.

Big Lord said—And what use burning lights anyway, Bonwari? You're saying it's Babathakur's wrath. So, yes, from what I'm hearing that's certainly it. In which case, light or dark, can that wrath be checked? Big Lord smiled a rather otherworldly smile, put his hand to his forehead, where destiny is written, and said—It's all this Bonwari, it's all this. A kalonagini snake bit Lakhai in the blacksmith's wedding chamber. God wrath, nothing can hold it back.

Big Lord's speaking right. Bonwari departed with a heavy heart. He stopped on the way and began to ponder. But light—how to go on without a bit of light? God wrath for sure. But giving a little water before death, seeing them one last time—how can these little things happen without light?

He went and stood at Babathakur's shrine.—O Babathakur! For a long time he stood, absorbed.

Suddenly that absorption of his was bathed in a reddish glow. Eyes struck by a red gleam. Field, bankside, sky, all turning red—far off, Kopai turn's waters can be seen, and it's as if a reddish luster is dancing on the current's wave crests.

It is almost evening, what's called—"glistery time." The sky had filled with red light breaking through clouds. Disc, which is to say the setting sun, has not yet sunk; as it sets it takes on a red-hued form and rotates quiveringly. Clouds in the sky have taken on a red color. Bonwari became a little concerned when he looked skyward. Tomorrow there'll be more rainfall. In the morning there had been a "curver," that's a rainbow, in the west; a bloody-eve at evening. Be heavy rain. Besides, if it rains crops will be damaged.

He was pondering as he lifted his head toward the western sky. Someone called him from behind—Uncle Beano!

Who's calling? Who's calling "uncle"? None of the village daughters' sons around. He frowned and looked around. Yep, that's Karali for sure! Bastard calls Bonwari Uncle these days, now he's in a relationship with Pakhi, daughter of Bashanta, of a village daughter. As soon as he heard the call he was doubtful. He did not reply, just stared at Karali expectantly with a severe face.

Karali yelled out—Been ta the 'amlet, me, came ta tell everyone. There'll be real 'eavy rain by day's end. Strong rain! News comin' by wire ta Channanpur.

Bonwari smiled. News of rainfall coming by wire! From Channanpur the boy Karali is telling of rainfall today! Speak blessed one, speak. News coming through the wires! Bonwari has no need of news through wires, Father's the diamond in the rough of the Kahar clan. Babathakur has spread news across the sky for Bonwari. Storm, rain—since the forefathers' times, Kahars have received news of this from sky, from ants, from rainbows, from windspeed; you've disappeared from the Kahar caste, become foreign infidel; you stick yer ear to telegraph poles in Channanpur an' hear all this news.

Karali asked him—Listenin'?

Filled with contempt, Bonwari said—I know that, I know it.

Karali pursed his lips, frowned, then turned away. But he turned back again and said—Mathla's boy died o' snakebite. If only someone'd taken 'im ta 'ospital!

What can Bonwari say to this upstart! Mathla's boy died! Well, he died because of *your* evil, *your* devilry.

Karali said—If summat like that 'appens again, take 'em to military 'ospital right away. Got snake poison injection.

Bonwari now spoke with annoyance—Hey, get off to wherever you were goin' to, all right? Go yer own way, right off wi' ya.

—I'm goin', I'm goin'! Goin' ta find out what 'appened to the kerosene. What did yer Big Lord say? Steals too much, that one.

Bonwari roared—Karali!

Karali didn't care. He hurried away. As he left he said—Ya didn't get any, that I do know.

∗∗∗

Rain fell. The news Bonwari got was true; the wire's news was also true. They were the same. It fell from morning onward—pitter-pattering. Cloud seemed to have descended over the top of Babathakur's silk-cotton tree. Cloud upon cloud, rushing past. Thin blackish coiling twisting clouds. The three worlds went dark.

Bonwari held the plow grip firm and halted the two steers. Conditions aren't good. These are like clouds of doom. Prohlad was riding a plow a way off; he called to him.

Prohlad paused, surprised. He spoke—Huh.

—Are ya gonna stop? Pellad?

Prohlad stared at the sky. Looking like a sign to stop. Elephant coming down. An elephant is coming down from the sky. King Indra of the Gods' elephant descends every couple of decades. Last evening its sign seemed to be there. Bonwari should have been able to understand. At eveningtime inside that sky-filling cloud spread with ruddy glow, a round little cloud, red like rouge, was pushing forth again and again. It's not a cloud, though. It is the round, rouge-smeared head of God's Elephant. So King Indra of Gods was enraged now. He'll rage indeed. There was rage of Babathakur; in 'forty-nine Paban of Winds went crazy; does King Indra not have means to rage, to get wild? Elephant'll come down! Come down? It's already down! There—there, you can see it in the southwest corner, far side of the Saheb Tracts, beyond the Barampal clay grounds, coming down from the sky—gigantic trunk of God's Elephant. From the clouds like ten palm trees—a thick, circular pillar coming down whooshing, sucking—toward earth. No pillar—an elephant! Elephant's trunk! A cry went up in the fields—Flee—flee—flee.

—Release the cows, release the cows from the plow. Gonna be a cow slaughter.

The moment they were freed, panting, terrified cows ran mooing, bellowing, with raised tails.

Cows calling calves. Calves calling cows. Goats bleating. Sheep fleeing silently. Quacking ducks out of water, sheltering in cottages. Shocked, frightened birds all screeching together. Monkeys clinging tight to branches and quaking in fear.

As Bonwari gazed toward the west his chest pounded within. Rainwater blurring all around. In its midst, huge and cylindrical like a cataclysmic pillar—the trunk of God's Elephant twisting and drawing near with a terrible pounding whooshing sucking sound. —Flee, flee. Fall there and you're gone. You'll tumble writhing to the ground, die breathless and be ground into the earth like mud, half buried. All the field folk have fled toward the northside. Bonwari has also run to wait in the shelter of Jangol's mango groves.

God's Elephant is King Indra's familiar. King Indra brings rain. Great King travels the seven oceans of cloud mounted on the elephant; his familiar sucks up water from the seven oceans of cloud and scatters it everywhere, splashing, spattering, dripping. Sometimes King Indra picks up his bolt—its name is "thundybolt," that's to say thunderbolt; Indra lashes that cloud ocean with his bolt. Fiery flashes leap from it. Flashes boom, roar, rumble. Now and again those flashes fall on some evildoer. Evildo-ers are not just human: trees, birds and beasts, bugs—evildoers among them all. Now and again King Indra's brother, Paban of the Winds, goes forth with him—that was typical. But sometimes King Indra's elephant gets crazy, breaks its chain free from the stable house, and plunges into the seven oceans of cloud. Then clouds get black and roiling. You'd think day had turned to night. Then that raging elephant lowers its long trunk even to earth and swings it to and fro. Wherever it goes it obliterates field and bankside in a deluge of rain. Paddy ripped up and washed away, fieldpath smashed, dancing the dance of annihilation. Maito Ghosh calls it—waterpillar. O Babathakur, O Kalarudra, don't take offense at Maito Ghosh.

Prohlad suddenly tugged on his arm. As he looked at Prohlad, Prohlad said—What's the matter wi' you? It's comin'!

Annihilation's waterpillar coming down. Coming with a howling roar. Everyone lying flat on the earth paying homage. Bonwari remembered, he lay down flat and paid obeisance—Bow down, bow down, bow down. O familiar of God! You coming to get repayment for great Babathakur's familiar? Killed by fire—you came to get repayment by pouring water? Bonwari slowly lifted just his head.

The elephant was heading from west to east. Making sky and earth one, swinging its trunk, God's raging elephant scourged earth and land with water and brushed past the heart of Jangol—it spared Babathakur's little shrine as it moved straight eastward toward river's edge. Ah, it de-stroyed a section of riverbank with an ear-splitting noise! Gone to the other side turning—turning. It came down at the edge of Buffalo Pit and Dompara. Ramkali Dom's cottage at that far end of Dompara. Who can say what the raging elephant's angry about. Who knows what Ramkali Dom's crime was? Fury fell upon Ramkali Dom's cottage. Its "nihillatin" trunk pushed down upon that cottage. Water poured down with a crash, the cottage broke apart with a smash; beside the cottage was a palm tree; the elephant tore it up by the roots and tossed it away. Then off it went. What happened? Stopped? Yes, the elephant had to stop, rolling up its trunk. Perhaps "King Indo" went out in search of the raging elephant and caught up with it; tapped it on the head with the driving stick. Eh up—thunder crashed with a boom. The elephant rolled up its trunk and went off to its own place.

So be it. Bonwari has meanwhile received reassurance. No harm came to Bansbadi. Babathakur is here. Didn't leave. If he said "I'm going," who'd let him go? Kaharpara will hold to him as fast as they held to the wood-apple tree and raised it up. Bonwari finished his weeping.

—O Father, Kaharpara's comfort, Lord of Punishments. If the raging elephant descends again, you'll save us. You'll point and say—Ye don't go hither, ye go thither. Instruct, point your finger—at those workshops of Channanpur. And to those airplanes flying in the sky—there's no day, no night, no rains, no wind and storm. Coming and going overhead, droning, whining. Give the order for it to grab with its trunk and smash them to the ground.

O, ho-ho-ho-ho! From where, from where, moving hidden inside the clouds—no way to know; only a whining can be heard.

O shame, shame, shame! Now who's started a "potheration," that's to say a quarrel, in Kaharpara? Shrill voices drowning out the whine of aircraft reached Bonwari's ears. He looked at the clouds but could see no more airplanes. He had to rush to the hamlet.

He never made it to the hamlet. Halfway there he met Big Ghosh's footman with a summons for him.—At once. Big Lord's shakin' wi' fury.

Big Lord really is shaking with fury. Big Lord is usually furious. He'll shake for nothing. Get in a rage for some trifling reason.

Big Lord screamed. —A complaint against me!

—Complaint! Against you? Me?

—Yes. You don't know anything? Didn't make a complaint through Karali?

—By yer leave? I can put me 'ands to yer feet an' say I don't know nothing. If I lie let a thunderbolt strike me 'ead. Let me limbs fall off.

Karali is lodging a complaint at the Union Board office in Channanpur, putting in a petition—why haven't the Kahars been given their kerosene? If they have, then who takes it? Let it be looked into. And let the document authorizing their receipt of fuel oil rations be given from this very office.

Bonwari put his hand to his head. He remained silent a while and then rose. He said—I'll sort the remedy fer this. I say this wi' me 'ands on yer feet.

He returned to the hamlet. Fight still going on—a terrible fight.

Today's fight has sprung up between Suchand and Noyan's Ma. Disaster!

Suchand is dancing a wild, hopping dance and screaming in a loud voice—Ya twisted the lad's 'ead, now ya won't even see. Ye'll put out yer 'and fer rice an' find a pile of ashes. Sayin' there's no ghost? Ye'll see, oh ye'll see. It'll break that whore's neck, it'll break 'er old man's neck, then it'll squish your neck. You'll nod, shake yer 'air, an' say—I'm Kaloshoshi. Suchand trembled from head to toe and shook her arms a few times as she finished speaking.

Meanwhile Noyan's Ma is speaking in a piercing voice—speaking at the same time as Suchand—O Babathakur, annihilate, Father, 'im that killed yer familiar, 'im that wrecked others' 'omes, that ignored village rules an' built a tall 'ouse, annihilate 'im—annihilate 'im. Just as ye smashed down that airplane today, smash 'im down likewise.

Bonwari was astounded. An airplane's been smashed down?

Nasubala brought tidings. An airplane crashed headlong into the Moyarakshi riverbanks at Saithiya today. It was descending, got caught in the elephant's trunk, which smashed it down. Karali went to Saithiya with those "Men." He passed the news to Bashan and went lamenting back to Channanpur.

Victory Babathakur! Victory King God's Elephant! Dharma's victory! Bonwari was filled with a marvelous tranquility. He felt strength in his breast.

He came proudly forward. But he had to stop in surprise. A fight's breaking out elsewhere. Seems to be Gopalibala's voice. And the other is Shubashi's. And Pana is sat in his cottage hurling insults too. What's happened?

In the tale of Hansuli Turn reasons for fights are as convoluted as they are various. Today two fights are coming to fruition together. On the one hand Nasu brought tidings that an airplane had crashed. Noyan's Ma heard that and is dancing with delight. On the other hand, this afternoon, that's when Bonwari was at boss's house, another drama was unfolding at Romon Atpoure's cottage; Romon's wife—Shubashi's aunt, Kaloshoshi's younger sister—suddenly fell down unconscious. She regained consciousness, of course, but now she's lying down indoors. People had no problem comprehending the matter. With her hair loose, she had sat to eat yesterday's rice with chili, salt, and onion today full on noon, at that exact time—. Today is Saturday new moon. At the moment she settled down to eat that attractive food, some restless dweller of the ghostworld used the chance of her unclean hands and the error of her loosened hair to take her. And, by grace of Babathakur and by the teachings of the tale of Hansuli Turn, there's no mystery for the Kahars about who that dweller of the ghost world was: none other than Kaloshoshi's spirit. She who died an unnatural death, whose desiring play of 'eat was not fulfilled; she who lost all sense of proportion in the game of 'eat, who died with the evil of destroying with her touch the caste of "Brahmbin"-equal Chotri, Master Bhup Singh, she'll obviously get to that ghost state!

Pana's joining in—he still can't get over his son's death. He's joining in—Incense and lamps of Father's shrine were defiled. It won't be! I'm being punished, many more people must be.

Meanwhile, niece Shubashi is objecting to all these points about dead Kaloshoshi. She had gone to sit and weep in the cottage. As she wept she called to her aunt's ghost and said—If ye've become that then all right, but tek—tek; tek the foe.

Bonwari's elder wife objected to this crying. She said—Don't cry like that at your age.

At this objection, Shubashi weepingly addressed her dead aunt—O 'ow ya loved me, O, 'elp me out. Tek—tek, tek my foe, tek your foe. Tek out me thorn.

"Thorn" means co-wife thorn. Co-wife also means foe. What greater foe than a co-wife? Thus began the fight between Gopalibala and Shubashi. Everyone in the hamlet went to watch. Because Pakhi was friendly with Shubashi and because of Bonwari's fondness for Kaloshoshi, Noyan's Ma took Gopali's side. And for that very reason, Suchand took Shubashi's side. Suchand was no longer angry with Karali and Pakhi. Karali's feeding her with prime liquor, giving clothing, clasping her feet, dancing in her embrace. Noyan's Ma said to Shubashi—If ye become ghost when ye die, an' if ghosts can 'ear us talk, I would've gotten a company o' ghosts: 'usband, son, pa- an' ma-in-law. An' they woulda broke ooever's neck I told 'em to. Go die!

Suchand immediately objected to this—Don't become a ghost if ye die? Ye'll unnerstan' when it comes down on your neck.

So it started up. Shubashi was objecting to the idea that her Aunt Kaloshoshi had become a spirit or specter. But in taking her side, Suchand's sharp objections are beginning to prove this—Kaloshoshi's certainly become a spirit and will exterminate Shubashi's foes.

Bonwari's own house was now silent and still. Gopalibala, Shubashi—each of them lying silently on the terrace of their room. Haven't even eaten. Bonwari's entire wrath had fallen upon his two wives; his anger with Shubashi was greater. Today he found out that Shubashi is friendly with Pakhi; what's more, she's calling Kaloshoshi's spirit. He took a stick, grabbed a handful of her hair, and began to thrash her. He thrashed her and then thrashed Gopalibala. Gave her fewer strokes. Then, stick in hand, he went to stand between Suchand and Noyan's Ma. Suchand immediately began to back off. She took a few steps back, then hurried off toward the fields. She'll sit there somewhere and curse, and finally she'll weep in remembrance of her dead father because nephew Bonwari had threatened her with a stick. But Noyan's Ma did not flee. She stood there steadily, glaring catlike.

No sign of Pana. He's locked up his cottage. His wife said—Got fever, lyin' down.

—Bro! Right then someone called from behind.

—Oo?

—Oo?

—Me, Bashan.

Yes, Bashan. Bashan's done no wrong; and yet because of Karali and Pakhi, Bonwari can't feel pleasure in seeing her. Bonwari spoke with grave face—What?

Putting a square of paper into his hand, Bashan said—Yer card.

—Card?

—Yeh. Keracheen, sugar—allowance of all that. Givin' 'em out at the Newnain-Bod, got it through Nasu. Seccetary gave ta Karali. Hedo Mondol from Jangol, 'is son came, 'e saw everyone, gave to everyone, this is yours.

Bonwari tore up the card and threw it away. Then he went into the hamlet. Which Kahar's telling Karali to go and say such things at the Newnain-Bod?

Nobody says anything.

Everyone remained silent.

—Throw the cards away.

Prohlad said—Beano-bro!

—No.

—Not no. He spoke a little harshly—That, bro, will be injustice. Think, will ya? Newnain-Bod's givin' cards. We give free labor. Why should we throw away our cards?

—Huh. But what if someone inquires, did Master Ghosh nab yer keracheen or no?

—Why'd we say this? Why say that?

—Won't even say it ta Karali?

—Nah, no one'll talk. Why'd anyone eat through the nose when they got a mouth? If they'd said, we'd a told ya.

—Enough. Enough. Prohlad began to gather up the pieces of Bonwari's torn card.

Back home, Bonwari lay on his bed and silently appealed to Babathakur.

Sky split and rain came pounding down. And will the elephant descend once more?

Now who's calling? Who's knocking at the door? Shubashi went to open the door, but Bonwari admonished her—Oi!

Who knows who! Who even knows if it's human or not! Who'll say it's not Kaloshoshi! Today Kaloshoshi's answering once more.

—Oo—oo're you?

—Kangal, I'm Kangal. Uncle Omon's wife died, came ta gi' tidings.

Yet it's Kaloshoshi who killed! Bonwari went out mouthing Father's name.

Five

Victory Babathakur! Shraban month has passed. Good farming. Passing very well; danger coming and passing. What can be better than this? Bhadra month arrived. In Bhadra sun the farmer becomes an ascetic. He goes out in terrible sun, through flourishing paddy fields, all limbs submerged, creeping from this end of the field to that end, cutting out weeds; body gets scraped all over, swells up rubbing against the scratchy leaves of paddy shoots; amidst paddy shoots, that sun's steaminess makes a body ooze sloughs of sweat. Then you think, quit home and hearth, work and duty, become a renouncer and go off someplace!

In the tale of Hansuli Turn, just as everywhere else in the world, Asharh and Shraban pass; Bhadra arrives. Kahars cannot know how and where Asharh and Shraban go by. Fields of Hansuli Turn chest-deep in mud and water, rain pours down overhead, clouds rumble with a boom. You figure that Shraban has finished when the work of transplanting in the fields is over. If transplanting is over then Babathakur is worshiped and preparation is made for the Indo ceremony at Babathakur's shrine. Indo is King Indra, he who brought rains, who has sent part of his heavenly kingdom's bounty to the "glube," which is to say the globe. Landlords make arrangements for Indo worship, and whatever little tasks need doing are done by the Kahars; the Mondol masters, landowners of Jangol, play headman. Landlords give goats, candies, sweets, chews, two annas priest's fee; Mondol masters get a reward of the goat "shanks," that's legs, and get God's leftover candies and sweets; Kahars sit until the end, and at the end of Indoraja's offering they take earth from the shrine and return to the hamlet. They build a woman-shaped mound with that earth at the shrine of the hamlet's assembly place, and on the eighth day of victory there's an offering for Goddess Bhanjo Sundari of Fertility. At Bhanjo Sundari's offering Kaharpara has "heatplay" for three days, an unaccountable orgy. Bhanjo Sundari's mound is built and decorated with vines, leaves, flowers; men and women drown themselves in liquor and sing and dance together. No sleeping at night—dancing, singing, staying up is the rule. From forefathers' times God's command has been that heat's songs, heat's games can be played with whoever one wants; whatever you see you don't tell, if you hear something you don't go look. You'll wipe everything of that day from your mind.

Bastard Karali is showing off this time, come back from Channanpur and has set up separately for Bhanjo with Kaharpara's old Bhanjo in his yard. He shouted—Smashed me 'ome an' I complained at police station, smash me Bhanjo an' I'll complain at military court. Two red-faced sahebs—those *Men* of his—have come with Karali. Took photos. They also shook their legs about and danced! They left. Drank some distilled liquor too, probably. Bonwari was filled with disgust at the sahebs. Karali's really looking like a saheb!

Oh bastard, Bonwari isn't afraid seeing all that. Saheb! *Pthu*!

Bonwari too gave a command—Put on a real show this Bhanjo. Tons o' paddy in the fields this time. No more worry about there being a heavy rain in Ashwin. Price of paddy rising in war markets, especially during the month of Shraban. Since the Swadeshi gents from all parts pulled up the "ail lines" at Channanpur, markets are leaping up even more. Let them rise, Kahars have no fear of that. Used to eating rice and salt. And why just eat that? Fish in the fields now, fish and rice, no lack of greens. If field waters dry up there are snails, shellfish, turtles, cockles in pond and lake, in Ma Kopai's belly. They're used to wearing torn clothing too, so there's no worry about hard times of war at Hansuli Turn. Instead, paddy will be plentiful this time—the Kahars will receive a plentiful share; if prices rises they'll profit. So go on and vie with Karali, beating your chest. The competition used to be with Atpoure Para, now it will be with Karali. Perhaps Babathakur is kindly. He's smiling a lot; if he's angry it is anger of raised eyebrows. Bhadra's clouds—like the play of sunshine. Now clouds will disperse. Bonwari had been the devotee at Kalaruddu's Gajon this time too; had got up on the iron spike-studded Charak bed, had put the flame-flower to Father's head; will all that go for nothing?

Father took the offering with smiling face. Its result is that times are now good in Kaharpara.

The thing is, Bonwari's getting very optimistic about all this. The elephant descended and did not harm Bansbadi; it smashed an airplane down. For these two reasons his fears from that quarter have been dispelled. Yet there is one fear—that fear of Kaloshoshi. Bonwari had forgotten that fear, but whoever killed Romon's wife has reawakened it. So on his arms are amulets of Ma Kali, Father Kalaruddu, Kartathatur. With the passing of fear, this promise of fields full of paddy had given him much courage. His mind glimpsing this, that things may not go badly for him now; this is his greatest moment, his fortune's returning. The fallow fields of Saheb Tracts land are now full of green paddy as far as the eye can see. What's called—"all round" paddy, that's it. The paddy is very good on the Ghoshes' share of land too. Meanwhile, paddy leaves need to be cut at once. The paddy sheaves are bunched like an ox's leg. Bonwari will now have to enlarge his threshing floor. Enlarge the threshing floor, build a strong granary. He also wants a "sonny," a scion; if he had that his desires would be fulfilled. He must live a long time. Bring the boy up, put him in headman's seat, then Bonwari could breathe his last in peace. In this regard he's afraid of Karali. Due to this wartime market he's making "earnins" hand over fist, and his body's powerful, an untamed bravery in his breast. If Bonwari dies while the boy is yet small, Karali will take the headman's seat at the assembly by force. Maybe he'd be able to kill the boy by hook or by crook. Lure him with greed of work in those workshops and shove him into the mouth of a machine. Bonwari will have to live on a long time. Must ensure Kaharpara's welfare, must take their trials and tribulations on his shoulders, must ensure great joy at feast and festival. Great joy.

Masters, big folk, Sadgops of Jangol call Bauris, Haris, Doms—little-folk castes! The kindhearted say—Wretched poor ones, living by unhappy toil. Both things are true. The poor unhappy ones love pleasure—if they find pleasure they run after it. Now the little mind reveals itself too, forever going where the pleasure is; if, today, newer pleasures can be had elsewhere than here—they'll always up from here and rush to there! Today Karali's wanting to do that. In the pride of his earnings he has set up a Bhanjo in his own "compown," or compound. He'll get rented lighting; he'll get a violin player, he'll get a "harmony"; he'll get all the casteless women of Channanpur, they'll dance with Nasubala. Sidhu will come, Pakhi will of course come. Many other people will come.

Let them come. Bonwari is also renting lighting. He's hiring really good drums, shanai, cymbals. He's giving the decree—all the gals, that's to say girls, Kahar maids and wives, must dance. He's distributing the green, red, yellow coloring he bought; dye your clothes in colors. Shubashi will dance too. He has bought her a colorful sari. Gopalibala will dance too. He has also bought clothing for her. He's ordering the lads— Pull up lotus and water lily flowers from all the ponds. Adorn Goddess Bhanjo's mound. He's leaving all this to Pagol Kahar. He who disappeared at farmwork time—he suddenly arrived the other day, the day just before Bhanjo. Full on noon, with nine or ten water lilies tied with their stalks around his head, a young kash-grass flower wedged in their midst; singing a song of the old and young, he came back to Hansuli Turn—

On which bank have you landed your boat, O my Bhanjo love, hey!
I cannot see you.
So I came to seek you on Hansuli's Turn—
Hiding in some bamboo grove, in some nook!
Give me a clue, O love, a sound
I roll my body at your red feet
O my Bhanjo love, hey!

Pagol's companions are elated.

Kudungtang-kudungtang-tak-tak-tak-tak, Bhanjo festival's drum sounded. No work in fields today, no going to boss's house today, today no Kahar is either subject to king or debtor to moneylender; no one will listen to the time signal of the train rolling over the Kopai bridge; nor will anyone look to see at what meridian Sun Lord's light traverses the yard. In former times, suckling calves were left unrestrained on this day; they'd drink milk to their fill. These days cows are milked in the wee small hours and then released. Release them to the banks of Hansuli Turn—to the sandbanks. Let them stay on the sandbank as long as they want. They'll eat a few measures of paddy—let them eat. Jars and jars of liquor are "juicing up" in Bhadra heat—as soon as lids are lifted an aroma wafts out on the breeze. Above Kaharpara a flock of crows is clamoring at that aroma; look earthward—lines of ants taking scraps of fermented rice, dogs circling around restlessly. Pagol turns his own mind into the beat of the drum; he's saying—Chores, duties, stop stop stop stop! Just dance, girls, just dance darlings! Go, from Kopai bankside bring back full pitchers, take clay platters for "five sprouties." "Five sprouties," that's to say five sprouting shoots that each woman will offer to Goddess Bhanjo.

Bonwari's sitting to filter liquor himself. He's throwing dregs, which is the filtered residue of fermented rice, to the dogs; he's putting some into coconut shells and giving it to the boys—Feed it ta cattle, steer, cow, calf—gi' to all. Wait, today everyone'll eat an' drink. Sheep, duck, chicken—gi' to them too.

Now all of you come, sit down. Sup away, sup away. Girls, take dears, take yer share away. Sup away. Set the musicians off, bro. Play, play real sweetly! Shanai man, let's see yer skill—bastard Karali's brought violin and harmonium, gotta put paid to that. Sup away.

Bhanjo the beautiful, platter of clay
Scarlet rouge on Bhanjo's brow.
I'll stain the earth with scarlet footpaint,
O soil, I'll tell my mind to you
Clasp my five shoots, O Earth.

Just this little was the song—mantralike. Every group must sing this little thing. Meanwhile Nasubala's group is coming out. Karali himself is playing the bamboo flute. They have really nice clothes. All "noo" clothes. Wages of Channanpur's evil, why not? And yet the most colorful glow comes from the clothes of Kaharpara's women. Old clothes newly dyed radiating intensity.

At one moment a clash broke out between two groups on the Kopai bankside. A clash of songs. It's always happened between Kaharpara and Atpoure Para. This time it's happening between Kaharpara and Karali's group. One side Pagol, the other side Nasubala. On this day of Goddess Bhanjo, Nasu does not tremble before Pagol's words, has no fear. Meets madness with madness. Face to face they compose insult songs—any insult. Yet there is no cursing in them. Heat's insults—juicy scandal's insults.

Then they began to return from the bankside to their own quarters to sing and dance. A first custom—an eternal custom—the elder women will begin the dancing. Suchand always starts this dance. This time she has gone with Karali's group. Who will dance here?

Pagol ran and got hold of Gopalibala. Gopalibala is drunk, yet she's a shy person; she's saying—Nah, nah. Moreover, recalling Pagol's wish to take her in a companion rite, she's getting even more embarrassed. Face going red with embarrassment. Everybody laughed heartily. —Nice one sis—nice one sis!

But Bonwari's mind is distracted. Remembering Kaloshoshi. He is smiling nonetheless; how could he not smile? Suddenly he noticed Noyan's Ma standing off to one side. She was caught in a daydream. Ah, having lost everything, she's standing there miserable! He went over and took her hand. Said—Come on, you an' me'll dance first.

Bhanjo Festival is a day of happiness. Heads feeling strange on liquor's intoxication; clouds dispersing in the sky; a flock of milk-white egrets flying under blue sky; lotuses and water lilies flowering in the indigo levee and the "gorakanda" field; drops of water trembling and sparkling in the sunlight on lily pads, like jeweled pearls; chaste tree flowers blossoming and patteringly falling. Lotuses coming out, they give light to Kaharpara; Kopai's floods have receded and muddy water's running clear; but where is Noyan's Ma's happiness? Autumn paddy is ripening, autumn paddy fields heavy as a ten-months-pregnant woman; in every pond snakehead fish are swimming around with shoals of baby fish; on every branch birds releasing their young ones—go, fly off and find things to eat; in Jangol and Channanpur clay has been applied to the framework of Mother Durga statues. Yesterday was her Sixth Night of Victory. Can Noyan's Ma forget Noyan today? Bonwari's mind also went back to that old business, the day that wheezing Noyan received a blow from Karali's hand. And to the day that someone had pulled Bonwari by the arm toward the dark kingdom of bamboo groves. But no more—no more. She got free of Bonwari's hand and fled in the direction of her own cottage. Then she called to Noyan first. —Come back, everyone's dancin', you're the only one not. Come back. Then she began to curse all Kaharpara.

Bonwari was shocked. Now what happened!

Pagol pulled him by the arm and said—S'nothin'. Don' listen ta that. Dance. He dragged Shubashi over. Shubashi is staggering drunk, wobbling like a drop of water on a lily pad. Eyes closing like two half moons, body feverishly hot.

Who's playing the bamboo flute, eh? Who?

Bonwari looked. Karali had at some point turned up at their Bhanjo mound, watching Shubashi's dance and smiling, playing along with the song on his flute. Such a hair parting, what fine clothes, perfume coming off his body!

Bonwari puffed his chest and came forward. But Pagol held him back.—Be careful! Remember whatta big man y'are. Remember what the forefathers said. Today's a day of 'eat—what's before yer eyes ya don't see, what goes in yer ears ya don't 'ear, what yer 'eart wants ya don't deny. Go, go, play the flute Karali, play the flute.

Karali kept staring at Shubashi. Pagol gave him a poke.—Why don'tcha play, eh? Whatcha lookin' at? Everybody broke into laughter. Pana's laughing most of all. The sound of his ringing laughter is like the striking of a gong. Shubashi also broke into shrieking laughter. Right then her glass bangles jingled.

Bonwari felt agitated all over. His body's getting overheated. But there's nothing he can do, forefathers' taboo. Yet can he really go to Karali's Bhanjo mound? Pakhi's dancing there too! Shame shame shame! O Babathakur! O Dharma-preserving Master, save us.

The Kahars don't smile along with those with whom they have no amity, but Karali's become different at Channanpur workshops. Even though gentry of Channanpur have no amity, they smile away. The Mister Mukhujees and Mister Chatujees are always coming at each other with lawsuits and proceedings, riots and affrays, but you'd never guess that if you saw them from outside. Those gents going to this gent's house in the morning; in the afternoon these gents coming to that gent's house, all smiles and cheer, jokes and jests, ribbing tales, singing and music. Bonwari is speechless to see this. Karali has seen it too, and is learning it. He said to Bonwari—Come along ta me Bhanjo mound, uncle. Prime booze—

Halfway there Bonwari rudely said—Nah.

Karali went on his way laughing. Seeing this laughter, Bonwari began to burn all over. Bastard went off with a joke, whistling away, wafting a fragrance over the whole Bhanjo shrine. Smearing sickly perfume on himself like the gentry!

Pana piped up with a rhyme. —"Don't weed in Bhadra an' the earth weeps at last; nourish the casteless an' he'll ruin yer caste!"

Bonwari stared at Pana with a hard look, but today Pana was not afraid. Today the gathering is not a fear-inducing gathering, it's Bhanjo Sundari's gathering, 'eat's gathering, pleasure's gathering; today there is no great-and-small; anyway, there's a vast amount of booze in his belly. Feet staggering, head splitting. Courage growing. Pana noticed Bonwari's harsh look and said—Say, whass gonna 'appen if ya stare a' me? Caste ain't gonna last no more, casteless comin' inside. If floodwater goes in yer 'ome—'ome's water mixes wi' it an' flows out. Look man, all the young lads gettin' together at Karali's party.

Bonwari was stunned. He sat there stunned for a while, then got up; got up, went to sit by the earthen liquor barrel, took a clay cup, and began spooning dashes of liquor down his throat. The earth seemed instantly to reel—began to dance before his eyes. In his mind he began to appeal to Babathakur. Shubashi is dancing, Gopali is dancing, Prohlad's daughter, wife of Gupi's son, is dancing, Pagol is singing. But Bonwari isn't seeing any of this. His gaze is toward Babathakur's shrine. The white ninth-night moon had set long before; the dark of Babathukur's shrine is deep and still. But Bonwari can see, Babathakur is standing with his hand on a branch of the wood-apple tree.

Father, don't just stand there. Call out now—Beware—watch out! At least give a sign. Let us know. Give them all a shocking warning. You've been there forever, Father; don't just stay silent today at this time of crisis. There are many precedents in the tale of Hansuli Turn. Suchand says— Whenever the Atpoure Para gang got caught when they went out ta rob, those times Babathakur 'ad given out a warnin'.

—Deepy-dark night, Srabon month, bitta scattered cloud in the sky. Atpoures went out ta rob. Great strong men. Twirlin their fightsticks wi' a *whoosh whoosh whoosh*. At first Babathakur's command was—Quit stealin', do farmin'. Kahars took up farmin' Atpoures, wi' their wild blood an' 'ot 'eads, didn't listen. One time robbin', two times robbin', three—four times 'e fergave 'em; on the fifth time, that Shrabon month, comes the consequence—they're crossin' the two-part field, then thunder, lightnin' strike crashed down at the edge o' Father's deeps, on toppa the palm tree beside Father's silk-cotton tree. But they didn't listen, an' not listenin', they got Father's reward soon enough. Three Atpoures got caught.

That time Master Chaudhurys were auctioning off the Jangol Bans-badi estates, that's when ye got yer sign: thatched roof o' the lean-to fer the Chaudhurys' song an' dance party caught fire; that one oo always lit lamps at parties—fifty-candle lamps, 'e was lightin' lamps, a spark o' that lamp caught the rope, climbed the rope an' the roof caught fire, fifty candles came crashin' down. "Keracheen" spilled out, caught fire. Father gave out signs—Beware! Ma Lakshmi's gettin' agitated, now's not the time for song, dance, boozy madness. But who're you speaking to? Who's listening? The Chaudhurys don't listen—within six months it's all auctioned off!

Give that kind of warning. Let Karali's cottage roof go up in flames, or else them who went and got together at that caste-wrecker's party— their roofs. Warn everyone, Father, at our Bhanjo party this very day. No, no, Father, don't set a fire within the village, Father. No use in that. Poor folk'll be ruined, Father. Head of the palm tree, that one in the yard of Porom's cottage, strike the head of that tallest tree with lightning. Or Porom's cottage is fallen down—Porom's a fugitive, Kalobou's dead—let that cottage catch fire and burn. Yes Father, let it burn.

Pagol said—Don' drink no more booze, Bonwari. Gettup. Tek Gopali-bou back 'ome, she's gone dee-sturbed.

Gopalibala had danced and danced into drunken madness and col-lapsed on the ground vomiting.

Bonwari stood up. Eyes turning red; everyone's eyes are doubtless turning red from drinking liquor, but Bonwari's eyes seem to be filling with redness.

Pagol was afraid; in that fear he called out—Bonwari!

Bonwari signaled with his eyes and pointed with a finger to indicate something and said—Kottababa, Babathakur!

—What? Whatcha sayin'?

—Beware! Father's speakin'. Bonwari staggered off toward Babathakur's shrine. Shubashi stopped her dancing. She followed Bonwari a way and paused, stupefied. She stood a while and turned, but not in the direction of the Bhanjo mound. Meanwhile at the Bhanjo mound they had all become anxious. Pagol said—Off, bastards; drinkin' too much booze! Get—get, sing songs, everyone. I'll tek Gopalibala 'ome an' get 'er laid down. Uh, hey, Pellad's Missus, go, will ya sis, grab Gopalibou an' bring 'er along.

Pellad's wife smirked. —Why, eh? Gettin' scared or what? Scared of 'eat?

Pagol smiled too; he broke straight into song—

That 'eat o' mine's floated off,
In Kopai river's water, O!
That 'eat took hold of my love
In a red water-lily flower, O!
(In Kopai river's water, O!)
Mind obeyed that lily flower
Forgot all my sorrow
The garland of your 'eat
You give it over too, O!
(In Kopai river's water, O!)
New lily blooms every day
Faded petals fallen down
(In Kopai river's water, O!)

The song began to move. Women dancing. Gopalibou remained fallen as she was. In an instant everyone forgot about taking her home.

Meanwhile Karali's party is getting very crowded. Their songs are the currently fashionable songs. Songs from gramophone *records*. Bamboo flute—bamboo-oo flu-ute, bamboo-oo flu-ute—girls are singing heartily along with Nasubala. But Karali's flute cannot be heard.

Bonwari suddenly came back shouting—Beware! Watch it! Looka that, looka that.

All around Bansbadi night's darkness thick and deep; in one place within, a fire's blazing bright. Smell of smoke coming. Smell of smoke from Bhadra month's damp straw burning. Fire! Fire! Bonwari crashed to the floor as if possessed by a spirit. Gopali suddenly sat up. She stared in bewilderment at Bonwari with her drunken red eyes.

All the men rushed to the fire's edge. Atpoure Para—not in Porom's cottage, in Romon's cottage. Romon's cottage is also standing deserted; he lives at Bonwari's house. After the death of his wife he became unwell and took his bedding to Bonwari's terrace.

The fire was quickly put out. A small cottage with little thatch, and wet too; it caught fire, and there's a big group of men from Kaharpara and Atpoure Para. They put out the fire and all went back to the Bhanjo mound.

Noyan's Ma is hurling abuse in a piercing voice—O Father, burn it all to ash, tek the fire that burned up yer familiar an' wi' that fire burn it all down.

Pakhi said—Where is 'e? Im? Meaning Karali.

Nasu said—Yeah, right! Where's 'e gone now?

Karali returned a little later. He did not answer anyone's questions and began to dance; what a dance! He took hold of Pakhi.

Bonwari came to in the morning. Dreadful agony and terror in his head. Gopalibala was lying in deep sleep, unconscious on the cottage terrace, her hair loose and disheveled. Shubashi entered the cottage after having immersed Bhanjo and taken her bath that morning. Young girl, tough constitution, she drank liquor but never completely lost consciousness. Bonwari glanced at her but said nothing. It's as if a fear is sleeping in his head.

Shubashi glanced his way with a little smile.

A sweet fragrance seems to be rising from Shubashi's limbs even though she's just come from bathing. But flies are circling around Bonwari's nose with a droning buzz—the smell of liquor is rising from every limb.

Six

The whole morning he sat strangely "out," that's to say stupefied. The whole hamlet still utterly soundless. It's never been so soundless on morning-after's Bhanjo, meaning the day after Bhanjo. But it seems the folk of Kaharpara were completely overwhelmed with fear because of that damp thatch on Romon's cottage catching fire last night. As long as liquor's fix is held up by orgies of enjoyment, the Kahars keep enjoying wildly; but if madness passes they fall into insensible sleep. They can drink liquor, pick up a palanquin, and travel twenty miles—but if they lower the palanquin, spread out their wraps, and lie down, it's deathlike sleep.

After that drama almost everyone in the hamlet fell asleep. Blood-red blazing fire of Romon's roof in midnight darkness is still floating before Bonwari's eyes like a dream. And in his ears his own voice ringing—Watch out—beware!

Then he remembers, he'd gone toward Babathakur's shrine—in that deep night. He remembers clearly that someone seemed to grab his shoulder.

Babathakur said—Beware.

Bonwari said to Father—Ripe Infernal Age, Father; in these times humans honor humans no more. You reveal your greatness, Father. Call out, Father. Resurrect your familiar; tell it, Father, to raise its hood in the sky—Karali, that evil Karali's brick house, breathe fire on it, Father; and burn Porom's cottage, Kalobou's destructive spirit is in that cottage.

Babathakur said—It'll be, it'll be. Bit by bit it'll be.

But why did Babathakur burn Romon's cottage instead of Porom's cottage?

The cows started to call. Mothers calling, calves replying; milk accumulating in the mothers' udders, teats smarting, so the mothers are calling. Or else the calves are getting hungry—they're calling and the mothers replying. Bonwari became conscious with these calls. He staggered to his feet.

Headman has many duties. The hamlet must be awakened. With lotus-flower garland, rouge forehead dot, jingling bangles on her feet, Bhanjo Sundari has gone to her rightful place beneath Kopai's waters; it will not do for folk of Kaharpara to stay in bed, they must get up. There are homes, doorways, there are cows, calves, goats, sheep, ducks, chickens; cottages and doorways must be cleaned, cows must be milked, goats, sheep, ducks, chickens must be chased outside. Milk deliveries must be made to the gents' houses in Channanpur. Green paddy in the fields is calling—Weeds growing all around me, pull them up, cut them out. Jangol's Sadgop masters and bosses are grinding their teeth in rage. They are absolutely furious about this Bhanjo festival in Bhadra; they just cannot abide this playing of drums, drinking of liquor, wild dancing, a whole day's absence at farmwork time. A whole day's absence already passed; if there's absenteeism today there will be no mercy. The Kahars are not afraid of beatings and insults, they fear for their stomachs; if the bosses stop paddy "rents," which is loans, it will be ruinous!

First of all he called Gopali. —Biggie, up, up. Biggie!

But Gopali did not respond. She was completely unconscious. What a disaster! Cows must be milked, cattle must be taken out. He has a lot of work himself, has to go and get things started on the Saheb Tracts plots, else weeding won't happen. For starters it's broken soil, new land too, water's drying up fast. Be no clouds in the sky from now. In Bhadra month King Indra gives the farmer two weeks, that's to say he gives pattering rain; and he gives the tanner two weeks, which is to say two weeks of earth-cracking sun; in that sun they dry out the skins they collected during the monsoon. If the sun comes up then it'll be two or three weeks of cruel sunshine. Saheb Tracts' water will dry up by then, and there will be no way to pull up the weeds. Bonwari must get to the Saheb Tracts.

Bonwari went forward and gave Gopali a shove, calling—Biggie!

He was shocked when his hand touched her body—Oh, yer body's burnin' so! It seemed so scorching that rice would pop if it fell onto her.

Bonwari called out—Biggie! Gopali!

Gopali opened blood-red eyes—Aaah! Then she suddenly spoke— Beware! Bonwari was shocked to hear this. He said—Whatcha sayin'? Gopali stared blankly at him.

Bonwari said—Ya got fever. Up an' lie in the room. Shubashi! Shubashi!

Shubashi came out of the cottage loosening her clothes. —What?

—Gi' a hand. Gopali's got a terrible fever.

—Fever! Shubashi spoke with a sneer—Won't be that, s'all that drinkin'! Mad love—that's it fer sure!

Bonwari told her off. —Listen ta what I'm sayin'! Gi' a hand—lay 'er down in the room an' then you finish the milkin' today. Tell Uncle Omon—take cows ta fields.

—Hey—hey! Whassat scent comin' off yer body? Eh? Bonwari asked when they had laid Gopali down.

Shubashi said—What kinda smell's it gonna be! Damn! Smell o' booze comin' off you.

—Nah, not smell o' booze. 'S a fragrant scent.

—Ye're angry?

—No.

—Yeh. Ye're angry! Remember whatcha did las' night? If they ain't angry folks don't talk like that—what's that sweet scent comin' off yer body?

Bonwari stared steadily into Shubashi's face.

Shubashi said—Was it you burned Uncle Omon's cottage las' night?

Bonwari was astounded.

—Victory Babathakur—Victory Babathakur—Kalobou, don't take offense, Babathakur's command.

—Cos you were mumblin' an' complainin', I 'eard everythin'.

A strange look entered Bonwari's eyes. He was staring steadily at Shubashi; it seemed like his two round eyes were going to pop out.

Shubashi backed away in fright.

Bonwari shook his head—No no no.

Inside the room Gopali was moaning restlessly—muttering complaints in feverish delirium.

Shubashi said—Go, wherever yer goin', go. Don't worry. Smilingly she went into her co-wife's room.

It seemed to Bonwari that Babathakur was coming down on his back again. Arms and legs shaking, sweat appearing on his brow, wanting to scream—Beware, watch out. Bonwari gradually pulled himself together, then went out into the hamlet. But what was that sweet scent?

Pagol is sitting alone at the Bhanjo mound with one of his brother musician's drums; instead of using sticks, he is tapping out a rhythm with his fingers and singing. The musician is prostrate under a tree. Here and there Kahar men lie sleeping deeply. The women are sleeping on cottage terraces. Of the women, Noyan's Ma has risen and is on the terrace, leaning on a post. She's still cursing as before—O Babathakur! Them what killed yer familiar, why've they been built up, Father? Is this yer judgment! Just bring yer wrath once, Father! Set fire a top o' the brick 'ouse in the village, Father!

Sometimes Bonwari wants to put his hands around this woman's throat and shut her up. And not just this woman, he wants to do this to all the argumentative women. But today he did not have this wish. Let her curse Karali. He forgave her for that.

***

In the tale of Hansuli Turn, whatever happens suddenly is Godly. God's wrath does not happen without a crime; it's written in the scriptures, that's what they believe. If gods are wrathful you must know: a crime has been committed, whether knowingly or unknowingly. And with that they also believe this—"He who kills a Brahmin will lose his life!"

On the third day Gopalibala suddenly died of that illness. People then said all those things. Everyone said—When it's a sudden death, and dying screaming, "Beware beware" like that, then you know it's God wrath! Manifest proof of God wrath—bad omen on the night of Bhanjo during the rains, an uninhabited cottage's thatch aflame. Babathakur has gotten enraged. But why did that rage fall upon Gopali? Some said—When it comes down then there's certainly a crime, fer sure! Some said—No one can blame Bonwari for the crime. It's someone else's crime.

Noyan's Ma says, as if she's speaking to someone—Ta smash the 'ome o' Noyan, marry Pakhi off ta Karali? Not undharmic? Not crime? Undredfold, thousandfold crime. That's why Babathakur smashed 'is established 'ome. This is sure, this is sure.

But where was a home smashed? Gopali's gone, Shubashi remains. Bonwari will suffer a bit of grief, but he has been saved from the fighting of two co-wives. After much consideration they said—Shubashi's fate is an altogether happy fate.

In reply to this, Noyan's Ma says—I don't 'old ta none o' that. What I'm sayin's right. I'm sat 'ere like Ravana's mother Nekasha, I ruined the fool's head, I can see it all. Tis first eve o' the Infernal Age. This is the beginnin'. Gopalibou was a fortunate one, so she went off first of all wi' a bang. Yet why'd she keep screamin' "Beware beware" till the end? Won't there be punishment for the one 'oo killed Father's familiar?

Suchand was the oldest woman in the tale of Hansuli Turn. Bashan and Suchand now have no quarrel with Bonwari about Karali and Pakhi; Bonwari is hamlet headman, how can you live in Kaharpara and be quarreling with him? Karali, that Karali who now wears military clothing, stomps around with shoes on his feet, wears a cap tilted on his head, who has pockets full of wages, could he really live here? He has a house, sometimes comes, stays an hour, comes on feast days and festivals, stays half a day and leaves; could you say he's living there? Doesn't live there for fear of Bonwari. Thus Bashan and Suchand don't have that whole quarrel with Bonwari. Nor does Bonwari fight; the headman has a dharma and he does not transgress it. And yet there's no meeting of minds. And Bonwari does not take Suchand's advice on every task. Nor does Suchand noisily involve herself in every task as before. Does not say—Little lad o' them old days, you; milk in me breast so yer life was saved. But today Suchand and Bashan could not stay away; Suchand hurried first of all, to beat her breast and weep. She wept, struck her breast, and said—What evil, what crime! O, which curse, what cursing! A good 'un, a lucky 'un, wi' a married woman's vermilion in the parting of 'er 'air, gone away wi' a bang in the fullness o' Bhadra month, O! Gone away smilin'-laughin', O! Didn't suffer the co-wife thorn fer six months, O! An' I'm left fallen 'ere, O!

Bonwari sat silently listening. He could not disbelieve what anybody said. He admitted it all. The words of Noyan's Ma were deeply clouding his mind. True though, if there is not a crime, then why did Gopalibou die like that? In Bhadra and Aswin months Kaharpara folk fall prey to bile, acid, fever. Baidya healers say—Chronic fever; doctors say—"Maloyria." Fever comes with shivers, with spurts of bile vomit; fever passes in sweating, comes again. Take "quinial," get your appetite back in a week or so, get out of bed, and in two or three weeks have a relapse. But this isn't that. Fever and immediate delirium. Not delirium, Babathakur's decree—"Beware beware"—screaming to the end. Bonwari remembers that Bhanjo night like a bad dream. His whole body trembles. He immediately recalls Shubashi. Every limb shudders with rage. But he cannot say a thing for fear.

Now when Suchand weeps she says—A good 'un, a lucky 'un! She believes this with life and soul; it's true though that she went off with a bang! Gopalibou is going off still married, with vermilion at her brow, rouge on her feet, in her very best cloth; sunlight sparkling all around in the last day's sky of Bhadra month, green paddy swaying in all the meadows of Hansuli Turn, bamboo grove leaves and leaves on tree branches are deep green, sparkling in the sun's glow; lotus flowers on lily pads flowering in ponds, lotuses flowering in yards, coral-jasmine flowers falling to the foot of the tree, Kopai's waters clearing—red waters becoming glassy-clear. Hansuli Turn is turning green, so the golden Hansuli necklace is taking a silver hue to adorn it. On riverbanks reeds have flowered, which is to say their flowers have bloomed. At Jangol and Channanpur Durga's awakening drums are beating. Mother Durga's coming, bringing Lakshmi, Saraswati, Kartik, Ganesh, her lion, and the Demon. Preparations are being made for offerings, threshing floors are being cleared; autumn paddy will soon be harvested. Autumn paddy's green has faded and taken a "reddy," or reddish, tinge. In this plenteous Hansuli Turn she has left husband, given co-wife the slip, and gone. People will surely give blessings.

Pagol, Prohlad, Roton—they'd all made preparations for carrying to the burning ground. Bashan came forward and painted on the foot rouge. She said—Ye blessed one. Ah, if only ye'd lived, taken my old age, an' I'd gone instead.

Bonwari was very moved by these words of Bashan's. Bashan is a very good woman. But on account of Karali Bashan has become an outsider.

Nasubala had come too. He too is weeping with the women's group.— Ah—ah—alas darlin' one! Aunt Gopali was one of my own, good as gold, dearest! 'Twas nectar flowed from 'er mouth, 'twas life's balm ta listen, Kopai's cool touch in 'er 'ands, ye'd fill wi' delight when she'd stroke ye. Ah, where've ye gone dearest—Ma Lakshmi o' the village!

Shubashi was off to one side, leaning against a wall. Nasubala suddenly said—Ah, makes me shudder seein' ya apart like that, Shubashi. I tell ya—pour on some vermilion—put some vermilion on yer co-wife's brow, I say—ignore yer 'ubby's orders, I've given ye the vermilion, you put mine on 'er.

Pagol called—Bonwari!

—What?

—Really need a piece o' new cloth. Needed at burnin' ground. Couldn't get it in the market. Said—No cloth.

Bashan said—Can I say a word, Bonwari-bro? Send someone ta Karali, 'e'll get cloth right out. There's this Company store—

—No. Bonwari shook his head and said—No need fer cloth. Go ta Jangol an' buy a gamcha towel from the weaver.

"What th'Infernal Age admits, I gotta do what fits." What to do? Time of war. Bonwari heaved a deep sigh. Last time war broke out the price of cloth rose—five rupees, seven rupees added to the price. In this war there's no cloth, can't be got. Let Gopali wear a gamcha towel. Let it be. What can Bonwari do? This misery will not leave him even if he dies.

Once burning is done he must place thorns in all manner of places on the way back. The ghost-soul comes after! Does the cherishing spirit of house and home let go with death? Bonwari placed many large acacia thorns on the path. Said to himself—Gopalibou, don't do any evil, your place'll be in paradise. Give up your hunger for home. I'm very sad for you. But I've got a lot of work now. Headmanship of Kaharpara and Atpoure Para on my shoulders. My—

Overhead a droning swarm of airplanes flew. Probably going to the new airplane hangars near Channanpur's workshops—on the turf of bastard Karali! Huh-huh-huh-huh. His chest pounding inside.

On the way back into the village he prostrated himself at Babathakur's shrine and silently said—Save me from the gaze o' Gopali, Father. Got a lotta work now. But who's that? Not Pakhi? Yes, it is so! She's standing beneath that very banyan tree outside the village where he met with Kalo-bou; she's having intense words with a few young lads. Lots of waving arms and moving legs. What's all that talk?

Leave it, let 'em go to hell, let her say whatever she wants; Bonwari's mind is not in a fit state to keep an eye on this.

Bonwari is not alone; the group of bier carriers is coming into view. Pagol said—Ah, I see Pakhi's jabberin' away!

Pana said—Yeah, Karali's got 'em well drawn in, that's what she's on about. Night o' Bhanjo, Karali sayin' 'e's got work at Channanpur. Lads've been twitchy since then. All that's bein' discussed. Don't come isself, sen-din' Pakhi.

Bonwari did not say anything. The closer he's getting to home, the more he's thinking of Gopalibou. Gopalibou, who joined her life to his and lived with him; so today it seems as if his entire life is empty. Let 'em do what they want, today he has no wish to say anything at all.

He was about to enter the house, but he could no longer remain silent. Karali's sitting in the yard of his house. Bonwari was surprised. Even from afar he's able to see clearly—late autumn sunlight falling on deep green paddy in the western fields, and a doubled glow falling on the terrace of his compound—some light falling through the open door into the room. Shubashi is sitting in there. She's really smart. Sitting there for no reason, "drawn over," which is to say with her veil up. Looking sidelong at Karali. Karali sitting with his back to Bonwari, he can't tell if he's glancing in his direction, but he understands well that he is glancing Shubashi's way. The lad's creating quite a get-together. Passing along stories and gossip heard at Channanpur. Saheb men have gone to war—England and Germany. Cannons, guns, bombs; Germany is winning, England is losing. Telling long, tall tales of airplanes. His engine workshop, wings, tails—all sorts of things.

Ah, bastard! Bonwari knows war. He too hears at the Ghoshes' house. War broke out once before in 'twenty-one of the Bengali calendar, nine-teen hundred and fourteen—he saw it then. What is it to your Father if war's breaking out? What gossip and stories of his at Hansuli Turn? Paddy and rice will be dear; price of cloth will go up. Is, will be; rises, will rise. There'll be a "lickle bitta" suffering and misery. Keeping dharma in your head, treading with caution the forefathers' "lines," or their paths, twelve months turn and however many years of war will pass away. Kot-tathakur will protect. Times will pass in his blessing, come good or ill. All lack will be wiped out if the meadows of Hansuli Turn take the dust of Ma Lakshmi's feet.

Bonwari entered the cottage and said gravely—Young master Karali, I presume?

Karali said—Yes, uncle. Eard 'bout auntie's dyin'. No break, so I couldn't come. I came now ta bring news.

—Do whatcha like. No rule against it, s'all stuff ta do; gotta do it. But kid, why 'ere with all this war stuff? Whatever country war's broken out in, what's that to do wi' bamboo-circled Kahars of Kaharpara on Hansuli's Turn? All those stories might dazzle the girls and make 'em 'ot, but that's not done 'round 'ere, kid.

Karali frowned, looked at him, and said—Meanin'? Whass all this yer sayin'?

—I'm sayin' right, ye're understandin' right. Yer wife comin', feedin' mantras in the lads' ears—Give up karma o' forefathers' clan work, come ta the caste-wreckin' workshops ta labor. You comin' an' the girls' minds—

Karali yelled—Tell ya, 'tain't gonna be good, Uncle Beano.

Bonwari said—Caste wrecker! Outcaste nobody! Ya got no shame, yer ma went off ta work on that line, went outside 'er own clan, quit this place, an' yer workin' that same line? Now yer comin' ta make the local lads bad in the 'ead? Smug wi' money, wi' yer coat an' long pants, comin' ta show yerself off ta the ladies—ye're such a big man!

Karali stood up, spoke—Oo's got caste? Any lad's dad got it 'ere? That old Suchand's sittin' there, let 'er say, let 'er say, I'm listenin'. Caste! None o' you's got no shame! Pure castes—gentryfolk, ye lick their feet, they take yer livelihood, take yer caste. Beat yer backs wi' shoes, ya put up wi' it in silence. Shame! Washin' yer faces at the riverside o' shame, are ya? Caste! Karma o' clan's work! So clan karma's herdin', diggin', tendin' fer the Jangol farmers? Ye'll go ta paradise on a chariot fer that! Not enough rice fer yer bellies, not enough cloth ta wear. Clan karma! Clan karma! What's yours? You're 'eadman, all set up, workin' some land, sowin' some paddy, gettin' wed at a ripe old age, showin' folk right dharma. Shame! You got no shame gettin' married in old age? Eadman! Folks'll work their bodies ta fill their bellies, clothe themselves, do it every day; show yer right dharma at that! Why'd people abide by your word? Why abide? I'm shoutin' it out—I'll get work fer ooever'll labor in the workshops. Five bits wages a day. Company'll give cheap rice, cheap soup, cheap cloth. Ooever wants can come. Don't abide by that oldie's word.

—Watch it! Bonwari shouted out. Bonwari now leaped up, having listened stupefied a while to Karali's speech, Karali's logic. Nobody ever utters this kind of statement face to face; and he's never ever heard a statement of such unjust yet such amazing logic, so he'd been stunned. As soon as Karali said, "Don't abide by that oldie's word" he awoke bursting with rage and screamed out—Watch it! Right away he leaped up and grabbed a fistful of Karali's long hair. He dragged Karali's head toward the dirt by the fistful of hair. By dragging he'll let him know to touch his head to the dirt; let him know it's law that you don't toss your hair and speak to Bonwari, headman of Kaharpara, by staring into his forehead. If you do speak like that then you're dragged to the dirt in this way. Bonwari pulled with a savage tug. But Karali works in Channanpur's workshops, he has forgotten to pay obeisance by touching his head to the dirt, he has got into the habit of saluting with his head straight; he's a tall, broad, tough man besides; pounding pickaxe and mallet has made his body hard as stone. Karali stiffened his neck and kept his head straight, bearing the agony; he didn't bow his head an inch.

Bonwari gnashed his teeth and pulled, yet Karali will not bow his head, his neck seems like it's getting hard as iron. He said—Leave off, 'eadman. I'm tellin' ya, leave off.

Bonwari bellowed—No.

Bashan screamed out—Beano-bro! Bro!

Suchand started to wail; Nasubala began to beat his chest and lament—O woe woe, whatta inhuman place! Lettit go dears, lettit go! Dearies, lettit go.

The veil's slipping from Shubashi's head, she's watching with popping eyes. Pakhi came running at just this moment. She leaped onto Bonwari like one nearly insane, and bit at his arm in ferocious attack.

People standing like they're stupefied. They're watching Bonwari's attack, the revelation of Karali's power. They're made speechless. After all this time Pagol came from wherever he'd been. He came; and as soon as he did, he ran to Bonwari, took his arm, and said—Bonwari! Fer shame! Let go, let go. They're comin' ta make inquiries at your place, ya gotta go clasp yer 'ands. Whatcha doin'? Bonwari!

Bonwari's fist loosened. Letting Karali's hair go he said—Get. Next time I won't letcha live.

Karali's neck was straight; he flicked his head, his long hair went down his back, he smiled a bitter smile and said—Next time I won't honor you, neither. Today I put up wi' it. Ye're 'eadman, this is me final honorin' of ya. Wouldn't have done that either. What ta say; today ye're burnin' wi' grief. Come on, Pakhi.

Pakhi's teeth and lips were stained with blood. Her teeth had torn Bonwari's arm and sunk in. Karali took Pakhi's arm and yelled out as they left—Ooever'll work at Channanpur workshops, come on. I've said so.

Seven

Babathakur Kartababa! Are you displeased, Father? It's something to make you displeased, sure; forgiving the one who killed your familiar. But can he have committed a yet greater crime than the one who killed your familiar?

The thought often steals into Bonwari's mind. Kaharpara's youth showing signs of disobeying him. Karali ignoring him, stubbornly coming every evening and holding a gathering at his house. That's where they're getting together.

And a female blacksnake has entered Bonwari's house. Shubashi blacksnake. Seeing her ways, Bonwari suspects—one day maybe *she* will sink her fangs into his breast!

Auntie Suchand used to tell a fable—King's daughter got married an' that very girl died. Like a stretched thread from the girl's nose, a thin snake came out; when it was out it puffed up, puffed and became a python. Then it bit the king's daughter's 'usband.

Bonwari thinks to send the girl away. But out of fear he cannot. Fear, fear of Kaloshoshi's ghostsoul; fear, fear of Gopalibala's ghostsoul. Shubashi—she can save him from their hands. Woman with a living husband—a woman's luck can save him from the hands of female ghostsouls. If he got rid of Shubashi he'd have to marry again. But another marriage at this age! That shames him. Besides, the moral character of the Kahars' women is virtually all the same. How many like Gopalibala are left? What's more, he's getting old; probably at least fifty. The restless nature of the Kahar girl who marries him will become yet more restless. So he does not send Shubashi away. Besides, even though he thought he'd quit Shubashi, the thought disturbs him. Shubashi has likely bewitched or enchanted him. Shubashi is strangely beguiling. So, it's Shubashi who'll strike his breast—with this suspicion he's keeping Shubashi under strict observation, not leaving her. When Karali gets his evening gatherings together Bonwari keeps Shubashi before him and sits home. Prohlad, Roton, Gupi, and the other elders come, Pana comes too—there's a meeting. But meetings don't gather without Pagol. Who'll sing songs, cut rhymes? Pagol has gone off again, quitting the "villidge." He left the day right after

Gopalibala's funeral. Bonwari is gloomy on account of Pagol. Without Pagol, meetings are only about work. Shubashi's Uncle Romon prepares tobacco. No kerosene, a lightless meeting, only a small fire burning. Ember flames' reddishness falls on everyone's faces. The topic of farming comes up, among other things.

Bonwari's apprehension, his mind's agitation, lessen a little if the topic of farming comes up. Here God is benign toward the world. Of course Hansuli Turn's Babathakur is benign, else why would there be so much paddy in the world? And now Hansuli Turn has the most paddy in the world. Would that ever happen if Babathakur wasn't benign? Fields full of green paddy taking on the thick darkness of black clouds. Each single sheaf of paddy cannot be held in two hands' grasp.

Everyone says—Yes, this has been a real year for it, indeed.

Pana says—Uncle Bonwari, do tell o' yer fortunes now. Dug up Saheb Tracts' land now, an' now look at what paddy ye got!

Bonwari silently admits this point but says aloud—Fortune ain't mine, it's gentry masters' fortune; I've 'eard that in war markets they're bringin' 'ome tens o' thousands o' rupees. My land's next ta their land, so—if it wasn't ye'd have ta be seein' summat different.

Roton said—If ya say that I ain't listenin', bro. Your paddy's strongest in the Saheb Tracts. Then, smiling and nodding he said—Yep, lovely paddy, what sheaves!

Pana said smiling—Auntie, ya gotta feed us at 'arvest festival this time. He speaks to Shubashi. Bastard Pana's not a trivial matter; if he's just a boy giving himself out to be a headman, what'll happen? What'll his nasty ways lead to? Somehow gets the opening to say a couple of sentences to Shubashi! Bonwari does not give Shubashi the chance to reply, and quickly speaks up—All right, all right, we'll feed ya this time.

Shubashi smiles, she can understand what's going on in Bonwari's mind. Smilingly she gets up and says in a soft voice—Damn you! No one understands who she is talking to.

At night Bonwari asks—Oo'd ya say that thing to?

—What thing?

—That whatcha said, "Damn you"?

—Ta meself, oo else?

—No!

—All right, ta you.

—Why?

—Why? Shubashi stares into his face for a while then says—Ye can't understand? Ye're not that stupid. If I spoke wi' that little ape Pana would I be destroyed?

Bonwari is silent a moment and then says—If Pana weren't a little ape but were like Karali, tall an' broad an' fashionable, what then?

Shubashi stares into Bonwari's face like a snake, unblinking. Exactly like a snake. Two eyes just glitter, no expression on the face.

Bonwari asks—No answer, then?

Without saying a word, Shubashi gets off the bed and goes out. Goes to the terrace and sits. Bonwari lies silently a while too, then rises, goes to appease Shubashi, and brings her back. He feels frightened in the room alone. Gopalibala, Kaloshoshi. Fears Gopali most. If the wife from a first marriage dies then she brings back the marriage's "urn," that's to say a water-filled pitcher, at her side. As long as the husband has not died she cannot throw away the pot. Just a few days before his death she throws that pot away. There's a noise. Nothing falls anywhere, and yet a noise can be heard. Now if there's the slightest sound of falling crockery in any house of the hamlet Bonwari is up with a jolt, sneaks out to check and be reassured. He always lies down touching Shubashi. Shubashi is very smart. She understands exactly what's going on in Bonwari's mind. Says—No fear, Biggie ain't standin' in the corner, sleep. She won't choke ya ta death.

Bonwari remains silently lying down; sleep does not come. Why will he die untimely? He must live. Now is the prime of his happiness. He is now master of many acres of land. There's a huge crop on that land in the very first year. He's newly married.

He sits up. Putting the palm of his hand near Shubashi's nose, he feels her breath. He checks to see if something threadlike is coming out.

Darkness broke at morning; the light spread, Bonwari became bold Bonwari. He rushed off toward the fields.

***

So much work, so much work!

Rains ending, sky becoming blue hued. In the space where Mother Durga's painted nimbus will be, a deep blue shines like blue paint. Kartik of War's familiar is sparkling like a peacock's neck. In Hansuli Turn's fields, elephantine paddy is rolling in the breeze, Sun Lord's rays are as if rinsed in milk. Kaharpara's men have scattered into fields. Submerged in four- or six-foot-high paddy, knees bent, they're moving around like wild boars, tearing up weeds, crushing them, and pushing them into earth where they will rot into compost.

But now and then there is an interruption to today's work; overhead, like great swarms of hornets, squadrons of airplanes fly with a droning noise; then everyone throws their work aside and stands to look. Even Bonwari looks.

Ah my, wartime, Father! There in Channanpur, and in every gentry "villidge" and town, they've started up all that weird Gandhi Raja stuff. Pulling up rail lines, burning government buildings; police-military shooting bullets, they're hit by bullets, dying, yet no fear, no dread.

Prices of paddy and rice rising rapidly. It's being said—they'll rise more. No worries if the price of paddy rises. Huge amounts of paddy this time. Just got to get through Ashwin. A "mizzle," that's to say a shower of rain, would be enough; what more's needed? Ears longer than half a hand coming out, fattening and ripening by the day, will fall to earth under their own weight. Now the bosses' account books are settled, the Kahars will bring paddy home. Bonwari has a wish; he'll summon Karali, say— Look! Look at Kaharpara's old Mother Lakshmi. A hope, that however restless the youth may be, Hansuli Turn's Mother Lakshmi will now give them a taste for working in service of the land. Yet he's having doubts.

War hasn't just set the paddy market ablaze. It's setting the markets for everything ablaze. Can't get cloth—Bonwari heaves a deep sigh when he thinks about cloth. He couldn't get hold of cloth for Gopalibala's final rites. Eternal indulgence of Kaharpara's women, they love to wear flower-bordered cloth. But they're going around in dirty cloth.

No kerosene. They don't eat sugar but need it in times of illness and distress, for worship and festivals. Can't get it with "Newnain Bod" ration cards anymore, either. Heard there isn't any left in the whole country. Meanwhile "maloyria" is starting to grip, but "quinial" can't be got either. Juice of night jasmine leaf a fallback. By the time a few days of Ashwin had passed the leaves of the hamlet's night jasmine were half gone. Fever starts from now—it will strike, lift, strike again; a few people will die in delirium. Most will die in winter. More of the elderly will die. It has ever been thus. Now a fear—no "quinian." In the midst of this there's work for worship—worship worries. Mother Durga of Ten Arms is coming, bringing son, daughter, familiar; Mother Birthgiver mounted on a lion, how great her glory! The place will be abuzz, drums will play, tom-toms will play, shanai will play, gongs will play; there'll be dancing, singing, eating, dressing up. He will stand at a distance from Mother's chamber, prostrate himself on the earth, and say—Save us, Ma, in danger an' mishap, in forest an' wood, on land an' water, save us. Gi' strength to our dharma, save us from the grasp o' greed; we're insignificant people, we're worshippin' wi' two arms, look on us from afar wi' a contented gaze, gi' to us wi' yer ten arms. Cancel all our evil an' anger, Ma.

Ten-armed woman, not exactly slight! Her worship! Homes must be cleaned up. Need new cloth. Shortage of money. Old paddy has run out at master's house, there's a delay with new paddy; this is a time for expenses. Now things are getting more difficult because of that war. Boss masters don't want to give out too much paddy. Keeping paddy locked up. At this time bosses always give more paddy than the basic ration. This time they're saying—No.

At certain times what Karali says seems to be true. They understand nothing but their own interests. The price of paddy is going up by the day; therefore they will not give paddy to the peasants. If they shut that down completely they'll also shut down farming—so give enough to fill a belly. Cloth must be bought, worship's coming up—he will not make a judgment. Roton said just yesterday—Bonwari, I couldn't keep me status up. Boss came an' gave a tickin' off about paddy. Says, cloth? It's not my duty ta see if there's cloth or not! Then says real nasty stuff. Finally gets mad an' hits!

Roton's boss, Hedo Mondol, is violent like this. Pana's boss, Paku Mondol, does not hit with his hands, he hits with words. Puffs bubblingly on his hookah and says—Hmh, hmh, hmh. It's the "hmh" that burns; finally he gets out his accounts ledger. Says—Mountain in arrears. More paddy on top of that? Certainly must give enough to eat; I'll give. Don't ask me to give more, sonny, I can't.

Pana sitting with his head in his hands. The young men saying to Bonwari—We started farmin' at your word. Make it possible.

They are grumbling in secret—We'd have made it if we'd taken jobs in workshops instead.

Bonwari is going to Jangol and Channanpur in breaks from work. Going to Jangol to see the farm masters; they really must give a bit more paddy and make more loans of manure. The Kahars will put down manure for the land. They'll put an extra cartload on the account rather than the money price. Masters are half willing. And he is going to Channanpur to see the storekeepers; need to keep back a bit of the cost of offering time's cloth. As soon as paddy's harvested the Kahars will repay the cash. I'll be responsible.

Mister Datta was agreeable. He deals in paddy as well as in clothing. He won't take the remainder in cash but in paddy, in the month of Poush. But he's saying—You have to give the paddy at that market price.

Bonwari was flabbergasted at first. Has Mister Datta gone mad! In Ashwin month the price of paddy is at its year's high; when new paddy comes up the price falls. Therefore—. It suddenly strikes him once it has turned around in his mind. The price of paddy is climbing—climbing so that even when new paddy comes up its price will not go down!

Will the price of paddy rise above four, four and a half rupees? Nobody has ever heard of this in the land of India! Eighty pounds of rice for nine rupees! O Babathakur, the games you're playing from age to age, Father! Ah! The granary will be filled with paddy from his two and a half acres. If it's a yield of three twenties per acre it'll be seven twenties in paddy. There will be more than that from sharecropping land; of course it will be shared with boss: shared twenty-two to eighteen. In the division of forty shares, boss will get twenty-two shares and Bonwari eighteen shares. Although he makes the final payoff of boss's loan from this share, he'll get between five and seven twenties. In each twenty there are a hundred and eighty pounds of paddy. Bonwari's head spins as he makes the accounts. He summons old Roton and says—Uncle Omon, come an' do the 'counts, will ya!

Oldie sits there night and day smoking tobacco—*hubble-bubble.* Takes cows out to the fields during work. That's it; besides breaking up straw, he won't contribute a thing. Eats rice by the heap.

The old man says—Counts? But that'll be a problem. Is Atpoure Para folk ever 'avin' anythin' ta do wi' paddy-rice business? Filled up sacks wi' stolen paddy, took it ta guard's place, 'e paid a wad. Ask Shubashi instead, she'll be able ta; was a paddy miller at Boss Farmer's place fer three, four years.

Shubashi doesn't make a bad job of the accounts. Fifteen twenties, each twenty one hundred sixty pounds—that makes twenty-four hundred pounds plus another three hundred pounds. She counts up on her fingers. She finishes the accounting, suddenly sits down with splayed legs, and laughingly says—Now I'm gonna weep. Yep!

Bonwari is very pleased. He smiles and says—Why, little precious, why gonna weep? Whatcha need?

—I'll 'ave a nice cloth fer this next offerin'—very nice.

Bonwari joins in the humor—No sweetie, don' cry. Course I'll buy for ya, 'course I'll give.

Shubashi counted up on her fingers—There's more offerins, Ram-two-three-four—

***

Those days too came to an end.

Hearing Noyan's Ma and Suchand's weeping, it is possible to understand. This was a rule in the tale of Hansuli Turn. The forefathers had said, at offering and festival, at wedding and nuptial, on happy days you have to be happy inside; those who are living, they're your own folk; the ones who loved you, those who you loved, those who are no longer, remember them and shed a teardrop or two. The recently departed come to mind; not just those from Hansuli Turn, even folk from the world of Channanpur come to mind—what heartrending words emerge amid weeping; eyes burst, flooding breasts with their own tears. Weeping for Noyan, that weeping for him of his mother's; all Kaharpara is embarrassed to listen as it joyously worships. Remembering Noyan, today her tongue is being washed of poison by tears. Weeping on the occasion of this worship and offering; from the very day she called out to Noyan she has not cursed a single person.

Suchand weeps tears of that rule. In the tale that is Hansuli Turn's, it's she who is the woman of ancient days. She weeps for her father, weeps for her brother, weeps for her husband, weeps for her son-in-law; then, taking each by name, she weeps for every person from Kaharpara who has died and strokes her leg bones; her pronouncements have given her "twingin' smarts" in the legs. Now and then she laments, ah, if I die no one in Kaharpara will follow this rule. The "omeplace" has changed from age to age, and with that people became indecent, filled with undharma. As she finishes her declaration she makes her lamentation palpable, saying—Ah! Ah! Oh woe!

She adds—Bonwari chased off my Pakhi an' Karali—'cos they've broke dharma, broke clan. Oo's got eyes, let 'em see—oo's kept dharma, oo's kept clan? But yeah, Karali's done a wrong. I'll say it 'undred times, say it a thousand times—wrong's that Father's snake was burned ta death. She folded her hands and paid obeisance to that dead snake again and again. As she was paying obeisance she suddenly began to weep in remembrance—O, come back in yer "varrygaited," or variegated, form on Father's worship day! Go around to 'eart's content in the bamboo groves lettin' out yer whistle; eat frogs, eat mice, O Father! O care fer the village!

Irritated, Bonwari stood up.—O she's annoyin'! Old woman's not dead yet.

Roton said—She's like that, indeed.

—Like that, indeed—like that, indeed! As he speaks he grabs the hookah from Roton's hand and begins puffing on it.

Prohlad says—So let's go one day ta buffalo pit on t'other side.

There is suddenly a shortage of water in the fields. Rain had stopped right from the start of Ashwin; field water almost dried up. Yet in Ashwin rice ears have developed in paddy heads' bellies, everything needs to be filled to the brim. The forefathers had said—Put five pitchers of water on each bunch of paddy every day; elephant-strong paddy in the fields this year. If this paddy goes bad, the Kahars will tear their breasts and die. If twelve-year-old male children died there wouldn't be such grief. So the word is, make a dam on the Kopai. Kopai's waters must be made to flood the fields by constructing a dam in Kopai's breast. Jangol's bosses have given the order. That dam is under way.

Bonwari is pondering many things. If the dam gets built, four or five people will go. When the dam's built, water pressure will go down; and there will be fights. If the dam gets built, folk from downriver will come to commit crimes. Sheikh groups will come. Besides all this, isn't Karali saying—Military won't allow dam ta be built. They've put an airplane base a little way away from Channanpur bankside—set up a "pumpu" there bringing up water. Bathe, wash down the airplanes, bring up all the food-cookin' water from that Kopai. No way they'll allow a dam ta be built.

Bonwari's idea is that Karali himself has done this through underhanded means. The bosses said—Nah, is the bastard capable of that! They mock the war and the saheb masters. They're saying that they'll go to the sahebs. Saying they'll help the Kahars. And they're saying—Look out at the offerings, this year Mother's coming on an elephant.

Bonwari said—Say Oton, let the offerin' pass first. Ma's comin' on an elephant. Won't the elephant sprinkle a bitta water? Then think—Ma'll eat up buffalo an' goat, needs water ta wash 'er mouth out.

***

On the sixth day of the lunar fortnight the Kahars were jubilant. Coming—coming. Clouds coming.

Clouds visible in the sky. "Blastering," that's to say blustery, blows the wind. Now and then bringing a fine, drizzlelike rain.

Bonwari spoke to the Kahars enthusiastically—Come, get cloth, come. Clouds up in the sky, Master Datta'll give cloth wi' no worries.

Nasubala is spinning around wearing a new sari. Laughing aloud. Saying—Is ours field money? Our money's from workshops o' the Infernal Age. Ching-ching-ching—cash cash! Our cloth ain't contemporary—it's ahead o' the times.

Before going, Shubashi said—But I want clothes like Pakhi.

It was as if blood filled Bonwari's head. —Like oo?

—Like Pakhi.

—Why, why, why? Why like Pakhi?

Shubashi was speechless. She remained frozen a few moments, then ran into the cottage and locked the door. Bonwari ground his teeth and said—Pouty's shot the bolt on the sulk room. Three kicks'd smash 'er body up. He put up the door chain and went off. Stay, stay locked up.

But at the store he bought the very best sari. Had to take out rather a lot of store credit for it. Even Master Datta made a joke. Roton and Prohlad began to laugh. The young men smirked at each other in private. Let 'em laugh. He was privately a little ashamed. After leaving the store they had to return home. Kottababa's offering on the tenth lunar day. On the tenth day of the Goddess's victory there will be sacrifice, offering. Cloth must be bought for this. He had an inner regret—he forgot to buy cloth for Father. Shame! Shame! Shame!

Shubashi did not accept such cloth with a smile, though. After much pestering, in order to get her out of the huff, Bonwari had to agree—tomorrow morning he would go straight to Channanpur and get "colorfill" cloth like Pakhi's that came down in an airplane.

Alas destiny, even cloth that came down in an airplane!

Now Shubashi looked at him askance and spoke with a smile—Hmm, I'll put on the cloth an' fly away.

Bonwari laughed. There's misery and there's laughter too. Now Shubashi came to him and embraced his neck. She giggled—Won't go alone, like a sprite I'll take ye with on me back.

At dawn Shubashi got him up with a shove. She needs her cloth before she can go and fill the offering's pitcher. But—what's this?

Thick dark clouds in the sky. Wind buffeting like a drunkard. Making noises like a wild boar. Oh, bad weather ahead—there'll be a downpour! End of Ashwin, ears at the head of every paddy stalk. If there's a storm! If top-heavy paddy stalks snap in the middle during a gust and lie flat in water, it'll be disaster. O Babathakur! If one of those disastrous Ashwin storms blows up, then, Babathakur, stand at once so your head touches sky, put your back to Bansbadi's bamboo edge, put your hands to hold the great banyan, fig, silk-cotton, rain trees. Smile a sweet smile and hearten the Kahars, say—No fear, I'm holding tree roots fast with my hand, let storm fly overhead, keep Kaharpara's human tribe safe, keep safe cow, calf, goat, sheep, duck, chicken, bug, worm; stand tall in the fields' gushing, sprout-filled paddy—wealth of the Kahars. O Babathakur! Not just Bonwari, all Kaharpara gazed at the coming storm and began to cry— "Plea" Babathakur! Which is to say, Please Babathakur!

Storm growing; instant rain. Treetops seeming to fling downward, bamboo flying upward in bamboo groves, Kopai waters rising in sheets, birds flung by wind blast sometimes falling into yard and terrace. He who always plays melodies in the heart of the earth can hear no sound on earth but the whining of the storm. Offering rite of offering rites; before rising from bed, sounds of drum, tom-tom, shanai, cymbal, gong, bell, horn; in their stead only noise—whining and roaring. Sometimes a groaning, crunching noise; then a gigantic crash. Trees breaking, falling.

O Babathakur!

Who seems to be screaming something in the middle of this? Who's saying what? What's happened to who? Shubashi dropped quickly down from the terrace. Bonwari was shrunk back in a corner thinking; he anxiously stood up—Don' get down, don' get down.

Shubashi said—That maniac. Else oo'd 'ave the guts?

—Oo?

—That one oo if I said 'is name ye'd get mad. Even in this tempest Shubashi drew her veil across her mouth and started to laugh. Bonwari came down from the terrace harsh, annoyed.

—Storm comin'. You-u-u-ge storm comin', "saikelone," "saikelone"— wire came from Calcutta ta Channanpur Station. No one go outdoors. Warnin'! Long tarpaulin clothes on his body, hat on his head, shouting and moving around: Karali.

Suchand screamed and wept—O Father, Kottababa!

Karali spoke through gritted teeth—Babathakur's boat's capsizin'. Wood-apple tree's uprooted, top's come down—lookit. Don' scream so. Get 'ome.

Bonwari was struck with terror.

Shubashi broke out giggling. Suchand's legs had been knocked from behind by stormblast and she had fallen over.

Bonwari gave her a smacking blow on the cheek. Then Shubashi began to laugh more. Bonwari rushed out into that storm toward Babathakur's shrine.

The wood-apple tree really was lying fallen again. Stonework half bursting open. Bonwari's whole body began to shudder and shake. Babathakur's tree finally uprooted! It's certain that Babathakur is here no longer; Hansuli Turn's God, the tale's godly legislator has gone away! Yet what of theirs remained? Bonwari couldn't stand upright any longer in the terrible storm; he sat down. Somehow he began to crawl toward the house.

In storm's midst Noyan's Ma forgot weeping for her son and wrapped her clothes around herself—in comfort of storm and rain—lazily gazing at the sky, she's speaking with great joy—Stronger, Father, stronger. Smash, crush, overturn, level it all. O Father!

Storm—storm—storm! Whining—howling! Terraces falling, trees falling, bamboo falling. In rain blasts all's a blur. Water torrent flowing with a smashing-crashing noise; Kopai welling up; indigo-levee's channel breaking; muddy water stretching desolate across all the fields of Hansuli Turn; now that elephant-strong, green-hued, seductive, eye-catching, intoxicating, field-filling paddy is going under water; here and there a green leaf floating up, like a hand stretching out to call for rescue before a drowning! But who will grasp her hand and pull Mother Lakshmi out? Babathakur gone, who'll pull out the Maiden Goddess?

Eight

Storm cataclysm ended on the third day. Yet the Kahars survived. Survive always. How often has there been famine, pestilence, flood, tempest; the Kahars have survived despite their dying. This time too a few died in the storm, a few were injured; Auntie Suchand broke her leg and is laid up in hospital—Karali took her to hospital. Noyan's Ma was critically ill. She somehow recovered. Bonwari gives her the odd handful of food. Homes gone, field-filling harvest laid waste, no paddy in the ears of the crop, just turned to husk; no kernels—husks, just husks, just husks left. Trees are broken-branched, shorn. Bamboo lying flat. Cows, calves, goats dead. Ducks washed away in the water torrent. After this, those who survived and remain are worrying—who'll save them? Babathakur's no more, who will protect them?

Bonwari is trying. He has stood the overturned tree straight again and rebuilt around the roots with fresh bricks and mortar. He also gave a great offering. Come back, Father, come back.

Meanwhile, worry about food is suddenly pressing forward. The fields' paddy has turned to husk; what's more, even cow and calf can't eat that husk. Price of paddy has gone from four to eight rupees—eighty pounds of husked rice is sixteen rupees. No one in the land of India has ever heard of such a thing, it is unthinkable to sages and wise men, it is not "writ" in scripture either. And war's eating up everything. Bosses are jumping for joy; they'll sell paddy and make money. They don't like to give the cultivators paddy. They only give reminders of dues—Be it husk, be it whatever, get paddy cut!

Bonwari understands their "yintenshuns," or intentions. If paddy is cut, straw will pile up in houses. Price of straw's going up steeply, just like that of paddy. It's being sold at forty rupees a bundle; it'll eventually rise to one, two hundred rupees. The bosses get straw at sixteen annas. The Kahars have only to come home with their share of husks. —Don'tcha eat husks in wartime? Roton, Prohlad ask this question. Bonwari has a little optimism. He'll get straw from the newly settled two and a half acres of land on the Saheb Tracts. He'll also get a bit of straw from the sharecropping land. The Saheb Tracts are fields of dry upland, not covered in water like the lower field flats; he'll get a little paddy there. Why, just a little, he'll do well. But what will the other Kahars do?

Roton questioned Bonwari as they cut paddy side by side on the land. Kartik month finishing then, Aghrayan beginning. This time, because of that rainstorm, it was getting pervasively cold there; streams of water still flowed in all the plots thereafter. Getting up to their ankles in water. Heads smarting, noses sniffling and dripping.

—What's gonna 'appen, tell me Bonwari? What we gonna eat?

Bonwari could not answer the question. Hamlet folk ask him this question every day. But what answer can Bonwari give? Everything has been messed up by the catastrophic storm of Ashwin.

Suddenly up ran that naked son of Prohlad's—Oi there, 'eadman, loadsa sahebs, so 'tis! Motor car, so 'tis!

—Loadsa sahebs?

—Yeah 'tis; Karali wi' 'em.

—Where, eh?

—At Jangol. Kalaruddu's shrine.

—Kalaruddu's shrine?

—Yeh. Puttin' up a tent at the place o' Kalaruddu's seat. There'll be an office.

—There'll be an office? O God!

—Goin' then? Beano? Roton asked.

—Course I'll go. Come on, let's see. What new wave has come in?

There is a great throng of people at Kalarudra's paved compound. Ten or twelve sahebs. These are not exactly Karali's *Man*. Karali is saluting them again and again.

Big Ghosh is also standing there; it's in his house the sahebs went to meet. Bonwari crept inside the house and asked Big Missus—What's up, ma'am?

—They're setting up a war office tent in Kalaruddu's shrine, little brother-in-law.

—War office tent in Kalaruddu's shrine?

—Not a war office. Contractor's tent, they'll buy bamboo, buy wood—

—Bamboo, wood? War needs bamboo an' wood?

Missus Maito said with a laugh—Little brother-in-law, warn your lovely second wife, eh. A creeper doesn't cling so hard to the tree when it's about to get cut down!

Bonwari was shaken. He left the house deeply anxious. He'll really warn Shubashi. War times! War times!

A few days later. As they cut paddy in the fields he was discussing the war with Roton and Prohlad.

A swarm of airplanes was flying overhead—looking that way, Bonwari was speaking. War breaks out in the world, has broken out how many times; there's rioting in cities, there's shouting and clamor, and it has nothing to do with Hansuli Turn. We hear a great earthquake's destroyed a city; nothing happens to the little cottages of Hansuli Turn. Like a little baby clinging to its mother's breast with two hands, they have miraculously survived the motion as the world rocked. War has now smashed Kalarudra's dominion and entered Bansbadi. Exerting its pull on every home. Karali brought it in. The gods are displeased with evil Karali's wrongs of karma. The gods' powers have a limit too. This time Father Kalaruddu will meet his end too. Kalaruddu's temple has been smashed; what's more, a war contractors' tent set up in his compound. A tarmac road is being built from Channapur to the edge of Bansbadi, motorcars will come. What else in store? War's coming to Hansuli Turn on a tarmac road in motorcars. Wood—bamboo—it wants everything! O God Hari! What won't war eat up? It eats up bamboo and wood? Word is that cows, goats, sheep, eggs, all this stuff will be consigned. And that there airbase next to Channapur, every day it needs herds of cows, goats, sheep, chickens, ducks; needs basket upon basket of eggs. Of course the Kahars will profit a bit from this. The price of goats, chickens, eggs has increased a lot recently, will increase more, a bit of money will come in. They never sell cows to the butcher, never will. Bonwari will not permit such a sale. But there's a doubt, will they be able to keep them? What'll happen?

Roton asks again—Bonwari?

Bonwari heaved a deep sigh and said—What ta say, Oton? Gonna tell me what Fate's decree is? What's writ will be.

—One thing I didn't say to ye, bro; three o' the lads have run off wi' their wives—. Larod, Nonda, an' yer Benka's gone.

—Ran off? Where?

—Oo knows, bro; took their stuff an' ran off at night's end. Yesterday evenin' they came an' were sayin'—Let Boss cut 'is own paddy, I'm neither cuttin' no paddy nor takin' no shares.

—Ow can they say that? That's a really unfair thing. It's me's responsible fer that.

—Unfair indeed. But what we s'posed ta say?

—Ya didn't forbid it?

—Forbid! Tell me oo's listenin' if we forbid? You forbade it yerself! Did they listen?

Bonwari became furious—They're not listenin'. Ooever don't listen can go off. But you lot, when ya knew this yesterday evenin', why din'tcha tell me?

—They all said they were goin' off, but 'ow were we ta know they were gonna go in the middle o' the night? Besides, it was late at night. Ye were lyin' down. Ye get mad if ye're called out at night.

There is a little salaciousness in these words. Bonwari gets mad if he is called out at night—behind these words is an intimation of the presence of adolescent Shubashi. But the words are half true. Bonwari's had a sharp eye on Shubashi since that day, and it's not a lie to say that he feels deeply for his adolescent wife; but there is more than this. He does not want to get up at night because of a terror of the ghostsouls of Kalobou and his first wife. If someone calls or there is a noise outside, he screams the question—Who? Who?

Bonwari angrily replied—When? When? When've I got mad, bastard? When?

Roton was astounded at the insult. Bonwari's insulted him?

Bonwari began to cut paddy; it scrunched. He had heard vaguely about this sort of thing, but had not understood so much before. If the topic of scarcity came up everyone was looking toward the tin roofs of Channanpur's workshops, toward Ma Kopai bridge construction, toward the arms of signals on rail-line poles, toward the red and blue lights visible at night; this he knows. But he did not think this kind of thing could happen. Humans can sell all and eat; no one can sell dharma and eat. Bonwari was worried, thinking on this very thing. He cannot understand how such a hidden fissure can become visible. The fissure has taken hold, collapse will follow. Karali! He must come to a final understanding with Karali. If so, Karali will stay; if not, Bonwari will remain at Hansuli Turn. Bonwari stood up and shook his head several times. Then he bent down again in silence and cut paddy; it scrunched.

Roton still remained standing. He was angry. Yesterday Roton's boss, Hedo Mondol, had given him a severe beating—had unfairly given him the beating. He had unfairly claimed that one of Roton's bamboo clumps was his own and Roton had protested this; that's why he'd given a beating. Roton can no longer take a beating with his mouth shut. There's also a lot of debt outstanding with boss. Roton won't get a share of paddy, and he won't be able to pay back the debt. He'll go to Channanpur. He said to Bonwari—Why'd ya insult me?

Bonwari stood up, loosened his waistcloth, and said—Did I insult you? I insulted yer deeds. An' why're you insultin' me? I said it once, you say thrice, bastard—bastard—bastard!

Bonwari stopped paddy cutting and prepared tobacco. He removed tobacco from a bamboo tube, a wisp of straw, a flintstone, and a piece of spongewood. Said—Come, sit. Smoke 'baccy.

They felt very relaxed sitting in the sun on the fieldpath, letting their wet feet dry. Roton said—Ah! Me body feels all right at last.

—Ere, smoke. Bonwari passed the hookah. Then he said—Good reason ta be angry, Oton! Lot 'appens in misery. "All eat if all is sold; none eats if dharma is sold." "If ye stay on path of dharma's right, ye'll have rice many a night." No one will understand in this Infernal Age—everythin's undharmic, unnerstan', everythin's for bad. Infernal Age is undharmic age.

Roton suddenly posed a metaphysical question—All right then, Jangol's mister Mondols are sayin' that it's end o' the Infernal Age—this time really the end?

Bonwari nodded and said—Maito Ghosh brought a book, a "warnin' me-sage."

—What sage?

—Warnin' me-sage. The sage said—Tis end o' the infernal this time!

—What'll 'appen? Everythin' endin' in downright chaos, jumble mix-up topsy-turvy shambles, skimble-skamble, or what?

—That could be. Jus' think, sky breakin' open wi' a crash smash—everythin'll be flattened, shattered.

In the tale of Hansuli Turn, the metaphysical narrative of this cataclysm is the oldest part—imaginings of an archaic era. And nothing would seem a more fitting event, of greater metaphysical significance for this, than today's ending Infernal Age. Roton had wanted to hear something just like this from Bonwari's mouth.

Bonwari said—All the omens can be seen. Is this not Hansuli Turn as Kartik month becomes Agrhayan? Are there any signs anywhere?

It's true. In Kartik-Agrhayan, in the tale of Hansuli Turn, the fields' color is golden hued. Cold, rustling breeze; spreading scent of ripe paddy. Krishna's Delight, Emperor's Delight, Golden Mountain, Vermilion Tip, Nayankalma—how various the paddy's scents! Each paddy its own fragrance, all mingled together they make one delicious perfume. Circling the breast of golden paddy-filled fields: glassy water, a flowing silver hansuli necklace—Kopai river's turn. On the banks, ripe kash grass stems and leaves make a golden-colored border. In every pond, wilting lotus flowers still have a little scent and have not yet completely shed their petals. In streams and ditches rivulets of water flow, shoals of little fish like slivers of silver stream along, seeking river. When autumn paddy is up, autumn fields are filled with green sprouts of spring crops. Trembling shoots of wheat, beans, potatoes, barley, mustard, flax, linseed are visible. Swaying in breeze, the tops of bamboo groves nod their heads in response. With a creaking—a tapping, sometimes sounding like a flute. Flocks of young birds fly and dance around in the sky. Cotton teals come flying in from the north, green parakeets come in flocks from the west; clamorous racket, as if the sky is a shrine compound on a festival day filled with madly dancing boys and girls. Flocks of birds come down at night and eat paddy; they fly into the sky in the day, perch on trees, circulate noisily. Sun scalds at midday; at night bodies tingle with cold.

Now fields are still full of water, winter has shiveringly descended. Sun has no strength. Birds came, but none staying; flock after flock is departing. No paddy, why would they stay? They come to the court of meadows' wealth, come like a group of boys to collect leftovers—there's no wealth, no leftovers, so they're leaving, weeping. Autumn's paddy fields are still waterlogged; if you step in your foot sticks, so there's not a trace of spring harvest; desolate fields are getting a reddish tinge. Bamboo groves—those ancient bamboo groves, will they sway now they've fallen flat? Ditches and drains still filled with gurgling, muddy water, pond lotuses torn up; that stormwater flooded ponds, making them putrefy and rot. Nothing you could call a reed. Everything finished off in storm and flood. Misery of miseries, voice thickens to speak of it, eyes fill with tears: field-filling paddy turning to straw, golden limbs stained with muddy water like a woman beggar smeared with dust and filth lying prostrate and motionless. Warning me-sage saying—End of the Infernal Age. Were these wise sage's words a lie? Omens can be seen.

Bonwari heaved a deep sigh and said—Oton, if it ain't gonna end, then why's Babathakur leavin'?

Roton gazed skyward. What and where's that sound!

Kaharpara's sky filling with a thumping drumbeat sound.

Roton and Bonwari were both shocked. A drum is beating, rhythmic thumping. What's up? It seems a drum is pounding in Kaharpara itself! Not seems—there's no mistake it's right in Kaharpara. What drum? They rushed toward the village.

The great gentry of Channanpur are sounding the drum.

The people who dug Saheb Tracts land must now cut paddy and bring it to the gentry's granaries. The gentry will not take rent, they will take a share of paddy. This does not include those who are using land on a tribute-payment basis. That means Jangol's Sadgop masters, who had paid tribute and taken land on fresh contracts. It does include Bonwari and the Atpoures.

Roton listened and said—Drum! Say, what a botheration, dear me! He was shocked. Still, has nothing to do with the land on the Saheb Tracts. That's why the thing's gravity was nothing to him. But the land his boss Hedo Mondol has taken is freshly settled. Therefore this is a waste of time for him. He went straight back to the fields. But Bonwari sat on the terrace of his own house with his head in his hands. No strength left in his legs.

Such desirable land in the Saheb Tracts. The gentry do not know the toil, the loving labor of the hamlet's folk with which he's preparing this ground; he knows, Babathakur knew; God Hari knows. A couple of handfuls are growing there because they're upland fields. That's where all Bonwari's hopes are now!

The gentry's command came down like a cloudless thunderclap. He sat silently for a long time. Then he rose. Where, where's Shubashi gotten to? She caused that quarrel—her nature's like a dancing girl's. Seems to fly fluttering around twenty-four hours a day, like a grasshopper or butterfly. As much as Bonwari likes this, it makes him equally fiercely suspicious. Suspicious about Karali. He knows—he knows—Karali wants to destroy Bonwari's prestige, his honor. Dharma-destroying Karali. He has no faith in him—no faith. He's slowly coming to believe that Karali was born just to annihilate him. He was born to destroy Hansuli Turn.

The lad is as fashionable as he is young and strong. Bonwari does not permit Shubashi to tread the road to Channanpur, but Karali comes at evening. He keeps Shubashi there before his eyes yet has suspicions. When Karali comes and maddens the hamlet with laughter and causes uproar, Shubashi jumps up startled. Just that's enough of a sign for Bonwari. Bonwari was unable to stop these visits of Karali's to Kaharpara— that remained a great irritation in his life. It's his loss—his defeat.

He stubbornly comes back every evening. Stays a few hours, whispers tempting phrases into the ears of boys and youths, departs in uproar; some people have seen him coming in daytime too, now and then. Saying, I've come on military work. O God, so many folk died by storm, Karali didn't die!

But where has Shubashi gone? Old Romon was smoking tobacco, bubbling away; he said—Oo knows?

Oldie's smoking away; he's fine. Won't do any work. What's more, he's pilfering things. It's clearly visible, a fistful of paddy heads under his torn clothes.

At this time he saw Shubashi emerging from among fallen bamboo groves near the river, a pitcher at her hip, head veil off, a bunch of flowers stuck in her hair bun. Milkwood flowers.

Bonwari's every limb began to burn. This really is not a good sign.

As soon as Shubashi got to the cottage he pulled out the bunch of flowers and tossed it away. He punched her full in the back twice and said—Put flowers in! I'll kill ya one day. Give, gimme some rice puffs.

Shubashi is an astounding girl. Even after a beating she starts to laugh. She said—Me lover gave me 'em, you'll chuck away the buncha flowers?

—Looka this? Again? I'll gi' ya a thrashin'.

—Me body's hurtin'. If ye thrash I'll be comfortable.

—Ye'll be slain by my 'and one o' these days.

Shubashi said—I'll put poison in yer food an' kill ya before then. Even as she said this Shubashi began to laugh.

Terrified, Bonwari stopped chewing the mouthful of puffed rice. Now Shubashi began to snigger loudly—No poison in the rice puffs. Eat up. Then she said—Ye're sure a bit of a mad 'un. People call ya 'eadman! Damn! So saying, she picked up the bunch of milkwood flowers and put it back in her hair.

Without saying another word Bonwari finished eating and set out for Channanpur. He knows nothing will happen; return to the magistrate, but the order won't be revoked. Yet he went. Just let the gentry leave off for this year. He'll give shares from the coming year.

He moved with bent shoulders and heavy feet.

A little way beyond Jangol he could hear—a rumbling sound in Channanpur. There was no such sound before. Since the coming of the rail line Channanpur's din has increased. Now what a terrible scene! A second line being laid down! Noise rising from the airplane base—rising. Ah, that droning whine, like when you throw a rock into a large hornets' nest! Sometimes a rail engine's steam hissing—earsplitting screeching whistles blasting.

He suddenly stopped in surprise. A few freshly broken-off leaves fallen on the fieldpath; he stared at them. Milkwood leaves. Seems there are a few more behind—one or two milkwood leaves thrown aside. Many have fallen here. It's not something to stop you still with amazement. But Bonwari recalled the milkwood flowers in Shubashi's hair. Right then he remembered, there's a milkwood tree on Mother Kopai's banks. Not in Jangol. And where else? Where? He couldn't think. Therefore someone else was beneath the milkwood tree with Shubashi. Either someone picked the milkwood flowers, gave one stem to Shubashi, kept another for themselves and came this way; or it's Shubashi who picked the flowers, put one into her hair bun, and put the other stalk into the hands of whoever it was walked this way.

Kosh-Shoulder Bonwari began to walk in the Kahar's "stride." If he's no weight on his shoulders he doesn't exactly begin to trot, but he strode anxiously.

He did not see anyone the whole way. Many people at Channanpur Station. He looked all around there and didn't find any clue; with a troubled mind he set off toward the gentry's offices. He suddenly stopped. Gravel road. He picked up several gravel stones and counted as he went along. If their number is uneven then the milkwood leaves he found on the way have nothing to do with the milkwood flowers in Shubashi's hair—if it's even then they do. One two three, seven eight nine—uneven. A bit farther on he stopped again when he saw a large rock by the side of the road. He threw one of the stones in his hand. If it hits that rock Shubashi isn't guilty. If it doesn't hit the rock she's certainly guilty. Direct hit. He threw again. Another hit. He threw again. And again and again— three times. If it hits this time Bonwari will not have any more suspicions. This time it did not hit. Yet it fell very near the rock. Bonwari approached and leaned over to see. No, it did hit. Not a direct strike, but it hit with a soft glance. That's it, Bonwari has no more suspicions. Shubashi picked the milkwood flowers for her own pleasure and wore them in her hair; some other person picked them up and took them away for their own pleasure. Suddenly yet another test occurred to him. He decided that if Gentry Master releases paddy to him now then Shubashi is definitely not guilty: if there is no dharma at home then Lakshmi's wealth comes not. If Lakshmi's wealth appears then there is of course dharma. And if not, then it's true; what Bonwari's thinking is true.

***

Bonwari was untroubled. Ah! Bonwari made it.

This time Gentry Master released paddy to Bonwari; and not just to Bonwari—as a result of Bonwari's audience he released it to everyone, including the Atpoures. But from next time there is a condition attached to sharecropping. They wrote a deed of agreement on legal paper and took his thumbprint.

In the tale of Hansuli Turn—there are no documents, no deeds, no registries, no time-limited repayments. Business being done by word of mouth since ancient times; giving and taking of money, buying and selling, are done with five witnesses. If there's a dispute you have to go to Lord's shrine, put your hand on the wood-apple tree root, and swear an oath. But the gentry masters have documents and deeds, they have ledgers, their business is not the tale's business; year, month, date, signatory's name, father's name, occupation, place of residence, reason for sale, rights, conditions, every single boundary must be described in writing—even physical condition, state of health, all must be revealed and be placed in that document.

Bonwari came away wiping off the black ink's head of hair from his thumb. Victory to Lord Hari, victory to God Dharma! Bonwari's wealth and dignity have been saved, Father. His is wealth of great hope. What's more, he has no more suspicions that Shubashi has committed a wrong. No suspicions at all. He thought that tomorrow he would see new leaf shoots on Babathakur's wood-apple tree. Babathakur will return. When he came out of the offices he saw it was getting late. Because of his arrival time. By the time he'd arrived at the offices, after eating, and counting and throwing stones on the way, it was already past twelve. Sitting in the offices till after three; during that time Bonwari lay down a while, sat a while, conducted a few more tests concerning the milkwood flowers. He came out from the audience with Gentry Master feeling pleased that the work was done, saw that it was getting late, and headed for the liquor store.

The Saha Masters' store is outside the village by a pond. The smell of fermenting liquor is intoxicating. The gentry cover their noses, but in the tale of Hansuli Turn this is the smell of life's mad ecstasy—if it goes in your nose, you start to salivate and you just need to drink. All are sitting in their groups. Channanpur's Jeles in little groups with their roasted fish. Santals have come with iguanas, mice, birds they've killed and are roasting them over a fire. Buyers for tanners purchasing the iguana skins. All around voices yelling, shouting. You see the prices in the war market and you'd think to strip off the skin from your own limbs and sell it. Many of them are drunk, songs are being sung—arguments are being had; sometimes a scrappy "shindy," that's to say a fight, breaks out. The folk of Hansuli Turn used to form their own group here too. Their spot is isolated and lonely. No money, what'll the folk of Hansuli Turn drink with? O Lord Hari! Bonwari heaved a deep sigh and sat. How great the might of Hansuli Turn's Kahars here! The number of times they have fought with other groups and returned home. Today there was no desire to sit in this place. He bought a pitcher of liquor and went back. He'll drink on the way. Won't take it home. He's headman of Kaharpara, which way could he get in there with a pitcher of liquor? Could he sit at home in the corner and drink alone without giving to anyone else? And then what if Shubashi wanted a swig? He'll drink on the way.

As he moved along the road he stopped now and again and took a drink. Finally, seeing a familiar bushy tree beside the road in the midst of the great uplands, he went to drink a little beneath it. He remembered how many scenes he'd enacted under this tree! When Kaloshoshi was a servant in the Channanpur gentry houses, this was their meeting place. The number of times they'd come here to share out earnings from a palanquin-carrying job. In the olden days the Kahars used to gather here under this tree before going out to steal. The final scene—this was the very site of his battle with Porom.

Ah, where did all those days go! When Babathakur went, everything went. The leaf-shedding wood-apple tree of Babathakur's shrine drifted before his eyes. If he repairs the shrine, what'll happen? The tree's drying out by the day. Just a little earlier he'd hoped that when wealth comes, there too is dharma; and in a time of dharma Babathakur will likely return. Tomorrow he'll surely see shoots like green needle tips. But as he drinks liquor he's thinking—No, no, never again. That undharmic luster glistening in Channanpur!

He took another swig of liquor. Drink's nearly finished, just a bit left. Two swigs, he was going to slurp it up when he let the pitcher fall from his mouth. He began to think, should he save a swig for Shubashi? Hmm. Shubashi's not alone, her old Uncle Omon is there. Noyan's Ma is there. Old Omon's endless tall tales. Work on work—cow grazing. The old man stole again today. He pilfers Bonwari's paddy seed and trades it at the store for eggplant fries to eat. Noyan's Ma is turning into an even bigger thief than him. Going into peoples' houses to steal from kitchens, eating up vegetable stew and coming away. These two will die in the coming winter. Bonwari's responsibility. Alas, headman! Auntie Suchand will surely go too. She's now in hospital. They've kept her in to put a cast on her leg, but does the leg need a cast? They'll cut her, but cutting will kill her. He told her this—To good folk beatification; to bad folk annihilation. Bastard Karali—wicked one, she'll fall under his influence, finally have the operation on her leg, take English medicines, and die. Bonwari pleaded—Don't go down that road!

Whose voices suddenly in his ears?

Who? Which ones? Now which ones started an argument in this empty field at night? A woman's voice, a man's voice. "Play of 'eat." Bonwari smiled. The woman's getting angry, getting in a sulk. Who? Whose voice? Bonwari stood straight. Pakhi's voice. Pakhi's saying—No no no. All yer sayin's lies. All lies. I understand everythin'.

—What, whatcha understand? Karali's speaking. They are returning from Kaharpara as they do every day after the evening gathering is over.

—I saw milkwood flowers in Shubashi's 'air.

—There's milkwood flowers on the Kopai banks, it's fallen.

—Fallen? Oo gave 'em? Ya left 'cos ya "got work" in the mornin'. Came back at midday wi' milkwood flowers. I got spicious then, ye'd definitely been ta Kaharpara. Said ta me—Brought 'em from riverbank near the bridge. But ya di'n't go ta bridge banks—riverbank work gang lads told me. So then where'd ya get the milkwood flowers? Why'd Shubashi laugh when she saw milkwood flowers in me 'air; why'd she say—Oo gave ya milkwood flowers then? Why'd she say that? Why're there milkwood flowers fallen in Shubashi's yard? Oo gave 'em to 'er? I don't understand nothin', eh?

—Ye've understood, understood. Ye know, in the month o' Poush a mouse marries ten times. Now all the twelve months are Poush fer me. I'm work gang leader. I'll take Shubashi an' tie the knot with 'er; ye'll live with that or get out.

Pakhi screamed—Whatcha say?

Just then it seemed as if the dark tree base howled. You'd think some terrifying tigerlike animal was screaming its way out from darkness. Karali and Pakhi were fearstruck at the scream. Frightened, sleeping birds began flapping out of the dark tree. Bats flew off with whistling sounds. Despite his shock, Karali turned around in a flash and stood firm; he called out—Who?

Howling and roaring like an animal, Bonwari leaped out and stood before him. Sky's spinning, earth's shaking, tongues of flame shooting out from Bonwari's head to his feet, his fingers like iron rods, nails like javelin tips! Gnashing his teeth with a crunching sound. He leaped and gripped Karali's neck in a flash—tear it out, he'll tear it out. Eyes burning. A whine coming from his throat. A raging howl.

Karali felt as if consciousness had disappeared before his eyes. But he must live. Not just live, he must get repayment for so many days of disgrace; Kaharpara's headmanship must be annihilated. The anger he'd suppressed for so long burst into flame. He won't take any more. He punched Bonwari in the belly. Now Bonwari had to release Karali's neck.

For a few moments the two stood frozen, staring at each other. Bonwari in severe pain. Karali too in unbearable pain. They're both overcoming their pain. Then they charged each other like wild boars. Bonwari charged first, Karali immediately after. They locked together in pitiless attack like two warrior monkeys and fell to earth, drowned in that darkness beneath the tree. Tear, bite, punch, beat, smash. Though war began one day in the shadows of Hansuli Turn's bamboo groves, it's not over. Today Bonwari won't quit until it's over. The darkness of Hansuli Turn's bamboo groves floods skyways, covers that tree's bushy leaves and branches, flowing downward each moment, thickening and deepening around the two men. Sound of savage beating, hateful howling, soft cries of pain are all that can be heard. Pakhi standing there like a clay figurine. She cannot budge, she cannot scream. Bats circling overhead. This way, that way, clicking, tapping, tocking—various reptiles calling. But Pakhi can't hear anything, see anything, understand anything of what's happening!

Who knows how long! Yet long later a figure stood up in darkness. It stood under the tree and began cautiously to wobble forward. Another one was lying unconscious.

At last Pakhi moaned an inarticulate moan.

Who won and arose, who? Bonwari—headman of Hansuli Turn, son of the Kosh-Shoulders? It's probably him. So Pakhi will find no escape today. She's Karali's darling. Bonwari will never let her off the hook, not today, right now. Dharma, society, he won't follow any strictures. She doesn't have strength to flee; her legs are shaking. Yet she desperately gathered her strength and spoke up—I fall at yer feet, on Babathakur's glory—

Ha ha ha ha laughed Karali. —Babathakur, phony!

—You! Pakhi was astounded.

—Yeh. So saying, Karali turned back and planted a kick on Bonwari's head. Then he returned and said—'S go!

Pakhi was startled when she put her hands to his body. —That blood?

—Yeh.

Blood dripping from every limb. The scarred and injured victorious hero staggered off.

***

The other one got back up. Much later.

In starvation, violence, famine, pestilence, storm, flood, the Kahars of Hansuli Turn do not die easily. They spend their whole lives half starved. In famine—though they eat leftovers, scraps, bad food, inedible food, yet they survive; they smash their heads in riots, chop bits off feet with spade blows, fall on their backs from broken tree branches. They're laid up in bed, suffer for weeks, apply herbal remedies to their bellies—recover oh so slowly; a limb might end up crippled, but life is not easily lost. Bonwari got up too.

Kaharpara's finest man, Kosh-Shoulder Bonwari, staggered to Babathakur's abandoned shrine and rolled on the ground sobbing. Beat his chest like a wounded forest monkey.

He wasn't sure of the time of night. But it's waning fortnight, moon up in the sky—half moon, coming up for a quarter way through the sky. Half sitting half standing, Bonwari staggered along. He entered Lord's shrine. Lord's rebuilt shrine is shining bright by moonlight. Bonwari began to tap his head on that plinth. Tears flooded his chest; ah-ah-ah-ah! His breast is splitting.

He suddenly raised his head in alarm. There is some jackal-like thing standing right before him. Just as the jackal yawned, a burst of flame flashed in its mouth. Again it flashed. Flash-flash-flash. Flashing on and off! Flames began to burn just like that in Bonwari's head. He got up. The jackal immediately fled. That's not a jackal. No way. Babathakur has sent an emissary. It's shown the way by lighting its flashing fire; he has received sign, Babathakur's decree. He must silently get his flint tube, it's hanging right outside on the wall. Then he must ascend Karali's brick house. No one stays in the unrepaired upper part of the house; Nasubala stays downstairs. Go upstairs and set fire to the strands of straw—. The brick house will burn—it'll even be visible from Channanpur. Babathakur's decree.

As he approached the house he came to a surprised halt. Who? Which ones?

—Hmm hmm hmm.

—Uh-huh. Yeh. Yeh.

Who is talking softly beneath that rain tree—at the edge of the bamboo groves? Who? Which ones? Who are they? Behind his house at the edge of the bamboo groves? Hmm. He beat him and came for Shubashi. Of course he'd come.

Bonwari moved forward cautiously. He grabbed a rock. It would have been better if it were an iron weapon. But he has neither patience nor leisure for that. It'll be this rock—a rock's enough. Karali himself had picked it up beside the rail bridge and given it to him a long time back. That same rock. Many tales of heads being bashed in with rocks in the bamboo groves of Hansuli Turn. Suchand says—Well, Bonwari's dad's dad's dad an' my dad's dad were the same man! So it's me granddad. That granddad saw me first grandma—that means 'is first wife—goin' out ta meet wi' one o' the Atpoures; 'e took the pestle off the grindin' stone an' bashed 'er 'ead in wi' it. Sat on 'er chest, an' wi' the pestle—

Not just wife Shubashi's head—he must bash in not one but two. He'll bash Karali's head in too. Karali's first. Then Shubashi. Despite half moon in the sky, shadows of ancient banyan, fig, and rain tree leaves mix with bamboo groves shade so it seems like new moon darkness. Ancient darkness of Hansuli Turn sitting here silent and eerie since ancient times. No waxing-moon fortnight here. No full moon. Forever new moon here. Darkness. Bonwari moved forward in that darkness, pestle in hand. Under the rain tree nearby stood a—where? Where? He can hear a very soft humming sound of speech. At one moment, in the depth of agitated Bonwari's alcoholic mania, it seemed as if two shadow figures came out clearly before his half-closed eyes. He clearly saw. Bonwari's chest leaped. There—there, Karali and Shubashi moving. He moved right after them. There, moving. There they're moving—there. By this time a Stone Age intensity, credence, passion were lodging themselves deep in his consciousness. Right before his disturbed gaze, two figures of his wounded and heart-stricken imagination clearly moving on ahead. Moving, let them move; how far will they go? Bamboo groves came to an end. Now he paused. Where are they, where? Suddenly two large birds flapped out of a thicket with a humming sound, ascending with outstretched wings right before his deluded gaze. He was shocked. To him it was just as if the figures had in an instant floated off into the pure lightless transparency of the lunar heavens. Slowly rising upward, they flew across to the other bank of the Kopai—settled on a branch of that silk-cotton tree above the deeps.

Bonwari began to tremble violently. Floated off into nothingness. So—so it's not Karali and Shubashi then! Who? Who are they?

These two are nocturnal birds. In these parts they are called humhum birds. They perch at night face to face and make sounds, *Hmm-hmm-hmm-hum uh-huh hmm*, as if they are talking to each other. Bonwari knows this. But today Bonwari's mind has spread its wings into the waxing-moon sky—he's roaming beneath that sky in the world of a primal age. So when the two birds flew off and perched in the silk-cotton tree, another imagining immediately played in his brain like a flash of lightning. The tale of Hansuli Turn's imagining. Kopai's sandbanks right ahead gleaming white in moonlight. You can see clearly—there's no one anywhere. But he clearly saw two figures in the darkness. Clearly heard their conversation. Yet now no one's there. The two black figures became spectral, unbodied, and flew away. They stretched their mysterious wings and perched on the branches of that silk-cotton tree. Kaloshoshi drowned in those deeps. Gopali was cremated right over there—Yet who, who are they? Yet, what—?

Bonwari began to shake again. Kaloshoshi? Gopalibala? Have those two come to fetch him today? Are they showing him those burning grounds beneath the silk-cotton tree? In his terror his blindly credulous mind recalled the two amulets of Ma Kali and Babathakur tied to his arms. He clutched his right elbow to his chest. Instant shock. Where, where's the amulet? Not there! Not there! The amulet had been torn away during the struggle with Karali. What'll happen? Who'll protect him now? No Babathakur. The banyan tree has dried up. Who will he call on? Babathakur has ascended to the sky, mounted his great snake-familiar, and departed. Who'll save him? Before helpless Bonwari's eyes, Gopali and Kaloshoshi sit on a branch and talk—*Hum—hum—hum—*

Hmm—hmm—hum—ha—ha—ha—! Now one of the birds called out loudly. Bonwari collapsed on the spot with an agonized cry. Lost consciousness. There beyond bamboo groves, in huts of Hansuli Turn, Kahars are having nightmares in their sleep. Here, on the last night between fall and winter, an autumn mist is rising on Kopai's breast like a light white cloud; on sandbanks a mist rising likewise from great rain-soaked piles of earth and rotting leaf debris left by the cyclone; clouds of mist, clouds sheltering thickets. Just such a blanket of mist slowly rose around the great body of Hansuli Turn's hero, Kosh-Shoulder Bonwari.

Final Part

A long sixty days, that's to say two months, later.

Strange sounds coming from all corners of Hansuli Turn, from Kopai river's every bend. *Khot-khot-khot-khot*. That sound running through the river's womb; running through, striking yonder turn, coming back this way. All at once tranquil Hansuli Turn is becoming noisy.

Today Bonwari got up from his sickbed. He was sixty days laid sick; unconscious for fifty of those days. He somehow managed to get up today with merely this skin-covered, big-boned frame.

Sixty days before, the Kahars had brought him home from the Kopai's edge fevered and unconscious. No one knows the reason. Bonwari was in no state to say anything. And in his delirium he just screamed—Babathakur, puttekt us. And he screamed—That's Kaloshoshi, that's Gopali! Ah—ah—o no, but I can't fly!

Treatment! That nontreatment. Medicines from Jangol's Sadgop healer. For five of those sixty days the healer shook his head and said—Won't make it through the night, son.

Yet Bonwari survived and arose. Kahar headman's life is made up of strong life-forces accumulated among Hansuli Turn's bamboo groves; he came through because it does not end so easily; so he survived. Yet perhaps it would have been better if he had died and not survived. This is what Bonwari himself said today.

The tale of Hansuli Turn is coming to an end. And what's the point of his living on? Why was I saved?—He said this again and again, shaking his head in profound disappointment. Tears poured from his eyes onto Hansuli Turn earth's breast.

Bonwari spoke this truthfully.

The tale of Hansuli Turn was probably ended. It cannot of course be said if it's going forever; but it's correct to say that it is either over or imminently ending.

As fruit of wrong, God went away. Babathakur has gone, war's office is being set up in Kalarudra's temple. Kalarudra is leaving too. War—times of war!

Bonwari spoke. He pronounced his words in a soft voice with deep sadness; tears flowed from his eyes as he spoke. He said—When war broke out it finished off Hansuli Turn. He shook his head disappointedly.

Shaking his head with a heartfelt spasm of grief, it seemed as if he wanted to scatter tears over all Hansuli Turn.

On day fifty, the fever lifted, and some days after that he was regaining a little consciousness. But all his senses were extremely weak. Even if he opened his eyes to see, it seemed he could comprehend nothing. In a while his eyelids would go down as if under some weight and he would fall asleep. Bit by bit, day by day, his consciousness became clearer.

His bed—a piece of torn rag for a bed—beside that bed waited Nasubala. Oh yes, Nasubala. From the first day Bonwari regains consciousness it's only him he sees. Nasubala with shaven face, dirty torn sari worn with feminine air, hair tied in a bun, bangles, iron and conch bracelets; Nasubala staying by his bed day in day out. He cannot see Shubashi. For the first few days the question didn't come to mind, he only wonders why none of his intimates is coming. There's one more person he sometimes vaguely recognizes—Pagol. Pagol? Buddy?

As soon as he tried to open his eyes that first day, Nasubala bent down close to his face and asked—Comin' round? Can ya recognize me?

—No. Bonwari had shaken his head. Then Pagol had come and sat beside him. Beano! After speaking, he'd taken Bonwari's hand into his own with extreme tenderness. And yet Bonwari could not recognize him either.

On the second day he had recognized Pagol. Seeing Nasubala, he'd asked—Shubashi? Nasu had sighed deeply, turned his head, and gone out.

On the third day he'd recognized Nasu and said—Nasubala?

Nasu had given a big grin and said—Can ya recognize me? Phew, whatta relief! I was dyin' o' worry. Ah, dear brave soldier-man!

Bonwari then looked this way and that, and not seeing her, he'd asked—Where is she?

Hearing this, Pagol had got up and left. Nasu had asked—Oo?

—Shubashi!

—She's around. Comin'. Stroking Bonwari's head with his hand, Nasubala had said—Gone off somewheres. She'll come.

But Shubashi did not come. Gone all day—yet she did not come. Now Bonwari could understand. He did not ask again. He knows how Kaharpara's tales develop. He merely wept a little. Nasu said—Don't cry. He wiped away the tears and put some water to his mouth, saying—Drink a droppa water. Then he cut a rhyme—"Krishna may your flute live long, plenty maids where Radha came from." I'll smack 'er face wi' a broom.

Bonwari didn't ask any more questions. He was remembering everything; in ten days his sense and power of deduction had come back to life. He can imagine where Shubashi is. He lay silently and just pondered—many old personal things. He'd never have thought he would be in the condition he's now in, or that this would happen. These days he has no one except Nasu. Had Babathakur in his benevolence formed Nasu with woman's nature for these very days? As he was creating, had he said—When I set off, leaving Hansuli Turn, Bonwari will be reduced to the level of a wisp of straw; I created you to take on this load at that time?

Khot-khot-khot-khot! Khotang, khotang, khotang! Noises going and coming back. Today he thought—What kind of sound is that, *khot-khot-khot-khot*? He's perhaps been hearing this sound since he became conscious, but it wasn't very clear then, he hadn't really heard it; hadn't really paid attention. His mind just seeking olden things this while. Today he has found the olden things. He's remembered everything. Today he's also able to hear. The noise seems to have become very clear to him today. Today he's seeming to hear clearly. Unrelenting noises rising. Sounding like someone's hitting wood with a hammer or something in silent and desolate fields—*khot-khot-khot-khot*!

The sound circling around from Kopai turn—*khot-khot-khot-khot khotang, khotang, khotang*! From morning until night—*khotang, khotang, khotang*!

He lay alone in his room. As he was hearing the sound a question arose in his mind.

He called—Nasu! Pagol!

No one answered. He slowly closed his eyes.

Strange kind of thing! No sound of human voices anywhere, no one shouting at anyone, calling anyone; no one weeping, no one laughing, no one arguing; no cows calling calves, no calves calling mothers. Have the young lads forgotten song?

Just noises rising—*khot-khot-khot-khot—khotang, khotang, khotang—*

Not just *khot-khot—khotang, khotang. Vroom-vroom vroom-vroom.* Probably airplanes flying around. Bonwari fell asleep as he listened. The next day he became aware of the outside world. He said—Will ye open the door nice an' wide? I'll see precious day now, up an' see. Then he asked—Traincar just goin' over the bridge, right? Shortly afterward that noise started up again—*khot-khot-khot-khot—khotang, khotang*! He frowned, looked into Nasu's face, and asked—What, Nasu? Sound?

—Cuttin' bamboo.

Cutting bamboo? Every single day from morning till night cutting bamboo? That's it. Master Ghoshes of Jangol are the owners, it's time to thatch buildings. That's it.

Soon afterward he fell asleep.

At dinnertime Nasu called to him—Eat a bitta sago.

Sound's rising—*khotang-khotang*!

He heaved a deep sigh. He started thinking of Shubashi, of his own state, of his terrible defeat at Karali's hands that day. Heavy tears began to fall from his eyes. He lay motionless on the bed so as to hide this.

In the morning Pagol called—Up, bro; say somethin'.

He took hold of Bonwari himself and sat him up. Now in his ears—*khotang-khotang-khotang-khotang*! Sound flying from this side of Hansuli Turn to that, from that side to this.

The next day the sound again began to rise. *Khot-khot-khotang*—

Today he asked in amazement—Still cuttin' bamboo today, Nasubala? Oo's cuttin' so much bamboo? Ripped out all the bamboos!

Pagol said—War contractors bought up all the bamboo, bro; Jangol's Sadgops sold it. Two stems a rupee. It's them's cutting bamboo.

Two stems a rupee? Eight stems-a-rupee bamboo being sold for two stems a rupee? War contractors cutting all the bamboo? O God! What's happened? Has the place caught fire? But why?

Pagol turned his face skyward and said—Terrible war's broke out in the world, there was never such war in the land of India. Japanese really makin' war. Droppin' bombs on Calcutta, smashin' it flat. Folk from there fleein' like dogs an' cats. Rent on a Channanpur shack is twenty rupees! Ten, twelve Calcutta folk oo couldn't find a place in Channanpur are rentin' Sadgop 'ouses in Jangol. Eighty pounds o' rice forty rupees; eighty pounds o' paddy twenty-four rupees. An then there'll be more folks fleein' 'ere from other places. I 'eard they're gonna go along the tarmac road next ta Channanpur rail line. Gonna go through Katoya and Dumka on the way ta the west country. They'll stay in Channanpur on the way; rest two days, bamboo huts bein' set up for that.

With a deep sigh, Pagol now said—It was 'im, bro, 'im oo put them on the trail—Bansbadi's bamboo, Hansuli Turn's wood. That Karali! Wrecker Karali!

Yes.

—Yes, 'ed do that. This is 'is dharma. Some 'e builds up, some 'e smashes. Now he heaved a deep sigh and said—So Channanpur's really jumpin'!

—Really.

Gesticulating with arms and legs, Nasubala spoke—S'a kinda giant village, ye know! Could fit nine, ten Kaharparas in it! My, my, my, what sights an' scenes! Settin' up a rope well for the place, doctor movin' in, forty thousand pounds o' pressed rice in storage, barrels an' barrels o' molasses. Cuttin' bamboo ta make sheds for all this. An' then northward where rail line's laid, where airplane base is, they'll need bamboo for all what's goin' on there. Order's come from government—bamboo's gotta be got, pay whatever price. Cuttin' down great big trees ta get wood fer cookin'.

Bonwari began to ponder in speechless amazement. He could not understand. This has never happened in the tale of Hansuli Turn. Floods, storms have come, fires in the village, plagues, even earthquakes—all that is in the tale of Hansuli Turn. There are riots, robberies, there are ghost-souls of Kaloubou and First Wife, but no war. That war has broken Hansuli Turn's slumber, cut into the tale; magnetized by the pull of the world's lifestream, the lifestream of this time's people mixes with history's course; that war is not in the tale's imagining. Babathukur never spoke of it, never showed it in a dream. Kalaruddu never made it known either. How would Kahars know? Not a bit of this entered the brain of vast-bodied Bonwari, dull-brained human of Hansuli Turn, he who goes with bent shoulders and great powerful thudding strides.

The next day the sound began to rise again. Bonwari said—Will ya take me outside now, Nasu?

—Ye'll go out?

—Yeh. I'll take a look at Birth Mother.

—Birth Mother?

—Oh yeh. I'll take a look at my Hansuli Turn Bansbadi Birth Mother, what state's she in? Ahh-haa! His chest cracked, releasing anguish.

—Able ta go?

—Look, 'course I can. He sat up on his own. Stood up. Big bones, stiff from lying down for so long, crackled as he got up.

Desolation all around, desolation. The bamboo groves of Hansuli Turn's Bansbadi have been uprooted. Not just bamboo groves, even the giant banyan and peepul are no more. Fierce light struck his eyes as soon as he stepped outside. Not a trace of green in the lap of the sky. Here and there just three or four thin, leafless rain trees, paper trees, wood-apples remaining. No shade anywhere, glare hits the eyes, harsh spring sunlight on all sides. All around you can see the perimeter of Hansuli Turn, right up to the river's edge. Across the river you can see villages and beyond.

Road gone off through some other place. As if no trace remains of that Hansuli Turn. You used to enter the village and be struck by a strange, hypnotic depth in entrancing shadows. Moving through shadows, it would be pleasing to pause in surprise, think your thoughts. All this destroyed by wiping out the deep shade of bamboo groves, banyan, and peepul. There would be no more free time for droopy-eyed slumbering under trees; there was no place remaining to linger in shade and compose the tale of Hansuli Turn's dreams.

He looked around toward Babathakur's shrine. Babathakur's shrine; and in its center was that banyan tree of Atpoure Para under which Kaloshoshi had blown out the lamp, under which he'd seen Shubashi and confused her with Kaloshoshi. Where's that tree? Which way is Babathakur's shrine? What place is that? What are all these motorcars? Whose? Have the Channanpur workshops expanded? So many droning cars. What a disgusting stink of smoke! Even here it's getting up Bonwari's nose.

Helpless and stricken, he turned to Pagol—Pagol, I don't reconnize any o' this, bro. Where's Babathakur's shrine gone? What place is that? All these cars? Pagol?

—That's it, bro! Babathakur's shrine ain't no more. It's where war's motorcars are gathered.

No trace of Babathakur's shrine. No wood-apple tree, no monkey-stick tree, no clumps of jujube trees, no creepers, no border of palm trees. An area spread with red gravel glistening inside an enclosure of white-painted brickwork. Whining motorcars coming and going.

Pagol said—They leveled out Father's shrine, makin' it a motorcar lot, Bonwari-bro. End o' the Infernal Age, end of us too. Bamboo, wood loaded up an' taken from there ta Channanpur. Makin' a tarmac road from Channanpur ta Hansuli Turn. Left nothin' behind.

There's that road. Wide regal tarmac road. Covered in red gravel, running straight from Hansuli Turn through Jangol to Channanpur; road straight as an arrow. Road tying a conjugal knot between Channanpur and Hansuli Turn. Cutting through paddy plots, filling in canals, blocking ditches, raising gangways. Cars come and go on this road with a vrooming roar.

Pagol said—Road's goin' all the way ta Kopai bankside. Next it'll cross the river an' go up the other side. They'll likely cut all the other side's trees.

Bonwari now groaned in anguish—Why did ya save me, Pagol? Hey, Nasubala, ya saved me ta show me this? O misery, why'd I live?

His vision became clouded with tears. He raised his eyes and gazed again at Kaharpara.

In time he noticed something else that concerned him.

It is not only the environs of Hansuli Turn that are desolate. Bansbadi Village, seat of the tale of Hansuli Turn, enclosed in Hansuli Turn—that too seems desolate. The cottages remain, but no bustle, no cows, no calves, no goats, no sheep, no quarreling women, no ducks crossing the levee waters, no boys playing; what's happened? Can't even see Kaharpara's dogs. Where have Kaharpara's black, beelike men and women gone, they who were contained within the tale's box, the tale in the bosom of Hansuli Turn?

Pagol laughed and said—They're around, even happy. Karali called 'em an' took 'em away. Toilin' in the workshops of Channanpur—they're gettin' by. Some o' them'll come at evenin'. Some o' them won't. Most don't come. They're right happy!

Bonwari did not show any more anguish. Fine, let them stay happy. Nasu said—Some died, some ran away.

Nasubala gave account. He told each person's story, one by one. Waving his hands before his face, he spoke—My, that old Omon! Very first to run off, that Uncle Omon o' yours. Exactly two days after you were brought in sick.

Just two days after that, old Romon took the cows out to pasture, sold one of Bonwari's best cows to a cattle trader on the spot, and fled off down the country roads. It's been heard that he's going around begging in Katoya, bent over with stick in hand. He says—I'm at life's final stage, so I came ta Mother Ganges' banks. If me few bones fall in the Ganges, I'll be reborn next life in an 'igher clan.

Noyan's Ma died. That death of hers was terrible. At least that's how Nasu told it—Arvest day, she departed on 'arvest day, end of Agrahayan month. Noyan's Ma stuffed herself full of ritually leftover food offerings from four Sadgop houses in Jangol; her breathing stopped and she died gasping and panting. She couldn't move, she couldn't speak, she died staring straight ahead.

Nasubala suddenly burst into tears—he remembered that incident. The image of Noyan's Ma's dying moments seemed to float before his eyes. He began to tremble. His eyes filled with tears. He dabbed his eyes with the hem of his cloth and spoke—Looka this, Noyan's Ma died over there, under that tree. She fell there alone, no one saw. You'd fallen sick, no 'eadman, no chief, oo was to look out fer the 'elpless, tell me? But there was a lotta fuss about you then too, people worryin'—what's up, what's up? So oo'd look out fer Noyan's Ma? I saw an' sat by 'er. I thought—Ah, 'usband gone, own son gone—'elpless, alone. Know what I thought? I'll be in that state at the end too. I ain't got no one either. I'll 'ave ta die like that, too. I put water to 'er mouth, she drank, then gapin' again. Drank again. Tears began to fall from 'er eyes. I said—What's up, Noyan's Ma? She couldn't speak from 'er mouth; wi' a lot of effort she just brought 'er 'and to 'er forehead. Y'understand, she said—Destiny—fate's writ. Then she started ta struggle. What a struggle; seemed she said the live long blessin', then she goes free. Does she go easily? Really late in the night, in the middle o' the dark, when she said live long, I understood.

—One o' the Atpoures died—that whatsitsname—fine name. But he could not remember.

Pagol spoke—Biswamitta.

—Yeah, yeah. Biswamitta.

Nasu didn't remember the name Biswamitra.

Biswamitra's father had given his son that epic character's name after seeing narrative poems performed by a traveling theater. Biswamitra died of fever. Then various folks' children died, young kids died—they're not worth counting. Nasu said—Ye don't count up the toes on yer feet, Uncle Beano; should I give account? After staying silent a while, he suddenly spoke up—An' yer Neem-oil Pana's in jail. Aha! Pankeshto went ta the foot o' the kadam tree fer a bitta flirting, an' ended up in the jailhouse.

—Jail?

—Yeh, jail. With great amusement Nasu said—Just deserts o' craftiness' crooked twists. Got into an argument wi' boss over accounts. Panu, me own Pankeshto; went ta get revenge on boss—stole boss's silver-inlaid hookah pipe. Well, ye know Pana's boss! Name o' Peko Morol! E's a Peko Morol in deed too, real pushy!

Pagol said—The lad wasn't caught. Caught pulled in by the wife. Kara-li got 'im caught. Peko Morol told the police. By then Panu'd gone into hidin'. No one knew where 'e was hidin'. Got snatched by bait o' goin' 'ome at night to eat. When you were laid out unconscious Karali was swaggerin' about; lad gets Pana's wife greedy about all sortsa stuff. Says—Come ta Channanpur, ye'll work, eat. I'll give good work. Cos o' that greed, the woman owned up that Pana comes 'ome at night to eat. Karali 'eard this an' laid in wait at night—grabbed 'im one day. Turned 'im over ta police. Ya know what Pana said? Said—So what, now I'm carefree for a while.

Nasu said—Pana's missus is now in Channanpur workin' in redface sahebs' airplane base. Barely a stroke o' work! Lotsa wages; what fashion!

Bonwari stared indifferently. His eyes fell upon the red tarmac road to Channanpur. The highway's glistening and shining. Everyone hurries along that road to work in Channanpur. Toil for five bits, for a couple of rupees. The ones who work night and day on those tarpaulin-covered goods wagons along the line get the most. They get coal; the rail people give them rice and pulses at a low price.

Bonwari looked suddenly into Pagol's face and said—Pagol, everyone gave up the clanwork karma? Oton, Gupi, Pellad—everyone?

Nasubala interrupted his words in reply—Everyone—everyone—everyone. No one left. Men an' women all runnin' off before dawn. No time. No respite. What'll they do, eh? Belly's needs.

Pagol heaved a deep sigh and said—Gut, belly—that's everythin', Bonwari.

Nasu said—Hell with it. Just the gut? Greed, wrong, unnerstan' Uncle Beano, wrong! The weight of wrong's increasin' in the world, there's nothin' else. I ain't seen a single person oo looks toward dharma. The Ghoshes—so long yer bosses, they let the sharecrop plots go. Plots on the Saheb Tracts, where you 'ad bit o' land ye worked wi' yer back. Channanpur gentry snatched it all. Uncle Pagol went along one day ta the gentry's place, an—

Bonwari looked into Pagol's face and said—Pagol!

Pagol picked at the earthen floor and said—Gone, s'all gone, bro. Gentry didn't leave a square foot o' shares!

The Ghoshes have got rid of land that has been sharecropped by Bonwari since forefathers' days.

Bonwari laughed. So what, so he's been utterly ruined then. Who cares?

A long while later, putting aside his own concerns and speaking of the Kahars, Bonwari said—It's good that folk went ta work in the workshops. Can't blame for that.

Nasubala said—Karali called 'em on that terrible day. Took 'em to the railway's commercial workshops in Channanpur. Gave work. Everyone snuck off quietly. You were so ill no one even asked.

Bonwari laughed—Let 'em not ask.

Nasu said—Get miserable if they don't come, o' course! Yer not miserable?

Pagol smiled—Are ye gonna be miserable or what, Beano?

The extremities of Bonwari's arms and legs are getting cold.

Nasu said—Only I don't go. Uncle Beano, I don't go outa hate an' shame for that monster Karali. All the love I 'ad for 'im's become poison. Shame-shame-shame! I'll die o' shame! Nowadays dresses like the soldiers an' says—*Military*! Wears shoes an' puts a cap on 'is 'ead.

***

Nasubala tells of Karali's hateful, shameful exploits. When Bonwari had been in a touch-and-go state on his sickbed a few days, they noticed one morning: no Shubashi. The previous day Shubashi had sold Bonwari's cows and calves on the pretext of Bonwari's medical expenses. She too vanished in dead of night with all the money, leaving Bonwari. News came by midday, Shubashi is in Channanpur—living at Karali's place. Karali used to call Bonwari "uncle." Didn't prioritize that relationship— shame-shame-shame! Bonwari was a sick man; Karali didn't think once about what'll happen to him if the girl leaves. Vicious heartless hateful Karali. He's stomped on dharma with sheer physical force, fiery blood, lust for money; he's blown decent conduct off into the air, spit upon it. Shame! Shame!

Bonwari stared fixedly at the ground. Even without it being spoken, he had understood this. His inner voice had told him—If Shubashi isn't near, not home, then Karali's taken her off. He knows she has gone off with Karali, laughing, hot like Kaloshoshi. Course she'll go; it's the rule. This is an old theme in the tale of Hansuli Turn. Pagol smiled, shook his head, he knows too—it's the rule in Hansuli Turn. Nasu was wiping his eyes. Once he'd wiped them he spoke again—I tell ya, Uncle Beano, a girl like Pakhi an' 'e didn't even look at 'er. Pakhi—ah—what ta say, Uncle Beano—O she wept like the cuckoo that calls "eyes-gone, eyes-gone" till it's worn out, wept just like that, wept so long.

Nasubala began to weep again. He wiped his eyes. He said—Ah, ah, my 'eart bursts in pieces if I think o' what 'appened ta Pakhi. He wiped his eyes again and said—I couldn't take no more, uncle. I cussed Karali out really bad an' came back—came back ta the village. Said—I'm wi' you fer life. Came ta the village. Got back an' I thought o' you. Ah, oo's lookin' after you? No other person at 'ome. Shubashi's run off, Omon's run off, oo'll look after ya? Sick person, terrible fever, unconscious condition— what'd 'appen to a person? Desperate state; Shubashi took off wi' as many belongings as she could. Where's the respite for those busy wi' the world, for those runnin' round like a mad dog given a bash on the 'ead! A couple o' women would come an' go, look in. But there was no wife at 'ome. Great fallen champion like Bonwari, 'ow could others' wives take care of 'im? Yet this many such a great champ, such an authority—to die uncared for? Ye won't get water in the night when ye're gasping for it, you'll die wi' a throat dried from thirst an' a crackin' chest? My mind said—Ain't you 'ere ta do it, then? God made you as man but gave you woman's mind; why'd 'e give ya the ability ta do woman's work? I didn't think one more minute. I came along, sat me down by yer 'ead.

Nasu made obeisance to God and said—Paid 'beisance at 'is feet, managed ta save ya.

Bonwari now said—Why'd ya save me, Nasu?

—It's the blessin' o' yer own assigned time an' my care.

Pagol smiled and said—Woulda been the end if ye'd died, Bonwari. Uman birth's a great piece o' luck; enjoy ta the full all there is to see. Death's sure. He suddenly breaks into song—

Hansuli Turn's story—tell it at a bad time, hey?
In Kopai river's waters—story floats away.

Meanwhile bamboo cutting and woodcutting are continuing. *Khot-khot-khot-khot! Khotang-khotang!* Cut trees falling with a groan, bamboo falling flat with a little sound—like poor folk when they're beaten. Trees falling, Hansuli Turn being cleared.

Khot—khot—khot—khot—khotang—khotang sound running in all directions. Ringing out from bank to bank of Hansuli Turn's boundary; a way off it hits Kopai bridge and comes echoing back. Perhaps, even as it announces Hansuli Turn's connection to future times and far-flung places, it's not content—borne back through echoes as if it's striking against all the epochs of the past.

Nasu's story is not ending. He began again—I'm so sad about Pakhi. Ah, dear golden "amber-jewel," oriole, with yer black head an' golden body—when I think o' that bird I think o' my other bird, Pakhi. Yes, woman, indeed. Get it, just as Karali took Shubashi away Pakhi began to beat 'er chest an' weep. Soon as I saw Pakhi's weepin' I came runnin' an' cussin' an' swearin'. That day evenin'-time, just as night's comin' in, 'round that time Pakhi came runnin' back ta the village to 'er ma. Cloth red wi' blood. Pakhi's eyes burnin'.

Course they'd burn! It's a Kahar girl going crazy! She's terrifying like the bank-bursting Kopai!

Evening time, when Pakhi stopped crying, she'd started a fight with Karali. She then picked up a chopping blade and, just about to deliver a blow to her own head she suddenly said—Why die alone? Karali tried to grab her hand, but Pakhi sank the chopper into Karali's head. The only reason Karali's alive is because of the kind of man he is, and because he had grabbed her hand; else he would not have survived. But Karali's head took a few blows. Pakhi wiped that blood off, fled here like a madwoman. Next morning Karali came to Kaharpara with his head wrapped in a doctor's bandage. By then Pakhi had died in the cage of desire. She's hanging with the noose of her wedding cord around her neck in the brick-built house of her desire; but yes, Pakhi has inscribed a permanent mark on Karali's forehead, his fate. Pakhi doesn't leave any way to forget Pakhi.

Bashan—Pakhi's Ma is an eternally good person. And everyone knows about her love story with the Chaudhury boy. Bashanta's an unusual Kaharpara woman. She had loved that Chaudhury boy and then never looked at anyone else again. Just as the lotus bud in a bunch of water lilies in Kaharpara's indigo levee looks fixedly toward the rising sun, so her mind, spirit, eyes, all were turned toward that one person. After the Chaudhury boy died she lived her life like a upper-caste widow from a respectable household. Tranquil, soft-spoken Bashanta—after her daughter's death she went and took refuge in that broken-down Chaudhury mansion. It's there she lives on leftover food offerings and awaits death.

Bashanta's Ma Suchand is in Channanpur. Amazing treatment at the rail hospital! She did not need to have her leg operated on. The old woman survived. She hobbles around with a stick, begging. She goes to middle-class houses in Channanpur and tells the tale of Hansuli Turn, tells it sitting under the station's tree. If anyone's there she tells it, if no one's there she tells it; tells it and tells it—bamboo-grove-circled, sleepy-headed, dream-loving, shadow-covered tale of Hansuli Turn is flower-filled, venom-filled, soft with love's heat, rough with unlove; the tale of Hansuli's Turn's Bashanta—her white brushmark of love's heat; Pakhi's blood writing. She tells this story in her own language. Carrying the tale of Hansuli Turn's cloth bag upon her shoulder, perhaps, she became the old woman of ancient days; Karali became demon or Satan—or else that same one became prince, headman of a new age. It was he who summoned war, he more than anyone who brought it to Hansuli Turn's Kaharpara. He who informed timber contractors. There was an old banyan tree from ancient times in the bamboo groves of Hansuli Turn. They cut down that very banyan. Cut that banyan as soon as they arrived. They cut out the bones, ribs, spine of the tale of Hansuli Turn; using them, according to war's decree, to build a house under the roof of history.

Creak, groan—boom! A huge noise stunned Hansuli Turn. A flock of birds flew off in tumult. A small flock. Flock on flock of forest birds' habitations have been wiped out in Hansuli Turn. A couple of wild boars did not dash out at the noise. Frightened cows didn't come running with raised tails; goats either. Little boys didn't come running to see, what's that noise! The Kahars take boys to work in Channanpur. Anyway, even if they'd been here they wouldn't have been shocked by this sound; Channanpur's howling din and weirdness are far greater.

Not a single cow or goat left in Kaharpara. War broken out. Packing them off. A two-rupee goat being sold for ten rupees. Price of a ten-rupee cow thirty rupees. Twenty-five rupee steer a hundred rupees. Not the price of milk, not the price of plow-pulling power, the price of meat. War has made the Kahars forget their cow tending and milk selling; it's wiped that business out.

Nasu stood and looked, what's up? He put his hand to his cheek and began to tremble. —My God, they've cut down that silk-cotton tree beside the deeps! Splitting and groaning, the great tree of ancient days coming swiftly crashing down. The force of its rapid fall still carrying in the breeze. Perhaps it is only through the tempo of the breeze that it's saying—I'm leaving.

Khot-khot-khot—khot-khot-khot. Cutting bamboo. Today one side has been completely cleared and Hansuli Turn has merged—with far-off places! In the end times of the tale of Hansuli Turn, the only sound is tree cutting. People have moved to Channanpur, merging into the rushing, tumultuous human stream of town, bazaar, highway. Great trees, immovable pillars, they who first formed the tale of Hansuli Turn's shadowy, sleepy-tranquil little village; it's they who are leaving now, they are passing. Amid all this sits Bonwari, last human of this age, like an immovable thing.

He grasped a bamboo post and stood. Stood and cast his gaze in all directions. Nothing—nothing—there's nothing left of Hansuli Turn's Kaharpara. No boundary of bamboo groves, no ancient arbor, no human, no people; no beasts, not even any birds. Of birds there are crows, gobbling up homeless insects from torn-up bamboo groves and scrublands. Just hard tarmac red-graveled roads all around. Just Kopai's bounds, Hansuli Turn's soil, and crumbling, unpeopled cottages from olden days. He brought his gaze back from there and looked—at nothingness of bamboo thickets. A small, sad smile grew on his face. Those cottages won't remain either.

At evening he said to Pagol—Gonna leave me body now, whatcha say?

—Leave yer body? Pagol was shocked.

—Won't live no more. No point in livin'. You've got the longin' ta see, you fill yer eyes an' see.

Pagol stroked Bonwari's body and said—Don' get yer mind down, bro.

—My mind's not down, Pagol, my mind's a rock. That's not it. My call's come. Ye get it—I can get it. If I'm on my own, inside it's sayin'—Let's go.

—That's yer mind's mistake.

—Huh! Bonwari shook his head.

Now he became a little feverish again. Pagol was taken aback when he put his hand to Bonwari's forehead.

Bonwari said—I 'ad a little wish, Pagol, a long-time wish. I've taken a few people for their last moments in the Ganges. Remember, we'd gone ta Kandra fer a weddin', dropped off bride an' groom at Atmangala, an' we're carryin' the empty palky back—we met an 'oly old ascetic under a tree?

—Course I remember. A great man. As if I wouldn't remember that! Sat leanin' against the tree foot in the midday sun, dust clogged. You gave water. Said wi' folded 'ands—Low caste, puttin' some water in yer mouth, don' take offense at me, Father. Father said—I got no caste meself, son, I'm a caste-renouncin' Vaishnav, ascetic. Course I remember.

—I asked—Why'd ya set out on the road wi' yer body like this, Father? Father said—Son, 'cos I'm dyin', this body isn't carryin' anythin' anymore. Remember? E said—It's carried me fer a long time, son; an' I gave it a lotta love. Ow I dressed it up, 'ow I scrubbed it, what pride I lavished on it; so I'm not comfortable just throwin' it away any old place. I'm goin' ta Mother Ganges' banks, I'll lie in the water, keep me 'ead on the bank—I'll depart callin' on the Lord; I'll depart leavin' this body in Mother Ganges' waters. Remember? Then we caught on—Come along Father, we'll carry ya there in this palky. Father smiled. —Come on, take me along.

Bonwari was silent a moment and then said—Ya know, on Ganges bank I asked Father a question, you lot weren't there; I asked—Father, ye're not sick at all, so how d'ya know? Father said—Son, me mind's sayin'. Midnight tonight—yes. Then 'e smiles an' says—Son, because our minds are so caught up in outer appearances we don't get the real story from inside. Don't go by common lore, son; when ye're engrossed in yer field work, ye don't feel hunger. You forget to eat. If the mind turns its eyes away from outside an' talks to its own inner mind, it'll rightly say—Bro, now I'm leavin'. My fixation on the outside's fleein', bro. I can hear what the one on the inside's sayin'. Sayin'—I'm leavin'.

Tears were streaming from Pagol's eyes. Bonwari said—Don't cry, friend. It's not in a Kahar's fortune ta die in the Ganges. Yet my Mother Kopai's still there; when I say so I want ya both ta carry me ta the banks o' the Kopai. Unnerstan'?

He grasped Pagol's hands firmly.

Pagol said—We'll go.

—An' give the Kahars tidings. If they come I'll see 'em an' depart wi' eyes filled.

He laughed.

A long time later Pagol said—Amaranth bush been hacked up, the story o' Hansuli Turn's finished. Hansuli Turn's finished too.

Bonwari shook his head—No.

No. Something remains. Lord has spoken, Kalarudra's whim, Hari's directive; if there's no flood then the tale of Hansuli Turn is not ended. All-destroying flood. In the tale of Hansuli Turn, the Kopai is like a raging Kahar woman; Kopai will fly into a rage and put an end to Hansuli Turn.

***

Flood came. Such raging flood. It overflowed Kopai's banks, whooshing, rushing, bubbling, gushing. An even greater flood than the one in which Babathakur walked across the floodwaters with his clog-clad feet. Devastating flood. But this time Kahars didn't die drowning. Didn't climb trees either. This time they were in Channanpur. Hansuli Turn drowned in the flood. With the bamboo grove barrier torn out, the flood now rushed a hundred times faster across Kaharpara. All Kaharpara was leveled flat. Not a single cottage remained standing. Indigo embankment filled with sand. Saheb Tracts land golden with silt. Sahebs' plantation buildings finished, not even a trace remained.

The flood story isn't tale, it's history. The Flood of 1350—1943 in the English calendar. That flood of thirteen hundred and fifty that washed away the rail line. Its story is in history. It's not just the rail line that washed away in the flood of the Damodar, Ajay, Mayurakshi, and Kopai rivers; like Hansuli Turn's, the tales and settings of numberless other places were also washed away, were transformed. History certainly does not obey Lord's word, Kalarudra's whim, Hari's directive. It says—contingency, coincidence. Let it speak—be truth what may; the Kahars will call it true and obey.

Pagol says—Bonwari knew. He'd smiled, lookin' at the cut bamboo border. I can see that smile wi' me own eyes.

Bonwari passed away, just before the powerful flood. He departed his body exactly as he had wished. Three days before death—he went and lay in a shack that had been built in the river's womblike hollows. He summoned all Kaharpara, filled his eyes looking upon them, and passed away smiling. The only one he didn't see was Karali. Karali—maniacal Karali, he's the only one who did not come. He came after Bonwari's death. Bonwari had also said—Burn me by these deeps. Where Kalobou had fallen into the water of the deeps, where his first wife had been burned—that place. So it was done. Karali came and stood at the time of this burning. He brought a fresh sal-tree sprig and ghee. He set them on the pyre, laid Bonwari out, and touched his head to Bonwari's feet. He said—Go, off ya go ta paradise.

The small rivulet of tale has joined the great river of history.

The Kahars are now a new people. In dress, speech, beliefs, they've really changed. They've exchanged smears of earth, dust, mud for engine oil; exchanged plow and scythe for dealings with hammer, crowbar, pickaxe. Yet even as they toil in Channanpur's workshops they die from starvation, die of disease; instead of dying from snakebite they're sliced by machines, crushed by wagons. But they don't appeal to Babathakur for this. Afloat in a boat on the river of history, they're looking to the compass—to the weathervane.

***

Yet they gaze toward that sand-filled Hansuli Turn from Channapur's dingy, cramped brick quarters. But how will they return, who will forge the first path?

Uninhabited Hansuli Turn stares into the sky. It is practicing ritual austerities like a childless woman desirous of new offspring. Heaps of sand flattened by flood—a great arid waste spread across Hansuli Turn's golden fields; it's only Nasubala goes there. Goes frequently. He can't not go. He goes to that Turn to collect cow dung, to catch crabs and fish, to break firewood. He sits with crossed legs, gazes at the sky, and weeps— Ah, Birth Mother dear!

Pagol sings songs from village to village, door to door—on the station platform—

I'll tell the story o' Hansuli Turn, ah clamity!

Pagol sings songs, beats a drum, and Nasubala dances, white-streaked hair braided with red ribbon and coiled into a bun, jingling anklets on his feet. Nasu prefers not to use a string of bells.

Pagol no longer drives Nasu crazy. Nasu doesn't get crazy either. Laughs. The two have come together since that time at Bonwari's cottage. Pagol sings—

The bamboo that makes a staff, bro, that bamboo'll make a flute
How I love that bamboo of Bansbadi.

Dancing, Nasu joins the song.

Under wood-apple tree, Babathakur, Father o' Kahar clan
In bamboo groves lived his familiar, python
Buzzing lifespirit lived there, protected,
(Ah me) Karali killed it in a burning!
Bamboo-ringed, inside a bamboo casket
Kahar clan's buzzing lifespirit set up home.
Military at last smashed the bamboo-ring casket—
Alas destiny, Kahars became wanderers.
Like hive bees they rove around and around
I'll tell of misery, o, in calamity!

Pagol starts a song—

Don't shed tears, don't shed tears from the eyes,
Just watch the games of destiny's old God, bro.

In the middle of the song Pagol sings Suchand's tale of Hansuli Turn, tells of Kaharpara from ancient times until today. First tells—cosmology; at the end sings that ending story—What's the sadness, why are you shedding tears? Destruction, creation—sport of destiny's old God. Destroys one, creates another—this happening since ancient times. Just as boys build sandcastles and then destroy them, chanting—To please my hands I built it, to please my feet I smashed it; it's just like that, just like that, just like that!

Sitting under a tree, Suchand tells the tale of Hansuli Turn. Some listeners hear the beginning, some the middle, and some the end. Meaning they hear a bit, then get up and leave. The old woman tells it to herself.

At the end of the story she says—Sonny, 'eard it when I were a kid. 'S an 'eart thing, ya know—keep it in yer 'ead, lice'll eat it; bury it in earth, termites'll geddit; 'old it in yer 'and an' yer nails'll mark it, or sweat stains; so I've 'eld it in me 'eart. If ya keep an 'eart thing in the 'eart—it stays there. None took this un, nor kept it. This tale's gonna end wi' me, yeh. But if ya can, keep it in writin'. Ah!—Hansuli Turn's done—I'm done too—story's done. Ah—ah!

But—. As she talks Suchand stops. She looks to the sky and thinks. Thinks, is there an end? Has anything ever ended? Whatever the time of sun and moon, there is no end after it; after that is eternal time. The turning of Father Kalarudda's Charak board. That turning has no end. No light, no dark, but no end to the board's turning. Now annihilation, now creation in that turning! Creation drowns in darkness, then rises in light. Yet how could it end? She thinks.

Suddenly one day Nasubala rushed up. Around two years later. He said—O hey, sis, sis, hey. Gimme me pair of anklets, will ya! Gonna dance.

Elder sister puts an end to it, saying—All finished, sweetie—it's all over.

Nasu laughed, bent down, and said loudly—'Tain't so, sis, listen. Listen ta what I saw 'fore I came. Saw bamboo shoots pushin' up through sand at Bansbadi's boundary levee. An' what new young grass! An' I saw that maniac 'fore I came.

—Bamboo shoots comin' up?

—Yeh.

—An' ya saw that maniac 'fore ya came? Karali?

—Yeh did so, Auntie. E'd gone there in secret—pickaxe in 'and. Diggin' the sand. Diggin' the sand. Diggin' the sand, an lookin' fer somethin'. Searchin' a while. Now gettin' up, now diggin'. Asked 'im—Whatcha lookin' for? Says—Earth. Build 'omes again. There'll be a new Kaharpara. Put a new levee.

Suchand raised her arms and says happily—A new bamboo barrier'll come up again—

Nasu said—No, 'e won't allow a bamboo barrier. This time 'e'll make a levee outa piled earth an' sand. Plant a reed fence on that. It's dark inside a bamboo barrier. E said a lotta stuff to me, Auntie—lotta stuff. A ton o' stuff.

Pagol began to nod his head. A song is coming to mind. New song—

He who creates, bro, he destroys; he who destroys creates—
O ye, come take a peek, in the workshop of destruction and creation.

Nasu immediately tied on his anklets and began to dance—

So snap-rap-tap—*the earthen pot rings out—*
Despite sister-in-law's decree—foot's ankle bells don't want to rest.
So snap-rap-tap—*so* snap-rap-tap.

Karali is returning to Hansuli Turn. He is wielding a pickaxe in his powerful hands, cutting sand, cutting sand, and looking for earth. He is cutting a path for tale's Kopai to merge with history's Ganges. New Hansuli Turn.

Acknowledgments

I would like to thank the following people for their help in making this translation possible:

Mrs. Gouri Bandopadhyay, Amal Shankar Bandopadhyay, Himadri Banerjee, Anjan Sen, Subha Chakraborty Dasgupta, Pradip Basu, Ritwik Bhattacharyya, Anirban Das, Mickela Sonola, Erin Soros, and Mandira Bhaduri. I owe a special debt of gratitude to Gayatri Chakravorty Spivak for helping me to grasp the how of translation. Geraldine Forbes generously agreed to let me use a painting by Rani Chitrakar from her collection for the cover image. Jennifer Crewe of Columbia University Press has been an editor supplying infinite patience and tactful pressure, and for both these things I thank her.

I would also like to acknowledge the intellectual and practical support of the Department of Comparative Literature at Princeton, a department founded by a translator that has kept the task of the translator at the center of its agenda. I also thank the Program in South Asian Studies at Princeton, and gratefully acknowledge Princeton's University Committee on Research in the Humanities and Social Sciences for its generous subvention assistance.

This work could never have been completed without Siona Wilson, ever the lightning in my cloud.